DEC   2010

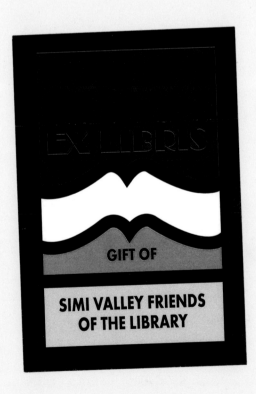

Twelve Rooms with a View

Also by Theresa Rebeck

Three Girls and Their Brother

Theresa Rebeck

a novel

Twelve Rooms with a View

Shaye Areheart Books

NEW YORK

Copyright © 2010 by Theresa Rebeck

Published in the United States by Shaye Areheart Books, an imprint of the Crown Publishing Group, a division of Random House, Inc., New York.
www.crownpublishing.com

Shaye Areheart Books with colophon is a registered trademark of Random House, Inc.

Library of Congress Cataloging-in-Publication Data

Rebeck, Theresa.
Twelve rooms with a view : a novel / Theresa Rebeck.—1st ed.
p.   cm.
1. Sisters—Fiction.   2. Inheritance and succession—Fiction.   3. Stepbrothers—
Fiction.   4. Rich people—Fiction.   5. Apartment dwellers—Fiction.
6. Apartment houses, Cooperative—Fiction.   7. Eccentrics and eccentricities—
Fiction.   8. City and town life—New York (State)—New York—Fiction.
I. Title.   II. Title: 12 rooms with a view.
PS3568.E2697T84   2010
813'.54—dc22   2009044560

ISBN 978-0-307-39416-3

Printed in the United States of America

Design by Lynne Amft

10 9 8 7 6 5 4 3 2 1

First Edition

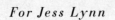
For Jess Lynn

Twelve Rooms with a View

I was actually standing on the edge of my mother's open grave when I heard about the house. Some idiot with tattoos and a shovel had tossed a huge wad of dirt at me. I think he was perturbed that everyone else had taken off, the way they're supposed to, and I was standing there like someone had brained me with a frying pan. It's not like I was making a scene. But I couldn't leave. The service in the little chapel had totally blown—all that deacon or whatever he was could talk about was god and his mercy and utter unredeemable nonsense that had nothing to do with her—so I was just standing there, thinking maybe something else could be said while they put her in the earth, something simple but hopefully specific. Which is when Lucy came up and yanked at my arm.

"Come on," she said. "We have to talk about the house."

And I'm thinking, what house?

So Lucy dragged me off to talk about this house, which she and Daniel and Alison had clearly been deep in conversation about for a while, even though I had never heard of it. Which maybe I might resent? Especially as Daniel obviously had an interest but no real rights, as he is only Alison's husband? But I was way too busy trying to catch up.

"The lawyer says it's completely unencumbered. She died intestate, and that means it's ours, that's what the lawyer says." This from Lucy.

"What lawyer?" I ask.

"Mom's lawyer."

"I have a hard time believing that that is true," Daniel said.

"Why would he lie?" Lucy shot back at him.

"Why would a lawyer lie? I'm sorry, did you just say—"

"Yes I did. He's *our* lawyer, why would he lie?"

"You just said he was Mom's lawyer," I pointed out.

"It's the same thing," she said.

"Really? I've never even heard of this guy, and I don't know his name, and he's my lawyer?"

"Bill left her his *house*," Lucy told me, like I'm some kind of total moron. "And since she died without a will, that means it's ours. Mom has left us a house."

This entire chain of events seemed improbable to me. I'm so chronically broke and lost in an underworld of trouble all the time that a stroke of luck like an actual house dropping out of the sky might be true only if it were literally true and I was about to find myself squashed to death under somebody *else's* house, like the Wicked Witch of the East. Surely this could not mean that. I continued to repeat things people had just said. "Bill left her his house?"

"Yes! He left her everything!" Lucy snapped.

"Didn't he have kids?"

"Yes, in fact, he did," Daniel piped up. "He has two grown sons."

"Well, did he leave them something?"

"No, he didn't," Lucy said, firm. Daniel snorted. "What? It's true! He didn't leave them anything!" she repeated, as if they'd been arguing about this for days.

"The lawyer said it wouldn't matter whether or not they agreed to the terms of their father's will," Alison noted, looking at Daniel, trying to be hopeful in the face of his inexplicable pessimism about somebody leaving us a house.

"If the lawyer said that, he's a complete moron," Daniel informed her. "I called Ira. He's going to take a look at the documents and let us know what kind of a mess we're in."

"It's not a mess, it's a house," Lucy said, sort of under her breath, in a peevish tone. She doesn't like Daniel. She thinks he's too bossy. Which he is, considering that we didn't *all* marry him, just Alison.

So we took a left out of the cemetery in Daniel's crummy old beige Honda and went straight into Manhattan to the lawyer's office. There was no brunch with distant relatives and people standing around saying trivial mournful things about Mom, which I didn't mind being spared. It would have been hard to find anybody who knew her anyway, but I did think that the four of us would at least stop at a diner and have some eggs or a bagel. But not the Finns. We get right down to business.

Before noon we were squashed around a really small table in a really small conference room in the saddest Manhattan office you ever saw. The walls were a nasty yellow and only half plastered together; seriously, you could see the dents where the Sheetrock was screwed into the uprights. The tabletop was that kind of Formica that looks vaguely like wood in somebody's imagination. I was thinking, this is a *lawyer's* office? What kind of lawyer? The overweight receptionist wore a pale green sloppy shirt, which unfortunately made her look even fatter than she was, and she kept poking her head in, first to ask us if we wanted any coffee and then about seven more times to tell us that Mr. Long would be right with us. Finally the guy showed up. His name was Stuart Long, and he looked like an egg. Seriously, the guy had a really handsome face and a good head of brown hair, but the rest of him looked like an egg. For a moment it was all I could concentrate on, so I was not, frankly, paying full attention when Lucy interrupted him in midsentence and said, "Can you tell us about the house?"

"The house?" said the lawyer, seriously confused for a second. And I thought—of course, they got it wrong, of course there is no house.

"Bill's house," Alison explained. "The message you left on our machine said Bill left Mom a house, and the house would be part of the settlement. You left that, didn't you leave that—"

"Well, I certainly would not have left any details about the settlement on a machine—I spoke to your husband, several times actually. Is that what you mean?"

"Yes, we spoke, and you told me about the house," Daniel interrupted, all snotty and impatient, like these details were really beneath him. I could see Lucy stiffen up, because Daniel clearly *had* told her and Alison that he had gotten "a message," when in fact he had been having long conversations with this lawyer that he had no right to have, much less lie about.

"You mean the apartment," Egg Man insisted.

"Yes, the apartment." Daniel was still acting above it all, as if he had a right to be annoyed.

"So it's not a house," I said.

"No, it's an apartment. Olivia was living there. Up until her recent death."

"Recent death—that's an understatement," I said.

"Yes, yes, this is I'm sure overwhelming for you," the lawyer said. He had very good manners, compared to everyone else in the room. "But I take it from your questions that you've never seen the apartment?"

"Bill didn't like us," I said. "So we weren't allowed to visit them."

"He was reclusive," Alison corrected me. "As I'm sure Mr. Long is aware."

"Mom told me he didn't want us to visit because Bill didn't like us," I said.

"That's ridiculous," said Alison.

"Could we get back to the point?" Lucy said. "What about this place—this apartment? We're inheriting it, right?"

"Yes, well, the apartment was directly willed to your mother," Egg Man agreed. "Because her death came so soon after her husband's, the title was never officially transferred, but that will most likely be considered a technicality."

"And it was her house," Daniel reminded him. He was really stuck on this idea that it was a house.

"Technically it is, as I said, specifically included in the estate," our round lawyer repeated. "Why don't you let me walk you through this?"

"Why don't *you* just tell us how much the place is worth?" Lucy threw in.

Mr. Long blinked but otherwise ignored her poor manners. "Obviously it's not possible to be specific about the worth of the property until we have a professional evaluation," he informed the room.

"You really don't know?" Lucy persisted. "Like, it could be worth ten dollars or ten thousand dollars or a million dollars, but you don't know?"

Before Egg Man could answer, Daniel tried to rip control of the meeting back to his side of the table. "She's just a little impatient," he said, smiling. "Sweetie, maybe we should let Mr. Long—"

Lucy rolled her eyes at this. "Just a ballpark, Daniel *sweetie*," she shot back.

Mr. Long cleared his throat, clearly uncomfortable. "Well, I guess I could—"

"Yes, why don't you," I said, trying to be nice, because I was feeling a little embarrassed by the way the others were acting. Also, I really wanted him to give up a number. "Just a ballpark," I said, smiling brilliantly, because sometimes that's all a sad, round lawyer needs: a pretty girl smiling at him. I thought Lucy was going to gag, but it did the trick.

"A ballpark. A *ball*park," he said, smiling back at me. "I don't know—eleven million?"

There was a big fat silence.

"Eleven million?" I said. "Eleven million what?" I know that sounds stupid, but what on earth was he talking about? Eleven million pesos?

"Eleven million dollars," he clarified. "That of course is almost a random number, there's really no way of knowing. But it is twelve rooms, with a view of Central Park, on a very good block. I think eleven million would be considered conservative. In terms of estimates."

So then there was a lot more talk, yelling even, people getting quite heated, worried about things that hadn't happened and might not happen but maybe were happening or had happened already, and the solution to all these things that no one understood, apparently, was for me, Tina, to move into that big old eleven-million-dollar apartment *right away*. Like that very day.

So it was odd how that happened? But that's where I ended up.

1

THE THING YOU HAVE TO UNDERSTAND ABOUT THESE BIG OLD APARTments in New York City is that they are more completely astonishing than you ever thought they could be, even in your wildest dreams. When you walk along the edge of Central Park at sunrise, and you look up at the little golden windows blazing, and you think oh my god those apartments must be mind-blowing, who on earth could be so lucky that they get to live in one of those apartments? My mother and her husband were two of those people, and they lived in an apartment so huge and beautiful it was beyond imagining. Ceilings so high they made you feel like you were in a cathedral, or a forest. Light fixtures so big and far away and strangely shaped that they looked like some aging star exploding in the heavens. Mirrors in crumbling gilt frames that had little cherubs falling off the top. Clocks from three different centuries, none of which worked. So many turns in the hallways, leading to so many different dark rooms, that you thought maybe you'd stumbled into a dwarf's diamond mine. The place was also, quite inexplicably, carpeted in mustard-colored wall-to-wall shag, and one of the bathrooms was papered in some high-seventies silver-spotted stuff. Plus there was actual moss growing on the fixtures in the kitchen—no kidding, *moss*. But none of that was in any way relevant. The place was fantastic.

There was nobody to let us in—we had to let ourselves in with the keys the nice round lawyer handed over, telling us about six times that he didn't think it was "necessary" that we take immediate ownership. He was so worried about the whole idea—that I would just up and move into this huge old empty apartment where my mother had died only days ago—that he kept repeating to himself, in a sort of sad murmur, "There's no need to rush into anything. Really. You must all be overwhelmed. Let me walk you through this."

"But you said there might be some question about the will," Daniel reminded him.

"No, no question—well, no question about Mr. Drinan's will. Your mother, as you know, does not seem to have left a will," he said, trying to drag us back into this nonsense. But now that the words "eleven million" had come out of his mouth, none of us was listening.

"We'd really like to get a look at the place," Daniel announced.

"Before we lose the light," Lucy said.

Sometimes I am amazed at the lines she pulls out. She just says this stuff like she really means it, even though she had said maybe a second ago that we needed to get over there and get Tina moved in to make it clear that we were taking ownership right away, because if there was going to be any contention or cloud on the title we'd need to have established a proprietary right to the property. She's not even a lawyer; that's just the way her brain works. She figures out the meanest truth, gets it out there and deals with it, then a second later pretends that what's really worrying her is some weird thing about the light. It's spectacularly nervy and impressive. And maybe Daniel doesn't like it because Alison is the oldest, which means that they should be calling the shots? But he just married into this situation, and there is no way around how smart Lucy is.

Meanwhile, I am the problem child who doesn't get a vote. She's caused too many problems; she doesn't get a vote anymore. Even when it's a question of where Tina is going to live, Tina doesn't get to vote. I didn't care. The truth was, I didn't have anything better to do than let my sisters move me into my dead mom's gigantic apartment on Central Park West. At the time I was living in a trailer park, for god's sake, cleaning rich people's houses out by the Delaware Water Gap. I didn't even have a bank account because I couldn't afford the monthly fees, and I had to borrow the fifty bucks for the bus to the funeral from my stupid ex-boyfriend Darren, whose bright idea it was to move out to that lousy trailer park in the first place. Oh well, the less said about the whole Delaware Water Gap fiasco the better, as it was not my smartest or most shining hour. So when Lucy leaned back in her chair and said, "We probably should take ownership right away, just to be safe—Tina

can stay there," I wasn't about to put up a fight. Move into a palace on
Central Park West, why not?

So we got the keys, crawled through traffic to the Upper West Side,
actually found a meter four blocks away from the promised land, and
there we were, before the light was gone, while the sun was setting. The
building itself was huge, a kind of murky dark brown stone with the
occasional purple brick stuck in. Strange and gloomy gargoyles snarled
from the cornices three stories up. Underneath them, two serious-minded
eagles with the tails of lions guarded the entryway; these characters didn't
look like they were kidding around, but they also didn't look like they
intended to eat you or spit molten lava at you, unlike the ones above. Plus
there were actual gas lamps, the old Victorian ones, burning by the heads
of the eagle-lions, and another gas lamp, a really big one, hung dead center over the door, right above a huge name in gothic type: EDGEWOOD.
In fact, all the windows on the first two floors had scrollwork and carv-
ings and inexplicable Latin words inscribed above them. It all added up
into a gothic sort of Victorian mess that was quite friendly while simulta-
neously seeming like the kind of place you might never come out of alive.

The foyer was predictably spectacular. Marble floors dotted with
black stone tiles, vaulted ceilings, and the biggest crystal chandelier
you've ever seen in your life. A huge black chair with actual wings, which
I later found out was carved ebony, sat right in front of an enormous
fireplace, with two more giant eagle-lions on either side. The fireplace
was filled with an enormous sort of greenery, which I later found out was
made of silk. The doorman's station, a nice little brass stand piled with
FedEx packages and a couple of manila envelopes, was empty. Behind
that were two brass elevators with elaborate doors.

"Wow," I said. "Check out the chair with wings."

"We'll have time for that later," Lucy told me grimly, giving me a
little shove toward the elevators.

"We should wait for the doorman, shouldn't we?" I said, looking
around. The place was deserted.

"Why? We live here," Lucy announced, pressing her lips together,
like don't mess with me, as she pushed the elevator button. She kept

tapping at that stupid button, as impatient as Moses whacking the rock, like that might hurry god up instead of just pissing him off.

"Seriously, we can't just go up there," I said. The whole situation suddenly seemed dicey. Alison started pushing the elevator button too, pressing it really hard. Both of them were in such a rush, like rushing through all this would make it okay. It reminded me of Darren and the whole Delaware Water Gap fiasco—things happen too fast and you end up stuck in the middle of nowhere with a complete shithead and a boatload of trouble. I was about to explain this to my sisters when the elevator dinged and Daniel swung open the outer door.

"You guys, wait a minute," I said. "We should wait for the doorman."

"Who knows where he is?" Daniel said. "We're not waiting."

And since no one showed up to stop us, I got in.

According to the keys the Egg Man had given us, Mom's apartment was 8A, so we took the elevator to the eighth floor, where it disgorged us on a horrible little landing. An old green fluorescent strip light flickered feebly, making us look like ghosts, and the venetian blinds at the windows were so old and cracked and dusty that even a hapless loser like me found them offensive. It was startling to find a landing so grungy in this fancy building, but this was the least of the improbabilities that were coming my way. It was taking Lucy a long minute to figure out how to work all the keys and I was in a bad mood by this time. I thought we really should have waited to tell the doorman we were there, and I was worried about a total stranger showing up and saying, "Hey! What are you doing?" A door to the side and behind the two elevators had been painted a sad brown maybe a hundred years ago, and next to it was another door, painted a gorgeous pearly gray, with "8B" in heavy brass. The "8A" on our door by contrast was in those sticky-backed gold-and-black letters that you buy at the hardware store. It was a sad little sight; it really was.

And then Lucy figured out the locks, and there was a click and a sort of a breeze, and the door to the apartment swung open.

You couldn't tell how big the place was right away. The blinds were drawn, and we didn't know where the switches were, so we all stepped tentatively into the gloom. It smelled too, a sort of funny old-people smell, not as if someone had died in there, but more like camphor and dried paper and mothballs. And far off, in with the mothballs, was a hint of old flowers and jewelry and France.

"Hey, Mom's perfume," I said.

"What?" said Lucy, who had wandered into the next room looking for a light switch.

"Don't you smell Mom's perfume?" I asked. It seemed unmistakable to me, even though she hardly ever wore that stuff because it was so ridiculously expensive. Our dad had given her a bottle of it on their wedding night, and they could never afford it again, so she wore it only once every three years or so when he had an actual job and they got to go to a cocktail party. We would watch her put on her one black dress and the earrings with the sparkles and the smallest little dab of the most expensive perfume in the world. Who knows if it really was the most expensive in the world, I rather doubt it, but that's what she told us. Anyway there it was in that huge apartment, in with a bunch of mothballs, the smell of my mother when she was happy.

"What was the name of that stuff?" I asked, taking another step in. I loved the apartment already, so dark and big and strange, with my mother's perfume hiding in it like a secret. "Mom's perfume. Don't you smell it?"

"No," said Alison, running her hand up the wall, like a blind person looking for a doorway. "I don't."

Maybe I was making it up. There were a lot of smells in there in the dark. Mostly I think it smelled as if time had just stopped. And then Daniel found the light switch, and there was the smallest golden glow from high up near the ceiling. You could barely see anything because the room was so big, but what you could see was that time actually *had* stopped there. Between 1857, say, and 1960, things had happened, and then just like that, they had stopped happening.

The ceiling was high and far away, with shadowy coves around the corners, and right in the middle of this enormous lake of a ceiling was the strangest old chandelier, glued together out of what looked like iron filings, with things dripping and looping out of it. It must have been poorly wired, because it had only three fake-candle fifteen-watt bulbs, which is why it gave off so little light. And then there was this mustard-colored shag carpeting, which I believe I have mentioned, and one lone chair in a corner. It was a pretty big chair, but seriously, it was *one* chair.

"What a dump!" Daniel whistled, low.

"Could we not piss on this before we've even seen it, Daniel?" called Lucy from the kitchen. But she sounded friendly, not edgy. She was having a pretty good time, I think.

Alison was not. She kept pawing at the wall. "Is this the only light? There has to be another light switch somewhere," she said, all worried.

"Here, I've got one," said Lucy, throwing a switch in the kitchen. It didn't really do much, because the kitchen was a whole separate room with a big fat wall in front of it, so there was just a little doorway-sized bit of light that didn't make it very far into the living room, or parlor, or whatever you wanted to call this giant space.

"Oh that's a *big* help," said Alison.

"Wow, this kitchen is a mess, you should see this!" yelled Lucy. "Oh, god, there's something growing in here."

"That's not funny," Alison snapped.

"No kidding," Lucy called back, banging things around in a sudden, alarming frenzy. "No kidding, there's stuff growing everywhere— ick, it's moving! It's moving! No, wait—never mind, never mind."

"I am in no mood, Lucy! This is ridiculous. Daniel! Where are you? Tina, where did you go? Where is everybody! Could we all stay in one place, please? DANIEL." Alison suddenly sounded like a total nut. It's something that happens to her—she gets more and more worked up, and she truly doesn't know how to stop it once she starts. No one is quite sure why Daniel married her, as he's pretty good-looking and certainly could have done a lot better. Not that Alison is mean or stupid; she's just sort of high-strung in a way that is definitely trying. Anyway, that apartment was literally starting to drive her crazy. She kept slapping the wall, looking for another light switch, and Daniel was ignoring how scared she was; he was heading across the gigantic room into the gloom on the other side, where that one chair sat, next to a big hole in the wall. Well, it wasn't a hole, it was a hallway. But from where we were standing, it looked like a hole, and the sloping black shadow that used to be Daniel was about to disappear into it.

"Daniel, just wait, could you wait, please?" Alison yelled, completely panicked. "I cannot see where you are going!"

"It's fine, Alison," he said, sounding like a bastard, then disappeared.

"Daniel, WAIT," she yelled, almost crying now.

"Here, Alison," I said, and I pulled open the blind at one of the incredibly large windows. A beautiful gold and red light shot through and hit every wall in that room, making everything glow and move. The sun was going down, and the light was cutting through the branches of the trees, shifting in the wind. That big old room went from being all weird and dreary to being something else altogether, skipping everything in between.

"Wow," I said.

"Yes, thank you, that's much better," Alison nodded, looking around, still anxious as shit. "Although that isn't going to be much help when the sun is gone."

"Is it going somewhere?" I asked.

"It's going *down*, and then what will you do? Because that chandelier gives off no light whatsoever, it's worse than useless. You'd think they'd have some area lamps in a room this size."

"You'd think they'd have some *furniture* in a room this size," I observed.

"Okay, I don't know what that stuff is that's growing in the kitchen," Lucy announced, barging into the big light-filled room, "but it's kind of disgusting in there. We're going to have to have this whole place professionally cleaned before we put it on the market, and even that might not be enough. Oh god, who knows what that stuff is? And it's everywhere. On the counters, in the closets. Who knows what's in the refrigerator? I was afraid to look."

"There's really something growing?" I asked. The more dire her pronouncements, the more I wanted to see the stuff. I slid over to the doorway to take a peek.

"Is it mold?" Alison asked, her panic starting to rev up again. "Because that could ruin everything. This place will be useless, worse than useless, if there's mold. It costs millions to get rid of that stuff."

"It doesn't cost *millions*," Lucy countered.

"A serious mold problem in an exclusive building? That's millions."

"You've never had a serious mold problem in *any* building, Alison. You don't know anything about it," Lucy said bluntly.

"I know that if the other owners find out, they could sue us," Alison shot back. "We would be the responsible parties if mold in this apartment made anybody in the building sick. It could be making us sick right now."

"Let's not get ahead of ourselves," Lucy said, looking at me and rolling her eyes. Everybody rolls their eyes at Alison behind her back, even if she might be right. She's just so irredeemably uptight.

"Holy shit," I said when I finally got a good look at the kitchen.

"What, is it bad? It's bad, isn't it."

"No, no, it's not that bad," I lied. The whole kitchen was green. Or at least most of it. "And I don't think it's mold. I think it's moss."

"Moss doesn't grow inside apartments," Alison hissed. "We have to get out of here. We have to leave immediately, it will make us all sick. It's probably what killed Mom."

"Mom died of a heart attack," I reminded her.

"We have to leave now, before we all get sick. *DANIEL! WE HAVE TO GO.*"

"There's another apartment back here!" Daniel yelled.

"What?" said Lucy, following him into the black hallway.

"There's a whole second apartment, another kitchen and another living room or parlor—there's like six bedrooms and two dining rooms!" he yelled.

"How can there be two dining rooms?" Lucy muttered. And then she disappeared. I looked at Alison, standing very still, arms at her sides. I completely did not want to contribute any fuel to the coming conflagration. But I did want to see the rest of that apartment.

"It'll be okay, Alison," I said. "It's not mold. It's moss! And Mom died of a heart attack. Let's go see the rest of this place, it sounds awesome." Realizing that I didn't sound particularly convincing, I bolted down the hallway.

The place *was* awesome. The hall was dark and twisty, and there were rooms everywhere that hooked into other rooms and then hooked back to that twisty hallway farther down. Seriously, you never quite knew where you were, and then you were in a place you had gone through six rooms ago, but you didn't know how you had gotten back there. And while some of those rooms were as empty and lonely as that giant front room, some of the others were cozy and interesting. One was painted a weird shade of pink that I had never seen before, with no furniture but with framed pictures of flowers on three walls and a gigantic mirror on the fourth wall. No kidding, the room looked six times as big as it was because of that mirror, and you'd jump when you walked in because you thought someone else was there with you, but it was just you. Another room had little beds that were only six inches off the ground and old solar-system stickers stuck on the ceiling, and someone had painted a giant sun setting over the ocean, right on one of the walls. Another room was painted dark purple, with stars on the ceiling and a little bitty chandelier that had glass moons and suns hanging from it. There was no furniture in that room either.

Twelve rooms is a lot of rooms. That apartment felt as if it went on forever, even before I got to the second kitchen and the two dining rooms. That's where Lucy and Daniel had ended up and were figuring things out.

"This is where they lived," Lucy observed, looking around.

She was right. There was furniture in these rooms, a couple of chairs and a comfortable couch across from a television set, and a coffee table with a clicker and some dirty plates on it. On one side was the so-called second kitchen, but it was really more of a half-kitchen dinette. It had the smallest sink imaginable, a very skinny refrigerator, and an old electric stovetop with a tiny oven. It was kind of doll-sized, frankly, but nothing was growing on it. And on the other side of this TV room–kitchen area was an archway, and beyond an old bed, with two bedside tables and a chair with some dirty clothes on it. The bed wasn't made.

"Jesus," I said, and sat down. Compared to the rest of that great apartment, this little TV-bedroom-kitchen space seemed stupidly ordinary. They lived in the most amazing apartment ever, but they just holed up in the back of it and pretended they were living in a boring normal place like the rest of us. It was overwhelming. Alison, arriving behind me, took a step forward.

"Look," she said, pointing to the coffee table. "Fish sticks. She was eating fish sticks when she died."

"Oh, for crying out loud," said Lucy, and she reached over, grabbed the plate, and turned back to the tiny kitchenette, where she proceeded to bang the cabinet doors.

"What are you looking for now?" I sighed, lying down on the couch. I could hardly keep my head up.

"It's disgusting," she snapped. "That's just been sitting there for days, I can't believe no one cleaned it up."

"Who would clean it up?" I asked.

"Someone, I don't know who. Who found her—wasn't it a neighbor? What did they do, just let the EMS people pick up the body and then leave the place like this? It's disgusting. It could attract bugs, or mice." Lucy started looking under the little sink for a garbage can. "Oh god, if there are mice, I'm just going to kill myself," she muttered. "It's going to cost a fortune to take care of that mold issue; I do NOT want to have to deal with exterminators."

"Relax," Daniel told her, turning slowly and taking it all in with a kind of speculative grimace. "We won't have to do a thing. What'd he say, eleven million? This place is worth more than that as is. With mold and mice and fish sticks on dirty plates and a shitty economy. This place is worth a fortune. We won't have to do a thing."

"Oh, well," said Alison, apparently having something like a philosophical moment. "She had a good life."

"She had a shitty life," I said.

"Look, there're actually some things in the freezer," Lucy announced, swinging open the little door. "Some hamburgers and frozen vegetables, and the ice-cube maker seems to work . . . plenty of food. You'll be all right at least for the next couple of days, Tina, then we'll

have to spring for some groceries, I'm guessing, because as usual you
are completely broke, is that the story?"

"That's the story." I shrugged. "Look, seriously, Lucy, maybe we
should wait a day. For me to move in? So we have time to like tell the
building super and stuff, so they know I'm here?"

"There's no reason you shouldn't move in right now," Lucy said.
"You need a place to stay, my place is too small, and so is Daniel and
Alison's. Where else are you going to go? By your own account you can
hardly afford a hotel room."

"This is—it's just—"

"It's our apartment. Why not stay here?"

There was a *why not*, obviously. There was a good reason to slow
things down, but not one of us wanted to mention it. Even me. You
split eleven million dollars three ways, even after taxes? Every single one
of us suddenly has a whole new life. I'm fairly certain that was the sum
total of all the thinking going on in that apartment when they handed
me the keys and told me to sit tight.

2

I CAN'T SAY I WAS SORRY TO SEE THEM GO.

The first thing I did was take my boots off. Alison would have thrown a fit if she had seen me. She had already moaned about how dirty the place was, and "who knows what might be lurking in that crummy shag carpet," like bedbugs or worms or slime from distant centuries might just be waiting for some idiot's bare foot to come along so it could spread fungal disaster into the idiot's system. Alison has that kind of imagination; sometimes talking to her is like talking to someone who writes horror films for a living. But I didn't care; my toes were so hot and tired and I just felt like being flat on my feet before checking the place out more carefully. As it turned out, the carpet was dry and seemed clean enough, just a little scratchy. It really was a pretty hideous color, but I think that's the worst that could be said about it.

By then the sun *had* gone away, as predicted, and I didn't have a lot of light to explore by, so I went back to the boring area where Mom and Bill had camped out. I slipped out of the dark blue skirt I had brought for the funeral, pulled on the jeans I had stashed in my backpack, and took a look around their rooms. Lucy had already cased the refrigerator, so I knew there was frozen food. A little casual probing in the cabinets yielded something like sixteen packets of ramen noodles, and then I noticed, on the teeny tiny counter, half a bottle of wine, open and useless, next to three empties. The search continued, and sure enough, when I poked around the laundry room behind the kitchenette I spotted a big pile of clothes on the floor, which looked like nothing until I nudged it with my foot and found two mostly full cases of red wine. I was feeling pretty good about that, so I kept looking, and up in the freezer of that skinny refrigerator, back behind the ice-cube machine, I hit the mother lode: a big bottle of really good vodka with hardly a dent in it.

Knowing my mother, I was sure that would not be the only bottle around. She liked to have a few in reach, so I was pretty sure I'd find some squirreled away in other thinly disguised hiding places. The two cases of pricy red wine told me that Bill was a drinker himself, and for a second I thought, well, at least she finally hooked up with someone who could pay for the good stuff as opposed to the truly undrinkable crap she had survived on the rest of her life.

Anyway, in the door of the refrigerator I found half a bottle of ruby red grapefruit juice, which meant I could have an actual cocktail instead of trying to down the vodka straight or over melted ice. So I made myself a drink, put the water on to boil for the noodles, and turned the television on for company. They had only basic cable, so I found one of those stations that run endless documentaries all the time and started to look around.

The bedroom was not really a bedroom, even though it had a bed. The enormous pocket doors were clearly meant to shut the room off, but they had been left open for so long they were stuck on their rails. Another set of pocket doors made up the entire wall on the other side of the room, but they were stuck closed, with the bed shoved up against them. There was a small alcove built into one wall, with fancy plasterwork up the sides and a crown at the top. That had a dresser in it. There were no closets—just clothes everywhere on the floor—which along with the pocket doors made me think this room was not ever meant to be a bedroom. Daniel had said there were two dining rooms, but I decided this bedroom was really the dining room, and the room behind it with the television was originally the kitchen, where the servants would cook, and then bring the food in through the pocket doors, which probably opened and closed at some previous point in history. Well, honestly, I had no idea what was supposed to be what in this crazy apartment in the other century when it was built. But that's what I thought.

I also thought, I wonder where Mom's perfume is? Because back in that freaky bedroom area I smelled it everywhere; it was in all the clothes and the blankets and the sheets, along with the red wine and the cigarettes and dirty laundry and mothballs. I kind of had it in my head that I might find that little black bottle and snag it before Lucy turned it into a big issue for no reason whatsoever. Seriously, you just never knew when she was going to get all twitchy and start making lists and arguing about everything, and Alison sometimes went along with that shit just because it wasn't worth arguing with Lucy. The next thing you knew, Lucy would be telling everybody that we'd have to put everything smaller than a paperback into a box and sell it all together because that would be the only way to be fair, and then she'd hand it over to some thrift store for ten dollars, not even enough to buy a pizza. It made no sense to let Lucy try that, so I started looking for that little bottle. I thought that if I found it I could stick it in my backpack and no one would ever know.

The first place I checked was the dresser in the alcove, which seemed like the only place Mom would have put anything of value to her; the rest of the room was nothing but piles of clothes, a chair, a couple of books on the floor, and the unmade bed. Besides, it looked as if she'd been using the dresser as a vanity; there was an old gilt mirror on the wall above it, with the feet of a cherub hanging down from the top. The top of the dresser held a few items—a hairbrush, a comb, an empty glass with a little dry well of alcohol stuck to the bottom. There was a tarnished small round silver box thing, with curlicues and a big French fleur-de-lis on top, and inside was a whole bunch of keys and an old wedding ring and three medals. One of them said CHEMISTRY. There were a couple of really old frames with old photographs of no one I knew, and behind them a couple of unframed photos with the edges curling toward the middle. One was of me when I was about fifteen and going on the first of many disastrous dates with Ed Featherstone. He was a mighty jerk, but at fifteen who knew? But it is a bit of a shock to see yourself seventeen years ago, with your arms around someone who is now seventeen years older and who made a fortune on Wall Street back when everyone was doing that, got out while the getting was good, and now owns lots of property in Connecticut. Whatever. I set aside the silver can of keys, which I thought might be useful for future exploration, and then I looked in the dresser.

The top drawer held her underwear, lots of sad bras and panties, several old pairs of neutral-colored support hose, and a quart bottle of that good vodka. In the drawer just beneath it was Bill's underwear, gigantic white and light blue cotton briefs. I so did not want to paw through that stuff—I mean, really, I wanted that little bottle of perfume, which I didn't think anyone else would want, but I was quickly losing my nerve. I had never even met this nutty alcoholic—who knew what lurked in his underwear? Rather than give up, I pulled the drawer all the way out of the dresser and upended it. There was nothing in there except all those huge pairs of underwear, and a wallet.

A wallet, there was a wallet, and the guy who owned it was dead, and everything he owned got left to my mom, who apparently left everything she owned to me and my sisters. I figured that gave me some rights, so I sat on the floor and looked through it, and lo and behold there were three receipts from a liquor store, a couple more pictures of people I didn't know, and a lot of money. Bill had seven hundred dollars in that wallet, which would be a significant windfall to pretty much anybody, I think, but it was a miracle to a person of my limited means. I pocketed the cash.

When I leaned over to scoop the now empty wallet and all that underwear back into the drawer, I also happened to notice the no-man's-land under the bed, which was crowded with boxes. These turned out to be really hard to get to, because they all were just a little bit too big for the space, which meant they were really squashed in there. They also each weighed a ton, as I discovered, since they were full of used paperbacks, most of them mysteries. After about twenty minutes of dragging the boxes out, I was ready to completely give up, until I got to the very last box, which was up by the headboard on the far side of the bed. That one was not full of books. It was full of junk—a crummy handbag, a little red change purse, two pairs of reading glasses, another quart of vodka, nearly empty, and an old cedar jewelry box filled with fake pearls and junky necklaces and a tiny bottle of French perfume.

It looked just the way I remembered it, pitch black and shaped like a heart. The ghost of the word *Joy* ran across one side in elegant gold letters. I tipped the bottle to one side, trying to figure out how much perfume was still in there after thirty years. It was impossible to tell.

It was not until that very moment that I remembered I had left a pan of water boiling on the stovetop this whole time. Which I have done several times in the past, in different apartments, with more or less disastrous results, so I jolted myself out of my mournful and useless reverie and ran back to that lousy kitchenette, where I put more water on to boil, made another cocktail, cooked up some noodles, had another drink, watched the end of a documentary about Egypt, and had a good cry. I thought about just passing out on that couch in front of the television set, but that seemed like a really poor idea, because it's the sort of thing that leads one to think one might actually be an alcoholic, which was a thought I didn't want to entertain that night. So I stood up, definitely wobbly, but I didn't judge myself, because Mom was dead and I was feeling hideous, and then I thought about climbing into her bed, and that was just not an option, so I wandered back through that maze of rooms until I found the one with the stars on the ceiling and the little beds on the floor, and one of those beds was made up with a couple of pillows and a kid's dark blue coverlet with rocket ships and planets all over it. I slid off my jeans and got under that cover and cried a little more, and then I went to sleep.

"Who the fuck are you?"

The next thing I knew, two guys were standing in the doorway, staring at me. One of them had flipped on the overhead light, so I could see there were two of them, two fucking huge guys staring at me sleeping in that little bed on the floor of that little room.

"What?" I said, blinking. "What?"

"Answer the fucking question! Who the fuck are you, and what the fuck are you doing here?" The first guy, standing inside the room with his hand on the light switch, was drunk, I could tell that right away.

"What time is it?" I said. I didn't know what else to say. And I really wanted to know what time it was. I was completely confused.

"It's two A.M. Who the fuck are you?" the first guy said again.

"Shit," I said. Which may not have been the brightest thing to say? But this guy was scaring me.

"Answer the fucking question. And get out of that bed. Get up. Get up!" Now he was barking orders and totally freaking me out. I was still blinking and trying to wake up and figure out what time it was and how much of a hangover I had, and this big guy was reaching over to grab me. Honestly, I remember thinking, what a fucking drag, I'm in a mess again, and this time it isn't even my fault—my staying here was Lucy's dumb idea, I was just doing what Lucy wanted, and here I am in a total fucking mess. I squeezed myself back against the wall, ducked my head, and threw my arm across my face because it was taking a long time to wake up and I was scared. Oh, what a drag, I thought, what a complete hideous drag.

"Stop it, Pete—you're scaring her," said the other guy.

"Good, I want to scare her. Breaking and entering is a fucking crime—she should be scared," said Pete, still coming at me like he was going to drag me out of that bed.

"I didn't break and enter, excuse me, EXCUSE ME, but do you think I could put my pants on?" I yelled. "Get away from me—BACK OFF, YOU JERK!" I smacked Pete's hand away before he could touch me, and surprisingly, he did back off. I continued yelling. "Turn around. Would you please TURN AROUND?"

Okay. Why this worked I have no idea, but it did; both of those guys did as they were told. I was freaked out, because seriously these were two huge guys, maybe six-two or six-four, and I'm a bit of a peewee, so I totally did not expect them to do as I said. I grabbed my jeans off the floor and slid them on fast. Being half-naked was not going to be an advantage in this situation, that much was certain.

"Who the fuck are you guys?" I said, trying to sound angry and sure of myself. I was scared out of my mind, no question, so I wanted to keep the upper hand as long as I could.

"We're the ones asking questions here," Pete said. "I hope you're dressed, because that's as much privacy as you're going to get." He turned around just as I finished zipping up my pants, and when I looked up he was taking a hit off a beer bottle. They both were tanked. This was a very bad situation. "So what's your name?" he demanded.

"I don't have to tell you my name. You tell me your name," I said.

"You're sleeping in my fucking bed, so yeah, you do have to tell me your name," Pete countered.

"Forget it, let's just call the police," said the other guy.

"I *am* the police," Pete told him, annoyed. "You can't call the police when the police are already here."

"Well, who cares who she is?" asked the other guy. "Just get her out of here." He looked toward the back of the apartment, like what was back there made him sad. Pete looked like he wanted to argue about this, but all of a sudden he was too tired to do it. He looked at me and reached out like he was going to grab me. I backed up. He didn't get mad this time, though, he just moved his hand, that little gesture that means come on, let's go.

And that's what he said. "Come on, let's go. I don't know how you got here and I don't care. Count yourself lucky. Just get lost." He wasn't even looking at me, he was half following the other guy, who was already heading down the hall. Pete took a hit of beer. He looked totally wiped and worried about the other guy, and also like all he really cared about was finishing the one beer and finding another. Now that he wasn't screaming at me, I could see he was not bad-looking; he needed a shave, and he was a little paunchy around the middle, but he had great eyes, dark brown, kind of shrewd and sad, which made him look like a worried kid even while he was being mean. Under the circumstances I wasn't falling for it, plus I truly didn't get what was going on here. These guys had barged in and woken me up maybe a minute ago. And now what, I was supposed to leave? Who the fuck did they think they were? I mean obviously I was grateful that they weren't rapists, but after my initial terror some sense of reality was setting in. What the hell?

"I'm not going anywhere," I told Pete. "This is my apartment. I live here. And and and I think it's a *good* idea to call the cops because you're the ones who, what the fuck are *you* doing here? Who the fuck are *you*?"

"You *live* here?" he said. "You live here?"

"Yes," I said. "This is my apartment. I own it."

"You own it?" he replied, taking a step back and calling down the hall. "Hey, Doug! Get back here! This chick says she owns this place!" He looked back at me, angry again, but in a calmer, nastier way. He also seemed to find my claim that I owned the apartment sort of quietly hilarious. He took a step back into the bedroom. "Maybe you should tell me your name after all, sweetheart."

"I don't, I don't—you tell me *your* name," I insisted. I shoved my hands into the back pockets of my jeans and felt the hard edge of the bills I had stashed there. I was glad I had taken the precaution of pocketing them right away; it looked like I might need that money sooner rather than later. "I mean this is like my house and you're like, you're like . . ."

"Your house?" said Pete, half laughing. "Your house. That would make you—what was your name again?"

"Tina Finn?" I said. Okay, I shouldn't have caved like that, making my name a question at the last minute, but it wasn't so easy keeping up the act that I was on top of this situation.

"Tina *Finn,*" he said, smiling now. "Tina Finn. One of the daughters of Olivia Finn, would I be too far off the mark assuming that?"

"Yeah, actually, she was my mom, and she just died two days ago, and and and—"

"Yesterday was the funeral."

"Yes, *yesterday* was the *funeral.*"

"Yesterday was the funeral, and you managed to slime your way into our apartment the same night. How very resourceful of you." This was a creepy guy, smart and wily and drunk and way too fucking good-looking. He was the kind of guy who knew he could get away with complete shit, and say and do completely shitty things because he *was* both great-looking and smart. I wanted to get away from this guy as fast as I could, but I couldn't give any more ground. If I did, there was no question I'd be kicked out of there, and where was I supposed to go?

"Okay, you got my name, how about you give up yours?" I said. "Somebody Drinan, yeah? Pete, that's your first name? So that makes you Pete Drinan. Bill was your dad?"

"Give the little lady a prize," he said with a smirk.

"Well, listen, Pete Drinan," I said. "I'm not going anywhere tonight. Now that you know who I am? Maybe you should just piss off."

"Maybe you should stop thinking you have any rights here."

"Maybe you should stop thinking I don't."

"And what gives you rights again? Your mother conned my father into marrying her, which gave her rights for a while, I guess, but you, I'm guessing not so much."

"He left her this place, so that does give me rights," I said.

"Really," he said back, like what I had said meant nothing. He took another hit of beer.

"Yeah, really. He left it to her, and she left it to us."

None of this seemed surprising to Pete Drinan, but it didn't seem totally familiar with the story either. He made that little come on, let's go wave with his hand again.

"I'm not leaving," I said. "I don't have to leave."

"Well, that's debatable, but I'm not asking you to leave. Hey, Doug!" he yelled, going toward the back of the apartment. "Listen to this!" Then he yelled at me, without even turning around, "Come on, Tina Finn, I think you should explain this situation to my big brother. Come on."

What a jerk, I thought, and boy does he know how to order people around. I followed him back to television land to see what fresh hell this great-looking asshole was about to cook up for me.

His older brother was sitting on the sad little couch in front of the TV set, sort of slumped over, looking at the empty bowl of noodles and the half-empty glass of vodka and grapefruit juice. When he glanced up, I got a better look at him; he had the same tired, smart brown eyes as his brother, but they didn't scare me as much for some reason. It might have been the rest of his face; his mouth was thinner and kind of kept in one line, like it was so used to being disappointed it didn't even bother to find another shape anymore. His hair was thinning too; I could see the beginnings of a bald spot dead center on the top of his head, and his hairline had crept so far up the dude looked startled all the time. So Doug Drinan managed to look shrewd, old, startled, and disappointed.

"There's hardly any furniture left," he observed to no one in particular. "I wonder what he did with it all? You think he sold it? He must've sold it, but why?" It sounded like what it was: a very good question.

Pete was on his own track, though. He turned to me and tipped his head, like I was some kind of circus animal he could order around with these little gestures.

"Tell my brother your name," he said, all arrogant and smug.

"Why don't you do it for me, you seem to think it's so funny," I countered. He really was the kind of guy who instead of doing the simplest thing he asked, you'd really rather just irritate the shit out of him.

Pete grinned. "Oh, no, I don't think it's funny at all. Tina Finn. Her name is Tina Finn, and she has just shared with me a few truly remarkable facts," he said. Then, before he could get around to narrating these fascinating facts, he glanced into the next room, which was just as I had left it: an unmade bed, piles of clothes on the floor, underwear and books and empty boxes everywhere. The place looked absolutely ransacked, because in fact I had ransacked it. "What the fuck?" He looked back at me, all angry again. "What the fuck. You went through his stuff. You went through my father's shit?"

I blushed like a teenager. "I didn't, I was just—um . . ."

"You were just what?" he asked, tossing underwear at me. "You were just casually going through my father's underwear drawer?"

"I'm sorry, I was looking—my mom had this old bottle of perfume, and I was—"

"You were looking for a bottle of perfume in my father's underwear drawer, and what you found was—his wallet." He unearthed it, looked through it swiftly. "And, oh look, there's nothing in there now, is there?" He closed the wallet and tossed it to Doug, on the couch.

"I didn't take anything from your dad's wallet," I said.

"That's a lie," he noted correctly.

"It's NOT a lie," I said, continuing to lie. "Yeah, I found it in there, but I mean there was nothing in it." It was clear that this guy was one hell of a bully, but I was pretty sure he wouldn't actually frisk me, so he had no way to prove I had the cash, which by the way I was not about to give up. "I was looking—"

"You were looking and looking and you also found—the vodka!" he exclaimed, picking up the bottle off the coffee table, where I had left it.

"Knock it off, Pete." The other Drinan stood, shaking his head, like he was used to this nonsense from crazy Pete but wasn't in the mood. "I'm sorry for your loss," he said to me. "You must still be in shock."

"Oh," I said, surprised. Doug Drinan expressing sorrow for my loss was strangely touching, under the circumstances. "Thanks. I mean, thanks."

"It was sudden, yes? I mean, she wasn't sick," he said.

"No, they, they said it was a heart attack. I don't know."

"That makes it hard."

"Don't make friends with her; she's not staying," Pete advised his sad big brother. He had pulled the cork out of the vodka bottle and started pouring it into a dusty glass, which he seemed to have located in one of those cabinets.

"You're going to regret that in the morning," said Doug.

"I'm going to regret everything in the morning; I regret everything now," Pete informed him. "But since you're so interested in making friends with our little intruder, maybe you should hear what she has to say about the apartment and why she's here." He took a hit of straight vodka. I was hardly listening. I was suddenly desperate for a drink myself and wondering if I could make one without losing any more ground with these guys. Doug looked at me with a kind of puzzled weariness, like he was sincerely curious about what I'd say in response to Pete's nasty prodding, but also like he didn't believe that anything really horrible was going to come out of my mouth. Seriously, he was such a tired and sad person, sort of like he'd already been through so much bad luck that he didn't think anything could get any worse.

"I . . ."

"According to Tina Finn, who claims she is not a thief, evidence on hand notwithstanding, Dad left the apartment to her mother, you remember the oh so lovely Olivia—"

"Jesus, Pete." Doug looked away, disgusted and embarrassed. "Knock it off, would you?" He stood and grabbed the bottle of vodka, then went over to the little freezer full of ice cubes. The drinking was apparently going to continue with both these fellows.

"I'm just getting to the good part. Dad left the apartment to Olivia—"

Doug turned at this, confused and concerned and about to interrupt, but Pete had more up his sleeve.

"And Olivia left it to her daughters."

This stopped Doug in his tracks. He turned and looked back at
me, skeptical but wary. The whole idea was clearly so ridiculous that he
couldn't take it in.

"She didn't actually leave it to us," I said, embarrassed as hell. "I
mean, she did leave it to us. She didn't make a will, and there's this, you
know, she died intestate. And that means—"

"I know what 'intestate' means," said Doug, going for the ice.
"This would explain what you're doing here."

"Yeah," I said.

"Is your mother even in the ground yet?" he asked in a sort of edgy
tone. No more friendly expressions, so sorry for your loss—now I had
to tough it out with both of them. To hell with it. If they were both
drinking, then so would I.

"The funeral was yesterday morning," I said, grabbing my half-
empty glass of vodka and grapefruit juice and following him into the
kitchen, defiant. "So we went from the cemetery to the lawyers and
then we came here."

"Very efficient." Doug nodded. He dumped some ice in my glass
and handed me the vodka bottle.

"Well, we didn't, it's not like, I mean I had no idea about any of,
any, you know, they didn't even tell me until after, I was standing there
at the grave, you know, honestly, when they told me about it."

"'They' being . . ."

"My sisters."

"Right, there are several of you," Doug reminded himself. "Four
of you?"

"Three. Me and Alison and Lucy. And Daniel, he's Alison's husband. But no kids. None of us has managed to, I guess."

"Fascinating." Doug nodded. "And someone told you . . ."

"This lawyer, he said he was my mom's lawyer."

"That idiot Long," stated Pete. He was lying on the couch now,
spread out the whole length of it, so there was nowhere else for anyone to

sit in this dreary little room. He had the cedar jewelry box open on his lap, the one that had Mom's perfume bottle in it. He was actually looking at it. "And he said you inherited our apartment. You inherit all my mom's stuff too?"

"That was *my* mom's." I wanted him to give it back.

"It was not your mother's," Doug informed me, cold. He was looking at me as if he was trying to decide what to do with me, like maybe he could just lock me in a closet and leave me there. I started to think he might not be the nice brother after all; maybe he was just a little less sparky than Pete.

"Yeah, it was too," I said. "She had it her whole life. So I just, that's why I was looking through their stuff. I knew it was in there and I wanted to have it." I set my drink down and walked over to the couch, reaching out my hand to take it from asshole Pete. He closed his fingers over it and dropped it back into the jewelry box and shut it.

"Everything's up for grabs, though, isn't it? Isn't that what Long told you?" Pete sat up, putting the jewelry box next to him, so close he was almost sitting on it.

"No, that's not what he told me. What he told me was everything was ours."

"Everything of ours is yours, that's what he told you?"

"He told me, he told everybody—"

"Oh look at this!" Pete found the tarnished silver box with all the keys in it; he had been lying on it on the couch. "You take a fancy to this too?"

"I wasn't stealing anything!" I said.

"Except our home," said Doug. He leaned up against the wall, looked out the window.

"Oh look, my mom's wedding ring," Pete observed, picking it out of the silver box. "Glad to know you weren't stealing that."

"Look, you guys are mad. Okay, I get it," I said.

"Like her mother, a regular rocket scientist," Pete murmured.

"My point being I'm not the one who fucked up this situation. That would be your dad, right? Didn't he tell you he was leaving the apartment to my mom? Didn't he even tell you that?"

"Who are you again?" said Pete, really pissed now. "Have we met? Do I know you? Then what the fuck are you doing here in my apartment! I grew up here with my family and my mother—my father was happily married to my mother for twenty years, not *two* years, *twenty* years. This is our apartment! What the fuck are you doing here, sleeping in *my* bed? What the fuck gives you rights?"

"Well, apparently some document that your father signed gives me rights."

"He was a fucking drunk!"

"Yes, that's real news, I was here for fifteen minutes I figured that out."

"Because booze was the first thing you went looking for—"

"No—"

"Just like your mother."

"Go tell the judge. Go tell Stuart Long. What are you yelling at me for? You think I'm making this up? You think I'd be here if they hadn't given me the keys?" I snapped. "Go yell at your father. Oh, sorry. Guess you missed that chance."

That shut old Pete up. He glanced at Doug, who looked at him for a second, then out the window. It happened pretty fast, but there was no question.

"Holy shit, he *did* tell you, didn't he?" I said. "You knew. That he was leaving her the apartment. He told you. That's why you're so mad. Because you knew." They both looked at me real surprised for a second, like it hadn't occurred to either of them that I might actually put that together.

"You don't know anything," said Pete, deflated as hell all of a sudden.

"Well, I don't know a ton, but I'm learning as we go," I retorted. "What'd you do, piss him off? That's just a wild guess."

"Don't push your luck," he said, but he was tired now.

"I don't think we should be talking about this," Doug observed, cool as a cat. Seriously, these two were a mixed set, like salt and pepper shakers. They maybe fit together, but they weren't alike. They both knocked back their vodka at the same time, but I could see it wasn't going to bring them any peace. Like vodka brings anybody peace, ever.

"Let's get out of here," said Doug.

"What, we're just going to let her stay?" Pete asked, offended by my very existence now.

"Unless you want to take her home with you, I don't know what to do with her," Doug said, shrugging.

"You know, you guys don't actually get to decide what to do with me," I said, all snarky and defiant again.

"Don't count on that," said Doug, rapidly moving into first place in the asshole competition that we all had going by this point. "And don't get too comfortable." He set his empty drink down on the kitchen counter and headed for the back hallway. Pete slammed back the rest of his drink and picked up the jewelry box as he stood.

"Listen," I said.

"What?" He looked at me. There would be no listening tonight.

"Nothing," I said.

He nodded and turned, following his brother down the hallway, taking my mother's little black bottle of perfume with him.

3

I CALLED LUCY FIRST THING IN THE MORNING. SHE WAS NOT THE least bit impressed with my story about Tina and the night visitors.

"They were going to show up eventually, that was a given," she announced.

"They were pretty pissed," I told her.

"Did you think they were going to be delighted to hear that they've been disinherited? I didn't."

"Man, Lucy, do you always have to be so mean about everything?" Lucy, she's, no kidding, it's very impressive how capable she is, but sometimes she just seems to think everybody should sleep on rocks. Plus I had a whanging hangover. I was in no mood for all this steely resolve.

"Just because I knew they were going to show up, that doesn't mean I'm particularly happy about it," she replied. "I think this could get pretty complicated pretty quickly, and I don't see any point in being naive about that."

"Yes, yes, *okay*," I said. "Actually, what I meant was couldn't you be like a little worried that I was stuck in this apartment by myself and these two big guys showed up and scared the shit out of me?"

"They frightened you?"

"Well, yeah, of course they did! I was sound asleep, and all of a sudden there are two big guys in this empty apartment with me, I didn't know who they were. It was terrifying."

"Did they threaten you?" Lucy asked, only idly curious.

"They were both drunk, and yeah, they threatened me—they threatened me a lot," I said. That cheered her right up; she went from being slightly interested to downright perky.

"That is absolutely unacceptable." I could hear her typing.

"Are you taking notes?" I asked, kind of wanting to strangle her.

"I just want to have everything on paper for the lawyers. We have to have a paper trail if they get aggressive. No point in putting it off. Listen, I have to run to a meeting."

"You're running to a fucking meeting? What am I supposed to do if they come back?"

"Tell them to call our lawyer," she replied. "Let's see—Long, tell them to call Stuart Long, you met him yesterday, he was Mom and Bill's lawyer, he put together the will."

"Yes, I remember, but I don't have his number."

"They'll know who he is, Tina," Lucy said. "Listen, I really do have to run."

"Wait a minute, would you wait a minute?" I said. "There's somebody here." And there was. Somebody was in the apartment.

"Is it them?" she asked.

"I don't know, but it's someone," I whispered. I was in that little couch-and-television island where Bill and Mom had drunk themselves to death. But the air in the back of the apartment was moving differently, like the wind that comes just before a train arrives in a subway station. And then I could hear somebody moving around.

"Tina, go find out who it is, and if there's a problem, call me back," she instructed. "I'll tell my assistant to come get me out of my meeting if you really need me. All right?"

"Can you just hold on a minute?"

"No, sorry, I can't. For heaven's sake. It's not like it's the middle of the night and they're walking in and threatening you. I can understand why that upset you, but this should be easy. Handle it, would you? You're not a child."

"Look, don't talk to me like that, okay?" I said, really annoyed now. "I don't appreciate it; we're all in this together."

"That's my point. If you need me, call me back." And then she hung up. No kidding. She hung up on me without saying good-bye.

"I hate my family," I said to myself. I knew that calling Alison would be useless in the complete opposite direction. She would get all uptight and start freaking out and have no idea what I should do, and then she and Daniel would come to the apartment and he'd try to take over. I decided I'd better go see what the hell was going on.

I heard another sound, like pots banging in a kitchen six miles away. "Hey!" I yelled. "Who's in here?" Which was not particularly sly, but I wasn't looking for the surprise element, since I assumed it was those two boneheads, or at least one of them. "You need to get out of here!" I yelled. I was charging through the maze of rooms now, all determined and cocky. The apartment looked considerably friendlier in the morning light. Even though there wasn't much furniture and the carpeting was shitty, the walls were painted all beautiful colors, which glowed in the morning light. It gave me courage, which was good because I didn't have much else to go on. "Get out of here and call your stupid lawyer and stop bothering me!" I shouted, charging into the giant room at the front of the apartment.

"Helllooooo," said a man. "Who are you?"

Okay, I practically jumped out of my skin. When I turned the last corner, there was a man, but not Pete or Doug, standing in the middle of that big empty room. He was quite short and very tidy, a tidy little person in clothes covered with dirt. I half expected him to evaporate, but he didn't. He just stood and stared at me until I recovered the part of my brain that wasn't completely hungover, and I flipped out.

"Who am *I*?" I said. "Who are *you*?"

"Oh wait, oh wait," he said. "I know who you are. You're Tina! Alison, Lucy, and Tina; you're Tina. Olivia showed me pictures. I've seen pictures of you."

"You've seen *pictures* of me?" I said.

"Look at you—you're pretty, you're much prettier in real life, you don't photograph well at all. I think that's strange, don't you, how some people look just lovely when you meet them, and then you see them in pictures and you think, well, *that* didn't translate. Well, anyway. I'm Len! Your mother . . . didn't? Didn't she?"

"Didn't she what?"

"Nothing," he said, kind of sad. "Oh well. She said you didn't talk; I didn't realize that meant you didn't talk at all. You and she didn't talk at all?"

"Listen, Len, I don't . . ."

"No, of course—not my business! Not my business. And honestly, it's not that we spent a lot of time on it, but she seemed, much more than Bill, to have a kind of yearning, you know you should have called her, you really, oh well. You don't have to answer that; I know things were complicated. She didn't blame you, so who am I?" He seemed to think this was a point worth making, but at the same time he didn't seem to want to continue our conversation. He glanced toward the kitchen, distracted.

"Look, could you, you know?" I was starting to get annoyed with this guy. Frankly, I was getting annoyed with just about everyone: Lucy, those shitheads who barged in on me while I slept, my mother, my ex-boyfriend Darren, everyone in New York City, the universe. "You know, whoever you are, Len, I think, uh, this isn't a great time for me to visit, and I'm not sure what you're doing here."

"Sorry." He smiled, suddenly looking down and dusting himself off, as if he remembered how actual people behave. "I'm being ridiculous, you're right to be upset. Did you stay here last night? You must have. I'm so sorry for your loss, it must have been a terrific shock. Well, it was for all of us. Such a shame. She was a terrific person. I'm Len Colbert, and like I said, I was a friend of your mother and Bill's. I live in the penthouse here on the top floor. Well, of course, it's the top floor—that's where penthouses are, aren't they?" He laughed at himself. "I'd shake your hand, but mine are not presentable. I'm a, well, it's complicated what I do." He sighed. "Not complicated. I'm an anthropological botanist. I was, that is—I don't teach anymore. But the, uh—the kitchen here—have you seen the kitchen?"

"The moss?" I asked.

"Yes, the moss." He smiled. This elflike character had a fantastic smile, charming and self-involved and devilish. He also had the most alarming blue eyes I'd ever seen, with dark edges but sky blue around the middle. For a second I was grateful he was at least thirty years older than me, because even though he was so odd, I could see the appeal of eyes like those. "Bill and I had an arrangement. He rented me his kitchen. He let me—that is, both he and your mother—let me use it as a kind of greenhouse. My own greenhouse, up on the roof, is not tenable for a mossery, not that I didn't try, but to maintain the habitat, the hydration alone would be a fortune. Of course, it may be possible that we just didn't solve the problems. But people were not enthusiastic overall, you can imagine. The terror of a few bryophytes! Anyway, it was finally impossible. I investigated the possibility of renovating the plumbing to provide the additional water to the roof, and I had no support from my fellow tenants. None whatsoever. One might even say there was open hostility. At least lawsuits were threatened. Anyway, you'll have to come see it."

"See . . . ?"

"The greenhouse. It's a rarity to find one in the city, but the light, as you can imagine, so far up, is utterly spectacular and alarming—even the views, not to mention what you can accomplish with that much light. I think I am not unduly proud, I'd love for you to come up; you should take me up on this. But it is absolutely useless for moss. Our solution—Bill's and mine—to our mutual needs was as you see." He made an elegant gesture toward the kitchen. "Actually it's a bit of a secret. There's a lot of misunderstanding in the building about moss. This confusion between moss and mold—it's ridiculous. They're not even the same order. Bill and Olivia were very understanding. And discreet." He smiled at me and nodded, apparently finished with this unintelligible explanation.

"So you have a key?" I asked.

"Oh yes. They spent most of their time in the other half of the apartment. This part of the place hasn't been in use for years."

"Well, okay, but it looks like I'm going to be living here now," I said.

"Reeeeallly?" Len asked, cocking his head as if it were the most extraordinary news. Actually, he made it sound like it was just the slightest bit too extraordinary to be believed.

"Yes, until the will is settled. I'm staying here."

"And what do the boys have to say about that?" Len the elf asked, sort of half to himself.

"I'm sorry, what did you say?" I asked edgily. He smiled, clearly amused by my tone.

"The boys," he repeated. "I ran into them last night in the lobby. They didn't mention to me that you would be living here. So I'm surprised to hear it. As I assume they were." He folded his hands in front of his chest with an odd little gesture of delight and smiled at me again, as if I would find his clever piece of deduction charming.

"Look, you're going to have to go," I said. "I don't know anything about this, and you know, you want me to be discreet and everything, but this is clearly some sort of illegal thing you have going here."

"Moss is not a controlled substance," he informed me, laughing.

"Oh sorry, I maybe misunderstood you before," I said. "Because you said how people in the building got all mad when you were trying to grow it up there on the roof, so I was thinking maybe they wouldn't like to find out that instead you decided to grow it on the eighth floor in the middle of the building, where it might actually *spread*."

"Ah," said Len. "I understand why perhaps you thought I said that."

"Yeah, it sounded a little like that, like people maybe wouldn't be so thrilled to hear what you were doing here."

"That's not what I was saying," he said.

"So I don't actually need to keep my mouth shut about this?"

Elfman laughed again, to himself this time.

"What's so funny, Len?"

"Nothing, no, nothing." He looked back at the kitchen, this time with real longing. "Do you like moss?" he asked me.

"Honestly, I've never thought about it that much."

"It is a rare spirit that appreciates moss," he said, as if this were news. "I have seventeen different species in this particular mossery. Some of them are exceedingly beautiful. The curators at the two public botanical gardens in the city would give their eyeteeth, frankly. It's actually a bit of an achievement that I could do what I've done, and under these conditions? Please. Let me show you."

"That's not necessary, Len."

"Please," he said, holding out his elegant dirty hand, like a prince at some ball, waiting to sweep me into a dance.

"What the hell," I said.

So for the next hour, this strange guy walked me through the intricacies of moss, gametophores and microphylls and archegonia—that's the female sex organ of moss, who knew—and how much water moss needs for fertilization and how long it takes for sporophytes to mature. He talked about liverworts and hornworts; he had mosses in there that were native to the Yorkshire Dales and mosses that grew only in cracks in city streets and mosses that grew only in water. In Europe during World War II, he told me, sphagnum mosses were used to dress the wounds of soldiers, because they're so absorbent and have mild antibacterial properties. Also some mosses have been used to put out fires. Don't ask me how they would do that, but apparently it's historically accurate. Old Len knew a ton about moss, and he made sure that I knew how great his mossery was and how no one builds them anymore and what a tragedy it would be if anything were to happen to his mossery.

"That would be awful," I agreed. I looked around the transformed kitchen. Len had even hung an old woodcut of a medieval tree on one wall, I suppose to keep the moss company. "So how much did Bill charge you to rent his kitchen like this?"

"Oh," he said, looking at me sideways for a second. "It was a very friendly arrangement."

"He didn't charge you rent for this? But they were broke, weren't they?"

"What makes you say that?"

"I spent the night here. There's nothing here. They were living on vodka and fish sticks and red wine," I said. "Which he paid for in cash."

"You *have* been busy, and you say you just arrived yesterday?"

"So he really gave you this room to grow moss in, for free?"

"I didn't say that." Len smiled. "I said we had a friendly arrangement."

"Like under the table, friendly like that?" I asked.

"Bill liked to fly under the radar," he admitted with a small shrug. "He did prefer cash."

"How much did he charge you?" I asked directly. Len looked at me sideways and then went back to examining one of his moss beds, poking at it carefully with his middle finger.

"Seven hundred dollars a month," he said, raising an eyebrow.

"You know what, Len?" I said. "I think this mossery is fantastic, and I see no reason why you can't keep it here for as long as you want. I'm gonna go make a phone call."

"Lovely." Len smiled. "I'll just continue my work, then."

I figured I might need to keep the cash coming, and it did seem reasonable to let this guy keep his mossery. So I went back to TV land and picked up the phone and started dialing, meaning I made it half-way through Lucy's number before realizing that the phone was dead. There was nothing on the line—no clicks, no beeps, no dial tone, nothing. I hung up and tried again, and I did that about eight more times, and then I plugged and unplugged the phone about eight times and then I tried it eight more times. Then I tried it in three other jacks, in three of the little bedrooms, before returning to the great room.

"Something wrong?" Len asked me, leaning out of the kitchen. I mean, obviously there was something wrong; I was holding the phone out and staring at it like it was about to explode.

"The phone doesn't work," I told him. "I mean, it worked just an hour ago, and now it doesn't."

He held out his neat but dirty hand and I gave him the phone, which he plugged into yet another wall jack. He listened for less than one second, then nodded. "Well," he said. "I need to introduce you to Frank."

Frank was the doorman. Len took me downstairs to the front lobby, and there was Frank, a good-looking Hispanic guy in a beige uniform with little gold things on the shoulders.

"Hey, Len, what's up?" Frank asked.

"This is Tina Finn, Olivia's daughter." Len made a little wave with his hand, like I might be some fancy dish that was being served up. I felt like bowing.

"Nice to meet you, Miss Finn," said Frank, reaching out and shaking my hand politely. "I'm real sorry about your mom."

"Thanks," I said.

"Tina is going to be staying in the apartment for now, while they settle things up with the estate," Len informed Frank. It was genius, seriously; coming from Len, "she's staying in the apartment" sounded pretty good. At least Frank the doorman had no problem with it.

"Well, welcome to the Edge," he said. "If you need anything, you let me know."

"There is something." Len nodded. "It looks like her phone's been cut off. Could you put a call in about it?"

"Sure, who's your carrier?" asked Frank, reaching for the phone receiver on his desk.

"You know, I'm not sure who they had," I said.

"Well, let's see then, maybe I'll put in a call to Doug—that's Bill's son," he told me. "There's probably been some mistake, maybe he cut the phone off. Did he know you were going to be staying up there?"

"Yeah, we talked, you know, we just talked yesterday about it," I said. "Look, you don't need to bother him, I'll call him myself."

"I got it right here," Frank said, dialing. "It's no bother." He was dialing away when Len tapped him on the shoulder.

"It's probably better just to give her the number," Len said under his breath, like he was trying to keep me from hearing what he said. Frank looked at him, confused, and Len did that thing with his hands, opening them up, apologizing to the universe for the stupidity of the human race. "I think there's a lot going on, Frank, you probably don't want to put yourself in the middle of it." It sounded so much like he was taking care of Frank that for a minute I forgot he was actually taking care of me.

However, it was starting to occur to old Frank that this story didn't quite add up. "But you did see Doug last night?" he asked, a little worried, while he rooted around for a pen.

"We hadn't figured out what we were doing last night when we talked, and everything was such a mess, with Mom's funeral, I was kind of a wreck and we hadn't actually thought about the practicalities. I mean, I was just like crying and crying, so I really didn't get the details straight," I fibbed.

"I know what that's like." Frank nodded. "I lost my mom fifteen years ago, I still miss her." He looked at me, and I swear to god, in that split second you could see the sadness rise up in his face, just enough to make his cheeks flush a little and his eyes well up. He got embarrassed right away and looked down, like he was still searching for that pen even though it was in his hand, and because that uniform looked so hideous on him, it made me feel kind of bad to be lying to him. I mean, he was significantly nicer than Len, who probably was just taking care of me so I wouldn't mess with his moss. But this guy Frank was just a nice person who missed his mom. He had a kind of bad haircut, which was so sweet and stupid I thought my head was going to split.

"Well . . . thanks, Frank," I finally said. "I'll go call Doug right now and make sure he knows about me staying here and all that and, you know, make sure that he knows not to turn anything else off." I turned away so Frank could have a moment of privacy to collect himself. And then old Len was at my elbow, showing me to the door, like a friendly undercover agent. "There's a Verizon store two blocks up and one over, on Columbus," he informed me cheerfully under his breath. "They sell those throwaway phones. You don't need a credit card, you can just pay cash, isn't that convenient?"

"Very," I agreed. "Thanks for the tip, Len."

A throwaway phone was exactly the thing, of course, because I had no cell phone and no credit card and now no landline. So Len was right to suggest it, and while I was out putting his sensible suggestion into action, I also poked around a couple of clothing stores so I'd have more than one skirt, one pair of jeans, and one sweater in my wardrobe. I could have called that bonehead Darren and asked him to put all my clothes in a box and send them, but I had no reason to believe he would actually do that, even if he said he would. So I ducked into a couple of really cute shops, where I learned that my seven hundred dollars, minus one throwaway phone, might buy me one pair of excruciatingly expensive blue jeans and half a tank top, which seriously annoyed me until I found a Gap, which had a whole lot of stuff on sale that fit fine and looked cool enough and cost quite a bit less. Then I was hungry, so I had a burger in a seedy deli, and then I needed underwear, and honestly I couldn't find anyplace to buy it except one of those really cute little shops, and that cost a complete fortune but I had no choice. So the seven hundred dollars was more or less whittled down to two hundred by the time I decided to go back home.

That was the first time my head said "Let's go home," and I know it sounds kind of ridiculous that I thought of it that way? But no kidding,

I was already in love with that place. All that stuff about my mother drinking herself to death there, and my sisters being so uptight and bossy, and the crazy drunk guys showing up in the middle of the night— none of it seemed that serious when I picked up my eighteen packages and thought about going home. I half wondered, what are you going to do when you get home? And then I thought, well, maybe I'll just make myself a cup of tea and read a book or something, there are at least a thousand used mysteries still shoved under the bed in Bill and Mom's bedroom. So on the way home I stopped at a little shop and bought some fancy tea, and I was well on my way to becoming a totally different person, the kind who lives on the Upper West Side, and drinks tea in the afternoon while reading mystery novels. Then I got back to the lobby of my fabulous new apartment where I found out I was still the same old Tina I had been just a couple hours before.

The lobby was packed. People were milling about, a bunch of kids in school uniforms were clustered around the elevator, arguing with one another and hitting the buttons on the elevator bank, and a woman in a bright red jacket with a fur collar kept trying to get Frank's attention at his little brass podium. Frank was talking to two men, and they were all yelling at once, and it sounded loud because the ceilings in that small space were so high and curved that the sounds bounced around in it. The lady in the red jacket was clearly related to the kids, because occasionally she would yell, "Stop it, Gail! All of you, would you just wait until I see if your father's package has arrived? Frank . . ." But Frank was dealing with whatever the two guys were saying, which I couldn't hear because of all the other noise. Two ladies standing behind the one in the red jacket were waiting a little more patiently, but not much. Both of them were spectacularly thin and wearing the kind of clothes you only see in ads in the *New York Times,* everything tight and fitted and slightly strange. I couldn't see their faces right away because their backs were to me. All I could see were those strange fashionable outfits, and one of the women had the most astonishing black curls tumbling down her back while the other one had short white hair flipped around her head. Then the one with black hair turned for a second, like she had heard some-thing just behind her, and she was one of those people who are so idiotically beautiful you think you're on drugs when you see them up close. Her eyes flicked in my direction, but then the woman she was with yanked at her arm.

"This is ludicrous," the older woman said. "I'll hail my own cab."

"That's what I said ten minutes ago," said the spectacular-looking woman. She turned around and headed right for the door. But the older lady didn't follow.

"We will get our OWN CAB, FRANK!" the old lady announced in quite a loud voice. "And I'm going to call the management company, do you understand? This chaos is NOT ACCEPTABLE."

"I want to talk to management as well, you get them on the phone," said one of the guys who was arguing with Frank.

"Maybe you could just take a second to look through the deliveries, then we'll just get out of your hair, Frank," said the lady in the red jacket, poking through the stuff piled on the console, trying to be nice but trying to get her own way too. The kids continued to scream as the furious white-haired lady turned away, muttering to herself about how nuts it all was.

Poor Frank was apologizing to everyone at the same time. "I can do that, sure let me—sorry, Mrs. Gideon, I am so sorry, so sorry, Julianna," Frank called after the ladies heading for the door. "If you give me just a second here—oh, she's here!" he said suddenly, looking both harried and relieved. And then the lady in the red jacket knocked all the packages off the top of the podium.

The whole scene was so complicated that it took me a second to realize that Frank was looking at me. He said to one of the guys he'd been talking to, "She says she's living there now, and that you met last night and you spoke about it—I'm not sure, but that's the young lady, she said that you know each other." Then he turned to me. "Tina, there's some kind of confusion here with Doug about the locks, he says he needs to change the locks, but you didn't say anything about that, so can you come talk to him while I deal with this? Hang on there, Mrs. Gideon, let me get you a cab. You can go ahead and look through all this, Mrs. White, but I didn't see anything." Frank rushed by me, opening the door for the infuriated Mrs. Gideon and her fabulous daughter Julianna. Mrs. White continued to yell at her children while she poked through the packages on the floor. Doug Drinan turned and gave me a dirty look.

Obviously this moment was a bit of a drag. The fabulous Upper West Side fashion plates were pushing by me while I tried to grab up my Gap bags, apologizing like a loser, "So sorry, sorry, sorry . . ." Frank practically shoved me aside while he raced after the women, trying to do his job. The loud, insane kids finally managed to get the elevator to arrive, but their mother was not yet ready to pile in with them; she was too busy giving me the once-over, like I was someone who was trying to break into their building. Which in fact I was.

"The doorman seems to be under the impression that you're living in my father's apartment," Doug announced. "And he thinks that I somehow agreed to this."

"Well, we did have a conversation about this last night, Doug, and I don't think you could have been really surprised that Frank told you that," I announced back. We were both pretending to be polite, but our voices were too forceful to count as polite.

"Last night we were decent enough not to kick you out onto the street," he told me. "The understanding was you'd be gone in the morning. You have no right to be here—your mother actually had no right to be here either, after my father died—"

"That's not what my lawyer tells me."

For some reason this caused old Doug to really lose it. He was suddenly furious, his face going all red, and he actually grabbed me, right up at the front of my shirt, and yanked me toward him, to do what I wasn't sure. I was not expecting it; even last night when he showed up with his brother totally wasted, and they were both really mad and reactive, they didn't put their hands on me. For one terrible minute I thought, oh no, this is one of those guys who's worse when he's *not* drunk; all that disappointment and sadness and thinning hair are just too much for him.

"Let go of me, let go let go," I said, real nice, real fast. I truly didn't want to find out if he had it in him to hit me.

"Look, I got a bunch of other jobs. Is this going to happen?" the guy with Doug asked. He had on a bad leather jacket and jeans and was carrying a tool kit, and he looked really bored. Somehow you knew right away that he saw this stuff all the time, people arguing about who had the right to change the locks to some house or apartment, and it wasn't all that earth-shattering. I realized I was probably not going to get hit. Anyway, the lock guy didn't seem to think so. He looked away like he didn't give a shit who won this battle, but also like he was pretty sure it was not going to be me, so there was no use even acknowledging that I existed.

The little interruption gave Doug a chance to recover. He let go of my shirt, giving me a little push, like he couldn't believe he had actually touched me. Then he turned and yelled back at Frank, who was outside trying to hail a cab for the fed-up Mrs. Gideon and her babelicious daughter. "We're going up!" Doug announced. Frank didn't even notice. Doug and the locksmith headed for the elevator, but they couldn't get in, because it was full of all those kids in school uniforms and the lady in the red jacket. But Doug was on top of his game now.

"We'll take the stairs," he announced, walking over to the other end of the lobby. The lock guy followed him. I did not. I finally got a clue, pulled out my brand-new throwaway cell phone, and called in the marines.

4

"OH FOR GOD'S SAKE," SAID LUCY, ALL ANNOYED, AS SOON AS I reached her. "Where have you been?"

"They cut off the phone," I told her.

"No kidding. I tried calling you three hours ago and got the message that the phone was no longer in service," she said. "Where have you been?"

"I went out to get a cell phone—"

"You've been out buying a cell phone for three hours?"

"Well, I needed some other stuff too and—"

"I thought you were broke, what are you using for money?"

"Would you listen to me, Lucy? They're here! At least one of them is here, and he's trying to change the locks, he has a locksmith with him, and he says I have no rights and—"

"Relax, I'm two blocks away, I'm taking care of it," she told me.

"What do you mean you're two blocks away? I called you at work," I said, all confused again.

"And my assistant patched you through to my cell."

"So you're on your way here? How did you know to come?"

"Tina, when the phone got cut off, what did you think was going on?"

"I don't know, I thought I needed to get a cell phone."

"Well, I thought a little harder than that. Just stay right there in the lobby; I'll be there in two minutes."

She hung up on me just as Frank trotted back in. He looked a little shell-shocked in a delirious kind of way. I thought he was going to be mad at me because I had just caused a huge scene, bringing utter chaos to his little lobby, with people threatening to have him fired and all sorts of unpleasant bullshit. Frank, however, seemed to have barely noticed. He was actually humming a little tune as he went back to his podium and started picking up the packages that were all over the floor. I thought for a moment that he was one of those strange sad people who need a little action to feel alive, but then I took another look, and it was like he was glowing around the edges, you could almost see beams of light coming out of his cuffs and collar. I thought, oh, he's in love, Frank is in love with the unspeakably beautiful Julianna Gideon. And he got to be near her, he got to hold the cab door open for her for half a second.

"She's pretty, huh," I said, testing out my theory.

"Oh my god," he agreed. "I can't even, when I look at her . . ." He glanced out the door, taking pleasure in seeing the place he had last been allowed to look at her.

"Does she know you like her?" I asked.

"What?" That was a bad question; it shook him out of his fantasy, and he remembered he had a real right to be mad at me.

"Did you get things straightened out with Doug?" he asked, suddenly stern. "He was quite certain that you are not supposed to be living up there in 8A. I didn't know what to say. This has put me in a very awkward position. I put a call in to building management, and I don't know what they're going to say. There's already been so much controversy around that apartment, I'm sure they're going to want to talk to both of you about it." He was trying his best to sound really mean, but the guy didn't have it in him. He was reading me the riot act, but he sounded like he was apologizing.

"I'll try to keep this out of your hair from now on," I said.

"I would appreciate that." He didn't sound angry, he sounded like he really would appreciate it. Just then Lucy walked in, wearing a sharp gray suit and heels, carrying a big briefcase, and looking like the queen of the universe.

"Lucy! Hey, this is my sister Lucy," I told Frank. "She'll have this solved in five minutes, I guarantee. You don't have to talk to building management."

"I'm sure they know all about this already," Lucy announced, a little clippy. "Tina tells me there's some confusion about the locks?"

"Confusion, I should say so," Frank said. "Doug Drinan, he's Bill's son?"

"I know who he is," Lucy said, nodding, trying not to make that little can we hurry this up please sign with her hand.

"Well, he's up there, having the locks changed," Frank told her. "He says he doesn't know anything about you having a claim on the place. I didn't know what to tell him. Your sister tells me she's staying there, I got no reason to doubt her, but Doug was Bill's son—"

"And we are his wife's daughters." Lucy smiled, completely professional. "No worries. We'll clear this up in no time." She took a couple of smooth steps over to the elevators and pressed the call button; as far as Lucy was concerned, this was as good as done. Frank smiled at me, relieved. When she isn't being annoying as hell, Lucy does have that effect on people. You know who's in charge.

Doug Drinan and his pal the locksmith were, sadly, not quite as easy to snow. We more or less fell over them on that eighth-floor landing— that is, I stumbled out of the elevator with all my packages, while Lucy popped out like a genie and presented Doug with a huge stack of documents.

"Mr. Drinan? Hi, how are you? I'm Lucy Finn, Olivia's daughter, it's a pleasure to meet you after all this time," she announced, talking quickly. "As you are aware, our mother passed only a few days ago, so obviously we are reeling, completely caught off guard, so I'm sure this is our fault. But I think there's been some confusion about the status of the estate. We spoke with Stuart Long just yesterday. He was in possession of your father's will—have you seen it? I brought an extra copy in case you hadn't." She handed it to him and kept talking. "Anyway, there is some real question about who the beneficiaries of the estate are at this time. Your father seems to have expressed in no uncertain terms that our mother was to inherit everything, largely meaning the apartment, it's unclear what else is included, but in any event I'm going to have to ask you to hold off on changing the locks for now. Until we get this sorted out." She smiled at him, very pleasant, but there was a definite don't-fuck-with-me edge behind it all. She works in PR and she can be very daunting.

Doug Drinan, unfortunately, didn't get on board with what she was saying. He barely glanced at the papers she handed him, then tossed them on top of the old radiator that was hissing in the hallway. "I'm aware we're going to be in a holding pattern for a little while with regard to the dispensation of the will," he told her. "Which is why I thought it important to secure the apartment. Obviously we can't have just anyone wandering in and out, disturbing the effects before we've even begun to probate this situation. I hate to say it, such a sad time—I mean really, condolences on your loss—but it sounds to me like this is going to get pretty complicated. This is just precautionary. Don't want things to get ugly down the line or anything."

Okay, the speech was good, but he was not as good as Lucy. He pressed those thin lips together, trying to smile and explain things like a nice guy, but he couldn't be bothered to pretend all that hard, so it came off like what it was, condescending and mean and like he was kind of enjoying messing with us. Which maybe he was. The more I saw of this guy the less I liked him. His hair really was dirty, and he had too much disappointment in him. Sometimes those are the worst people to deal with because they aren't even thinking anymore, they're just hoping they can make you as miserable as they are.

Lucy didn't care. Honestly, she has ice water in her veins, so this guy and all his unhappiness were just no match. "I completely agree," she said. "That's why we felt it was best to have Tina camp out here for the time being, to have someone on site making sure nothing untoward happened to the property while we sorted this all out. For instance, I think you and your brother stopped by in the middle of the night last night and removed some items?"

Doug Drinan stared at her, aghast at her nerve. She looked right back at him. "My mother's wedding ring," he said finally, as if the righteousness of the situation would mean something to her.

Lucy shrugged. "We have no way of ascertaining that."

"Except that she saw it." Drinan turned his cold stare on me, like I was the one who was fucking with him.

"I never said it wasn't, I didn't—ah—" I started.

Lucy raised her hand, fearless, and cut me off. "Tina, your actions are completely blameless in this matter."

"How do you figure that?" asked Drinan. "We got there, she'd already completely cased the joint."

"I was looking for my mom's perfume," I explained again.

"You went through my father's underwear drawer," he sneered. "You managed to find his wallet, which was conveniently empty by the time we got there."

"I didn't—"

"It doesn't matter what you were doing, Tina," Lucy said. "The point is, you did not remove anything from the premises, nor are you—or I or Alison—doing anything except insisting that we hold to the status quo until our lawyers and their lawyers have a chance to work through the documents and finalize the legal status of the estate. That's all we're trying to do. Protect everyone's rights."

"Look, I don't know what any of this is about?" said the locksmith. "But somebody's got to make a decision about these locks. There's a kill fee, you call to have your locks changed and then you change your mind, that's a fifteen-dollar charge."

"Not a problem," Lucy said, reaching into her purse.

"I don't agree to that," Drinan snapped. He put his hand out, stopping the locksmith from pushing for the elevator button. "I want the locks changed, and I have every right to change them."

"You legally have no right to change the locks," Lucy said. She was so coolheaded there was no way the locksmith would not do what she told him. But he did feel bad about it.

"Listen, man, I'll wait downstairs and let my boss know what's going on. If the situation changes, I can come back up and do the job. But I can't get involved in something that might, you know, be illegal."

"This is my apartment. I grew up here, this is my apartment." Drinan's temper was fraying again.

"Unfortunately, we have a stack of legal documents indicating that there is a very real chance that in fact it is not your apartment," Lucy said, not quite so nicely anymore. "And if you insist on pursuing this course of action I will be forced to call the police—"

"Go ahead. My brother is a detective with the NYPD, and you want to know something? They take care of their own."

"Listen, buddy," the locksmith said, desperate to get out of here. So was I. Bringing up the cops just made everything ickier.

"Wonderful. Your brother works in law enforcement, and I work in publicity. He can bring in his friends, and I can bring in mine. I know several writers for several prominent newspapers who would be only too happy to write about the NYPD superseding the law and forcing people from their homes."

"This *isn't* your home!" he shouted, starting to lose it.

"It is *Tina's home*," she told him in no uncertain terms. "Our mother died here, and every legal document I have studied so far tells me that this apartment is now *our* apartment, and she has no place to live, so for now she's living here, and it is her *legal right to do so*."

"I don't even know you people," Doug observed, as if that mattered.

"I suspect we will have plenty of time to get acquainted," Lucy said. She looked at the locksmith like she couldn't believe he was still standing there. "If you want to call your boss, now would be the time. I think we both know what he's going to tell you."

"Yeah, I don't have to call him; I'm not getting involved in this," he said. "But I do need that kill fee."

She reached into her purse, lifted out a neatly folded bill, and handed it over to him. The whole move took three seconds. "Keep the change," she announced. "For your trouble."

"Thanks." He nodded, then ambled over to the exit sign, pushed through that crummy brown door, and went on down the stairs. I didn't blame him. I wouldn't want to hang around waiting for an elevator under those circumstances either.

Drinan likewise didn't want to wait. He picked up his pile of legal documents and followed the locksmith.

"Perhaps you'd like my card," Lucy cooed, holding one out to his back.

"When I need to talk to you, I won't have any trouble finding you," he said as the door to the stairwell slammed shut behind him.

"What a lovely character," Lucy said, putting the card away. "I thought you said he was good-looking."

"The other one, the cop," I said.

"What does this one do?" she asked. "Run a charm school? Let me have the keys."

I handed them to her. "I don't know what this one does. Last night he didn't say much. They were both drunk."

"You should write down everything that happened last night. Have you done that yet?" she asked me.

"No, of course not—why would I write it down?"

"Well, we're going to need a paper trail on everything, Tina, this isn't a joke. I want it established that we are keeping records. Things are going to happen really quickly, and obviously the Drinan brothers have no compunction about playing hardball. We need to be prepared, as much as we can, for whatever they throw at us. What the hell is this?"

We had stepped into the front room, now filled with light from top to bottom. In spite of the hideous wall-to-wall shag, and all the crazy trouble with Doug Drinan, that room was really gorgeous, so I got distracted for a minute just staring at it and didn't know what she was talking about.

"Tina, helllooooo," Lucy said, waving her hand in front of my face and snapping her fingers.

"What?" I said.

"What," she asked, impatient, "is this?" With her toe, she nudged a small wooden toolbox, placed neatly against the wall beside the door-way to the mossery.

"Oh, that's Len's," I said.

"Len," she repeated, looking at me as if she knew that once again I had slept with someone I shouldn't have.

"He was a friend of Bill's and Mom's, that's his moss in the kitchen. They let him grow it there, he's some kind of botanist person, he lives in the building," I explained. "He was here when the phone got cut off, and he, you know, he said I should go get a cell phone." Lucy flipped the light switch. Nothing happened.

"Yes, I see," she sighed. "And what did you do once you bought the cell phone? Did you call me at work, as I asked you to, and say, Lucy, the phone has been cut off and they're probably going to try to cut the electricity as well and maybe change the locks, could you come over and help me handle this? Did you do that?"

"No, I didn't do that," I started.

"No, you didn't," she said, continuing to flip the useless light switch for effect. "You went shopping."

"Why would I assume this guy was going to do all that stuff you said? We don't even know these people."

"Tina, honestly, would you try to *think* for once? Hello, Monica, hi." She was on her cell now, firing on all jets. "I'm going to need you to call Keyspan *and* Con Ed, the gas and electric got turned off in my mom's apartment and we need to get it turned back on right away, and I mean now. My sister is living here, and she obviously can't stay if there's no gas or electricity, so if you need to run down to their offices, then do it. I left three copies of the will on my desk, take them with you so if they give you any trouble you can prove we have the right to put the accounts in my name. You can also give them the number of the building, tell them the doorman can verify that we've taken possession. What's his name?" she asked me.

"Frank," I said.

"Frank," she said to the phone, and then she rattled off the Edgewood phone number, which of course she knew even though I did not. She finished up the call by snapping her cell shut and then continued to explain things to me as if there had been no interruption at all. "I checked in with Stuart Long, the lawyer, from yesterday?"

"I remember, Lucy, could you not talk to me like I'm an idiot?"

"Don't get snippy, Tina, you almost completely blew it today—"

"I told you, I didn't know."

"No, you didn't *think*; you just took off for three solid hours on a *shopping* spree, and I'm not going to ask where you got the money because I don't care. But while I don't think Doug Drinan has any sort of legal claim on this apartment, I don't necessarily think he is a *liar*. Did you find money here?" She waved her hands idly at all the shopping bags I had dumped on the floor.

"I didn't have anything to wear," I said, trying to get to the beginnings of a defense. She was not interested.

"You listen to me," she snapped. "If I hadn't gotten worried about not hearing from you, and showed up, what would have happened?"

"I don't actually care what would have—"

"You'd be locked out. We all would be locked out. We would not have access to the apartment or the building, for that matter, for months. We'd have to go to a judge to get an injunction for permission to even look at the place, and by that point the Drinan brothers would have filed to legally contest their father's will, which, depending on how long that took to get through the courts? Would cut us off for years. *Years.* I checked this out with Daniel's friend the real estate lawyer, who assured me that contrary to what that idiot told us yesterday, a scenario like that leaves us with virtually no standing whatsoever. If they can prove that Bill was of unsound mind and Mom was of unsound character, and none of us had ever met Bill and had never set foot in this apartment, it is not that far a leap to claiming that Mom *tricked* him into changing his stupid will and that we have no right to this place. And that is what they are going to try to do. So do me a favor and don't make their case for them, would you? We put you here for a reason. Stay put."

"You expect me to never leave."

"Not unless you pick up your handy new throwaway cell phone and call me first and let me know that you have to go out for two hours and that Alison or I need to come by and be on site while you traipse about."

"Well, so how long—"

"As long as I say! If you don't like this deal, let me know. Let me know, and you can go back to Darren and the trailer park and the Delaware Water Gap now instead of later. Because if you don't help me make this work? That is where you're going to end up anyway."

I really thought Lucy was overreacting and being a total nightmare, but her argument made an impression on me. Even though I couldn't follow all the dastardly legal turns she had worked out about where this situation could go, it was pretty clear that if we didn't pull this off, it was in the cards for me to get booted out of there and back to cleaning houses in New Jersey.

"Okay okay okay," I said.

"Not okay okay okay!" she snapped. "I don't want to hear some sort of snotty okay! I want to hear, Yes, Lucy, I Will Do Whatever You Say."

"Well, I'm not going to say that," I snapped back. "I'll do it, but I'm not going to say it."

"Fine," she said, clearly sick of me. "Now, what's the story with all this moss? This is actually here for a reason?" Look, I find it impressive when she does that. In the middle of all that arguing, she remembered the one thing I had told her about the moss.

"Len, it's Len's moss, he lives on the top floor."

"Well, Len is going to have to get his moss out of here," she said, shoving his little toolbox with one of her slick black heels.

"I don't have his number," I said. "But I could go downstairs and get that doorman to buzz up and see if he's there."

"That's a good idea," she said, only half paying attention.

"Maybe I should get the keys copied while I'm down there."

"Now that, actually, would be useful," Lucy noted. She dialed her cell, then popped it to the side of her head while she held out the keys, which I took. "Listen, don't panic, there's nothing to get upset about," she said, so I knew she was talking to Alison. "But I'm over at the apartment. There's a lot going on."

Now, you do have to wonder why someone like Lucy believes people like me when we suddenly cave and agree to all sorts of nonsense in the middle of an argument. Because really, I had no intention of calling Len and telling him he had to move his moss. Instead I went downstairs, waved to Frank, walked over to Columbus and found the one bodega that inexplicably hovers there, and I bought myself a box of Dots. Then I walked around the block, ate the Dots, and thought about what I was going to do next. I wandered around the Upper West Side until I found a crummy little hardware store, where they made some new keys for me. While I was there I bought a few more choice items. Then I went back home, feeling more and more that I had every right to think of it that way.

5

"THE MOSS GUY ISN'T IN. FRANK BUZZED HIM ABOUT EIGHT TIMES, but he didn't answer," I told Lucy. "So I asked for his phone number, but it's unlisted and the doorman isn't allowed to give it out. Anyway, I left a message with the doorman for Len to call as soon as he gets in, and I'll tell him we need him to move all that stuff. Here, I got a set of keys for you and also an extra one, in addition to the ones I have." Soaring right through the lie about Len, I started fumbling with the keys. She didn't even look up as she took them from me.

"You didn't leave my number as well?" she asked, pecking away at her laptop, which she had set up on the coffee table back by the TV. There was a whole mess of documents and file folders falling out of her briefcase on the couch, so I knew she had decided to spend the rest of the day there. I felt like I had been invaded.

"He and I got kind of friendly, so I thought it would be better for him to call me," I said.

"You thought it would be better if I let *you* handle it," she said, making this sound like a stupendously idiotic idea. I looked at the floor and acted like I was really sorry that I was such a stupid person, which worked, because that's what she thinks I am anyway. It's easy to fool smart people about really stupid things. It's all about the assumptions.

The door to the bathroom behind the laundry room swung open, and a woman appeared. I just about jumped out of my skin, but Lucy kept on tapping at her keyboard.

"Fantastic," the woman said, smiling at me like we were old friends. She had blond hair very close to her head and she was exceptionally tan. She was wearing a tight beige microsuede pantsuit—pants and a jacket made out of synthetic beige polyester—and actual panty hose and boring-looking low brown heels. I'm sure that everything she was

wearing cost more than I made in a month of cleaning houses, but
frankly I don't understand why people dress like that.

"This place is *fabulous*," she informed me, striding over and holding out her hand for me to shake. "Hi, I'm Betsy Hastings. Did I hear
you saying something about the moss in the front kitchen?"

"We haven't been able to get hold of the guy who owns the moss,"
Lucy announced, "but it's being handled."

"No worries, no worries," said Betsy. As opposed to my sister, she
couldn't have been nicer. "This whole place is amazing. It's incredible
when a place like this comes on the market. Just thrilling."

"You're the real estate person," I said, guessing.

"A lot of people are interested, Tina," Lucy informed me. "And a lot
of questions need to be answered. Things are very preliminary at this
point."

"No question, no question," Betsy agreed. "I would love it if you
would let me handle this. I have a number of corporate clients who would
pick it up immediately, as is. I don't think you need to worry about
anything—the moss, the carpets, the appliances—you can let the buyer
take care of all that. Even in this market, which, as we know, has cooled
considerably in the past couple years. But you don't have anything to
worry about; this place is *amazing*."

"We've noticed," Lucy observed.

"Absolutely. Absolutely." Betsy Hastings nodded, running her
hand over the pocket doors. "A property like this, my advice would be
to let a professional pick it up and do the renovation, even at eleven or
twelve million it's going to be considered undervalued, which is good;
you want them to see the potential for a fast turnaround and a big
profit. You don't want to get involved in the level of renovation a place
like this would need, to pull in the really big numbers. There are agents
out there who will tell you that you could take in twenty or even
twenty-two on this, but that's going to require an enormous investment on your part up front, and I would say, let someone else take care
of that."

"Why don't you put together a strategy and call me tomorrow,"
Lucy said, holding out her card and not even looking at Betsy. She did

everything but tell Betsy to her face that her wild enthusiasm had put her out of the running.

"That's not to say, if you're looking for the bigger numbers, I can work with that too," Betsy explained, taking the card with a little shrug. "This end of the market, it's always a question of how long you want to wait. If you can afford to take the time and put a few million into it yourself, then we're talking about significantly larger numbers. It's just a different approach. As I said, I'd love to work with you on this. Really, it's a great place. Just the size of it, and the details! I love it when these old places open up. New York. There's no place like it, there really isn't, you just get such a sense of history. Fantastic. Fantastic. I'll give you a call tomorrow, we can go over a couple of different plans."

I had to give it up to old Betsy Hastings; it was pretty inspired bullshit. I mean, everything she said was true, and I totally agreed with her excitement about the apartment. But obviously she was mostly talking about money, which contributed to making everything she said sound kind of fake.

So Betsy took off, and then this swank young Indian character showed up, who went into overdrive explaining how if we could take a year and sink a million into the joint and break it down into three spectacular *separate* apartments, we could pick up twenty-two easy. Which made me like Betsy better, because she totally called that, that some other agent would tell us this version of events, and then that happened within the hour. And then this older white guy came by, wearing an extremely expensive suit, and he just looked around and acted like the place wasn't so great after all. The fixtures were all inappropriate, and the appliances were from the seventies, and he would have to think about whether he was interested in taking this on even if we could work out the legal difficulties. He was the only one who brought up the "legal difficulties," which perversely seemed to cheer Lucy up. She just shrugged and said something like, that would be up to you. They were quite snippy with each other. He may have thought his approach would make us want him more, which didn't make much sense, because clearly we were sitting on the mother lode in real estate terms, legal difficulties or not. Anyway, by the end of the day, when Daniel and Alison came by so we could have a powwow over Chinese food, it all felt very nerve-wracking.

"There's no way we can push through a sale before they slap a cloud on the title, if that's their intention, and it sure as hell would be mine," Lucy explained as she picked pieces of chicken out of the little white carton. "It's going to cost a fortune, and the legal tangle will be considerable. What'd your friend tell you, inheritance taxes are due within the year?"

"Six months," Daniel said. "Although it's apparently not much of a problem getting an extension when the will's being probated. We can get Wes to file for us if it becomes necessary."

"When," said Lucy. "*When* it's necessary—there's no use being naive about this."

"How much is this going to cost us?" asked Alison, all worried as usual.

"Much more than we have," Lucy admitted. "The only way we're going to be able to afford this is to get into a partnership with a real estate agency. I'm going to talk to Sotheby's about it tomorrow."

"That guy from Sotheby's was an asshole, he was the least interested of anybody," I pointed out.

"That's how I can tell he wants it," Lucy said, spearing a shrimp with slashing efficiency. "We need someone who's willing to work around the legal problems. Those other two were too spooked to even mention it. Losers."

"What if Sotheby's gets behind the Drinan side of this?" I asked.

"I sent over a packet of the documentation. They'll look at it and decide, but it's pretty clear we're going to win." Lucy shrugged.

"How can you be so sure? I just don't see how you can talk about all of this like you know what's going to happen. How can anyone know what's going to happen?" asked Alison.

I thought this was a pretty good point, but Lucy didn't even respond. Daniel reached for some beef and broccoli, not bothering to answer Alison either.

"These legal situations aren't sure. They never are," Alison persisted.

"And if we spend all our money and it isn't enough to cover the costs if the costs go through the roof—instead of everything, what if we end up with nothing?"

"*Alison,*" Daniel finally snapped. "I spent the day on the phone with four different lawyers; all of them gave us the same answer. This is a no-brainer. We're in the clear."

"If it's so totally clear that we're going to win this, how come it's all such a surprise to those Drinans?" I said. "I mean, they knew he was leaving it all to Mom."

"They told you that?" said Lucy. "Wait a minute. They *told* you they knew he was leaving the place to Mom?"

"They didn't say it, I just kind of figured it out," I said, looking over the remains of all that Chinese food. "Anyway, they definitely knew."

"That he was leaving the place to Mom."

"Yeah, they knew that part. But they totally didn't know that we would show up and get it. Like, why would they know that part but not the other part?"

"What else did they say?" asked Daniel in a tight voice. When I finally looked up, they were all staring at me. For a second I considered lying some more, because Lucy and Alison and Daniel were acting like such unbelievable sharks. But I didn't see any point in protecting those Drinans either. Already it was hard to know whose team I was on, and we had only been at this for a day and a half.

"They were just sad and drunk and kind of mad, that's all," I said, opting for a nonanswer. "One of them talked about all the furniture being gone, like it was so sad. He was a little surprised that so much of it was gone."

"Why would that surprise him?" Alison asked.

"Not totally surprised. But sad. Like they hadn't seen the place in a while, and they knew what it was like in here but not all the way. Sort of like that."

"They probably weren't allowed in very much." Lucy stared into her spicy shrimp, putting it all together. "Apparently Bill was a Howard Hughes–level freak. Then, when he died, if Mom didn't want his sons around, she didn't have to let them in. Maybe she was afraid they'd

kick her out. They probably would've tried that—they haven't been exactly civil, have they? Anyway, it was only three weeks ago, they didn't
have a ton of time to figure out a game plan. Maybe they didn't even
know they needed a game plan. Most people don't think ahead."

"What was only three weeks ago?" I asked.

"When Bill died."

"Bill only died *three weeks ago*?" I blurted.

I honestly do not know why I didn't know this. But I didn't; the
situation with my mom was that screwy. A few years ago she was living
in Hoboken and working at some H&R Block office, filing tax returns;
then all of a sudden she was getting married and moving to Manhattan.
And then it was all "Bill's private, he doesn't see a lot of people," or "we're
really busy this month, maybe the fall would be better." The fact is, I
hadn't even spoken to her since the three of us took her out to dinner a
year and a half before all this. Mom suggested it, and then, when it looked
as if it would happen, she made a big deal about not going too far from
home, because Bill might get upset if she did. Alison said Daniel didn't
want to come all the way in from Queens on a Saturday, and then Lucy
got bent out of shape about finding a place we could afford, since she
assumed we'd be treating Mom, and she didn't want to split the bill
two ways with Alison because she always got the short end of the stick in
these situations—"Alison" included Alison and Daniel, which meant that
Lucy was stuck paying for me as well as half of Mom. So even a not-so-
expensive place quietly got really expensive from her point of view. Of
course, she was completely blunt about all this, which I took exception to,
because even though I'm consistently strapped it's not like an occasional
nice dinner out is a complete impossibility. But Lucy was right—we
ended up at a place that charged twenty-two bucks for a plate of spaghetti
with red sauce, which made everyone, especially me, uptight.

So that set the party off on an unfortunate foot. Mom had a vodka
tonic, which I think cost fifteen dollars, and the rest of us drank tap
water. Lucy, as usual, monopolized the conversation, blathering on about
the big corporations she did PR for and how difficult it was to work with
corporate jerks and none of them really want to talk to a woman and
they're all in love with themselves and their own power and she really

thinks they're all closet cases anyway. Alison got on the bandwagon about the prices on the menu and kept letting us know how worried she was about the money, and then she got Daniel to keep a running tab on the paper tablecloth, which he did methodically, with a mechanical pencil. I told them all I was going to move out to the Delaware Water Gap with Darren, and how he had this business plan set up—so many really wealthy people had summer homes out there, and he was putting together a company that would do caretaking year-round, and he already had six or seven clients and I was going to help him with the bookings and also do personal services for people, like shopping, say.

So that was the dinner. And Mom was fine, really. Maybe a little too perky, like she was trying too hard to seem happy. But how can you know something like that? She didn't say anything at all about Bill or how it was going with him, even though Lucy made a couple of stabs at it.

"So are we ever going to meet our so-called stepfather?" she asked, sipping her cappuccino. Since none of us had wine with dinner, Daniel and Alison had relented and let us order cappuccino and biscotti after the expensive spaghetti.

"You're all grown, you don't need a stepfather," Mom said, laughing a little and looking at the last traces of her second drink.

"Wait a minute. You guys haven't met him yet?" I asked. This had somehow gotten by me. I assumed I hadn't met Bill because I was the last one who still lived in Jersey. The fact that Lucy and Alison, who lived close by in Brooklyn and Queens, hadn't met him caught me off guard.

"He's so private. I told you, sweetheart. That's just the way he is. Someday we'll make it work out," Mom said, patting my hand.

"You live like right around the corner from here, right?" Lucy persisted. "Let's do it now. He's home, right?"

"I don't think he'd like that."

"We won't stay. We just want to come by and see where you live!"

"I'll tell him. Maybe we can work something out for next month."

"Is it a dump? Are you living in some sort of crazy dump?"

"No, not at all. He's just private."

"He's crazy is what it sounds like."

It was pretty uncomfortable for all of us, frankly; Lucy's questions to Mom made the situation sound as creepy and weird as we worried it might be. Mom just shrugged a little and looked down, and then she sighed, like this was all too much.

Lucy took offense. "It's a fair question, Mom," she pointed out, kind of edgy. "You've been married to this guy for almost two years— why can't we meet him?"

"He doesn't want to, is why," Mom said. And she wasn't apologetic about it at all.

"But he's nice to you, right?" I said.

"You don't have to worry about me, sweetheart, I'm fine!" she said, and she smiled and squeezed my hand. Which is maybe why it occurred to me after she was dead that what she meant was, worry about yourself, you dingbat; you've just agreed to go to the Delaware Water Gap with another loser.

It also occurred to me that she didn't want Bill to meet us because she was ashamed of us. Sitting there on the floor of that ridiculous TV room, eating Chinese food out of cartons, and trying to figure out how to screw over the two guys who grew up there and whose father had died just three weeks before Mom did, it then occurred to me that maybe we weren't behaving well.

"Are you crying?" Alison asked me suddenly.

"It's this kung pao chicken, I bit into one of the peppers. I wonder if there's any Kleenex around here." I stood up and looked around, confused. Lucy held up a wad of those lousy paper napkins that they dump in the carry-out bag and breezed on with her clever plan. "I'll have the Sotheby's guy call Long in the morning. Eventually he's going to have to transfer the files anyway, and they'll have a better sense of how soon that needs to happen. Surely they know how to work this so we can proceed with the sale even though the property's still in probate," she told us, licking her fingers like a cat. "There's no question they'll fight it, but we could at least get a jump on those Drinans. Potentially we could leave them in the dust."

"They're already in the dust, their father just died," I reminded her.

"Their father, who disinherited them," she retorted.

"Precisely," I said. "Precisely."

"You're not going to get all moralistic about this," Lucy said, looking up. "Oh, no no. This is not a situation of our making."

"You're sitting here—plotting!" I said.

"Plotting to make you rich. Oh, a couple million dollars, that would suck. You might have to give up cleaning houses."

"I wasn't cleaning houses," I told her, suddenly feeling peevish as hell. "I was *managing properties*."

"Well, my way you can own the properties you manage, how's that for a thought?" she said, starting to close up the food cartons. "And you can go back to college and finish your degree in pottery, and you can start your own little pottery shop and throw clay around for the rest of your life and never worry ever ever *ever* about whether you make one red cent off any of it. That's what can happen to your life, Tina, if you just sit still and let me make you rich."

"That was mean," I said.

"What?" she said, looking at me like I was nuts. "That was *mean*?"

"Yeah, mean, you're being mean to me again, Lucy."

"We're all tired, it's been a long couple of days," Daniel chimed in, trying to be soothing. He was being Mr. Good Brother-in-Law now, asking quietly supportive questions and making sure Lucy knew We Are in This Together. "Lucy's worked hard to protect us all, and I for one appreciate it." He smiled at her. I wanted to smack them both. Instead I smiled wanly and nodded my sheepish little head.

"I'm sorry," I said. "I'm still a little shook up about Mom."

"We all are," Alison said, like she also thought maybe I was being a bit too morally superior.

"I know I know, I mean, I didn't get much sleep last night," I said, fully in retreat mode, because what other option did I have? I rubbed my eyes for effect. "I think I'd better go lie down."

"Be my guest," Lucy said, shrugging. Which was her way of letting me know that this wasn't my apartment, it was her apartment, and I wasn't calling the shots. As if I ever called the shots with this crew. I went and hid in the bedroom with the little beds on the floor. I stared at the stars on the ceiling and waited for my so-called family to leave.

Which they did not do, and after a while I started worrying that maybe they were plotting about how they were going to cut me out of my share of the loot once we got our hands on it. And once that occurred to me, I worked myself into a complete paranoid frenzy. I almost went back out to let them know they weren't pulling any fast ones on me, that I was a full member of this little tribe of pirates, and there would be no sneaking around and cheating. Then I decided I probably shouldn't be so confrontational, because it would make them think I was weak. The smartest move, I thought, would be to sneak through the pink room and into the empty room next to the TV room, where I could hide behind the door and eavesdrop on their diabolical maneuverings.

I was about to put this idiotic plan in motion—I was literally sneaking to the door of the pink room and easing it open as silently as I could—when I heard them coming down the hallway. So I had to sneak back to the other room, and the little bed against the far wall, so that when Lucy looked through the crack in the door she could see me sleeping peacefully and tell herself that I was a mess but not a problem. Her shadow hovered in the doorway for a moment, watching my back, curled against the light in the hallway. Then she left.

I lay there for a good five minutes after I heard the door thump shut and the three different tumblers turn in their locks. And then I waited another five minutes. I didn't want one of them coming back and interrupting me, which was completely possible, given my older sister's devious mind. But after fifteen minutes I was fairly sure that they had gone away, so I turned on the light, pulled out the bag I had hidden under the clothes I had bought, and began to inventory my afternoon's purchases.

6

So this is what I had: one Phillips-head screwdriver with inter-changeable heads, one zinc-plated steel four-inch spring-bolt lock, and two brass chain door guards. Both the spring bolt and the chain guards came with their own screws, but I had bought an extra half dozen just in case. I spent the next fifty minutes locking myself into that apartment. I knew it would piss off absolutely everybody that I was doing this—Lucy, Alison, Daniel, those Drinans, maybe even Len the moss lover and Frank the doorman, both of whom had been really nice to me. Nobody was going to be happy that I had figured out a way to be the one who said who could come in and who couldn't. But I didn't see that I had much choice. In case you hadn't noticed, in spite of the fact that I had been in-vaded the night before, not one person had spent one second figuring out how I was supposed to protect myself, given that the Drinan brothers had keys and that they clearly thought they were within their rights to use them. Lucy was spending all her time cooking up plans to pull one over on those guys—well, if you ask me, it wouldn't take a brain surgeon to figure out that they were doing the same thing to us. I needed protection. I needed a spring bolt and two security chains.

And I was right. I mean, within ten minutes of finishing the instal-lation process. I was in the kitchen pouring myself a tumbler of vodka-grapefruit surprise when the yelling started. You could hear it all the way back in the kitchen.

"What the fuck? HEY. WHAT THE FUCK!" Then pounding, and yanking, and more pounding on the door. It was enormously satisfy-ing to hear.

"GO AWAY!" I yelled in return, while I sauntered to the front of the apartment. "I'M CALLING THE COPS!"

"I *AM* THE COPS!" he yelled. "OPEN THE FUCKING

DOOR." By this I knew it was the Drinan with the sexy eyes. Not that I was surprised.

"I'M SLEEPING IN HERE AND I'M NOT BOTHERING ANYBODY. GO AWAY," I yelled.

"OPEN THE FUCKING DOOR," he yelled back.

"What, you've got like three sentences, is that all you know how to say?" I asked him through the door. "Open the door, I'm a cop, what the fuck—is that all you know how to say?"

"I'd open the door, Tina Finn," he warned me.

"Oh yeah? Why?" I said to the door, kind of bold and cocky. It was weird. All of a sudden I felt like I was flirting with someone in a bar. "What are you going to do to me, Officer?"

"I'm going to arrest you," he announced.

"I'm not the one trying to break in and harass an innocent citizen in her home, dude," I retorted. "I put a call in to 911, you're the one who's in the shithouse."

"There's a stay on the apartment, Tina," he informed me through the door. "No one's allowed to fuck with the locks. You're in violation of the law."

"Except I didn't fuck with the locks, Pierre," I said. "I put in a spring bolt and some chain guards. The locks are fine. When I'm not here? The locks work just fine. When I am here? YOU'RE NOT ALLOWED IN."

There was a pause, and then a bump right at my shoulder. "Shit," I heard him mumble. He must have been right up against the door. For a second I thought, wow, this door is so thin I can hear everything—and if I can hear everything, he can probably bash it open with one of those little battering-ram things cops carry, whether or not I have the spring bolt in place. And then I thought, is he the kind of cop who carries those things? What kind of a cop is this guy anyway? Does he have a gun on him? He didn't have a gun or a uniform the last time I saw him, but there was no knowing if he had any of those things right now. I took a step back, because it did occur to me that if he started whacking at the door I didn't want to be leaning against it. But that did not seem to be on his mind. For the moment, at least, he was quiet.

And then someone else started talking.

I couldn't hear what the other person was saying. The voice was much softer, more distant; I heard a murmur, and a question. Pete answered, only now I couldn't hear him either; he was practically whispering to whoever was out there. This should have been good news—let's face it, having an angry cop screaming at me to let him in was not an ideal situation—but the whispering voices actually made me more anxious than the yelling had. I stepped back to the door and put my ear up against it to see if I could hear what the other person was saying or what the angry Pete Drinan was saying. But now I could barely hear Pete. He wasn't up against the door anymore; he was over by the elevators. The other person asked him a question that I couldn't hear, and he answered, and again I couldn't hear. I thought the other person might be his brother, that would make the most sense, but it didn't really sound like Doug. This person was talking more thoughtfully, and Drinan was talking thoughtfully back. I truly couldn't tell what was going on.

Given my options, I decided to go for it. I slid back the spring bolt very quietly and carefully, which was exceptionally difficult; those spring bolts hold pretty tight—what use would they be if they didn't? Luckily, Drinan was far enough away, and the conversation was apparently riveting enough that he wasn't super-attuned to the sound of a spring bolt being slowly scraped back. He had already thrown the tumblers in the three door locks, so all I had to do was make sure the chain guards were in place and open the door as silently as possible.

He was past the elevators, his back to me, and he was talking to whoever lived in the other apartment. It made so much sense when I saw it that I almost laughed out loud about how paranoid I was being. The lady—I could see it was a lady with kind of messy brown hair—was standing in her doorway, like all the yelling had woken her up and she had come out to investigate. But she didn't seem angry. She had her hand on Drinan's arm, and every now and then she would pat it, like she was comforting him, and he would nod and look at the floor. He had a bottle of beer in his left hand and was holding it behind him, like a teenager who doesn't want his mom's friend to know he's got a beer. His thumb was hooked into the top to make sure the fizz didn't go.

They didn't know I was listening, so they just kept talking. "God rest her soul I miss her every day," said the lady. Her voice was sort of odd and low, which was why if you couldn't see her, she sounded like a man.

"I miss her too," he told her, quiet.

"It would have killed her to see this, just killed her! Oh my god, when they were selling the furniture, all I could think was this would have just killed Sophie, the way Bill is letting everything go."

"Actually she hated most of that stuff," Drinan noted.

"So many beautiful pieces. Worth a fortune! And then the paintings, I thought I would just cry, when the paintings—"

"She didn't like them either." With every answer, he sounded like he wanted to take a hit off that beer bottle, but she wasn't giving him an opening.

"Your inheritance, it was all your inheritance, gone—that's what she wouldn't have liked. Your father should be ashamed of himself."

"Yeah, well, he never was."

"God rest his soul, you got that right. And he never asked me if I wanted them. I thought, at least ask, I would have been happy to step in and keep them in the building. I would have done that for your mother, god rest her soul. I told him! But you couldn't talk to him. Well, you know that."

"Yes." He shifted on his feet, and for about fifteen seconds I got a better look at the woman, who had an intelligent face underneath that big messy head of hair. I wasn't liking her much until I saw her face, then I wasn't so sure, because she seemed sort of sensible, even though she was saying slightly dotty things and clearly was cranky that she didn't get her hands on those paintings and all that furniture. She had on some kind of silk robe, sage green with a burnt-orange stripe, and the bit I could see hanging off her shoulder suggested it might be spectacularly beautiful if I could get a better look at it. Drinan shifted again, and I lost the sight line.

"Well, thank you for your thoughts, Mrs. Westmoreland," he started. The hand holding the beer was getting a little slippery, plus I could see from the way his shoulders were scrunching together that he was getting pretty desperate for that drink. Before he could take a step backward and turn to take a fast hit, she touched him on the sleeve and held him there. Ai yi yi, I thought, this is getting interesting.

"But these people—who are these people?" she asked, all concerned. "Coming and going, acting like they own the place, Frank says one of them has moved in. I'm *horrified*." I went back to not liking her. What on earth was she complaining about, she was "horrified" about me living in an apartment I had every legal right to live in? She was just an Upper West Side snob who had the hots for a dude half her age, I decided, on the basis of hardly any information at all.

"It's something to do with Dad's will," he told her. "He left everything to Olivia."

"You're kidding!"

"Look, it's fine, it's going to be fine." You could hear that he was already kicking himself for telling her that much. And it did seem to be a terrific mistake.

"He left everything to *Olivia*? He barely knew her!"

"They were married two years," he corrected her.

"Did you know he was doing that? Did you agree to it?"

"He didn't actually ask us to agree," Pete said. His voice sounded really uptight. "He told us. Doug tried to talk him out of it. He wanted to do something for her."

"But why?"

"He was worried that she wouldn't have anything if he died. That's what he said."

"She didn't deserve anything!"

"Well, that's what he felt, anyway. He, you know, he knew he was dying, and he wanted her to have some security after he was gone."

"Surely you could have put a stop to this."

"We had a big fight about it. Doug, you know, he pretty much felt the way you do, and Dad got real mad. It wasn't . . . we didn't really talk much after that."

This was so much more information than I'd ever had about Bill and his marriage to my mom that I was momentarily thrilled. I had forgotten how useful snooping at doors could be. I was also happy to have a shred of good feeling for the guy, since he had tried to do the right thing by Mom in the face of opposition. He was instantly transformed in my imagination from a selfish drunk into an eccentric recluse who had lousy kids.

"But Olivia is dead now. And these other people, what rights do they have?"

"I don't know. Honestly, I just don't know." Pete trailed off, clearly wanting to get out of this conversation. But she was a sharp one. And she was as fascinated by what he had told her as I was.

"He didn't even know them, he refused to meet them!" she told him. "He was afraid of just this scenario, that complete strangers would come after his property—that's why he told her they were never to set foot in the building!"

"She told you that?"

"She did! I asked her one night. She had just come back from having dinner with them apparently. It was so rare that you ever saw either of them leave the apartment, so when I saw her in the lobby, I said, this is a treat! You and Bill don't go out much, do you, and she said, I was having dinner with my daughters, and we rode up in the elevator together, and I said, are we going to meet your daughters? She said, oh no, Bill prefers to keep me all to himself! And I said, well, that hardly seems fair, you must miss them a lot. And she said she did, very much, and that she had tried to speak to him about it but he was very worried—those were her words—he was worried that other people were after his property, and he had to protect it. Those were her exact words. And then I saw him one day not long after that—I actually saw him putting trash in the bin, which he never did—and I said, why Bill, there you are! He looked terrible, I don't need to tell you that, he was sick for a long long time and I know he refused to see a doctor—"

"Yeah, but you said you talked to him?"

"I did. I took the opportunity. I said, Bill—Olivia tells me you've never even met her daughters, aren't you curious to meet them? She's your wife! I was reluctant to say anything to him at all, I couldn't believe he brought another woman into your mother's apartment. It's the Livingston Mansion Apartment, it is a historic property! He should have let it go, is my opinion, when your mother died. He should have sold it to someone who would take care of it, someone in the building who would appreciate it. He never appreciated it. She was the one."

"But he said something? About these daughters?"

"Yes, he said they were trash. He said, those daughters are trash and I'm not meeting them. That's what he called them. *Trash.* And he said all they wanted was his money." At which point old Bill went back to being an alcoholic asshole in my mind.

Pete Drinan thought about this. It was not an uninteresting bit of information to him. "Was he drunk?" he finally asked.

"Well, I only saw him for a moment, so I couldn't really say," Mrs. Westmoreland admitted. "I know he did like to drink."

"Yes, he did," Pete sighed, his hand still curled around the beer bottle behind his back. "Listen, Mrs. Westmoreland—would you be willing to talk about this? To our lawyer?"

"Oh, a lawyer . . ." she sighed, all worried but excited too, like she was secretly happy to be asked. "You mean, officially?"

"Well, yeah," said Pete. "It might make a difference—that you spoke to him directly and he told you he didn't want the property going out of the family. That that was his intent?"

"That was my understanding. But if this is an official situation—I don't know. I want you and your brother to have your inheritance. But obviously I don't want to get into some complicated legal mess. I did love your mother. Maybe you'd like to come in and have a cup of tea?"

"Oh," said Pete, his fingers twirling around the neck of that beer bottle. I thought about how the beer was getting all warm and flat, and I guessed he was thinking that too. And sure enough, he leaned back on his left leg, ready to edge away again. But she was not letting go. She actually had her fingers twisted in his jacket sleeve now. Her door had swung completely open, and what little I could see of her place was gorgeous.

"Your mother was my neighbor for thirty years, this whole story breaks my heart," she explained, leaning up against the doorway.

"Mine too, Mrs. Westmoreland." He nodded, leaning back.

"Good heavens, Peter," she sighed. "After all this time I think you could consider calling me Delia."

"Yeah, well . . ."

"Come in, let me get you that tea. Or a drink! Maybe a whiskey—that sounds like a policeman's drink!" she said with a smile.

He turned, finally, planning to get a hit off that beer bottle, and saw me looking out through the crack in the door. He looked tired. And then he remembered what was going on and took a fast step in my direction. I remembered too, and I slammed the door and slid the bolt back in place. I thought he was going to start pounding again, but he just waited. I could hear the woman in 8B start to gripe about how awful it all was; I couldn't really hear the words, but the tone of her voice was not complimentary. He didn't say anything back to her. I stood at the door and listened, but he didn't say anything at all. I wasn't sure what was going on. Finally Mrs. Westmoreland stopped talking, and it got really quiet. I thought maybe he was gone. And then a little white card was slid under the door. At the last second, it kind of wafted, like he had pushed it. I picked it up. It was a really plain business card, with the NYPD shield, and his name, Detective Peter Drinan, right in the middle, and a cell number. On the back, in little block letters in ink, it said, CALL ME WHEN YOU'RE READY. I thought about that for a second, as I kept listening at the door. He was still out there; in fact, from the shadows it looked like he was sort of hovering down near the floor to see if I had picked the card up. So I took the paper bag from the hardware store, and I looked through my backpack, which was still right where I had dumped it, for a pen, and I ripped a piece off the paper bag and wrote: OKAY. I shoved that through the door, And then I watched through the bottom of the door while he picked it up. And then I heard him laugh. The lady in the other apartment asked some more questions, and he said something to her, but then I heard the elevator ding, and the door close.

And when I went in the hallway in the morning, he was gone.

7

LEN'S GREENHOUSE WAS SO BIG IT HAD ROOMS: THE DECIDUOUS room, the desert room, the rain forest room, the heirloom plants from other centuries room, the plants that only grow on other plants room. Some of these were subsets or extensions of rooms, and some of the rooms overlapped before growing into new rooms—the plants growing on other plants room turned into the orchid room, which evolved into the spectacularly gorgeous and weird plants room, which turned a corner and became the poisonous plants room. So the whole greenhouse seemed to be growing. In some places it covered the roof and threatened to crawl down the side of the building. It was the only greenhouse I had ever seen that was big enough to get lost in.

I told Len that I was surprised he could get enough water up there for a greenhouse that big, especially one with a rain forest, and yet he couldn't get enough water for a little bit of moss.

He said, "I know, it is surprising, isn't it?" By which I knew he really was full of shit, and there was no reason he had to stash the moss in my apartment, except that he had run out of room in his. That, and there really was quite a lot of sunlight up there. He got light on six sides. It was like living on Mount Olympus with a whole bunch of plants.

As much fun as it had been to talk to Len about his moss, it was nothing compared to hearing him go on about plants. He started by delivering information like a university lecturer, which he had been at some point. Everything was all about the genus and the species and the Latin name and the common name and the historical sources of the names. But he couldn't hold on to the formality. In no time he was talking to the plants, checking out the texture of the leaves, telling the pretty ones how lovely they were, telling the ones that were all spiky and weird-looking that looks don't matter, the pink coleus is just a slut for showing off like that, beauty comes and goes so quickly, and she's only an annual anyway. He thought the cactuses were sly and devious, the "tricksters of the desert," which I didn't quite follow, because all those spikes didn't look sly to me; they seemed pretty direct. When I pointed that out, Len just laughed, like there was so much about cactuses that I didn't know. And how could you argue with that? I *don't* know anything about cactuses; I was just making an observation. Then he took me into the orchid room, and I got an earful about the orchids. He had more than a hundred different kinds, each one stranger than the last. Some had spots all over them, which I had never seen on any flower. They were pink and purple and yellow and white and dark red with black centers, and one was black all over, which was strangely frightening. Some looked like stars and some looked like butterflies, some looked like tarantulas, and some like hornets or some other kind of stinging animal, and then of course there were dozens that looked like sex organs. Seriously, all of those flowers looked like they wanted to have sex with humans. It was a bit creepy, honestly. I was somewhat afraid to touch them.

This turned out to be a good impulse on my part, as Len casually informed me once we were done with the orchid room.

"Some of them are poisonous," he admitted. "The pollen, the ovules, the nectar, this little darling here—don't touch—not that it would hurt you permanently, but you very well might lose all feeling in your arm, at least for a day."

"Come on, Len," I said.

"Do you want to try it?" he asked, raising those eyebrows at me.

I didn't. "But if orchids are poisonous, how come everybody has them in their houses?"

"Only certain species, Tina. Use your head," he said, pulling out a very small pair of clippers and snipping some extraneous vines away from a line of bright yellow star-shaped flowers that wound down the side of a tree. "Please don't touch that."

"You can't touch any of them?" I asked.

"Until you know which ones are poisonous and which aren't, no, in fact, you can't touch any of them."

"How did you find out which ones are poisonous?"

"The hard way," he said. "I studied."

The place smelled like growing things and sounded like water. He had little fountains in corners, and strange pools behind tree trunks or alongside a hillside of ferns. That greenhouse was so big it had hills—small hills, but definite undulations. And everything was green, a thousand different greens, each one more subtle than the last. In spite of the pink coleus and the startling sexuality of the many-colored and poisonous orchids, green was what you saw everywhere.

And then all of a sudden you turned a corner and were back in his apartment. The apartment was quite small in comparison to the greenhouse; it was one little room right at the center of the roof. There was a kitchenette with a linoleum counter, completely cluttered with pots and pans and a blender, and lots of mismatched dishes on open shelves. And across from the counter was a wall with a lot of books about plants, and a chair and a little table. To one side was a big, overstuffed blue couch with magazines and books piled all over it, and behind that, in a corner, an unmade bed. Next to the bed was what seemed to be a closet, and then a very small bathroom with a skylight and lots of plants in the tub. On the other side of the bathtub was one of those clear acrylic doors they sell in fancy bath stores, and just beyond was the room with all the ferns. Seriously, you could step out of that bathtub and into the greenhouse. I mean, the apartment did have some walls, just not as many as most people have. The greenhouse seemed to have grown out of that tiny apartment and then just kept on growing.

"Would you like a cappuccino?" Len asked me. He gestured toward a large silver contraption that took up all of the counter space between the very small stovetop and the equally small refrigerator. The only thing that wasn't utterly minuscule in the kitchen was the enormous cappuccino machine. Len considered it with an air of bemused resignation, like it was an old but hapless and worrisome friend. "I have this wonderful machine someone gave me, but I can never get it to work," he admitted.

"If you can't get it to work, why are you offering me cappuccino?"

"Well, I was thinking that if you wanted a cappuccino, you could try to make it yourself, and then, if you were successful, you could show me how to do it," he said, offering up that dazzling smile.

"Fair enough," I said. "Where's the coffee?"

"Oh, coffee . . . oh," he mused, looking around the tiny kitchen.

"Never mind, I'll find it," I said, and started poking around. There weren't that many places to look. I landed on the stuff my first try: in the freezer.

"You know you're not really supposed to freeze your beans, it dries them out," I informed Len, looking for an expiration date. "How long has this been in here?"

"Oh, not long. A week? My daughter brought it by, she brought me one of those baskets of food they give to invalids in hospitals. I think there are chocolate biscuits somewhere." He started poking around the bookshelves, as if he might have hidden the biscuits in with the books.

"You have a daughter?" This was real news. I mean, it was hard to imagine this strange person having any human relations. I thought he was half plant himself by this point.

"Oh yes, she's, well, you know, she's my daughter, you know what that's like," he replied, as if all girls with parents somehow must share the same frontal lobe. "I can't find the biscuits."

"Here they are," I said, pulling them out from behind the cappuccino machine. Len looked at them with a sort of stern surprise, like the biscuits had done something offensive, locating themselves in such an unusual spot.

"What are they doing there?" he asked.

"Maybe your daughter put them there," I suggested. "Maybe she was trying to clean up your kitchen and she thought it was a good spot to stash the cookies. You know, by the cappuccino machine. What's her name?"

"Oh, who remembers," he sighed, suddenly bored to the point of apathy. "Her mother always called her Charlie. I dislike it when girls have boys' names, it's confusing enough as it is without things like that."

"Is that the name on her birth certificate?"

"What? No. Do you think I'm crazy?"

"Well, yes, a bit," I said, looking around.

"Her given name is Charlotte. We named her *Charlotte*," he stated, with some heat.

"Well, why don't you just call her that?" I asked, pouring a bunch of coffee beans into what seemed to be the grinding part of the machine; at least, the clever little chute that opened up off one side implied that beans might go there.

"I rarely see her, so I don't call her anything." Len sounded increasingly annoyed with my questioning.

"Why don't you see her?" I said, looking for the switch.

"Well, let's see, Tina, why would a parent and child become estranged? Let's speculate on that, shall we?" He ducked his head into the refrigerator. "You'll need milk, I think."

"This is a very nice machine, Len," I told him, flipping the switch. Nothing happened. He set a red-and-white carton of whole milk on the cluttered counter between us and watched as I flipped the switch again.

"Stop it—it makes no sense to keep flipping that switch. One try is plenty. It doesn't work, I told you; I've had that machine for years, and it doesn't ever work."

"So why don't you get another one?"

"Oh, I don't really like cappuccino anyway," he sighed, opening the tin of cookies.

"Then why am I making it?"

"Well, you're not, as far as I can see, you haven't gotten that thing to work any more than I did. And now you have to figure out how to get the beans out of there; you're going to have to turn the whole thing upside down, and doubtless the beans will simply go everywhere. It's a complete waste of time."

"Wait," I said, plugging the machine in. "Hang on." I flipped the switch. The machine started to hum and rumble as the beans swirled in the chute.

"Oh," said Len, arrested for a second. Then ground coffee began to spit all over the counter. "Well, that is—interesting."

It took twenty minutes to figure out how to get the ground coffee into the other part of the machine, make the espresso, and then steam the milk, but the whole project was pretty entertaining and relaxing, compared to the other stuff that had been happening to me for the past few days. Len had a lot to say about everything except his own personal history. As long as we stayed off the subject of his daughter Charlie and her mother, he was a complete motormouth. He left out a lot of things, but if I didn't push too hard and just let him keep yakking he produced plenty of information, which I was happy to have.

"So what's the story on the lady who lives on the same floor as me?" I said, serving up a perfect cappuccino—which, as it turned out, Len liked a lot.

"You've met Delia Westmoreland!" he noted, admiring the foam on his coffee cup. "How was that for you?"

"How was it?"

"Yes, did you find her charming? She can be, if she likes."

"But not if she doesn't like?"

"I didn't say that. Where are those cookies?"

"We finished them, but there are some cheese-twist things here," I said, finding another little foil bag from a fancy food store. "Is this all you eat, gourmet snack food?"

"I have a hard time in grocery stores, they confuse me," he admitted. "Delia Westmoreland. She's a strong personality, I would say. And she had strong ties to the previous tenants of your apartment."

"Yeah, I noticed."

"You noticed? How so?"

"One of them came by a couple days ago, the Drinan who's a police detective or something?"

"Yes, I know who he is," Len responded drily.

"Anyway, when he couldn't get in, he stood out in the hall and yelled, and she came out and talked to him. She's pretty ooh la la for a lady her age," I observed.

"She's fifty, darling, it's the new seventeen," Len informed me. "Although 'ooh la la' does cover it. Why did young Mr. Drinan find himself stuck out in the hall yelling in the first place? It was my understanding that neither you nor the Drinans were allowed to change the locks."

"Where'd you hear that?"

"Everyone in the building is talking about it, Tina. You'll have to get used to it, the walls have ears in a co-op. One of you is going to need a court order at this point to change those locks. You didn't do something foolish, did you?"

"I didn't change the locks, if that's what you mean, I just put in a couple of chains and a spring bolt, so people can't barge in whenever they want."

"Oh," said Len, startled at this idea. "Oh! That's clever. Good for you."

"He didn't think I was so clever—he was pretty pissed off."

"Well, he's an open wound. You know that legally you're not allowed to forbid them access to the apartment until claim to the title is established."

"I didn't say he couldn't come in, I just don't want him barging in while I'm sleeping there."

"Well, you put yourself in that situation, darling."

"My sister put me in it."

"Oh yes, I see," he said, raising his eyebrows.

"What?"

"A girl who knows how to put in a spring bolt and two chain guards is hardly a victim, Tina."

"I didn't say I was a victim."

"Didn't you? I thought you did."

"Could we get back to this horny Westmoreland character who lives on my floor?"

"Horny? Why do you say that?"

"She was coming on to Drinan big-time. She kept trying to get him to come into her apartment and have tea."

"You're up in my apartment having cappuccino, do you think I have designs on you?"

"No, you have designs on making sure nobody bothers your moss."

"Well, along those same lines, allow me to inform you that Delia Westmoreland does not lust after young Mr. Drinan. She lusts, but not after human flesh."

"She said she was mad that Bill didn't offer her all the stuff in the apartment when he started selling everything off," I remembered. "But now it's all gone. You've been in the place, there's nothing left for her to want, is there?"

"That's not what she's after," he told me, eating one of the cheese twists. "No, darling, she wants the same thing everyone else in New York is pining for: square footage. If she could get her hands on the Livingston Mansion Apartment, she would own the entire eighth floor. Minor renovation, and she's sitting on one of the most spectacular apartments in the city. She's been trying to buy that place for years—she literally hounded Bill about it."

"She wants to own the whole eighth floor?"

"Of course she does."

"I thought, I mean, she kind of—doesn't she live alone over there?"

"There's the occasional visit from estranged children, but yes, for the most part she lives alone."

"Well, how much room does she need?"

"It's never about need when it comes to real estate." To a girl who last lived in a mobile home in a trailer park, this did not completely make sense, but he was dead serious.

"So if she bought it, she'd have like—how big an apartment would that be?"

"Twelve thousand square feet."

"That's a lot."

"With park views and walk-in closets? All those freaks over in 10021 would commit collective suicide out of sheer envy if Delia managed to pull off that coup. A place like that would be worth forty million in any market."

"So she's like mega-loaded."

"Not particularly, no."

"Come on, she's got to have some money, she lives here."

"She inherited. Her husband's parents bought the apartment she lives in back in the twenties for something ridiculous like thirty-five thousand. They died—that was in the late eighties, just before the market tanked and I managed to grab the roof here, which is a whole different story—anyway, that's how she got in. He was in finance, but he was never a major player, so in some ways they were just scraping by. I think she's got twelve or fifteen million on a good day in the market, apart from the apartment."

"So she's worth, like, twenty-five million. And that's not loaded?"

"Well, it's certainly not enough to make a grab on 8A unless she leverages her place, which may be her thinking. If she puts up two, let's say, she should be able to find a bank to lend her the rest. Another million goes into the renovation and voilà, for the up-front price of three million dollars, she owns an apartment worth forty. But my suspicion is, she hopes to lay her hands on that place for nothing at all."

"How's that supposed to work?"

"Well, I'm not saying it will work. But if she can convince a developer to put down the money up front in exchange for right of first refusal to buy the place from her estate when she dies, that might be of interest to any number of speculators."

"People do that?"

"That's actually a fairly tame and sensible scenario. For instance, it doesn't involve homicide, although if Delia made it into her nineties I am sure there would be some discussion of poison. Even in the most catastrophic of markets, a twelve-thousand-square-foot apartment with park views on the Upper West Side will never depreciate. It's win win win win win for everyone. Oh yes, I'm sure all of these options have been considered by now. And not merely by her."

"Who else?"

"It's an old and elegant building, Tina. People have lived here a long time."

"What does that mean?"

"It means it's an old and elegant building and people have lived here a long time," he repeated mysteriously.

"Well, if any of these 'people' want to buy our apartment they should call Sotheby's. Why is this woman sucking up to Pete Drinan in the middle of the night if what she really wants is to buy the stupid apartment?" I was getting a little peevish. I turned back to the cappuccino machine, thinking I'd make another round, even though I was so caffeinated I thought my head was going to explode.

"Is something wrong?" asked Len.

"All these rich people make me nervous. She has a zillion rooms herself, and she wants our place too? But she doesn't want to pay for it? That's just incredible. Plus you should have heard her going on about how horrible it all was, we're horrible, Mom was horrible, like we're just crazy skanks from Jersey or something—and meanwhile she wants to take over our apartment just because she's lived on the same floor for a bunch of years. That's classic, it really is."

"It wasn't your place at all, I might remind you, until three days ago."

"It was my mom's. When she died, the deed was in her name, was it not? Was it not?"

"So I'm told," said Len.

"So I'm told too. By *lawyers*. My mom lived there, oh and by the way, she died there too. That doesn't give us rights?"

"I don't imagine that Delia Westmoreland thinks so, no. I don't believe the Drinan brothers think so either. And I have a suspicion that the co-op board will not feel that it gives you rights."

"Well, they don't get to say, do they? The *law* says. The *LAW* says we own, it's ours by *law*."

"That's not going to do you any good if you can't sell it, Tina. And if you can't sell, how will you pay the inheritance tax? Have you asked yourselves any of these questions?"

"We are going to sell it."

"Not if the co-op board can stop you."

I truly didn't know what he was talking about, but it had that peculiar sound of a true thing. "Okay," I said, trying not to get too worked up. "Okay, so tell me what the problem is with the co-op board. I don't even know what a co-op board is."

"They are the twelve residents of this building who will inform you and your sisters—repeatedly, I am afraid—that even if the courts decide that you do own the apartment and that you very much have the right to sell it, in fact they will not permit you to sell it."

"They can't do that."

"Alarmingly, yes they can."

"Why would they do that?"

"Because they don't know you. You're an outsider. Your mother was an outsider. It's an offense to everyone here that you and your sisters think you can just come in and take over that beautiful old apartment. You and your sisters can talk to Sotheby's all you want; every offer they put on the table will be rejected out of hand until someone, or more than one person, in the building has been permitted to make an offer."

"They can't do that. They said, that lawyer said, there isn't a cloud on the title. It means, that legally means—"

"I know what it means, Tina, and I'm afraid there is very much a cloud on the title, whether it is a legal cloud or not."

"I have to call Lucy," I said, digging into my pocket for my cell phone.

"She knows all about this, Tina, I'm sure."

"No, she doesn't, she didn't yesterday—"

"Does she tell you everything?" he asked me pointedly. I looked at him. He was considering me like I was some kind of interesting plant that was growing in odd directions, or my leaves were drooping and gray, and he couldn't quite understand why.

"Why—why are you telling me all this?" I finally asked. Truly, none of this was good news, but it wasn't like he was trying to scare me off. If he had had a watering can, I was pretty sure he would have been pouring it over my head.

"Well," said Len, looking around. "You did fix the cappuccino machine. Besides which, I had pneumonia last year, and I ended up in the hospital for two weeks, and your mother took good care of my moss. There aren't many people who would have bothered."

"You're nice to me because my mom saved your moss?"

"There are worse reasons, Tina Finn. She was a nice woman. She was a caretaker at heart. I'm sorry you didn't know that about her."

"I did know it," I said.

"Well, then you should have visited her more," he replied, turning away and putting our dishes in the tiny sink. The air from the greenhouse drifted through the kitchen, a little chill now, and he looked up as if someone had spoken. "Oh, the rain-drip mechanism is off again in the deciduous room, I'm sorry, you'll have to go," he told me.

"But—"

"I have a lot of work this afternoon. Thank you for coming up and telling me about the spring bolt; when I need to come down, I'll be sure to check with you first, so I don't startle you."

"*You* don't startle me," I said, a little confused at the change in him. "I just—"

"I'm sorry, but I really do have work to do—is there something *else* you need?" He was seriously impatient with me now. I had no idea what had happened. We had been doing so well.

"Why are you mad at me?" I said.

"I'm not angry—I have no feelings at all," he said, like that was going to make it better. "Are you *crying*?"

"I just don't know what to do," I said, and the fact is, I had most definitely teared up. It was really mortifying. "If everybody hates me just because I'm here, what do I do?"

"Oh, for heaven's sake. Get a grip," he said. "If nobody likes you, the thing you need to do is *make friends*."

8

THE WHITES' APARTMENT WAS ON THE NINTH FLOOR, DIRECTLY above me. Like mine, it had way more hallways and rooms than you could figure out or follow, but unlike mine there were people in all of them. There was Mrs. White, who wore really cute jackets and skirts and panty hose and short heels, so she looked great while she ran around like a lunatic, shouting at everyone and carrying books and piles of laundry and stuffed animals and spoons and forks and empty juice boxes everywhere. Then there was a cook—actually two cooks, who came on different days—and a Polish woman named Anna, who was always doing laundry, and a Hispanic woman, Magda, who seemed to clean the bathrooms constantly, and there were lots and lots of girls, little girls and big girls, mostly wearing pleated plaid skirts and dark green cardigans. The Whites had six kids, all girls. It took me more than a few days to learn all of their names: Louise, Jennifer, Gail, Mary Ellen, Katherine, and a two-year-old named Barbie. They actually called the kid Barbie, which I thought was a mistake, but I figured she would grow up and tell them to cut it out, and that would be the end of that.

A week after Len gave me my instructions, when I went up to 9A to introduce myself to the chaotic Whites, I had no idea what I might find there. After he had kicked me out, I went back to my apartment and poked around the kitchen and the laundry without knowing what I was looking for. I put a call in to Lucy, but her assistant told me she was in meetings all afternoon and would not be able to return calls until the next day. I thought about arguing with her and telling her there was an emergency at the apartment, but I was pretty sure Lucy would not consider my musings about the devious co-op board and the greedy Mrs. Westmoreland an emergency, so I said thanks and hung up. I thought about calling Alison, but that didn't seem likely to calm me down, and then I picked up the clicker for the television and thought about channel flipping for a while. In previous times I had spent entire days aimlessly trolling basic cable for traces of common sense or answers that never appeared. Then I considered throwing the fucking clicker against the wall but decided just to set it down on the coffee table, which is where I found the card for Stuart Long, Esq. And when I got up the nerve to call a couple days later, he actually got on the phone as soon as his receptionist told him I was on the line.

"Hello, Tina, how are you?" he asked, all kind and concerned. "Are you still in the apartment?"

"Where else would I be?"

"Well, I heard from the Drinans that they'd prefer for you to stay elsewhere, because they are planning to litigate," he observed sagely, as if this were big news.

"Listen, Mr. Long, I actually called about a slightly different question. The co-op board over here, they could make it difficult for a sale to go through when we try to sell this place, is that right?"

"They will have to approve the sale if or when it gets to that point, of course. I don't think it's anything you need to worry about now, though. You have a lot of hoops to jump through before that."

"That's not what Lucy thinks. She's already had real estate agents coming through here, she thinks we're good to go."

"Your sister is clearly someone who likes to move quickly; I noticed that when we met," Long agreed. "Nevertheless, I'm sure she doesn't expect this situation to resolve itself overnight. Probating even a simple will takes months, and this is far from simple. The courts have not yet probated Mr. Drinan's estate, and the deposition of that will bear directly on your situation."

What he said made almost no sense to me, so I stuck with the subject at hand. "Yeah, well, what about the co-op board?" I asked.

"Have they contacted you?"

"Is that what happens next?"

He paused for a moment, with that kindly concern. "Tina—your sister indicated to me that you are employing other counsel. Are you aware of that?"

"No, she didn't mention that either. Sorry, Mr. Long, I didn't know, I'm so—uh, look, could you just tell me who's on the co-op board, and I'll take it from there?"

"Well, that information is included in the documentation about the apartment, which I gave to your sister."

"So you don't have it anymore?"

"Of course I have it. I represented Bill Drinan for thirty years, I have everything on file."

"Could you give me those names?"

"You don't want to ask your sister for them?"

"Well, since I have you on the phone I thought it made more sense just to get them from you." I did not want to get into a discussion of my problematic sister with this nice man, especially if he wasn't going to represent me anyway.

There was a little silence on the end of the line, and then he sighed. "Let's see what we have. Here we are. There are twelve people on the board. It's a rotating board, of course, but this slate was elected last spring, so it should be current. Alice White, apartment 9A. Roger Masterson, 11B . . ."

Twelve people to suck up to and make friends with. One of them was Len, which I did think he might have mentioned when he brought the subject up in the first place. I found that to be a worrisome oversight on his part, but I couldn't dismiss the commonsense idea that I should try to present a good face to the people in this fancy building and start pretending to the neighbors that I really did belong there. I thanked Stuart Long and hung up.

A couple days later I had a plan. I decided to start with the Whites because they were the closest, just one floor away.

"Hi, I'm looking for Mrs. White," I told the edgy teenager who answered the door. Her plaid skirt and green cardigan looked terrible on her, as it would on any reasonably attractive person.

"Mooooom!" she yelled. "There's some lady here!"

"Louise, don't shout, *please*," shouted Mrs. White from two or three rooms away. Louise shrugged and walked away; I had no choice but to let myself in and watch her pass her mother in the hallway. Mrs. White was carrying a baby, and had a crying child glued to her leg. But she was wearing a really cute pink suit that looked terrific on her.

"Who is it?" she asked Louise, looking toward the other end of the apartment, as if I might be back there. I think she was confused for a moment about where the front door was.

"I don't know her name. I think it's that lady who moved in downstairs," said curt Louise, not even bothering to pause as she answered the question.

"Oh, that's ridiculous," said Mrs. White. "You didn't ask her name?"

"It's Tina Finn!" I called, trying to be all friendly. "My mother was married to Bill? My mother was Olivia? Did you know my mom?"

Mrs. White was too startled to answer this at first. She just stared at me. I took a step in and held up the bottle of wine, like a trophy. "I wanted to come introduce myself and say hello. I'll be staying downstairs for now, so I wanted to say hello." I was hoping this didn't come off as ridiculous and dopey as it sounded in my head. If it did, Mrs. White's manners were really just too good to let me know.

"Of course!" she said, trying to unpeel the kid from her shin and take a few steps toward me in the foyer. "Yes, I did see you the other day, didn't I? Downstairs in the lobby, I think—sweetie, let go of my leg, Mommy needs to say hello to the lady."

"Tina," I repeated.

"Yes, Tina, it is—lovely—to meet you," she agreed, reaching a bit to shake my hand. I took the last few steps in to make it easier for her, at which point the kid on the floor lost her footing and started to go down.

"Katherine, be careful—Katherine—oh, thank you, thanks," Mrs. White said, as I scooped the child up.

"Wow. That's your name, Katherine?" I asked the kid. "You're so pretty." At which point the baby started to wail.

"Now, now, Katherine, don't bother the lady," Mrs. White instructed the kid, who was now glued to me. "Thank you for the wine."

"She's not bothering me," I offered, ignoring her not so subtle hint that I should leave. I had made it through the door, which was farther than I ever thought I'd get, and I wasn't going to give ground so quickly.

As the baby got going, wailing and writhing with that peculiar rage that comes out of nowhere to really little kids, Mrs. White was suddenly helpless.

"Barbie—Barbie—oh, for heaven's sake, sweetie. Barbie!" She turned to me. "I'll be right back." And she scooted off with the baby, down one of those endless hallways, leaving me and Katherine staring at each other.

"Do you want to see my toys?" Katherine asked.

"Sure," I said, following her down another hallway to a room so far back in the building I would have gotten lost if I had to try and find it by myself. There was a comfortable daybed covered with a pink-and-yellow bedspread, and on the wall behind it was an enormous quilt cross-stitched with little pictures for the different letters of the alphabet. The walls were yellow and the rug had a big rainbow on it. Itty-bitty wooden and plastic people were clumped in small groupings everywhere, like they were having discreet parties in every corner of the room. Some were standing around toy plastic playground sets or, in one corner, beside a little wooden castle.

"Wow," I said, flopping on the daybed casually so I could sneak a glance out the window. It looked out on an alley I had never seen before, which convinced me that there was another room in my own apartment that I had not yet found. "Is this your room? It's so cute."

"This is my bed, and these are my animals," Katherine said, pulling about seventy stuffed animals out from behind the sweet little trundle bed that sat tidily in the opposite corner. "This is Blackie. This is Lulu. This is Betty."

I climbed down to the floor to get a closer look at the dogs and cats and rabbits and bears and ponies and ducks and sheep and llamas pouring out from behind the bed. We were deep into some game that had to do with animals living in the forest when one of the teenagers finally found us. It was not Louise, the one I had met at the door, but a slightly younger one who seemed even more unhappy about wearing that hideous school uniform. Her hair drooped all over her head as if she couldn't be bothered with it, which was a shame, because it was that great dark blond color with streaks of red that only teenagers get to have, and only for a little while. She had pretty gray eyes, but they were narrowed together under suspicious eyebrows. The kid definitely needed a makeover.

"Who the fuck are you?" she asked, a tad hostile, from the doorway.

"You said the f word, you owe me a dollar," Katherine announced without looking up.

"Fuck fuck fuck. Fuck," the hostile teen replied.

"Jennifer!" Katherine gasped, truly appalled by this outrageous breach of decorum.

"It's better for you, now I owe you a five," Jennifer announced as she picked the kid up and kissed her, then set her back down in the middle of her animals with a move that was both careless and careful at the same time. "Are you the person who moved into 8A?" she asked, flopping on the daybed.

"Yeah, my name is Tina," I started.

"I know your name," she announced, utterly bored. At least she was acting bored, but I know plenty about teenage girls, having been one, and I was well aware that she was completely desperate for information about me and the empty apartment beneath our feet.

I was only too happy to share. "My mom died, so, yeah, I just moved in. Downstairs. I guess I'm right downstairs." I started to smile, decided that was too much, so I turned back to the game. Katherine was in the thick of it, waving a spotted pony in my face. "No, no, go away!" she yelled.

"I'm gonna get her," I announced, picking up the unicorn and pretending to eat it. She started laughing, completely beside herself with glee.

"Yeah, but you're not like staying there," Jennifer informed me. "Like I heard they were kicking you out."

"Who told you that?" I asked.

"Everybody." She shrugged.

"Everybody who?" I pressed.

"Just people." I knew I'd get nothing more out of her until she felt like talking.

"We'll see, I guess." I shrugged. "Do you want to see it?"

"See it?" she asked, not quite getting me. "You mean the apartment?"

"Yeah, you want to come down and see it?"

Such a stroke of blind good luck had never occurred to her. But she was far too well versed in the etiquette of cool to acknowledge any excitement. "Are you *allowed* to let people in?" she asked, choosing to completely dismiss my invitation rather than express any interest in it.

"I have the key," I pointed out. "My stuff is there. They haven't kicked me out yet."

"But isn't it just like this place?" She suddenly and cleverly decided to feign indifference, pretending to be bored with the possibility of seeing the mystery apartment downstairs. "It's the same layout and everything—it's the same apartment, right?"

"Are you kidding? Your place is totally normal, you should come see my place, it's pretty weird. Like they were selling off all the furniture, so there's nothing in there but light fixtures and moss and some clocks and those crazy mirrors from like the nineteenth century? All sorts of cracked stuff."

"Moss?" said Jennifer, disbelieving this. "I mean, like, are you kidding? What is it, like *mold*?"

"No, it's really moss, the guy who has the greenhouse up on the roof needed a place to put his moss."

"You know that guy?"

"Len? Yeah, he was a friend of my mom's; he's great. Have you ever seen his greenhouse?"

"No," she said, an edge of sullen jealousy creeping into her tone.

"It's amazing. If you want, I'll take you up there." I knew this all sounded so unbelievable that she was tempted to believe it. "Anyway, you have to at least come by and see the moss, he's got twenty different kinds in my kitchen. One of the kitchens."

"You have two kitchens? 'Cause we only have one."

"Yeah, it's different down there. The layout is completely different. Like this room, the one we're in right now? It's not there."

"Well, where is it?"

"I don't know, maybe it's part of the Westmoreland apartment. Do you know her, Delia Westmoreland?"

"Do *you* know her?"

"Not really."

"She wants that apartment, she's been trying to buy it for like fifteen years," Jennifer stated. "She's going to try and get you kicked out. She's hell on wheels."

When Jennifer wasn't pretending to be bored with the universe, she had a curious beam going, like there was a spectacularly intelligent person in there who was perfectly capable of utterly devious behavior.

"I'm not going anywhere," I announced, feeling far less sure of this than I sounded. "You want to come down?"

"I'm not allowed."

"Come on, it's only one floor," I persisted. The idea of having an idle teenager to show off my cool apartment to was suddenly very enticing.

"Seriously, I'm not allowed," she said. And the devious person went away again.

Jennifer was telling the truth. When Mrs. White showed up two minutes later, she shooed Jennifer back to her room and described the facts of life as they were lived in 9A.

"Their father is very strict," Mrs. White explained, as she politely ushered me back through the many hallways to the front of the apartment. Their place was easier to navigate than mine, but it was a bit of a maze nonetheless. "Raising six girls in Manhattan, you can imagine how that would be necessary. The things that go on in the private schools, you don't want to know about."

"Drugs, boys, blow jobs?" I asked, kind of all concerned and quiet.

She shot me a look, none too pleased with my slightly too careless display of insider information.

"Of course, you would know about this," she observed, smiling a little too tightly.

"Oh, I just know what I've read, it's all over the Web," I countered fast. "Isn't it? I went to Catholic school in Jersey. All girls, only nuns. We didn't even have priests. Well, and thank god for that! I mean, what the priests turned out to be up to, a kid would be safer in prison."

"You went to Catholic school?" This seemed of some interest to her, so I was glad I had made it up.

"Saint Ignatius, over in Jersey City. They finally closed it a couple years ago, which is too bad, I got a great education there." To my own ear I sounded like a pretty desperate liar, but she was dealing with a writhing baby and wasn't paying full attention. "Your girls are in Catholic school, right?"

"Saint Peter in Chains, up on Ninety-eighth," she said.

"Saint Peter in Chains!" I smiled, like I knew it well. "I love their uniforms, they look so cute."

"Well, it certainly makes life simpler. With six girls you can imagine what kind of chaos we would have to deal with in the clothes department if we didn't have the uniforms," she agreed. "And my husband wants them to learn a broader system of values."

Eyeing Mrs. White's gorgeous pink outfit, I felt a sincere moment of sympathy for those teenage girls learning a broader system of values. I mean, their mother was running all over New York City in designer suits, and they had to throw on the same ugly pleated skirts every morning before heading uptown to hang out with a bunch of nuns. It seemed like a pretty nasty fate, especially considering that they lived in Manhattan, where I would have thought that nobody, and I mean *nobody*, went to Catholic school to learn values.

"Well, I know I loved my uniform, maybe not every day of high school, but afterward, definitely," I said. "I come from a family of girls too. Not as many, there were only three of us, but obviously we were in something of the same boat in terms of the clothes, I mean. My mother was always up to her eyeballs in laundry." I was definitely starting to sound like a suck-up. Mrs. White, mother of teenage girls, recognized the sound, and her already chilly attitude became logarithmically less friendly.

"Thank you for coming," she said, opening the front door. Behind her I could see Katherine watching from the hallway. Off in the distance teenage voices were suddenly raised in heat—Jennifer and Louise sniping over shoes or hair clips or who was hogging the phone—and then a third voice chimed in, topping them both. I thought for a second about the two girls whose names I didn't know yet and hadn't even laid eyes on. Mrs. White turned for a second, impatient.

"Girls, no yelling! Gail! Louise! NO YELLING IN THE HOUSE!" she yelled. And then she looked back at me, clearly waiting for me to just go.

"I have two sisters," I repeated.

"Yes. So you said."

"I'm the youngest. We didn't live in a very big house, so we were really on top of each other all the time. And we would argue about everything. Sometimes I think of the stupid things we argued about and wonder how my mother didn't go stark raving mad just listening to us. Did you ever meet my mother? She lived downstairs. She died just a week and a half ago. It feels like a long time already, but it was just a week and a half. I mean, it was a shock to everybody, we had no idea she was even, well, I guess that's how heart attacks work, nobody sees them coming. And maybe it was good for her, to go that way, just fast like that. If you're going to die, that would be the way, right? I just worry. I'm staying down there and I'm seeing all her stuff, and I'm telling you, she—did you know Bill? Because we didn't—anyway, I just hadn't seen her in such a long time. I think maybe she was lonely. It's nice to meet you. It's nice to meet your girls. I'm happy to be here."

Don't ask me what I was trying to do, because I didn't even know. I just didn't want her to think I was whatever she thought I was. Katherine was still watching me from behind her mother. I gave her a little wave, low, so she knew I could see her. She waved back. The voices of the girls at the other end of the apartment rose again, unyielding in their fury. For a moment a few words shook themselves free of the sound and made the argument comprehensible: shampoo. They were mad at each other over shampoo.

"GIRLS, HONESTLY YOU DO NOT WANT ME TO COME BACK THERE!" Mrs. White hollered. "I'M NOT KIDDING. DO YOU WANT ME TO TELL YOUR FATHER ABOUT THIS?"

Silence bloomed instantly around the question. She turned back to me, newly determined. "Well," she said. "Thank you for coming by." She raised her hand, but with the palm up, so it was more like an offering and less like she was pointing at the door, which was in fact what she was doing.

"I would be happy to babysit sometime, if you need anybody," I said.

"We'll give you a call," she said, politely shutting the door in my face.

Okay, so that didn't go exactly the way I wanted, but since I hadn't put a ton of thought into the plan, I decided not to take it personally. Besides, I had made definite inroads with two of the kids, and I had left the dangling possibility of cheap local babysitting in the back of Mrs. White's busy brain. Even though she had been less than enthusiastic, I decided it might be worthwhile to capitalize on my introduction to her, so I hopped into the elevator and went down to the lobby, where Frank was leaning on his podium, head in hands, talking quietly in Spanish to someone on the phone who was clearly bugging the shit out of him. He didn't raise his voice at all, but the speed of the conversation kept increasing until Frank was careening through sentences and thoughts so fast I expected him to crash and burn any second. But he didn't. He just looked up, saw me standing there, and switched into English.

"I got to go," he said, and hung up.

"Hay una problema?" I asked, in friendly lame Spanish.

"Dos problemas. Dos hermanos, dos problemas, not as big as the problem with *mi padre,* but what can I do for you, Tina? I heard you were moving out soon."

"Ohhhh, not yet," I said. "Who'd you hear that from?"

"Well, who you think?" he said, starting to sort mail. He was a lot less friendly than he had been before, but having just come down from Mrs. White, who was downright rude, I didn't take it personally. I saw how right Len was, that I had a lot of work to do if I wanted to try and stay here.

"Yeah, I heard that Doug wants me out, but I think Pete's okay with it, isn't he?" I asked. "Did you talk to Pete?"

"No, I talked to Doug, he said you were moving out," Frank repeated.

"No, not yet. Listen, Mrs. White asked me if I could babysit for her sometime, so I said okay, but I didn't remember the number of my cell phone because I just got it? So is there something I can write it on, and you can maybe give it to her with her mail?"

"You're going to babysit for the Whites?" He looked up at me, surprised, and I could see that his eyes were kind of red and sad around the edges. Then he looked away again fast, and I thought, oh hell, he's not mad at me, he's upset, that phone call really upset him. He took a second to press his eyes as if he had a headache, but really so that the tips of his fingers could catch the tears before they actually existed. Then he started sorting the mail with extremely fierce attention, so I knew I'd better say something fast or it would be impossible for us both to keep pretending that nothing was amiss.

"Yeah, I went up and said hello because my mom always talked about how much she liked Mrs. White, and we talked about me babysitting, but I didn't have my phone, so I went back to the apartment and got it and then I was going to run back up with the number, but they were in the middle of homework and stuff when I left, and I thought it would be easier to leave it for her with you, and you should have it anyway," I said, acting all casual and sticking my fingers in the back pockets of my jeans, pretending I was looking for something there. "And of course I'm so retarded I don't even have a pen. Do you have a pen? Do you have anything I can write on?"

"Yeah, I don't know, here, here's a pen," he said, handing me one of those skinny ballpoints that nobody buys, but businesses get in truckloads and give out to people they don't care about. He went back to sorting the mail, then stopped and said, "There's paper too, hang on, I got a notebook here under the mail." And he lifted up the whole pile, which was quite an awkward maneuver, and I saw a spiral notebook, which I slid out before he could drop something. The whole move was so complicated that by the time we were on the other side of it we were both in the clear, and I was writing down my cell phone number and he was putting it in with Mrs. White's mail, as if that was all that was going on anyway.

So we were busy when Vince Masterson showed up.

There is almost no point in describing Vince Masterson. When you first meet him, he seems to look like nothing; his features are so regular that he doesn't look like anybody in particular. He's about thirty, you think, and he just looks normal. Then he starts to talk, and you realize that his eyes are a perfect light blue and his nose is long and beautiful and he's tall and jaw-droppingly gorgeous. And then he keeps talking and you realize that he's actually kind of an asshole and he doesn't really know as much as he thinks he knows and he's not that handsome after all. And then he keeps on talking and you think wow what a gorgeous guy, maybe I'm wrong, maybe he does know all this stuff, and I'm the one who's stupid. And then he talks some more and you think, what an asshole. And then you think he's handsome again, but maybe not really. It's like that.

So this was the first time I'd laid eyes on Vince. He announced his arrival pleasantly enough. "Hey, Frank, how's it going?" he called from the doorway. Frank and I both turned, and I thought, oh, it's just some guy who knows Frank, stopping by to say hello.

"Hey, Vince," said Frank, holding up his hand in a polite, friendly wave.

"Anything in there for me?" asked Vince, and he sauntered over, stuck his hands in his pockets, and leaned over the podium to watch what Frank was doing. I was standing right in his way, so his arm kind of brushed my shoulder and I took half a step back. He's tall; I'm short, and when he stood that close that fast, it became immediately clear that I would fit perfectly under his arm. He smiled down at me, and I was thinking, holy shit, this guy is gorgeous.

"Hi," he said.

"Hi," I said, and I swear to god, I turned all red. Seriously, that's how great-looking Vince sometimes is: you just go all red.

"I got a couple days' worth here," Frank mentioned. "Hang on a second." His head disappeared below the podium. Vince continued to smile down at me, but didn't say anything. The effect was insanely flirtatious.

"Hi, I'm Tina. Tina Finn." I suddenly got it together and held up my hand for him to shake. "I just moved in. Do you live here? I'm in 8A."

"Oh, the Livingston place, I heard about this. You're squatting there."

"I'm not squatting there, no, I, no," I said, both flustered and defensive. "My mother was, she left the apartment to me and my sisters. It's our apartment."

"That's not what I heard." Vince shrugged as he accepted a slender pile of mail. "Thanks, Frank." He stood there, ignoring me now, while he glanced through it.

"Most of it's for your dad," Frank offered. Vince looked up with a fast flash of annoyance, and I had an utterly ridiculous moment of feeling glad that he didn't get any mail, that it was all for his dad.

"Yeah, thanks, Frank, I'll get it to him," he said, tossing the junk mail onto the podium, right on top of what Frank was doing, sorting everyone else's mail. It was so condescending you could tell that he really thought he was better than Frank and didn't care if Frank knew it. I mean, people do that to me all the time, and I don't love it, but it doesn't piss me off as much as watching people be mean to some nice doorman like Frank.

"Here, I'll take care of that for you, Frank," I said, and I grabbed the junk mail before he could reach for it. "He's the doorman, not the garbageman," I informed Vince as I carried it across the foyer.

"It's okay, Tina," said Frank, a little confused and nervous. And why not, I was being unspeakably rude on his behalf.

"Are you up or down, what's your name—Tina?" Vince said, looking me over again, sort of like he was skinning me alive.

"What?" I said, shocked.

"Up or down?" It sounded like he was talking about sexual positions. He smirked, like he knew I was thinking that. "Are you on your way up, or have you just come down?"

What a creep, I thought and was about to say something completely inappropriate and aggressive when I glanced down at the junk mail I was about to dump into the trash can and caught the name *Roger Masterson*. One of the names on the list, one of the kings of the co-op board.

I took a breath and dumped the junk mail in the trash. "I'm on my way up," I said. "Want to share an elevator?"

9

VINCE MASTERSON HATES HIS FATHER. HE LIVES IN HIS FATHER'S apartment, which is quite nice but small compared to, say, my apartment. Vince has a trust fund, which his father set up, so Vince gets a check in the mail for many thousands of dollars—more than fifteen, as it turns out—from his father *every month,* while he lives in his father's apartment and hates his father. Vince talks easily and exhaustively about how much he hates his father. It is his favorite subject.

"It's not even his money, that's the thing you have to remember." We were in the big room, downing red wine while Vince took off his gorgeous but slightly uptight jacket, and I gave him a tour of the place. "He *inherited* it, and it's not like he inherited a small fortune and then was such a blinding genius at investing that it grew into a significant fortune, that's not what happened," he explained, as he launched into his favorite subject. "He just got it handed to him from my grandfather, who had it handed to him, and god, let me tell you, it's not like either one of them added to it—it just *sits* in the *markets.* Someone else, some completely anonymous but clever underling at Goldman Sachs or Morgan Stanley or Chase Manhattan, moves it around or leaves it where it is, and it grows, even in a shitty market it just keeps growing in these underground vaults, and every so often Dad or Grandpa will go and lop off a wad of this stuff and blow it on something ludicrous, a house in Palm Beach or an estate in East Hampton. So that's the family business, spending money, even though there is no way to use it up. No one does anything and it just *spreads.* It's that kind of money. Because if you *did* something meaningful with it, you would have to *be* someone, you know, actually be someone whom people *dealt* with on a cultural or political or even global level. You'd be a *player,* even though I hate that word. You'd have to risk everything to have real power, you know what

I mean? Honestly, I think that would be the better option—you'd have to risk losing it and then risk being the person who lost the fucking family money, but at least you'd be yourself."

Vince took a huge gulp of wine and looked out the window over the park, posing like a model in a fashion shoot. It was quite a performance. He sounded like a complete idiot and at the same time a broken-hearted old soul. "And that's what scares him!" he exclaimed, turning back to me with complete anguish in his eyes. "The man is so terrified of his own existence he can barely speak. You say 'hello, Dad' and he looks at you with complete and utter *contempt,* but it's not really contempt because it's terror that's driving him. Trust me, the *contempt* is just the cover, and not a very good one at that."

The heartbreak careened into superiority. "All the sneering and spending and *womanizing,* it's positively mun*dane,*" Vince explained, as if I could follow this. "I have not two but three stepmothers, all of them so exactly identical I can't keep their names straight, and he's cheated on them all with women who look just like them. A couple of them tried to take him to the cleaners, but the money's tied up, as you can imagine; the lawyers aren't letting anyone, much less a trophy wife, walk away with anything meaningful, no matter how big a shit my father is. But what I don't understand is the endless repetition. Honestly, why trade in one for the other if they're exactly the same model? And what on earth do they talk about? You can't fuck all the time—I actually don't think he fucks them at all, if you want to know the truth. These women are not getting laid, every last one of them has this look of pinched terror hovering around the corners of her bottom lips, although that could be the plastic surgery or the fact that they're all starving to death. Has anyone ever thought about the irony of all these ridiculously wealthy white women starving themselves to death on the Upper West Side of the richest city in the richest country in the world, because the instant they look healthier than a fucking Holocaust survivor their husbands will divorce them? Although, trust me, I waste no sympathy on any of the brainless twigs who married my father. Christ, the whole thing is so *stupid,* it's so fucking *stupid* I can't even bear to talk about it. What a fucking waste of time. Is there more wine? You know, this stuff is actually quite good. And just cases of it lying around, that had to be a nice surprise."

He carried his half-empty glass of wine loosely in his right hand and poured with his left, not even glancing down to make sure he didn't spill anything. While I found the guy annoying, I couldn't help noticing that he had a great chest, because at some point the top three buttons on his shirt had sort of magically come undone.

"So what's under here?" he suddenly asked, kicking at a tuft of the mustard-covered shag.

"I haven't looked," I said, staring at his chest. He smirked like a thirteen-year-old, and I turned red. "I mean, we haven't had a chance to do an inventory or anything like that."

"I heard you already had the place appraised."

"Who'd you hear that from?"

"I'm asking the questions, Ms. Finn. Did they give you an estimate?"

"Yes they did, we got three separate estimates. One from *Sotheby's*." I held my glass out, opting suddenly for a stance of deliberate and overt sexuality. It always works. He came to my side and refilled it with sloppy generosity, finishing off the bottle.

"So how much did they tell you you'd get, without even bothering to glance under the rugs?" he asked, coolly appraising the place himself.

"I don't know you well enough to discuss my personal finances, Vince."

"We just drank an entire bottle of red wine together in under twenty minutes, Tina. I think you know me pretty well, or at least you will within the hour." I couldn't help it, it was so cocky I had to laugh.

"What's so funny?"

"You're just a really good flirt," I tossed at him.

"Thank you," he said, following me around the room like a dog on a leash. "I appreciate the compliment. Must be this place. Down in the lobby, I could have sworn you didn't like me."

"I don't like you," I said, smiling up at him. "That doesn't change the fact that you're a really good flirt."

"You're not so bad yourself," he said, with a dazzling smile full of smug self-assurance. And why not, he really was beautiful, especially standing in front of a view of Manhattan with his shirt half open. Vince glanced over my head and out to the spectacular expanse of Central Park, visible from all six windows along the big room's front wall. "Christ, this place really is amazing. It's got to be seven thousand square feet, and this view! What did Sotheby's tell you? Come on, I want a number. Everybody in the building is guessing you'll get at least ten for it—if they let you sell it, that is."

"Are they going to try and stop us?"

"I'm still the one asking the questions today. Come on, what did they say you'd get?" Wandering across the room, Vince stuck his head into the kitchen and jumped. "Holy shit, what's this? There's mold everywhere in here, have you called the super?"

I laughed. He glanced back at me, flushing with annoyance, and you could see that mean streak flare up. Mean, handsome, hypersensitive, rich, arrogant, sexy, and drunk; there was no question where this was going. I followed him across the room, passing him in the doorway of the kitchen, where he hovered like a scared rabbit.

"That guy who lives in the penthouse—Len? The botanist? He had a deal with Bill; he rented the kitchen to him. It's a *mossery*." I leaned on the word to make it sound like I thought he was a bit stupid.

"A what?" He followed me in but stayed behind me, still completely creeped out by all that moss. I flipped the wall switch, and the place started to glow. Len had tucked itty-bitty light fixtures into odd corners amid the moss, so it looked like you were lost in some gnomish netherworld. There were three fountains that propelled tiny streams of water through the various trays of bryophytes. The pump that kept the water running hummed, so the dark, mossy room seemed to vibrate a little and shift in the light. I took a step in and fingered one of the mosses Len had shown me; the tiniest of purple knobs skimmed the surface of that particular tray.

"It's a *mossery*," I repeated. "They used to have them all over the place in the nineteenth century, now people don't do them much, except for places like botanical gardens. But Len wanted to build one, and he gets too much light up in the penthouse, so he rented one of Bill's kitchens. Look at the cedar-plank boxes, he built them himself. And some of the moss—like this one—grows on *concrete*. But mostly he has to create an environment that approximates the floor of a deciduous forest." Len had told me some of this stuff, but mostly I was making it up. "Here," I said. I put my hand on Vince's, lifted it, and moved it onto a particularly dense thicket, pushing his fingers into the softest part of the growth. "Feels weird, doesn't it?"

Vince looked down at me. "Fantastic," he said.

No surprise, Vince knew exactly what to do in this situation. He just leaned down and kissed me carefully, right on the mouth. His right arm went around me, he tossed his wineglass onto one of the moss beds without even looking where it landed, and then he had my back up against the wall while his other hand moved easily up under my shirt, pushing it out of the way so that two seconds later, when his half-buttoned shirt was somehow completely undone, my skin was right up against his. I mean, both of us still had our clothes on, but who could tell? His tongue was so far down my throat I was seeing stars. I thought about coming up for air and decided I'd rather faint, if it came to it. Seriously, I knew it was bad news, this guy was so good at making a pass at someone he barely knew, but he was so good I really didn't care. He kept me pinned against the wall, with both hands on my waist, and then he slid his fingers down into my jeans, and I almost leapt out of my skin. I could feel his erection pressing against me, and he made a little sound in the back of his throat, like he knew he was an animal and he wasn't going to give me a chance to pretend I wasn't. I mean, it was one hell of a kiss. Vince made out the way he talked, with so much reckless confidence it didn't really matter that everything he said was bullshit.

By the time we stopped kissing we were both gasping for air. He set me down, took a step back, and leaned against the opposite wall, knocking over a pile of wooden trays that Len had stacked next to a bag of plant food. The trays went flying. When he reached out to stop them from collapsing into the room, he bumped into something else that bumped into something else that knocked his wineglass off the counter and onto the floor, where it shattered with a loud crack.

"Holy shit, the moss is attacking me," Vince muttered, shoving the trays back against the wall with his foot. "They seem to be very protective of your honor."

"Too late for that." I laughed, sounding way too shaky. Vince looked up from the broken glass and considered me from the darkness on the other side of the room.

"Thanks for showing me the mossery," he said. "But maybe we should take another look at the bedrooms."

"You know, now is not such a good time," I said. "But thanks for stopping by." I went out of the kitchen and turned toward the front door, which surprised him. After all, there was no hiding the fact that I was dying to leap on him again and let it take me wherever it would. But I thought it would be a bad idea to give him the satisfaction. He had too many character flaws, most of which I already knew. "So maybe I'll see you around the building," I said, turning the locks on the door with casual determination.

"I'd like that," he said at my shoulder.

I turned to smile a good-bye to him, my hand on the spring bolt. But before I could open the door, he grabbed my shoulder, flipped me around, and got his tongue down my throat a second time. I considered resisting for about half a second, but honestly, it is not always easy to consider consequences at moments like that. So much for walking away, I thought, my hands going after the top button of his jeans. He already had mine unzipped when we heard a voice in the hall.

"Tina? Are you in there? Tina?" There was a little rapping on the door, the sound of keys. I stopped.

"Yeah—Lucy—just give me a minute." This made not the slightest impression on old Vince, who was wrapping his arms around my waist. I very weakly tried to extract myself. "Put your clothes back on, come on," I whispered, dragging him away from the doorway.

"Tell her to go away," he murmured in my ear as his fingers continued in their determination to undress me.

"I would, but she doesn't do what I tell her," I said, shoving him. The locks were flipping. I was not going to have Lucy find me in a clinch with Vince Masterson with my clothes half off.

"She can't be your mother, your mother's dead." Vince laughed, as I desperately buttoned my jeans.

"She's worse, she's my sister," I told him. He laughed again and leaned against the wall, completely amused by my predicament. Lucy stepped through the doorway. Her eyes swiped over us, then raked the room, finding the empty red wine bottle in the middle of the floor, where Vince had simply dropped it. She looked back at us and didn't say anything. She didn't even set her briefcase down. Vince stifled another laugh. I elbowed him.

"Ow, what'd you do that for?" he said, acting like a frat boy. "Hi, I'm Vince Masterson. I live on the fifth floor, Tina was just showing me the apartment. It's fabulous, congratulations. What did you say your name was?" All his sexual and class confidence merged into one dazzling bit of arrogance as he ignored the utterly disheveled state of his clothes and held out his hand for Lucy to shake. She looked him in the eye before glancing down at his hand, trying to decide if it was clean enough to touch, because it was not at all clear where his fingers had recently been. I wanted to hit her.

Vince just laughed and brought his hand up, touching her carelessly on the elbow as if that had been what he intended all along. "Terrific meeting you," he said, smiling. "Tina, you were just showing me out, weren't you?"

He looked back at me and held out his hand. I obediently reached for it and let him drag me to the front door, which was still standing open. He leaned down and kissed me on the cheek. "I feel like I got caught in the back of the schoolhouse with the parson's daughter," he murmured in my ear.

"It was *so* great to meet you, Vince," I said loudly.

"Likewise," he agreed. "Give me a call."

I shut the door and turned to find Lucy picking up the empty wine bottle. She held it out to me.

"Do you think you could put this in with the recycling? I don't want this place turning into a dump," she said.

"It's one empty wine bottle," I told her with deliberate indifference.

"It's trashy," she informed me. "And we're not going down that road this time, is that understood? It's not happening!" And then she shoved me. I think she just meant to poke me in the shoulder for emphasis, but her anger got the better of her and she *shoved* me. It really hurt.

"Hey," I said. "What's your problem?"

"*You* are my problem. Jesus—I would just, I would just like to fucking kill you!" she hissed. I didn't particularly enjoy the fact that she had walked in on me making out with a cute guy, but this was a bit out of control.

"Chill out, will you?" I said. "That guy—"

"I don't want to hear about that guy."

"He lives in the building."

"He lives in the building! Terrific! Is that enough of a reason to bring him up here and have sex with him?"

"I didn't have sex with him! I was trying to make friends with him—"

"Well, you seem to have succeeded. Well done, Tina. And what's this?" She looked at the front door, where my rigged-up spring bolt and door chains sparkled in the afternoon light.

"It's my security system," I said. "Too many people have keys to this place and seem to feel they can let themselves in any time they want. We're not doing that anymore. If I don't want people to come in, I'm not going to let them in."

"I didn't agree to that."

"I don't give a shit if you agree or not," I said, turning back to television land. It was rough coming down from near-sex with a really hot and deeply problematic guy to getting yelled at by your bossy sister. I needed more wine.

"Don't you dare walk away from me," Lucy snarled over my shoulder. She was spitting mad. I headed down the hallway.

"Relax, would you?" I said. "I'm getting myself a glass of wine."

"Don't you think you've had enough to drink?"

"No, actually, I don't. Want some?" I cut through the TV room and back to the laundry room to score another bottle from the stash.

"No," Lucy countered, tossing her briefcase onto the couch. It landed right next to Vince's jacket and tie. "Oh look. Your friend, whom you're not sleeping with, left his clothes."

"Yeah, great, I'll get them back to him. It'll give me an excuse to go up to his place and not fuck him there."

"This is no joke, Tina!"

"Lucy, if you want to sell this place, we have to get by the co-op board," I said, returning with the fresh bottle. "And they can stop a sale if they feel like it, and right now that is how they feel, they don't like us. Oh wait! One of them likes us—Vince likes *me*."

"He wants to have sex with you. It's not quite the same thing."

"For most people it's close enough. And if you had sex on a regular basis, you might know things like that."

"Thank you for once again elevating the conversation. Really, it's terrific having you around to put things in perspective." Lucy stood there in her tight gray suit, not even looking at me, her thumbs moving restlessly through the air above her ever-present BlackBerry, and I knew that nothing I said, sensible or otherwise, would make an impression.

"Look, is there a reason you're here?" I said. "Is there some dazzling legal maneuver you're about to pull, or did you just stop by to make me feel shitty?"

Lucy paused for a good long time before deigning to answer. She kept reading her BlackBerry, then decided she was done with that, pocketed it, and reached for her briefcase before glancing in my direction. "Well, let me just tell you this much: we don't have to worry about the co-op board for now," she finally said. She snapped open the clasps on her briefcase, flipped the cover up, and reached inside for a crisp manila envelope, which she tossed onto the coffee table. I could tell by the way it hit the wood that it contained freshly minted documents.

"What's that?" I said, feigning indifference. I was pretty sure it was something big, but she was really working my nerves so I thought I'd return the favor.

"You can read, right? I mean, you did acquire that skill before you dropped out of college to run off with some loser, didn't you?"

"Yes, I can read, but since I'm stupid it takes me a real long time. Maybe you could just summarize in ten words or less and tell me what I'm supposed to get myself all upset about today."

"We have a court date."

"A court date for what?"

"The Drinans are objecting to the will."

"Well, what does that mean?"

"They're claiming that their father was mentally incapacitated when the will was executed and that Mom used undue influence, and that we came into possession illegally, so they're suing for damages."

"Well, they *are* damaged, but whose fault is that? Not mine."

"They're suing you for it. And they're suing me, and they're suing Daniel and Alison to the tune of twenty million dollars."

"Come on."

"You asked me to summarize."

This sounded so bizarre I couldn't believe it. I decided it might be smart to take a look at the documents myself, so I opened the envelope. Lucy went back to making love to her BlackBerry.

"There's a preliminary hearing in Surrogate's Court on December seventh," she said. "That's three months from now. It's unheard of to get a date set that quickly, so they're clearly pulling strings. They also went judge shopping—we're scheduled to be heard by the one judge who thinks she can do whatever she feels like with the law. The one who's a cop, he probably had enough clout in the legal system to put this where they wanted it. The other one is some sort of principal at the Dalton School, so he knows absolutely everybody. In any case, they pulled strings."

I paged through the papers in front of me and tried to make sense of them. They seemed utterly incomprehensible, and for a moment I thought, *Maybe Lucy's right, maybe I never really did learn to read properly.*

"They're suing us—like *suing* us, for money?"

"That's a separate action, they're just trying to scare us. They want us to make a counteroffer."

"What kind of counteroffer?"

"Well, let's see, what do they want? The apartment! I think if we offered them the apartment, this would all go away."

"What if the judge gives them the apartment?"

"We're not going to let that happen."

"But they're suing us? So we could lose the apartment, and then if they win the lawsuit we'll have to pay them money too?"

"You're not going to have to worry about that, though, are you, Tina, because you are completely without resources. Isn't that right? Do you have any money left from the stash you found in Bill's wallet?"

"Some," I admitted.

"How much?"

"Maybe a hundred?"

"You're going to have to come up with some more and buy some decent clothes. And I do mean decent, none of this boho-loser-chic stuff you think is so cool. A skirt and a blouse and sensible shoes. Something good and ugly. You're going to have to stop dressing like a slut."

"Anything else, mein führer?"

"When there is, I'll let you know." She picked up her briefcase and looked at me, sprawled on the couch, wineglass in hand, watching her with my best sullen disregard.

"Before you take off, can you at least tell me who my lawyer is? You said you were going to replace that nice Egg Man. Did that happen?"

"We have a new and very good lawyer, yes. His name is Ira Grossman, he's very experienced in these kinds of litigious inheritance situations."

"Can I call him?"

"No, you can't call him! Every time you call him it costs a hundred dollars, which you don't have!"

"Yeah but—"

"Tina, please, I don't have time to hold your hand on every single thing. If you have questions about your legal status in this situation, read the pleadings."

"I can't understand this shit!"

"No? Then I guess you're going to have to rely on me and Daniel and Alison to tell you what to do. Get that shit off the door, buy some decent clothes, and keep this place clean. Oh, and tell that guy to come down here and get rid of the moss. Sotheby's has agreed to represent the apartment as a historic property, and no one is going to understand a roomful of moss when they start to show the place."

"How come—"

"That's all you have to worry about. Okay? Okay?"

"Okay."

She smiled grimly, as if she found it satisfactory to hear me say "okay," but she didn't look satisfied. She looked like her suit was too tight and she wasn't eating enough red meat and her shoes hurt. She had little gray smudges under her eyes, and her hair was pulled back in a bun, which was an extremely bad look for her, and usually she knew better than to try it. Her mouth was pinched together, bitter and worried, and for the first time I saw what Vince had seen instantly under the skin of my smart, ferocious sister: an old schoolmarm in a rage because the world had overlooked her.

"Hey, Lucy," I said, feeling completely awful all of a sudden. "No kidding, Lucy. Maybe we should just offer to split it with them. Even split five ways, we'd all end up with a ton of money. Has anyone offered to split it?"

"I don't believe that's been discussed, no," she said, with a kind of infantile brightness that had yet another sneer behind it.

"Yeah, I guess that's pretty stupid," I said. "Sorry. 'Compromise.' What a boneheaded idea."

"You said it, not me," she murmured under her breath.

She left. And I decided to stop asking questions nobody had any answers for anyway and just let things happen.

10

THREE DAYS LATER, WHEN LEN CAME BY TO CHECK IN ON CURRENT events, he was not particularly happy with the state of his mossery. He was thoroughly appalled that someone had been messing with his trays, knocking over bags of mulch, and tossing shards of glass all over the floor. During our abortive but completely memorable makeout session, Vince and I had also, it seems, damaged a display containing a delicate species of hornwort, several large sections of which had turned a distressing shade of mottled brown. The picture of the tree was so far askew it looked like it was about to fall off the wall.

"For seven hundred dollars a month, I think it's understood that the mossery is protected space," he informed me, straightening the picture with annoyed precision. "Your mother took great care with it; you, I see, do not have her touch. I'm going to have to ask you to refrain from even entering my room unless I am here to supervise you."

"It's not your room, Len," I reminded him, a tad defensive, since I knew he was right. "You're just renting it."

"Renting it from whom, that's the question," he said with a sharp little nod of contempt. He leaned past me to open the tiniest sliver of a closet door that was squashed between the refrigerator and the wall. He retrieved a whisk broom and a dustpan, which had been hung just inside the door at eye level. I watched as he swept the shards of glass together and disposed of them in the plastic dustbin next to the sink. Then he swept the floor again, and then he did it a third time, each time picking up ever more delicate pieces of broken glass. Then he reached up, pulled a roll of paper towels out of the cabinet above the moss, and dabbed carefully at every corner of the linoleum, finding little sparkles of glass dust everywhere. He folded the paper towel, put it to one side, and considered the dirty red wine stain that had spilled in ugly blotches everywhere.

Honestly, when Vince knocked his wineglass over, it hadn't seemed like there was much in it. But there was more than I thought and now those little spots of wine had set. Len glanced up at me, his face a mask of disappointed annoyance. "How long has this been here?" he asked, exhausted by my incompetence.

"Just a day. I was going to clean it up. I forgot," I said, trying a little too hard not to sound like a ten-year-old.

"And how did it happen?" he asked.

"I, um, I met that guy, Vince Masterson? He lives on the fifth floor?"

"Yes, I'm aware of where he lives," Len said, even more coolly disinterested, if that was possible.

"He wanted to see the apartment. So I invited him up. And I was showing him around and he dropped, he had a glass of wine and he dropped it, so—anyway I met the Whites too, I might be doing some babysitting for them." Len considered this possibility as he ran a paper towel under the faucet and started working on the wine spots.

"Babysitting?" he said, raising his eyebrows, as if he'd like to see that one.

"Yes," I said. "I'm good with kids. And, you'll be stunned to hear, I could use the money. "

"Your mother never had any money," Len observed, glancing up. "Bill didn't either. I used to ask them about it. They were both eligible for Social Security. But Bill wouldn't cash the checks. There was some sort of pension out there, but Bill wrote to them and told them he had moved. So those stopped coming too. Neither one of them had any money, really, at all."

"They didn't cash the checks?"

"Bill wanted to live off the grid."

"He lived in New York City!"

"Yes, that's true. Nevertheless. His need for privacy went beyond any other concern in his life. Except, perhaps, his love for your mother. If you had any real interest in the details of their life here together—"

"Of course I'm interested!"

"You might have put two and two together and realized that for Bill privacy was everything. *Everything.*"

"Why are you so mad at me?"

"Why are *you* letting people parade in and out of your home?"

"Well, the Drinans parade in and out because they think it's *their* home—"

"Which you are determined to dissuade them of, even though they were both raised here."

"The only other people parading in and out are my sisters."

"And?"

"And, okay, the real estate people, but what am I supposed to do about that?"

"And?"

"And you, you're the only other person 'parading' in and out. I don't know what you're talking about."

"Stop acting like a child."

"What is the big deal! It was one person!"

"A trustworthy person, I'm sure. Someone with unassailable character. Who will treat this apartment and its history with the respect it deserves."

"You were the one, you told me to make friends—"

"Whatever you say."

"Oh, for crying out loud. You're a guy who talks to plants!"

"Then why do you care what I think?"

He turned back to check on his hornwort. He was right; I did care. I so did not want him to be mad at me.

"I'm sorry," I finally said. "I mean it. I won't let it happen again. I didn't know. I mean, I knew that privacy was important to Bill, but how was I supposed to . . . I mean, people knew they were in here! Didn't they? They went out and stuff."

"They did not."

"But they—they weren't really off the grid, were they? In the middle of the city? You can't live off the grid in New York City. They had heat and water and telephones, and television."

"Bill set up a trust that his lawyer took care of. The rest was absorbed by the building."

"Absorbed by the building?"

"Honestly, Tina, I don't have time to explain everything to you. Just do me a favor: next time you have friends in to take a look at this wonderful and very private old place, please do *not* let them in the mossery. It is officially off-limits to you now, is that understood?" He actually tried to shoo me out of the room so he could continue cleaning up in peace.

"They want you to get it out of here. Lucy says you have to take it out by next week."

"Quite frankly, I don't believe you'll be here that long," he said icily.

"I wouldn't bet on it if I were you." I leaned against the refrigerator and watched him work. The place was almost back to normal. The floor was spic-and-span, the cedar boxes were restacked, and the half-spilled bag of plant food was tidied and tucked back into its corner. Now that Len had bent his attention to the tray of hornwort, his anger had cooled, and he was murmuring comfort to the things.

"You're okay. Oh, no no, this isn't a tragedy. We'll fix you right up," he cooed. Seriously. The guy was talking to *moss*.

"I'm not kidding, Len, Lucy is dead set on you getting this stuff out of here pronto." He looked over at me, annoyed again. "Look, I'm sorry to interrupt your conversation with the hornworts," I said, "but you can't just boss me around and expect this problem to go away. I'm going to need a little more help than that."

"How about two hundred," he said suddenly. "Will that help?"

That wasn't what I had been going for, but given the life I lead, I am never averse to taking money. "Yes, I think that will help me figure out how to solve this. I really do."

"Why don't you let me finish up here," he said, turning his gaze back to his wounded moss. "Maybe twenty minutes?"

"Great," I said. "I'll go take a shower."

After Len had finished tending his moss, and I had dried my hair with the thirty-year-old blow-dryer I found underneath a sink, we took the elevator up to the greenhouse, where Len apparently kept piles of hundred-dollar bills hidden in corners.

"Seriously, you have that kind of money lying around?" I asked him, impressed.

"You live in New York City, you have to expect that someone will come along and try to extort you at any time of the day or night. As you seem to have managed to do today, Tina."

"Come on, Len, you offered," I started lamely.

"Are you saying you don't want the money?"

"We have a court date, I need some decent clothes," I protested.

"And of course I would be responsible for that," he replied, not impressed with my logic. When the elevator dinged, he slid the grille back, pushed the outer door open, and stepped onto the landing. I stepped out behind him and slammed right into him because he had stopped. Literally, he just stood there, holding the elevator door open.

"Hey, Len, is there a problem?" I asked, trying to look over his shoulder.

"No, no problem." His voice had fallen back from the bossy exasperation he had come to use as his regular tone with me, into a kind of effortless chill that I had come to recognize as bad news.

"What is it?" I said. He still hadn't moved. I had a feeling he might shove me back into the elevator and send me off, so I turned and nudged him with my shoulder, just enough to get the right side of my body past him and onto the landing. He looked back at me, annoyed.

"That hurt," he announced.

"Well, why are you just standing there?"

"Hello, Dad," said the person leaning against the door to the penthouse. Len smiled at me, tight and unamused, and waved his hand with his little elfin flourish toward the person at the door.

"Hello, Charlie," he said. "This is my friend Tina."

"Hello, Tina," said Charlie. She was tall, much taller than Len, but she had his air of earthy capability. She also had his strange blue eyes. Her light brown hair was pulled back in a ponytail, and despite her height she looked even more like an elf than he did. Unlike Len, though, she behaved like an actual human being. She reached out, smiled, and shook my hand, as if she believed that we might soon be friends.

"Hello," I said, smiling back at her. Beside me, Len bristled. "Are you okay, Len?" I asked.

"I'm just surprised. I'm surprised to see you, Charlie, very surprised, and I think you know I don't particularly like surprises. I'm busy now. I think you can see that I have a guest and we're very busy."

"It won't take long, Dad," she said, completely ignoring his rudeness. "I have something I need you to look at. Benny, this is my dad, whom I told you about." She turned back to the doorway, where another person was hidden—a boy, maybe ten years old, in jeans and an old dark-red T-shirt with an insurance company ad on it. His skin was so black you could barely see him in the shadows, and he was so shy you could barely see him in the light. He looked up at Charlie with complete bewilderment and trust.

"Show it to him," she said.

Benny looked down at something in his hands. And then he dutifully held it up so we could see what it was. It was a plant, a small plant in a small white plastic cup with some dirt. I hadn't noticed it at first because I was trying so hard to make out the kid, who struck me as being the most nearly invisible person I had ever seen. But Len saw the plant. He took a step forward and reached his hand out. The boy lifted the plant to hand it to him, and I saw Len's fingers curl and shake for a moment. I swear they went all bony with greed. I think I may have gasped, because he turned to me sharply, as if to tell me to shut up, when in fact I hadn't said anything. But Charlie wasn't going to let him grab the thing and scare the kid like that; she stepped forward and folded her arms across her chest like a soldier. Which, I discovered later, she was.

"Let's go inside," she said. "There's not enough light here."

Inside the greenhouse there was plenty of light. Len pushed into the kitchen, impatient to get a look at the plant, leaving Charlie to hold the door for me and the kid, who stopped in the doorway and gasped, completely and instantly overwhelmed at the sight of all those plants. Charlie glanced back at him, then up and around with the same wonder; she smiled at all those plants like they were old and dear friends.

"I told you," she said, as if she was hearing the thoughts in his head. Then she took the cup out of the boy's hands and ushered him into the kitchen, which was still relatively tidy from the cleaning I had given it over a week ago. "Place looks good, Dad," she noted, letting her eyes brush over me. I don't know what she thought was going on between us, but she didn't much care. What she cared about was the kid and the plant in the cup.

"Why don't you tell me what we have here?" Len prompted her. He was staring at the plant in the cup too.

"Okay. Benny grew this on his window ledge, didn't you, Ben?" She smiled at the kid, who smiled back shyly; growing this plant on a window ledge was some great achievement, apparently. "And then he looked through all his books, and he couldn't figure out what it was, so he got on a bus and rode all the way in from Crown Heights to find me in the Botanic Garden and see if I knew what it was. And I wasn't sure. But I told him I knew someone who would definitely know. So I brought him here, Dad. Do your stuff." She was sensational, this woman. She kept her hand on the kid's shoulder and let him know that he was safe and she was taking care of him and his plant, and even though her own father was being so rude he could barely look at her, she didn't seem to notice.

"Where did he get it?" Len asked, completely focused on the plant now. Charlie made sure there was enough space at one end of the counter so we could get a good look at it from all sides.

"Tell him where you got it, Benny."

Benny looked at her, not at all sure that would be a good idea.

"He won't tell anybody, I *promise*," she said, and then she laughed. "Trust me. My dad is not going to want anybody anywhere to know about this."

"So you do know what it is," Len murmured, half to himself.

"I think I do, but I didn't think it was possible," she admitted. "You think that's what it is?"

"Let's not get ahead of ourselves," he said, wiping his palms on his gardener's apron before he finally allowed himself to reach out and touch the plant.

Charlie took the boy's hand and led him one step aside so Len would have a little room. There was a hanging fern right beside the refrigerator, which she reached up to touch, as if she were saying hello. Len kept staring at the tiny plant in his hands. These people really were their own tribe.

"Where did he find it?" Len asked suddenly. He turned his eyes on Benny and considered him with more interest. "Where did you find it, young man? What's your name—Benny?"

"Yes," the kid whispered. He was overwhelmed, and who could blame him? *I* was overwhelmed, and it wasn't even my plant.

"Did someone give you the seeds for this or did they bring you a cutting from another plant?"

"It was some seeds," he said.

"And who gave you the seeds?"

"It was some friends of my mom's," he said.

"How many seeds?"

"Little bag. Maybe six or seven."

"Can I see them? The seeds?"

"That's the only one that growed."

"You planted them all."

"Well, yeah."

"You should see where he lives," Charlie said with pride, putting her hand on the kid's shoulder, like he was her own. "He's got plants growing everywhere, in every corner of this shitty little apartment. His mother's hardly ever home, from what I could tell. He's got two older brothers, and who knows what they're up to, so he's almost on his own there. Dad, you can't believe what he's gotten to grow in those rooms with no light, no fresh air—he's a miracle worker."

"I'm impressed already." Len nodded, smiling, at the kid. "Now, these seeds. Where were they from? Did they come from Africa?"

"That's what they said."

"And why did they give them to you?"

"I don't know. It was one guy, my mom knows him. He saw I liked plants."

Len tore his attention away from the plant to look at the kid, who was now looking at the ground, completely overwhelmed with shame. It wasn't a stretch for anyone in that room to know he was lying.

Charlie crouched down next to him, keeping her arm around him. She looked up at Len. "Some friend of his mother's took their welfare check. He told Benny he would trade the seeds for the check. Benny got into a lot of trouble for it, even though it wasn't his fault."

"And how old were the seeds—did he tell you?" Len asked, not giving a rat's ass about how much trouble Benny got into for letting this friend of his mom's con him out of their welfare check.

"He said they were magic," Benny admitted. "I wanted to see if I could make them grow."

His eyes filled with tears at the admission of his own gullibility. Len turned back to the plant. He didn't give a shit about Benny's gullibility either.

"But he didn't tell you how old the seeds were or where, exactly, they came from?"

"No sir."

"And you didn't save even one? You planted them all? Did you plant them all like this, in separate trays?"

"You mean the cups?"

"Yeah, the cups, you planted each one in a separate cup, yes? Did any of the others come up at all?"

Benny nodded, still miserable, but regaining his equilibrium now that they were back on the subject of plants and seeds. "Two sprouted but never flourished, they just turned yellow and got some brown spots, then they shriveled up and that was it. The other ones never even sprouted."

"Did you save the unsprouted seeds?"

I didn't think this was the least bit likely, and neither did Len. There was a sort of hopeless moment of expectant disappointment, as we waited for the kid to tell us he had just tossed the unsprouted seeds. But really, you never know what's going to happen, you just never know. Benny reached into his pocket and took out a rolled-up paper towel. "Yeah, sure. I dug 'em up to see how far they gestated."

Len looked up, startled, and caught Charlie smirking at him. She knew all along that the kid had the other seeds, and she knew that Len would underestimate him.

Len didn't waste any time. He turned back to the kid and held out his bony, greedy hand. "Good for you, Benny. You saved the seeds to see how far they gestated. That was the smart thing to do. May I see them?" Benny handed him the rolled-up paper towel, and with the meticulous care of a jeweler revealing a trove of uncut diamonds, Len opened the towel to consider the second half of this apparently unheard-of treasure.

"I see, I see," he said. He reached over, plucked a pair of tweezers out of a pencil tin hidden somewhere in the mess on the phone table, and delicately picked up something that looked like a fossilized raisin. "Wonderful," Len whispered. He set the raisin back down and turned his attention back to the tiny plant, which looked a little like a cross between a tiny cactus and an orange African violet. "Wonderful," he said again.

"What is it?" I asked.

It was a mistake; I can see that now. In the extreme excitement surrounding the kid's extraordinary plant, they had completely forgotten I was even in the room, which was the only reason I had been allowed to stay. Announcing my presence with a completely boneheaded question more or less shattered the spell.

"What are you doing here, Tina?" Len said. He had utterly forgotten why I had come up to the greenhouse with him.

"Well, we were—you were down at my place checking in on the moss, Len," I reminded him.

"What moss?" asked Charlie.

"She's just a neighbor I was doing a favor for. We will have to talk about that later, Tina." Len held up his hand to silence me, then swiftly went over to the desk, turned his back so we couldn't see what he was doing, and retraced his steps to the door, which he opened. "This I think covers it," he said, shoving some folded bills into my hand. "Thanks for the help."

"What's going on?" I said to Len under my breath. "What's with the plant?"

"You're quite welcome," he said, coldly polite, as if he barely knew me. He took my arm, pushed me gently out the door, and closed it.

That was it, I was not one of them. I just stood there and looked at his closed door for a full minute as I tried to get up the nerve to knock with some excuse that would persuade them to let me back in. But nothing came to me. Grabbing that extra two hundred from Len seemed embarrassing and trashy, just as Lucy always said I was. I couldn't pretend that Len and I were friends now, that I was someone he might include in the cool secret surrounding that plant. Because you don't extort your friends, do you?

I was so depressed by my own horrible behavior, I spent the next week contemplating personal improvement. Not much immediately came to mind aside from absolutely everything. Then, one afternoon, when I returned home from a minor shopping spree—a tube of toothpaste—I found myself considering the old boring landing. The floor needed a serious scrubbing, and the plastic plants didn't just need to be dusted; they needed to be tossed and replaced with something you could actually water. The blinds covering the one dirty window needed to be replaced as well. At which point my rather gloomy mood lifted into something resembling hope. I can do this, I thought. I used to clean houses for a living, out there at the Delaware Water Gap: a bucket of water, some Lysol, new blinds, and thirty bucks' worth of plants would make all the difference. I could make the landing a better place and then see if that made me a better person. It was a far-fetched idea, but not *that* far-fetched. A lot of people think cleaning things up is the first step to moral improvement. Why shouldn't that be true? It was at least something I could accomplish. So I was actually contemplating the possibility of this when I heard a door creak behind me. Not my door, the other one. I looked over and saw that it was open, just a few inches, and someone was watching me.

"Mrs. Westmoreland?" I said. "Hi, I'm Tina Finn, I'm living in 8A."

The door stayed cracked, it didn't close, but it didn't open any farther either. I could see just a little of the entryway; the marble floor was polished within an inch of its life. Farther in, I could see the end of a couch in the living room, with a perfectly folded throw in gold and orange hanging off one side. It didn't look anything like my crazy apartment, but I stepped forward with determination. "My mother was Olivia, she was married to Bill? Anyway, I, uh, I'm living in the apartment until we can get everything sorted out with the wills. I wanted to introduce myself." I was talking way too slow and too loud, like I thought maybe she was a retarded deaf person. "Anyway, I was thinking I might clean up our landing, get rid of the plastic plants, get some new blinds, would that be okay with you? You wouldn't have to do anything. I just think it might make the place look a lot nicer if I took a scrub brush to everything . . ."

"You got to go."

"What?" I asked, moving closer. Mrs. Westmoreland had finally answered, but her voice was so soft I could barely hear her. I leaned in to listen.

"You've got to get out of here. The police are here," she whispered.

"The police?" I said. Her door shut quickly, just as the one behind me opened. I turned, not knowing quite what to expect, but I was beginning to get a clue. A uniformed officer stood in my doorway. He was young and buff and kind of mean-looking. I'd seen his type before.

"You Tina Finn?" he asked.

"Who's asking?" I gave him back.

"This your stuff in here?" He held up my backpack and a pair of underwear.

"Is that my 'stuff'? You mean is that my underwear? Yeah, that's my underwear. You got a reason for breaking into my apartment and going through my underwear, Officer?" Look, I knew that you're supposed to shut up and just do what you're told when they come at you like that; believe me, I had been warned. But sadly, I always seemed to forget.

"Could you come in here, please?"

"Yeah, you bet, whatever you say, Officer. I'm sure your reasons for pawing through my underwear are excellent." The sarcastic tone is also not a good idea when talking to police officers. What can I say? I walked to the doorway and looked at him with what can only be called disgraceful disregard, considering that we both knew what was coming.

"You're going to have to step aside," I said. "You're so big and strong and scary, I just can't squeeze by you."

"You think you're helping yourself here, Miss Finn?" the guy asked.

"Would that even be possible, Officer?" I asked. Behind him were two more uniforms waiting for me.

"I don't think so," he said.

"Then could you step back, please?" He did, and I stepped into the apartment.

"You're under arrest," he said.

"I'm stunned to hear it," I replied.

11

W̲ʜᴇɴ O̲ꜰꜰɪᴄᴇʀ M̲ᴀᴄD̲ᴏᴡᴇʟʟ ʀᴇᴀᴅ ᴛʜᴇ ᴄʜᴀʀɢᴇs, ɪᴛ ᴛᴜʀɴᴇᴅ ᴏᴜᴛ
that an injunction had in fact been issued by some court and had been
subsequently received by one Ira Grossman, Esquire, who was acting on
behalf of Alison and Daniel Lindemann, Lucille Finn, and Christina
Finn of a lot of different addresses. The injunction stated in no uncertain terms that we were not permitted to trespass on the premises of
cooperative apartment number 8A in the Edgewood Building, address
819 Central Park West. Service having been accepted on my behalf by
Ira Grossman, the legal system assumed that I had been duly informed
that further trespass upon the premises would be treated as an unlawful
act and I would be persecuted to the fullest extent of the law.

So that's what happened. The arresting officer informed me that I
had violated the injunction and that he was hauling me down to the
precinct. So I smirked and said "yes, sir," like I thought he was a complete idiot, so he asked me if I had a problem and I said, *no, Officer, you're*
so big and strong and mean I'm just terrified is all, which as usual was not
the right thing to say. One of the other officers said, "Phil . . ." like
a warning, because you could see Officer MacMean go seriously red
around the corners of his face, like he had a spectacularly shitty temper,
which anybody could see just by looking at him. He paused for a few
beats, said he was fine, grabbed me by the arm, and shoved me through
the doorway with significantly more force than necessary, considering
that he weighed probably 240 pounds and I come in under 115. He
didn't insist on handcuffs because he couldn't—I wasn't technically
resisting arrest; I was just tossing around attitude—but he did make
sure he hurt my arm.

I didn't know which precinct they took me to, but since it was the
Upper West Side, it was actually not too bad as precincts go. It was

alarmingly ugly, with fluorescent lights, linoleum floors, and weird green plasterboard walls, and it had venetian blinds on the inside office windows, which made the place look like a third-rate medical clinic. But trust me, the fact that there wasn't a layer of grime on every conceivable surface put it in a whole different league from the other precincts where I'd landed after being arrested. The mean cop was still being a little too rough, so one of the other two cops kind of stepped between us in a very casual way, like all he meant to do was show me where I needed to go to get processed. He didn't give me any eye contact, just leaned over and said, "You're going to have to leave your valuables at the window," but then he stayed where he was while he traded greetings with the guy at the front desk, and that effectively stopped MacMean from shoving me around anymore. I waited for the lady cop to show up, because they always pass you off to a female officer, who takes your valuables, puts them in an envelope, gives them to the guy behind the window, and then leads you to the back for your interview. Then, if they decide to hold you, someone comes and takes you off to the holding tank for girls. In my experience, the procedure is pretty straightforward and consistent, precinct to precinct.

This time, though, they didn't take me to the little room for the interview; the lady cop walked me down a depressing hallway straight to the holding tank.

"Don't I get an interview?" I asked.

"What are you going to tell them, that you weren't there?" she said.

"There might be extenuating circumstances," I suggested as she unbolted the barred door.

"I'm sure your lawyer will make that clear," she said. And then she shut the door and threw the bolts back in place. Which, in spite of the notable differences in procedure up to this point, had an unfortunately familiar ring to it.

But the holding tank was not bad as these things go. Except for the bars on one side, it could easily have passed for a hospital waiting room, with rows of blue plastic chairs bolted to the walls. Apparently it was a slow night for crime on the Upper West Side, because only one other woman was in there, a sorry-looking teenager with black hair and a lot of tattoos. She wore a ripped T-shirt and a kilt, which is a look that honestly works for no one, but what can you do, some trends take forever to die. She glanced up at me with tired eyes, and I could see that earlier in the day they had been lined with the blackest eyeliner out there, but an unknown number of hours in a police tank had taken its toll, and now she just looked like an eighteen-year-old kid who had done something dumb that landed her in a holding cell.

"I'll be back in a second so you can make your call," the lady officer informed me.

"Hey, can I have another call? I need to make another call, can I have another one?" the kid said. "Please?"

"You only get one call," the police lady said.

"I need to make another call! I called my friend and she's not coming, I need to call somebody, I need to call my mom!" The police lady didn't even seem to hear her. She disappeared down the icky hallway, so bored that you could see it in her walk. Goth Girl leaned up against the bars, squeezing her eyes shut in a concocted rage that she clearly hoped would keep her from crying.

"Is this your first time?" I heard myself saying. I didn't mean to sound like some jaded old creep; it honestly just slipped out. Goth Girl tipped her head back and looked at the ceiling with her mouth open, as if she could not believe she was stuck in this holding tank with such a colossal idiot.

"So you're like an old hand at this," she said.

"Not an old hand. But it's not like I've never been arrested before."

"Good for you," she mumbled, staring off through the bars, dismissing me entirely. The phone, a huge old industrial model that looked like it had been designed by the Army Corps of Engineers, hung on the painted cinder-block wall three feet away. "This is so fucked," she told herself. "I have to get home. This is just fucked. I am so fucked." There was no way to reach the telephone from where we were, but she could barely stop herself from shoving her arm through the bars and uselessly trying to grab it.

"When the public defender shows up, he can call people for you," I offered, leaning against the bars. I had no idea how long I would be stuck there, so I had no interest in sitting down just yet. Plus those chairs looked fiendishly uncomfortable. You know they put in separate seats like that just so people can't lie down.

"I've been waiting for four hours for the fucking public defender! When's the fucking public defender supposed to fucking show up?" She was fraying at the seams.

"Sometimes it takes a while," I said.

"This is so fucked," the girl repeated, glancing down the hallway. The lady cop was coming back now with her slow, bored walk. I couldn't figure out why she had left in the first place—probably she had to go to the bathroom.

"So who are we calling?" she said as she handed me the receiver through the bars. This was the usual drill; they give you the receiver, you tell them the number you want to dial, they dial it for you, and you talk. I thought for a second about calling my so-called lawyer, Ira Grossman, whom I had never met. I thought about calling Lucy. Then I thought about calling Alison and Daniel, who would just call Lucy, who would then call the lawyer. And then I'd have to go home with one of them, because I wasn't allowed to stay in the apartment anymore. If it was Lucy, I'd have to listen to her bitch at me all night, even though this clearly wasn't my fault. If it was Alison and Daniel, I'd have to listen to them hanging out in their tiny kitchen, whispering about my sleeping on their crummy couch, and whether Lucy would be able to put me up, and wasn't there anyone else Tina could stay with, and why doesn't Tina ever have any money or seem to be able to hold down a job. I had lived through this delightful conversation more than once, truth be told, and I was not looking forward to hearing it again. The thought made my head hurt.

"Hey, Kilt Girl," I said. "What's your mom's phone number?"

"What?"

"Is that who you want to call?"

"She's not allowed another call until the PD shows up," the lady cop informed me, irritated.

"Yeah, but I get a phone call," I said.

"You want to call my mom?" the kid asked.

"Isn't that who you want to talk to?"

"Yeah, but . . ."

"So what's her number?"

The girl looked at me. The cop looked at me too. She was moving out of irritated and more firmly into pissed off. "Look, this isn't up to you," she told me again. "She's not getting another phone call."

"It's not her call, it's my call," I said.

"You aren't getting another call. You call this kid's mother? That's your call."

"I know that's my call."

"You call her, you're stuck here," she said again, like I wasn't getting it.

"What's your mother's phone number, kid?" I asked.

"And she's not allowed to talk to her."

"She's not going to talk to her; I'm going to talk to her. Kid, what's the number?"

The kid spit out the number so fast I almost didn't get it. I mean, this sudden stroke of good fortune had definitely commanded her attention, and she had no time to affect disinterest or suspicion. "Tell her I really need her to come down," she said. "Tell her they said I was doing drugs but I was totally not doing them at all. It was totally these three other kids at this party. And it's a total mistake."

"I totally will tell her that," I said. Now that she had a shred of hope that someone was going to help her out, she was sort of charming in a way that made me suspect she was not in fact eighteen. Someone picked up the phone at the other end of the line.

"Hello," said a kind of tony fake voice. You could practically see the whole apartment from the sound of that voice.

"Hi," I said. "I'm a friend of . . ."

"Colette," Kilt Girl said, fast.

"I'm a friend of Colette's," I said, thinking this kid looks nothing like a Colette. "Is this her mother?"

"Yes, I am her mother," said the voice, sounding a little worried now but also kind of exasperated, like someone who was already exhausted by Colette's recent shenanigans and not looking forward to a new chapter.

"Well, I'm afraid Colette, unfortunately she's having some trouble with the police right now, nothing serious—"

"It's a mistake, a total mistake," Colette dictated.

"A total mistake," I repeated. "But she does need for you to come down to the precinct and pick her up."

"Oh my god. You're kidding. She's at the police station?" said the tony voice, rising an octave. "PAUL! COLETTE'S AT THE POLICE STATION! What is it, has she been arrested? Is she all right?"

"Oh yeah, she's fine, she just needs you to come pick her up," I reassured the voice.

"It's a little more complicated than that," the lady cop sneered.

"Maybe, maybe not," I told her. "What precinct is this again?"

"The Forty-ninth."

"We're over here at the Forty-ninth Precinct, I don't know the exact address, but you can look it up. Oh, and can I ask—how old is Colette again?"

"How *old* is she?" asked the voice, all frosty now. "She's sixteen, why?"

"Okay, you might want to mention that to the guy at the front desk. When someone under seventeen gets picked up, the police actually aren't allowed to hold them unless there's an adult present. Colette may have lied about her age, so I wouldn't be too mean about it? But you know, it's not legal for them to hold her without you being here."

"Who is this again?" asked the voice.

"Okay, see you," I said, and handed the phone back to the officer. She stared at me.

"You're quite the expert on juvenile arrests," she observed, hanging up the phone.

"Yeah, weird, huh," I said. "I'm going to need a PD."

About twenty minutes later she came back and picked up Colette, which I thought was a good sign—I mean, her folks didn't make her sweat down there; they came right away and got her. She didn't even look at me, she just followed that lady cop down the hall.

"You're welcome," I yelled, but I didn't watch to see if she even flinched.

So now I was stuck there by myself. I sat down in one of those ridiculously uncomfortable chairs, and then I tried to lie down across three of them, which was truly backbreaking, so I ended up sitting on one of the corner chairs and stretching my legs out to the second chair in the row across from me. This position turned out to be just barely comfortable enough to sleep in, once I took my sweater off and figured out how to lodge it between my head and the cinder-block wall at an angle that held up my neck. Then, of course, as soon as I managed to pass out, a different lady cop, this one Hispanic and skinny, woke me up.

"HEY!" she yelled. "Tina Finn! You Tina Finn?"

"Yeah," I said, picking my head up way too fast, given the crazy position I was in. My poor neck felt like it was in pieces, and one of my eyes seemed to have glued itself together, so I figured I had slept longer than it felt like, but it was clearly one of those odd sleeps where you pass out so thoroughly you don't have any sense of what day it is when you wake up.

"What day is it?" I said.

"They want you in interrogation," she answered. I nodded and picked up my sweater, which had fallen on the floor, and then I followed her down the hallway. The fluorescent lights are always on in those places, so it really is impossible to tell what time of day it is. I had utterly no clue until I got into the interrogation room, where a clock informed me that it was a little past two in the morning.

"It's two in the morning," I said to the officer.

"That's right."

"Well, the PD isn't coming at two in the morning," I said, still feeling kind of stupid and like it was taking too long to wake up.

"This is interrogation, they want you for interrogation," she said, and then she left, like this made any sense at all.

"How come they didn't interrogate me when I got here?" I said, but the door had already closed behind her. So there I was in a totally empty room again.

The whole thing seemed completely surreal, and I'm someone who has a relatively high tolerance for strange adventures. I looked around for a minute, thinking about the shit that goes down in a place like this.

There was no sign of it here—like everything else in this too-clean police station, the walls gave up nothing at all. I felt like I was trapped in one of those science fiction movies where they bore you to death and then suck your brains out and everyone becomes a complete automaton; seriously, I was feeling significantly creeped out when the door opened and Detective Pete Drinan walked in. At which point, nothing seemed surreal anymore.

"Oh, it's you," I said. "Such a surprise."

"Yeah, how you doing?" he asked, tossing a manila file folder on the table. "You want anything, a cup of coffee or something? You want a Coke?"

"A Coke sounds kind of good, sure," I said. Drinan went to the door and leaned out, yelling, "Hey! Can somebody bring me a Coke?" It sounded so much like cops on television I almost started to laugh. Nobody answered immediately, and after glancing up and down the hall for a minute he disappeared, letting the door swing closed behind him. After a few minutes I was bored, so I picked up the manila file and started to read it.

The door swung open again. "Hey, what are you doing? Don't do that," Drinan said. He came over behind me and took the file out of my hand impatiently. "What's the matter with you?"

"What's the big deal, it's my record," I said. "It's not like it's a big secret."

Detective Drinan took a seat and gave me a look. "You always act like this when you get arrested?"

"I do when the cops are acting like jerks," I told him.

"Most people would have the sense to keep their mouths shut when the cops are acting like jerks, Miss Finn," he said. He tossed my file back on the table and ran his hand over the back of his neck, like he was trying to figure out some big annoying puzzle. "What happened to your arm?"

I looked down to see what he was talking about. I hadn't noticed anything when I had my sweater on, but now, with just a tank top and in that horrible green light, I could see that my arm was covered with bruises from elbow to shoulder where the arresting officer had yanked me around. I suddenly felt so embarrassed I didn't know what to say. Even more mortifying, my face turned red, and I was so surprised by my own embarrassment and so exhausted that for a second I thought I might start crying. Drinan was really watching me, so I stared at the broken corner of the tabletop and tried to focus. The tabletop was fake-wood Formica, and I wondered why they kept trying to make plastic look like wood, when even a half-wit like me knows it's just not possible.

The door opened again, and the skinny Hispanic police officer stuck her head in.

"You wanted this?" she asked.

"Yeah, thanks," Drinan said, and he reached out to take the can of Coke she held out to him. While his back was turned, I picked up my sweater and wrapped it around my shoulders, fast, so the bruises didn't show as much. When I looked up, Drinan was watching me with those sad brown eyes, which registered nothing more than a mild detective-like curiosity. He shrugged a little, put the can on the table, and popped the seal with one hand. He held it out to me, then sat down and started reading my file while I drank my Coke. It tasted amazing, frankly.

"Don't bolt it," he advised. "I'm not going to get you another one."

"I'm thirsty," I said. "I've been here since god knows when."

"Since 4:37 P.M.," he said, reading off the front page of the arrest report. "You resist arrest?"

"It doesn't say that," I said.

" 'Belligerent and provocative' is what it says, right here." He held it up briefly to show me.

"We're not allowed to talk back?"

"No, in fact you are not allowed to talk back to your arresting officer. What are you, a moron?"

"I come home and find my apartment full of police officers and I haven't done a fucking thing and I'm not allowed to have an opinion about that?"

"It's not your home," he informed me.

"Far as I can tell, it's not yours either."

He paused without looking up, like he was thinking about responding to that, then got more interested in why I persisted in my stupidity. "You might want to watch your mouth," he finally suggested.

"Yes sir," I said. He looked up at me, but he wasn't annoyed by my problematic tone of voice. Now his face was bent around the words that had come out of my mouth.

"Wait a minute, what did you say before? You came home and found them there?"

"Yes sir."

"So, what, you opened the door and found them in your so-called apartment?"

"No."

"So what happened?"

"I was out buying some toothpaste and then I came home, and I got off the elevator, and I was going to go in, but Mrs. Westmoreland told me the cops were in there and I should get out. So—"

"You know Mrs. Westmoreland?"

"I saw her that night she was trying to get you to come in and have a drink with her."

"That night you were spying on us."

"Yeah, that night."

"Well, maybe that night you heard she's not someone who's going to go out on a limb and do you any favors. And now you're claiming what, that she *warned* you there were police officers looking for you? Why would she do that?"

"I don't know. Maybe it wasn't her, maybe it was someone else."

"She lives there alone."

"Well, I don't know who it was. She was standing behind the door."

"And whoever this person was said get out of here the cops are here."

"Yes."

"So then what did you do?"

"Well, then the arresting officer—"

"The one who put his hands on you?"

"Yeah, that guy, he stepped out into the hallway and said could you come in here, please?"

"Did he put his hands on you then?"

"No, he just told me to come inside."

"So that's what you did."

"Yes."

This seemed like bad news to Detective Drinan. He was in a pissy mood now, you could see it in his face. His eyes were hooded and his hand covered his chin, which made it look like he was trying to be businesslike while he looked at my file. But he was biting the inside of his lip like he had a canker sore that was giving him hell. He shifted in his seat and looked up at me.

"You knew there was an injunction barring you from the apartment and that cops were waiting in there for you, and you walked over and stepped into the apartment anyway?"

"I didn't know there was any injunction."

"You were served."

"I *wasn't* served."

"Your representation was served. Your legal representative accepted service on your behalf two days ago." He leafed through a pile of documents in another manila folder and shoved one across the table to me. I couldn't even read it.

"I was served?" I said, sounding really stupid all of a sudden, like someone who was completely exhausted and hadn't eaten in twenty-two hours.

"What's the matter with you?" he asked. "Was this deliberate? Is that why you went in there and mouthed off at Officer MacDowell, so you could provoke him into shoving you around a little bit? We going to see all this in the newspapers tomorrow?"

"Oh, knock it off, this isn't my fault," I said.

"The hell it isn't. You walked right into this. You defied a court order and forced an arrest—"

"You're the one who got this fucking injunction."

"Yes, I did, that's right, I did; I fucking well did."

"You said you'd wait. You said let me know when you're ready, you'd come by when I was ready to let you in, and then you sent a bunch of creepy police officers to arrest me."

"You wanted to be arrested."

"Oh yeah, I love being arrested, it's just a total blast having police officers manhandle you."

"According to your record, you have something of a problem with men shoving you around. Maybe you enjoy that type of thing a little more than you like to admit."

"What did you say? You think I like it when men hit me, did you just say that?"

Now it was his turn to go all red. He didn't say anything for a second, like he was thinking about what to do next, and then he just shrugged. "Sorry," he said. "I apologize."

I had no idea where this was going. He wore me out, Pete Drinan, he really did. I looked up at the ceiling and noticed a fan, and while it twirled around I tried to keep focused on one of the blades and watch it spin so I could see each one individually instead of just watching them blur together. I suddenly felt so tired I thought I was going to fall over. It probably had more to do with bolting down that Coke than anything else, but who's to say.

"You didn't use your phone call," Drinan finally observed, still consulting my file.

"What?"

"There was some kid in the holding tank, you called her mother, told her to come get her?"

"Yeah?"

"Why'd you do that?"

"I don't know. It was stupid."

"Yeah, it was stupid. Now you're stuck here until some useless PD shows up and gets your bail posted and calls your sister for you. And I got to be honest, Ms. Finn, you strike me as a lot of things, but I wouldn't put stupid on the list."

"Is there a question in there?"

He bit back a snappy response and tossed down the file. Then he rubbed his eyes. "Yeah, okay," he said. "Here's the question. Did the arresting officer ask you to step into the apartment before he arrested you?"

"Yeah, he did, I just told you he did!" I said, standing up finally.

This whole situation was really making my head explode. "I told you—I told all of you—I—"

"Relax, Tina, just relax." He sighed. "Sit down." Then, "Are you all right?"

I really wasn't. I felt exceptionally sweaty, my tongue seemed stuck to the inside of my mouth, and fireworks were erupting in my brain. "Oh, shit," I said, and keeled over.

12

WHEN I CAME TO, I WAS LYING ON THE FLOOR OF THE INTERROGA-
tion room. My sweater was off, and the Hispanic lady cop was waving
her hands around my face in some strained attempt to stir up a breeze.

"What are you doing?" I asked, trying to shove her away. My arms
didn't seem to work. "What happened?"

"You fainted," said Drinan's voice somewhere behind me. "Here,
can you pick your head up?" A couple of hands I couldn't see lifted my
head a few inches off the linoleum and cradled it briefly before shoving
something that turned out to be my sweater underneath it.

"I'm okay," I said. I wanted to sit up, but I was afraid to try, and
frankly I was still confused about what I was doing on the floor. "I just
got hot."

"They've been working on the heat for three months, and still nobody knows what the problem is," the Hispanic officer said. Up close,
she was kind of pretty. Her hair was pulled back too tight, but she had
crazy eyebrows that looked like some sort of unusual punctuation. She
was still flapping her hands in my face, but I didn't find it so annoying
now; she was so matter-of-fact and determined that the fanning seemed
good-natured and odd at the same time.

"Maybe we could prop the door open," Drinan suggested. The lady
cop stood and went to prop open the door, and for a moment his hands
came back and stroked my hair away from my forehead, even though my
hair wasn't on my forehead. A breath of air moved across the floor. I
hoped I didn't look too stupid, spread out on the floor like that.

"Could you get us a bottle of water?" he asked the lady cop. Then
he leaned over so his face was in my line of vision. "You think you can
sit up if I help you?" He didn't wait for me to answer; he just put his
arm under my shoulder and lifted, then stopped carefully when I was

halfway up. It was a good thing he did, because the whole room started to spin again, and I almost fell over a second time. "Hold on, hold on," he repeated, holding on. I was really having trouble with the air.

"I'm okay," I said. "Seriously, I'm okay. I just drank that Coke too fast."

"Yeah, a cold can of soda, that would make anyone pass out," he observed. We sat there for a moment, while he propped me up and I leaned against his chest, trying to breathe. "When was the last time you had anything to eat?" he finally asked.

"Who knows," I said.

"They give you anything when you got here?"

"You mean like carry-out?"

"Yeah, like that," he said. "Never mind."

He stood me up very slowly. Then he led me into the hall and leaned me up against the wall. Eventually Officer Martinez of the Extraordinary Eyebrows delivered a plastic cup of lukewarm water, and Drinan watched as I dutifully took sips. The hall was something of a major thoroughfare as hallways go, and even at three in the morning, there was a good deal of foot traffic. Mostly it was the night-shift officers taking bathroom breaks in between falling asleep at their desks. But then a detective came through with a couple of younger officers dragging some perp who'd been picked up. As they cut through, the detective nodded to Drinan.

"Hey, Pete," he said. "What are you doing over here?"

"Just talking to a witness," he said.

"Out in the hallway? Some hospitality. You want to use my desk, it's free for at least twenty minutes."

"Yeah, thanks, I might do that," he said. "See you, Mitch." He looked back at me as Mitch disappeared down the hallway with his arrest. "You feeling better? You want to sit down?"

"So this isn't your precinct, huh?" I asked.

Drinan laughed. "Jesus," he said, "you don't miss a trick. How many times have you been arrested, anyway?"

"Not that many. Three."

"Is this three or four?"

"I haven't been processed yet, so I can't tell."

"Yeah, well, you're right, it's not my precinct. Come on, let's go. I'll buy you a burger."

"I'm not allowed to just leave, you moron," I said, although I didn't lean on the "moron," so it didn't actually sound that bad. "I'm under arrest."

"Thanks for explaining the rules," he said. "Now, could we get something to eat before you pass out a second time and we have to put you on an IV?"

He straightened up and took a step back, as if to show that although he was in charge and I was going to do what he said, he was also going to be a gentleman about it. "There's an all-night diner around the corner on Broadway," he said. "It doesn't look like much, but the food is okay. Burgers, omelets, fries, that sound all right?"

"Boy," I said. "Who knew that fainting was so effective?"

"Yeah," he agreed. "You figure out how to do that on cue, the world's your oyster." He put his hands in his pockets to make it look like he wasn't really in charge of this march, but he stayed just the tiniest bit behind me so there could be no question in anyone's mind. I was completely starving by this point, so I was less interested in my perpetual impulse to argue just for the hell of it. I let him nudge me toward the front door of the precinct house.

"Can I have my sweater back?" I asked as we neared the front desk.

"You cold?" he asked.

"No, I just want my sweater."

"Then why don't you let me carry it for you." He waved to the officer manning the desk. "Hey, Randy, how's it going? Pete Drinan, we met last year at the Mets game with Jimmy Marks and Brian Cahill, you remember? They were playing the Royals, Jimmy scored those seats off some reporter he did a favor for over at the *Daily News*."

"Sure sure sure," Randy replied. "How's it going, Pete? What're you doing here this time of night?"

"Phil MacDowell brought in a witness on one of my cases," Drinan lied. "She's been hanging out here all night, I need to get her something to eat. Tina Finn, this is Officer Bohrman."

The guy behind the desk, a huge black man with a nice smile, stood, which made him eight times as big as me and Detective Drinan combined. "How you doing, young lady?" he asked.

"Great," I said. "Just a little hungry."

"My fault entirely," Drinan said, still the perfect gentleman. "She's been waiting for me all night. Whoa, Tina! What happened to your arm? Randy, look at this! She's covered in bruises!"

Randy glanced at Drinan, then glanced at my arm, then back at Drinan. "That is a shame," he said, cool and formal. "You need to take better care of yourself, Ms. Finn."

"Thank you, Officer, I will, I will do that," I said.

"See you, Randy," Pete said.

"You take care, Pete," the officer replied. Drinan put his hand on my back and steered me right out the front door.

"So what was that about?" I asked him twenty minutes later, when I had an enormous, dripping hamburger in my hand. Actually I had less than half a hamburger in my hand by then. I was so hungry I couldn't even talk until I had consumed most of it, in addition to two dozen enormous and fairly mediocre fries. Drinan was picking at a piece of apple pie.

"What?" he asked, pouring sugar into his second cup of what had to be truly shitty coffee. The place he had taken me to was linoleum central. A single waitress was propped up against the fry window, and apparently another person was back there somewhere; the place was barely more populated than my apartment. But the burger was good.

"With Randy at the front desk. 'Oh, Tina what happened to your arm?' You practically made him take a picture of it," I said.

"Are you complaining?"

"I'm asking a question."

"You want to end up in the Tombs for the rest of the week?"

"Is that what you do to people who ask questions?"

"Why didn't you call your sister? Why didn't you call your lawyer?"

"Oh, for crying out loud."

"I'm giving you an opening here, Tina. You might want to consider taking it."

"You were the one who had me arrested in the first place."

"You let yourself get arrested. You saw MacDowell standing there and you let him arrest you. Why'd you do that?"

"Maybe I wanted to see you."

"So you got your wish. Keep this up, you'll also see the inside of a jail cell for a second time tonight. Or you could go home."

This was news to me, honestly. I could tell he was feeling vaguely lousy that I had been roughed up and nearly starved to death by his friends in the local precinct, but it had not occurred to me that this might amount to a get-out-of-jail-free card. But as soon as he said I could go home, I couldn't help but wonder what good a get-out-of-jail-free card is to someone who has nowhere to go.

"What's the matter?" he asked. "You look like I just killed your dog."

"I'm just surprised," I said. "So how come you arrested me if you're just going to let me go?"

"How about we pretend that I'm asking the questions for a little while, Ms. Finn. Why'd you walk into that arrest?"

"I didn't, strictly speaking," I said, going for the dregs of my Coke.

"Didn't strictly speaking *what*," he said, waving to the waitress to refill my drink.

"Strictly speaking, I didn't know about this injunction."

"You said that before. It won't stand up; they served the papers legally."

"But they didn't tell me. I don't know why."

"I find that hard to believe."

"Look, it's what happened. You guys never make mistakes? They didn't tell me. I mean, that it was illegal, that I could get arrested. They never told me."

"Your sister never told you?"

"You think she knew?" It had not occurred to me that Lucy would know something like that and not share the information. It suddenly sounded so plausible that I turned all red. I mean, Lucy sometimes behaves in questionable ways, but would she set me up to be *arrested*? "Come on," I said, trying to shrug off this thought, but I sounded like I was being an idiot about the truth. "There was just a screwup somewhere."

Drinan was listening in a bored way. He reached over and took a limp fry from my plate, doused it with salt, then licked the salt off the fry and went after it again with the saltshaker.

"That is really gross," I said. "You're going to give yourself a heart attack."

"I'm touched by your concern."

"Well, what are you doing? You're acting like some wild boar at a salt lick. That's gross. Stop it," I said, slapping his hand and taking the saltshaker away.

"There's something else I'd like to know."

"I told you everything, there isn't any more." I sighed. "Come on, you've been grilling me for hours, this is stupid."

"No," he said, licking the salt off the disgusting french fry and dropping it on his plate. "Even if this was all just a technical screwup, you still haven't said why you didn't call anybody. Why spending a night or a day and a night or a week in jail is preferable to calling one of your sisters and asking her to come get you out."

He picked up the paper napkin next to his coffee cup and wiped his fingers. He looked at me hard, and his eyebrows went up just a little, like *you think I'm going to let you avoid that one?* I never did think that. I'm just not sure why everyone thinks you'll get what you want or need by saying the true thing that's in your heart.

"I can't," I finally admitted.

"Can't what?"

"There's no place for me. Lucy won't let me stay with her, and Alison and Daniel don't want me. So. It's like that."

He waited, like that wasn't good enough, and I was going to have to give him all of it.

"They think I'm a loser," I said. My voice was getting steadier. It didn't sound so bad, honestly, when I just said it. "They don't want me. I'm not allowed to stay in their apartments. And I don't, I don't have any money and I don't have friends here, I don't live here. Seriously. I have no place to go. So why should I call Lucy and let her come down to the precinct and make a big deal about it, like she's doing me some huge favor?

Then, when she gets me out, she'll act like her shitty couch is too good for me. Why give them the opportunity to let me know I'm some huge hideous problem that they always have to deal with? Why not just stay in jail?"

"You ever been in jail? I mean, I can see you've been arrested, but have you ever actually spent a night somewhere other than a lockup?"

"You mean like jail jail?"

"Yeah, 'jail jail,' Miss Smartypants. You ever actually spend any time there? Your so-called record says three arrests but no actual jail time, is there something I'm missing here?"

"No."

"Okay, then stop acting like it's an option."

"You want me to call Lucy?"

"I'm not going to tell you what to do." I couldn't tell if he was bothered by my lack of self-regard or disgusted with the lot of us. He finished wiping his fingers and set down the crumpled napkin, then checked his nails, as if it had just occurred to him that they might be filthy, which in fact they were not. He leaned back into the vinyl of the booth and seemed to be thinking about what I had just said, but at the same time I could see that his eyes were scanning for where the waitress was, so he could ask her for more bad coffee or the check. I decided he must be a pretty good detective, because even though I kept mouthing off and acting like I was running the show, he had found out everything he wanted to know, and I hadn't found out anything at all.

"Did you ever meet my dad?" he finally asked. Over my head he caught the waitress's eye and tipped his chin a little bit. He reached for a toothpick, even though he hadn't eaten anything other than sugar, pie, coffee, and salt while I pigged out. Good-looking, mean, and he doesn't eat; maybe he's a vampire, I thought.

"Hey, are you with us?" he asked.

"What was the question—did I ever meet your dad? No, I never did. Did you ever meet my mom?"

"A couple times."

"You did? You met her?" This seemed like really great news, that he had seen my mother after she went away from me and into that other world up in the beautiful strange apartment with that crazy old drunk. "What was, what—wow. I didn't know you met her."

"Before they got married, when she was cleaning house for him, I met her a few times."

"She was cleaning *house* for him?"

"You didn't know that?"

Why was the news that my mother had been cleaning houses the worst news I could get, when in fact it was exactly what I had been doing? I had let her go so far away for so long that I thought the guilt of such distance had burned itself out. But she had still lived in the world, and she found herself cleaning houses. And this sad-eyed detective had seen her with buckets and rags, on her hands and knees, and I had not.

He wasn't volunteering any more information. I hated the way I had to pry facts out of this bonehead. "Did you see her often?" I asked.

"Just a couple times."

"How did she look?"

"I didn't pay much attention until he married her."

"Were you at the wedding?"

"No, I was not invited. My brother and I were not consulted about the marriage, we were told about it after the fact."

"So what happened then?"

"You know as much as I do about that part."

"I *don't* know as much as you; I don't know anything, I think *that's* pretty obvious. Which is why I'm asking. I only saw her the one time, which you already know about from Mrs. What's-Her-Name who I wasn't spying on, she was spying on them, and we weren't allowed, your dad—we didn't—oh fuck it." I moved almost instantaneously through losing my cool to picking up a phony version of it as it occurred to me that I had to keep my mouth closed about how Bill was shutting us out of their life. Lucy had warned me not to let the Drinans know that Bill didn't want us around, that it would hurt our chances of getting the apartment. I remembered the rules and managed to stop myself from giving up any more information. But I still wanted to know what he knew. "Did they, did they have a wedding dinner?" I asked.

"No," he said, laughing a little at the very idea.

"Well, when did he tell you? That they got married?"

"A couple days later."

"Did you see them?"

"Yeah, we did. We were over at the apartment, and we saw them and they told us."

"And they were happy?"

"You know, it's hard to tell about people and happiness, Tina. That's one thing you learn in police school." He looked down, and I could see that he had pulled a small wad of neatly folded bills out of his pocket and was rifling through them swiftly, counting to himself like a little kid.

"What does that mean?" I asked, trying not to get mad. He wasn't objecting to my asking questions, so I didn't want to piss him off with my famously bad attitude, but my nerves were running on fumes by this point. "I mean, did you see them, what did they—wow. Okay, okay," I stumbled. "When was the last time you saw them?"

He looked up from his counting, caught by the question, like he couldn't immediately remember the answer. "A long time," he admitted with some shade of sorrow or reluctance. "I don't know. A couple years maybe."

"A couple years, like two years?" I asked.

"Yeah, like two years."

"Like when they got married, that's when you stopped seeing him?"

"Yes, that's when I stopped seeing him."

"So he married my mom, and he told you, and you guys had a fight and that was the end of it for you, like how could he have married my *mom,* and so then you just—stopped even talking to him. Was it that horrible for you and your brother? You just cut yourself off from him because he married her? Is that what happened?"

"Something like that."

He looked down, still trying to count those bills, a task that was mysteriously beyond his ability all of a sudden. "Look, she was cleaning his *house,*" he said, and he sounded truly pained that he was the one

who had to tell me this. "And then he married her? What were we supposed to think?"

"Just whatever you thought, I guess. How do I know?"

"Exactly."

"Look," I said. "She was a really nice person." Somehow I thought
this would make a difference. It didn't. Detective Bonehead raised an
eyebrow as if he was pondering my loyal burst of sentimentality. Then
he went back to asking questions.

"So how come you abandoned her?" he said.

"I didn't," I said. "I didn't. I didn't."

My assertion that my mother was a nice person did not get through
to this guy, but the idiotic desperation behind those three denials
apparently did. He shrugged. There was a mournful pause as we both
considered how pathetic I sounded. "Well," he said, with a truly hopeless edge to his voice, "I didn't abandon them either."

"No, I get it," I said. "I do. Here, let me count out the money, you're
like retarded all of a sudden." Before he could argue, I reached over and
took the ones out of his hand and started counting. "How much is it?"

"I don't know," he admitted, looking around helplessly. We had
been abandoned by the waitress.

"We just had a burger and a Coke and pie and some coffee, it can't
be that hard to figure out," I noted, counting out about twelve bucks.
Somehow everything had shifted, and now we were just two people
talking about our fucked-up families. And it was late.

Drinan sucked in his breath and then blew it out slowly, as if someone had taught him that in the one yoga class some hippie girlfriend had
gotten him to take before he became a cop. But he still remembered the
breathing, so he did it as he sat in that booth, like that one good yoga
breath was going to put him back in control of his whole messy life. His
face looked like four in the morning. "Yeah," he said. "Let's go."

"Oh, wait, hang on," I said, remembering my situation. My heart
started pounding way too hard. "Jesus, wait, hang on." Reality was setting in; I wasn't going to be spending the next three days sitting in a
booth in a shitty diner; I was going to jail. I suddenly felt as old and tired
as he looked.

"Relax, Tina," said Detective Bonehead. He stood and dusted the crumbs of salt off his jacket. "I'll take you home."

So we went back to the precinct and picked up my stuff, and then he drove me back to the Edge in his old blue Buick. I sat in his car for a long minute, trying to figure out what to say.

"Are you going to get out of the car?" he said finally.

"Yeah, I'm getting out. Sorry. Yes, sorry, I'm just trying to figure out what this all means. Does this mean I can stay in the apartment?"

"It means you can stay tonight."

"What about after tonight?"

"After tonight is tomorrow."

"And after that?"

"You know what, Tina?" He tilted his head quickly left and right, like he was working a bad kink out of his neck. "I'm not going to try and tell you what happens the day after tomorrow. Nobody knows what's going to happen. If you think you do, you're wrong."

I was looking down the street past a couple of drunks staggering up the sidewalk toward us. The sky was starting to turn that strange dark purple that meant the night was on its last legs. "Well," I said. "The sun's coming up, I know that much."

"That's just an educated guess," Drinan said. "Listen. If anyone tries to arrest you again? You might want to mention that you got roughed up the first time. That sergeant at the desk, his name is Bohrman. Randy Bohrman. You think you can remember that?"

"I think so," I said.

"They're not going to bother you. That's just in case."

"Thanks," I said.

"I'll see you in court." He was gripping the steering wheel, but he didn't seem angry; it was more like he was trying to stay awake.

"Look," I said. "You want to come up?"

He tilted his head away, like that kink in his neck was not going to let him alone. Then he glanced back at me with a weary, coplike regret. "That won't be necessary," he said. I turned red yet again.

"I didn't mean that," I said. "I just meant, since you haven't seen it. In so long. Just that one time. And you were drunk that night, and

I thought . . . Do you want to come see it? Just see it. Oh, whatever. Whatever!" I think I yelled it as I started to get out of his stupid loser car. "That is just classic, and you know what? I'm too tired to even be embarrassed by you thinking I'm trying to come on to you right now. Like I'm so tired I'm not even awake enough to think, 'What did he say? This moron thinks I want to sleep with him even though he tried to have me arrested? He thinks I want to have sex twenty minutes after eating a pound of hamburger and six dozen French fries?' Men are such geniuses. I'm so tired I can't even articulate any sarcastic bullshit for you, Detective. So when you want to see the apartment you grew up in—when you want to see your old room and what's left of your mom's crazy paint job—you'll let me know."

I was almost up to the door of the building when he yelled after me. "What did you say?"

"Oh, man," I said. "I'm not kidding. I'm done. I'm going to bed."

"About my mom's paint job."

"What about it?"

"How'd you know it's my mom's?"

I couldn't remember. I couldn't even remember what I said about his mom, and I had said it like seconds ago. "Come on, man. It's four in the morning."

"Yeah yeah yeah, okay." He looked down at his hands on the steering wheel, and he sat there for a second like he wanted to ask me about something else. Before he could ask, I went inside. I went into the apartment and lay down and didn't get up until Lucy appeared and told me to get out of bed.

13

It took me a second to catch up. She was watching me from the doorway, impatient, while I groggily fumbled around with the covers. My little adopted bedroom had two windows overlooking an exhaust shaft, so there was not much light even when the old pull-down shades were up, which they were not at this time. So it truly was dark.

"What time is it?" I asked.

"It's three-thirty in the afternoon. What is the matter with you?" Lucy asserted, stalking in on her low sensible heels and yanking the shades up. "Are you hungover?"

"No, I'm not hungover."

"Right," she replied, all pissy as usual.

"I don't have a hangover, Lucy," I said. "I was arrested yesterday afternoon, and I spent the night in lockup, thank you very much, because someone forgot to inform me that there is a fucking injunction on this place."

That did get her attention, although she was completely unapologetic. "You were arrested?" she asked, with more than a shred of disbelief.

"Don't give me that," I said, disgusted. "You knew all about it. And don't even bother lying to me about it—"

"I am not—"

"You forgot to inform me. You and that lawyer, although my bet is he told you and you told him that you would tell me, but then you didn't even bother to tell me."

"I am not sure what you're accusing me of here, Tina. But if you were arrested—"

"What do you mean, 'if'? Do you think I'd make up something like that?"

"I don't know what you'd do."

"Why would I make that up?"

"Well, why would I want you to be arrested? Isn't that what you're accusing me of, trying to have you arrested for some unknown reason?"

"Oh *forget it*," I said.

"You know, Tina, you're increasingly unstable," she noted, starting to dial her CrackBerry.

"I'm, excuse me, I'm what? What am I?"

"All these crazy accusations. If you had been arrested, I would know about it, wouldn't I? If you were arrested, you would have had to call me—hi, it's Lucy Finn, could I speak to Ira? Thanks," she cooed into the phone.

"I'm not making this up!"

"Or Alison. Or anybody, you would have had to call somebody, and they would have had to call me. Which to my knowledge did not happen."

"I'm going to go take a shower."

"Hi!" she chirped. "I'm over here at the apartment, and Tina has just told me an interesting story."

Right across the hall was a bathroom—the one with the silver-spotted wallpaper—but it needed a good cleaning, and several tiles had come up around one of the corners, so it was frankly too depressing to take a shower in. There was also a pretty capable blue bathroom right behind the kitchen off the great room, but Len had all sorts of apparatus set up in there. And just to the right of the TV room and the bedroom, there was a quite tidy peach-colored bathroom, but it had one of those shower chairs in it for people who are too old and decrepit to stand up, which was simply too depressing to contemplate. But if you walked down the hall off the TV room, past the laundry room, and around a corner, there was a fourth bathroom, which was painted periwinkle, and had a lot of sixties-looking groovy flower stickers stuck to the ceiling and all over the cheap plastic door of the shower stall. So although it was a little inconvenient to walk a quarter mile to take a shower, it was a nice bathroom and worth the effort. I left my nightmare of a sister to her devilish shenanigans and hiked off to take a shower to clear my head.

By the time I got back, Lucy was done with her phone calls and having a cup of tea. She glanced up at me, set the cup down, and stood. Then she smiled, like we were good friends who had had some sort of minor misunderstanding. "I talked to Ira," she informed me.

"Good for you."

"He told me that they do in fact have a record of you being taken down to the Forty-ninth Precinct."

"Did you think I was lying?"

"Well, Tina—it didn't make sense. And by the way, you weren't actually arrested. They just had you in for questioning, at least that's what they have on record."

"They have anything on record about an injunction?"

"Well, that's the interesting part," she said, still smiling. "There was in fact an injunction. Ira accepted service, and he did tell me about it, but he assured me that he didn't think it would stick."

"And then you just forgot to tell me."

"I didn't forget, for heaven's sake, no one thought they would *arrest* you."

"So you deliberately didn't tell me?"

"This is not my fault, Tina. I am not the one who had you arrested," Lucy claimed, staying right on point. "And if you would just calm down long enough to listen, it might interest you to know that the injunction is gone. Obviously it would never have held up to a court challenge, which Ira was going to file this week."

"They just dropped it? When?"

"Just this afternoon apparently. So no worries about that, okay, Tina? Although honestly, if the police come by, you will call me, right? Even though they just took you in for questioning, that is completely unacceptable, and you should never *ever* talk to the police without a lawyer present. Ira got really upset when he heard that you let them take you down there and no one called him."

"I don't even know him," I said.

"But you should have called me, and I would have called him. Listen, tell me you understand this. If you're being harassed, it's important that you let us know."

"Why, because you're so worried about my safety? Is that why you didn't even *warn* me?"

"I'm not going to get into some long argument about this, Tina, especially when everything came out all right. I already said I'm glad it was nothing worse. I don't know what more you want out of me, but then I never do." She sighed, looked at her CrackBerry, and started doing that little thing with her thumbs.

"Why are you here?" I asked.

"What?"

"You never just show up. You always have a reason," I said. "So what's your reason today?"

"A friend of mine is coming over."

"What friend?"

"His name is Dave, he works on the city page of the *Times,* he's going to come take a look at the apartment. He might be interested in writing about it."

"No. Come on," I said, suddenly overwhelmed. "No."

"What do you mean, no?" she said, looking up at me sharply.

"I mean *no.* No reporters in here. No." I thought about Len talking about privacy, and Pete Drinan not even setting foot in his home for years and years, and that tenderhearted paint job in the kid's bedroom, and I just couldn't bear the thought of some fucking reporter wandering around my apartment. "No," I repeated.

"You know, I don't actually need your permission, Tina," Lucy observed, with that nasty edge she could not keep out of her voice. "You can stop acting like you own the place, when you're just staying here for all of us."

"I can't believe you," I said, trying seriously not to lose it. "I spent the night in jail because you—you—"

"I'm only taking care of my interests and yours. And as to spending a night in jail, it's not the first time, so I don't know what you're making such a big deal about." She stood up, turned away, and went to the little kitchenette, where she started wiping down the counters deliberately, like I had not done a good enough job.

"Fuck you," I said, sounding like a peevish teenager. "Fuck you. Call me when he's gone."

"He might want to talk to you," she said, all deliberate and chilly and mean, like some nasty old high school nun. "About being hauled into the police station. We're in the middle of a real estate war! And they had you arrested? You should tell him about it, it might help sell the story."

"Go to hell, Lucy." As I left I slammed the door behind me, good and loud. I am sure Mrs. Westmoreland heard it and took notes.

Wandering the Upper West Side of Manhattan can be entertaining when your life is less screwed up, but when you're in a bad mood, both about having been arrested and having a sister who consistently behaves like a jerk, it is not all that much fun. I walked up and down Amsterdam for a while, then cut over to the park and wandered around, hoping that a little urban nature would make me feel better. It was a lonely and pathetic endeavor, but after an hour it started to have a little bit of a positive effect. That section of Central Park was in fact particularly utopian; old ladies and their dogs wandered along charming, curling pathways where young boys and girls on Rollerblades flew by, calling to each other with hopeful, nonsensical glee. College kids lay on the grass and laughed at each other while inching ever closer to having sex. I passed a mossy lake and a giant statue of an angel coming down to earth. An Arab guy at a little Plexiglas stand under a green-and-white umbrella was selling falafel sandwiches and cans of soda. Life was coming back into focus, and the exhausting, endless night finally seemed over.

Which is when I tried to buy a can of lemonade. It seemed like a sane enough idea, as I had been walking and thinking for quite a while and was feeling rather thirsty. Unfortunately, I was so thoroughly peeved with Lucy when I left the apartment that I had been more concerned with making an exit than with grabbing my backpack. All I had on me were my house keys and a dollar twenty-five in my back pocket, and the Arab guy in the falafel cart wouldn't spot me the quarter.

In fact he was dismissive. "One *fifty*. You need one dollar and fifty, young lady," he explained, which I was perfectly willing to accept, if he hadn't so quickly and needlessly worked himself into a lather over it. "What is the matter with you?" he asked before I had a chance to scrounge the three quarters, four dimes, and two nickels out of my pocket. "Can you step aside, please? If you are not going to purchase something, step aside!"

"Cool your jets," I muttered. This sent him even further over the edge.

"You have no money! Step aside! Step aside, please! You have no money!"

"Could you just relax for a second," I said. "I *have* it. For fuck's sake."

"Why are you using obscenity?" the guy howled suddenly. "STEP ASIDE," he raged. I couldn't move. I was in trouble, serious psychological trouble. After my awful night and day, I had nothing left. I was actually contemplating leaping onto his little cart and hurling cans of soda at him when some girl came up behind me.

"I'll buy her a lemonade," she said.

"It's fine," I said, trying not to sound as insane as I felt. "I didn't want his stupid fucking lemonade."

"This crazy woman is cursing me! I do not have to serve people who speak to me with this language!"

"Yeah, I'm sure you've never heard that word before," said the girl. "Relax." She reached past my shoulder and handed the guy a five. "Make it two," she said. I turned to snap at her and stopped. It was Jennifer White, my sullen teenage neighbor from 9A.

"Oh," I said.

"Yeah," she said. "You're welcome." She handed me my can of lemonade and turned back to reach for her change.

"Here, here is your change, now please go!" growled the way-too-uptight Arab. "There are customers who are waiting!" Jennifer ignored him, holding her lemonade under her arm while she slowly took the two dollars off the Plexiglas stand and carefully folded them into a tiny pink change purse. "Please!" he howled, but he sounded now like he was begging. Still ignoring him, she dropped the change purse into the side pocket of an enormous backpack and finally stepped aside.

"I AM SO SORRY, HOW CAN I HELP YOU!" the guy shouted at the next man in line, with a kind of friendly fury.

Jennifer looked at me, unruffled. "Are you heading home?" she asked.

"I guess so," I said. "Thanks." She popped the lid of her lemonade and took a long slow sip, as if this were the most natural thing in the world. The leaves were glowing above us. We sipped our lemonades silently, as if that were a solution to something, then turned toward the path. Jennifer walked so slowly we were barely moving at all.

In the golden light of late afternoon, Jennifer White looked like a young goddess. A slight breeze moved carelessly through her hair, and her cheeks had the slightest lift of color in them. She was wearing that dopey school uniform, but the boring white blouse was open a bit too wide at the neck, and the plaid skirt looked witty, somehow, like an outfit in a hip-hop video. Heroic-looking young men in shorts and running shoes kept glancing back at us in fleet, happy admiration.

"This lemonade is pretty good," I said.

"It's all right," she agreed.

"I don't want to go home either," I told her.

She didn't respond, as that would have amounted to admitting something. I decided to just keep talking. "My sister is a fucking nightmare," I said. "Sooner or later, she'll leave, but I can't go home until she does."

"What's so bad about her?" asked Jennifer.

"All she thinks about is money."

"That's all anybody thinks about."

"Yeah, I know, but trust me, Lucy is off the deep end. I think inheriting this apartment has driven her insane."

"I heard you didn't inherit it," Jennifer volunteered. She didn't exactly sound like she was fishing, but I knew she was.

"My mom was married to Bill and he left it to her, so they say we inherited it. It sounds legal to me, but what do I know." This came out sounding snottier than I meant it to, since I realized that Jennifer might be able to shed some light on a few things. "Anyway, that's what they're going to figure out, if we did inherit it. Nobody knows yet."

"They think they do."

"They who?"

"Everyone."

"Everyone who?"

"They're having meetings about it, you know. You are so totally not supposed to be there. It's driving them nuts."

"Them who?"

"The *building*," she said.

I knew what she meant, but it was unnerving to hear it stated so definitively by a teenage girl.

"The building doesn't get to decide, does it?"

Jennifer shot me a bored look, like she didn't believe that a person as old as me could be so stupid.

"What?" I said, trying to laugh. "It's not up to them."

"They *think* it's up to them," she said. "They didn't like your mom."

This last bit, offered up with no prodding or prying on my part, landed like an atom bomb on my heart. For a second I hated that bored kid in her snotty pleated skirt and her shitty little white blouse and her perfect blond hair, but before I could come up with a cutting remark to avenge this completely obscure and meaningless slight on the mother I had barely spoken to in the last years of her life, Jennifer flushed, ashamed of herself. "Not me," she apologized. "I liked her. I mean, she was always nice to me. But she was like a cleaning lady. That's what they're hung up on. And Mr. Drinan was kind of weird. And they're all obsessed with that apartment, everybody knows it's the best one in the building, and they're all *so* hung up, it's so, whatever. I'm just telling you. That's what the problem is."

She felt so bad about telling me the truth that I didn't know what to say.

"It's okay," I said. "I appreciate the information."

"Yeah, okay," she said. Neither of us said anything for a little while, and then, as slowly as we were walking, we were there. We looked up at the Edgewood looming above us, elegant, enormous, the *building*.

"I love those lions," I said.

"They look like guard dogs to me," she replied, tossing her empty can of lemonade into the cast-iron trash can on the street corner. She looked over at me and made one of those half smiles, like you expect people to know how unhappy you really are. It was the most human expression I'd seen cross her face.

"Look," I said. "Do you have to go in?"

"They're probably flipping out already," she said, and the half smile evaporated. She just looked sad.

So that's how I got into that apartment again. I took Jennifer up to the Whites' apartment and rang the doorbell and started talking. "Hey, Mrs. White," I said, all friendly and helpful. She was, as usual, wearing an absolutely glorious suit. "I hope you haven't been too worried about Jennifer. She's been with me."

"We have been worried!" Mrs. White said. Her entire ensemble was the most extraordinary shade of sea green. She must have had the shoes dyed to match the suit; there could be no other way to get the color so exact. "I was just about to send for the police!" she announced, checking herself out in the mirror.

"Oh, I am so sorry, we should have called, but she was really upset," I said humbly.

"Jennifer is not allowed to go off and have activities after school, certainly not with people she barely knows! Your father will be beside himself, Jennifer. You know the rules!"

"Would you relax, Mom?" Jennifer started. I reached over and squeezed her hand, her new best friend.

"No no, don't get angry, of course your mom was worried, she didn't know what we were doing!" I explained. I looked at Mrs. White and smiled. "I was helping her with her math!" This was completely improvised on my part, and Jennifer looked at me with real surprise. "We bumped into each other in the lobby—I mean, literally, it was ridiculous and completely my fault, because I was just not looking where I was going—and her homework went everywhere, and when I was helping her get it back together she told me she didn't have a clue how to make it through today's problem sets. And there were so many! Let me reassure you, those nuns are doing their job up there at Saint Peter in Chains, she's getting a workout in the math department. It is almost laughable how much homework she's got. Anyway, she was a little upset, so I told her— well, I'm actually, you know, I'm pretty good at math." Improbably, this part was true. "And I felt bad that she seemed so overwhelmed, so we went to my place just to look at a couple of the most difficult problems, and we seriously lost track of time. And when I realized how long we had been working, I was appalled, and I thought about calling, but obviously it made more sense to bring her home. I'm really, really sorry." Jennifer was staring at me now. It is possible that I was laying it all on a bit thick, but I could tell that Mrs. White was not particularly interested in facts, so the more I gave her, the less likely she would be to examine them too closely. And as usual, seven things were going on at once in that apart- ment. Kids were screaming off in the distance, a washing machine was chugging along, and then something in the kitchen fell with a crash. Under the circumstances, Mrs. White couldn't waste a ton of time wor- rying about me.

"Oh, well, thank you," she finally said, picking up a small child and kicking a pile of coats and scarves into the closet off the foyer. "That really was kind of you, I just wish—Anna, where are you going? I have to meet Bob any minute, is dinner ready for the girls?"

"Is Wednesday," Anna, the Polish cleaning lady, announced, as if that were an answer. She was putting on her coat.

"Wednesday?" said Mrs. White. "No no, it's not Wednesday. Or, I mean, it is Wednesday, but we talked about this, this is the Wednesday you're staying. Barbie, please!"

"I'll take her," I said, and as I untangled the wriggling child from her arms, Mrs. White tried to explain to Anna that she had agreed to stay until midnight, because she and Mr. White had made arrangements months before to attend an auction this evening benefiting the Museum of Modern Art. His firm had bought a whole table at great expense, and there would be some extremely important Korean clients at that table, and they would not understand if his wife failed to make an appearance.

Anna the cleaning lady seemed to feel bad, but it wasn't clear that she even understood Mrs. White's explanation. She kept saying, "Sorry, so sorry," while Mrs. White kept telling her why she couldn't leave. After a little while, Anna just walked out the door, leaving me and Barbie and Jennifer as witnesses to Mrs. White's problem and her beautiful suit.

Mrs. White looked over at me. She really had no options, so I knew better than to push it. I kissed Barbie on the cheek and started to hand her back. "Here's your mommy," I said. "Don't mess up her pretty suit."

"You couldn't—I'm sorry, but you did say you might be interested in babysitting sometime. You wouldn't be available right now, would you?"

"Right now?" I said. "Gee."

Once we got rid of Mrs. White, things really started to cook. The first hour or so was a bit of a mess, because six sets of coats and shoes had to be hung up and put away, the baby needed a new diaper, and dinner had not even been started. Katherine decided that because she had seen me first, no one else had any claim on my attention whatsoever. She followed me around, silently worshipful but with big confused tears in her eyes, while I dealt with all sorts of nonsense instead of going back to her room to play stuffed animals with her. The other two girls, whom I had not met before, didn't want to eat anything, and they argued incessantly over total bullshit. There were three cooked casseroles from a fancy gourmet store in the refrigerator, but nobody was interested in them. Louise, the oldest daughter, made herself a shake with flaxseed and wheatgrass and ignored me. Jennifer sat in a corner of the kitchen and picked at a salad.

"Is that all you're going to eat?" I asked.

"Are you my mother?" she asked back.

"No, I'm the person who wants to know if that's all you're going to eat," I told her.

She smiled to herself like she thought that was amusing in a minor way, then she looked at the ceiling. "Yeah, this is all I'm going to eat."

All of this eating and not eating was going on around the kitchen table, which was apparently a real treat for everyone, whether they were eating or not.

"We're not *allowed* to eat in the kitchen," said one of the middle kids, whose name I couldn't remember.

"Your mom didn't tell me that," I told her.

"*I'm* telling you. We eat in the *dining* room."

"I want to eat in the kitchen, it's easier," I said.

"You don't get to *decide*," she informed me.

"Sure I do; I'm in charge."

"You're not *old* enough to be in charge," she insisted.

"Don't you think it's boring to eat in the dining room all the time?" I asked.

"It's the way we *do* things," she told me.

"It *is* boring," Jennifer announced from her corner. "This is better."

"How old are you, anyway?" asked Louise, the eldest, who had been helping me feed Katherine and the baby with a sort of effortless ease.

"I'm thirty-two."

This made everyone stare. The two monstrous middle kids, Jennifer, Louise, Katherine, even the baby, seemed startled to hear that I was so old. I was startled myself.

"You're in your *thirties*?" said one of the monsters.

"You don't look that old," said the other one.

"It's just because I'm short," I told her. "If you stretched me out a little, I would look older."

"You would look *taller* maybe," Jennifer corrected me. The two monsters thought this was a riot and started giggling hilariously, burying their heads in each other like little animals. That made Katherine start laughing too. Then Louise started laughing, just because everyone else was. The baby looked bewildered. For a second, Jennifer's mood lifted, and she actually smiled, like she really liked having gotten the whole room to laugh, even inadvertently.

"Thirty-two, that's bizarre. That's like *old*," said Louise.

"Yeah, I'm pretty near death," I admitted. This made the monsters laugh even harder, and things were pleasant for about ten minutes, until I told them that they would not be allowed to have chocolate ice cream and watch television unless they ate their dinner and finished their homework. They started whining and yelling again, and then Jennifer sighed and told them to fuck off, which pretty much put an end to all the fun. The monsters went back to their room, where they argued with each other over nothing for another hour or so. The baby fell asleep in her high chair, then woke up screaming while I wiped her off, and Katherine started crying because no one was paying attention to her. The kitchen looked like a disaster because I didn't have time to clean up before Louise announced that Katherine and the baby really needed to have baths and be in bed before eight, and she couldn't help me because she had so much homework to do.

For a moment I wondered how much people got paid for this, because I had not nailed Mrs. White down on the details of the baby-sitting plan before she fled the apartment in her hot little sea green suit. But I really had no time to think about that missed opportunity. I gave the baby a bath and then Katherine, who then proceeded to prance around the apartment naked and screaming while I tried to put the baby to sleep. Louise said I shouldn't have let her fall asleep in her high chair even for a minute because now she would not go down for hours. The two monsters suddenly came out into the hallway, declaring that they were hungry for dinner but didn't want the cold food that was congealing on plates in the kitchen; they wanted the leftover Chinese carry-out they had had earlier in the week with some different babysitter who, they insisted, had shoved it all in the back of the refrigerator. Louise told them that Anna had tossed the leftover Chinese food when she came in that morning, which started another unfortunate round of whining. I wanted to smack Louise, who really seemed to be constantly full of bad news, but then she sighed and told me to go read to Katherine, that she would put Bee to bed. I didn't know what she was talking about until she reached for the baby, whom she called Bee instead of Barbie, and that made me like her, even more than the offer of help. Then Jennifer appeared out of nowhere and said, "I'll feed them," propelling the two hungry monsters toward the kitchen.

That left me to lead the naked Katherine back to her little yellow
room, find her some pajamas, and look through a pile of books with
her. This was extremely pleasant after all the chaos. Katherine carefully
and quietly picked up one book after another and considered which
ones she wanted read. The books all had brilliantly colored pictures of
talking animals and princesses and elves and happy families with small
but significant problems, all of which got worked out by everybody
being kind to each other. Seriously, the pictures in these books were so
pretty and the people in the stories so decent and sensible that you
wondered how we all ended up being such assholes in real life.

After about twenty minutes of lying in bed and paging through
peaceful and lovely picture books, I was quite frankly drifting off when
Katherine whispered, "There's the ghost."

Because I was only half awake, I thought she was talking about the
story we were reading. I shook my head slightly to clear the fog and
considered the picture we were looking at, confused. The story had to
do with a talking teddy bear who was left in a large department store by
mistake, then had a series of charming misadventures before the little
girl who owned him came back and found him. "What ghost, there's
no ghost," I said.

"Listen, *listen*," Katherine said, worried. She put her small hand up
in the air, like the ghost was in the room with us and might flee if I kept
talking. We had turned off the overhead light and were reading by the
bedside lamp, so the room was dark. I put my arm around her and looked
up to listen, meaning to take just a moment before telling her there were
no ghosts in her room, only night and shadows.

And then I heard the ghost. I tensed up a little, so Katherine knew
she was right. "See?" she said.

She was right. There was a kind of whisper in the walls. It was a
female ghost, and she was upset, talking fast in a different language in
her other world, which seemed to be sort of adjacent to this one, or
maybe in a slightly skewed dimension. It sounded truly spooky, like a
river of dead words with nowhere to go, trapped in the air all around us,
some past catastrophe frozen between places where things moved. It

was definitely a ghost. Katherine looked at me with solemn confidence. She knew that I knew she was right.

"That's not a ghost," I said. "Come on, that's just some person who lives in the building."

"Then why is she on our floor? We are the only people who live on this floor, and that's not us."

"It's somebody on some other floor."

"Shhhhhh," she said. "She's crying." Sure enough, the ghost had stopped her mournful complaints and now was sobbing, long pain-wracked moans that clung to the insides of the walls.

"That is not a ghost," I repeated. I sat up to go look for it and caught sight of Jennifer in the doorway.

"You hear the ghost?" she whispered. She glided into the room and joined us on the bed.

"That's not a ghost!" I said, with so little confidence that they both looked at me triumphantly.

"Shhhhhh," whispered Katherine. "If you talk too loud, it goes away."

"I'm not going to be loud," I said, whispering as well. "I'm just going to go listen." I left them on the bed and got down on my hands and knees so I could crawl silently through the wool pile of the carpet and get to the wall without the ghost knowing I was closing in on her. She was talking again, a fast, anxious complaint, like she knew she was trapped forever and simply couldn't make peace with it. Katherine sat up on the bed, clearly worried that something was going to happen to me. She leaned into Jennifer, who put her arm around the kid in a gesture of such careless affection it wounded me to the core.

"Come back, come back," Katherine whispered, waving her hands at me like I was doing something way too dangerous and had to be ushered back to the one safe spot in the room—the bed—or the ghost would get me. I didn't answer right away, I just put my ear up against the wall. The murmuring river of grief got louder; there was no question that the ghost was inside the wall. "Oh," Katherine said, really worried. "Come back!"

"Does the closet go all the way over here?" I asked, still in a whisper. "How big is that closet?"

"We've checked out the closet. The ghost is not in the closet," Jennifer said.

"Yeah, I know, I just want to check out something else," I murmured. I crawled over to the closet door, reached up for the knob, and carefully swung it open.

"No!" said Katherine, in a terrified little wail.

"There's no ghost in the closet, Katherine, we already went through this, the ghost doesn't live in your closet," Jennifer told her. I was not so sure. The ghost's voice was distinctively louder there, and it seemed to inhabit the closet space with more authority. The walls were holding on to the sound and carrying it into the room, but the sound did seem to come from the closet. I put my ear to the floor and listened. The ghost was in the floor. I tapped quietly on the floor with my index finger. The ghost fell silent.

"Hey," I said. "Hey, who are you? Are you okay?" There was another moment of silence, then the sound of air, some things bumping, and the sound of a door closing. Then nothing. I turned back to Jennifer and Katherine, who were watching from the bed as I talked to the floor.

"You scared her away," Katherine reprimanded me. She was clearly not pleased with my behavior.

"I did scare her away, isn't that what you're supposed to do with ghosts? Most of them are not quite so cooperative." I reached up, flicked on the closet light switch, and started shoving around all the shoes and kids' costumes and stuffed animals that were thrown willy-nilly around the floor.

"What are you doing?" asked Jennifer.

"I don't know, I'm just looking to see if there's a trap door or something," I said. "It doesn't make any sense. This room is right above my apartment, right? Would she be in my apartment?"

"You said you didn't have this room," Jennifer noted.

"No, I have this room, I just don't have this view," I explained.

"So the ghost is in your apartment?"

"It's not a ghost, sweetheart, it's a person. That's a person who's downstairs, and she's upset, and it sounds like she's in my apartment, but she can't be," I explained.

"You said you didn't have this room," Jennifer repeated, mostly to herself. She was ignoring me now as she dropped off the bed, got on all fours, and started shoving the stuffed animals out of the closet and into the room. The closet floor was also carpeted with yellow wool. Jennifer started peeling back its edges.

"What are you doing?" said Katherine, excited.

"I'm looking for the trapdoor."

"There's no trapdoor," I said. "I was making that up."

"There might be," Jennifer said. "There's clearly something down there. And you say it's not part of your apartment."

"I don't know if it's part of my apartment or not, Jennifer, but you can't just rip up the carpet in here, your mother will kill me."

"She won't even notice," Jennifer muttered. By this time Katherine had crawled off the bed and was helping her pull up the carpet.

"What on earth are you *doing*?" said Louise, from the doorway.

"We're looking for the trapdoor," said Katherine, quite matter-of-fact. Louise looked at me as if I were completely insane.

"You told them it would be okay to take the carpet up? Mom is going to flip out," she stated.

"I didn't tell them it was okay. We just heard something in the wall, so we were trying to find out where the sound came from. It's okay, Jennifer. Katherine, get back in bed, please. We're fine. The ghost is gone."

"The *ghost*?" said Louise, raising her eyes to heaven as if someone might glance down and agree with her assessment of this whole mess, which was not good. "You know my parents are not going to be happy to hear that you're telling her ghost stories, it's not part of our religion."

"I didn't tell her a ghost story, she *heard* the ghost in the *wall*. We all did. Come on, sweetie, you have to get back in bed now." I leaned over and grabbed Katherine before she could crawl farther away from me, swinging her into my arms and plopping her on the bed in one swift move that left her giggling. Louise continued to watch with disap-proval, but I was not letting her get to me. "Come on, Jennifer, Kather-ine has go to bed. There's nothing there, I was kidding."

Jennifer looked up at me, and for the first time I saw her smile, a big, happy, excited grin. "Then what's this?" she said.

14

It didn't look like much, but there was no question that she had found something: a perfect square, about three feet by three feet, that had been cut out of the wall and then dropped back in, tightly fitting the hole from which it had been cut. Then it had been painted over, and a laminated picture of Noah and the ark taped over that. It was pretty well hidden, but there it was, right in the wall.

"Wow," said Katherine. "How do you open it?"

"It doesn't open, Katherine," Louise said. "It's not a door, it's just a hole, left over from the crawl space for the workers who built the building. After they finished, they made a plug and sealed it up. They were all sealed up ages ago." Not content to have made such a deflating statement, Louise droned on, "This is an old building and it has its quirks, but there's nothing more to it than that. This isn't one of your storybooks. I don't know why you're encouraging her, Jennifer, you're not a child. And isn't it past her bedtime?" This she directed to me with a kind of pointed superiority. Those nuns are doing a good job with this one, I thought. Louise moved to the closet and flicked off the light with a quick impatient gesture, then stood in the shadows with her hands on her hips. "Mom really wants the little kids to get to bed on time."

Jennifer stood up and glided into the hallway, then, quiet as a ghost herself, disappeared behind the door to her own room. Sanity regained its footing. One by one my charges went to sleep, and at half past twelve their parents returned, paid me a surprising amount of money, and sent me back downstairs to my own life.

I let myself in to my apartment with all my multiple keys. Lucy was long gone, of course; the place was deserted. There was no sign of the guy from the city page of the *Times,* if in fact he had shown his face and prowled around and invaded the empty corners of my enormous empty apartment. And compared to the Whites'—so cluttered with children and toys and furniture and uneaten dinners and coats and shoes and arguments over nothing—my apartment seemed especially enormous and empty. Feeling both exhausted and spooked, I went into each room and turned on all the lights everywhere, as if that would populate the vacant spaces. But a lot of the bulbs were dead, and the ones that worked put out only the shadow of an actual glow. The effect was so painfully lackluster and grim it made everything worse, and I started to panic. As I looked around that empty apartment, I honestly didn't know how I was supposed to go on. After spending the night with six messy and unfinished girls who hadn't yet made a single disastrous life-altering mistake, I was not in the mood to spend any time alone with shadows. Besides, I was now somewhat convinced that there was a ghost in my apartment.

It occurred to me that I could at least replace a few of those bulbs. I remembered seeing some dusty packets of lightbulbs somewhere during my early searches, so I went looking again, poking around in a few closets in the empty bedrooms and some of the many bathrooms. There I found only some empty plastic bags and a couple of old sheets, so I went to check out the laundry room, where the light was marginally better than anywhere else in the apartment, and started looking through the plywood closets nailed to the wall above and alongside the washer-dryer. In the first one I found more old plastic bags shoved in a corner next to a dozen or so crisply folded paper bags. Then a packet of bright blue sponges shriveled together like frightened old ladies, still in their shrink wrap, and behind that an unused toilet plunger, also still wrapped. The sponges and plunger were covered with dust, as was an old red plastic bottle of liquid Tide, my mother's detergent of choice. Behind that were three different kinds of stain remover, two flashlights with no batteries in them, and behind that, neatly folded and stacked, a pile of old sheets and pillowcases so worn and drained of color that you honestly wouldn't know they existed if you weren't bent on emptying the whole sorry cabinet just to see if there were any lightbulbs back there.

The other two cabinets yielded similarly dispiriting prizes: a half-empty bottle of Windex, a container of tarnish remover, more withered sponges, tile cleanser from the past century. It was truly dreary to find so many different household cleansers covered with so much dust, and I was starting to feel pretty sure that these plywood cubicles were never going to yield any lightbulbs, but I was so wired I just kept looking without really caring what I found. A floor-to-ceiling closet that had been shoved into the corner next to the dryer was full of dusty mops and a couple of broomsticks with bent yellow plastic bristles on the end. There was a folded metal footstool that was so rusted you couldn't open it anymore and more old plastic bags crumpled together in such a dirty and disgusting heap that I was vaguely afraid something horrible might crawl out if I moved even one. I kicked the pile cautiously a couple of times and nothing scurried out, so I reached in with both arms and started to paw it all aside, pulling the mess out into the room along with the ancient brooms and mops and the dusty cleansers that I had dumped in the middle of the floor. And then, because I had taken all the stuff out of it, the closet lost its balance and almost fell on my head, because it wasn't really fastened to the wall. So I had to catch it and wriggle out from underneath it and somehow keep it from braining me.

And I found that I had been right all along; the layout of my apartment and the Whites' did not line up. There was another room, and that cheap little plywood closet had been shoved right up against its door. There was the extra room, right underneath Katherine's, and somehow a ghost had gotten into it.

15

It took me a whole day to get up the nerve to go in. The room was quite dark, and the light switch on the wall, like so many of the others in that apartment, was completely useless. Eventually I found a flashlight that worked, and this is what I found: sixty-seven ancient cardboard boxes, taped shut and stacked neatly on top of one another. Six oil paintings in dusty, broken wood frames. Six ornate oak dining-room chairs with turned legs and an orange-and-yellow-vinyl folded-up baby's high chair. An old bed frame, a giant wingback easy chair with torn pink upholstery fabric. An eight-foot-long solid oak Stickley dining-room table leaning up against the wall with the legs removed. In a far corner, stuffed between the last two rows of boxes, a cracked black garment bag with three floor-length evening gowns.

This is what was in the boxes: six Waterford crystal tumblers, three with chips. Two dozen plastic jars filled with two dozen different colors of dried-up poster paint. Four pairs of battered gym shoes, two pairs of low black pumps, one pair of bright gold four-inch spike heels, and sixteen pairs of cowboy boots. A dark gray-and-black hand-knit Fair Isle sweater. Four Indian-print cotton scarves, three silk scarves, seven wool scarves, and one scarflike shawl with Tibetan coins stitched around one edge. Four shoe boxes filled with dangly silver earrings, tangled-up bracelets, and inexpensive sparkly necklaces. Another shoe box full of Mardi Gras beads. A box of red, blue, yellow, black, and white Lego blocks. Another box full of Tinker Toys and Matchbox cars, along with about sixty pieces of orange plastic Matchbox car track. Two boxes of old phonograph albums, by bands and girl singers I'd never heard of, except for the Beatles and the Rolling Stones. Two broken plastic light sabers and three plastic swords. A whole box of hats—a bowler, four fedoras, a Robin Hood hat, a really well-made French beret, an equally well-made wool cap from Ireland. Five leather gloves, none with a mate. Six pairs of worn jeans, a bunch of T-shirts, eight Indian-print skirts, four pairs of eyeglasses. Dishes. Glassware. A shoe box full of expensive flatware. Two table lamps with strangely carved bases and even stranger Dr. Seuss–like lampshades. Two broken laptop computers. Three unspeakably beautiful glass vases with a swirled gold and blue finish. A funny cookie jar in the shape of a fat man carrying a suitcase. Two half-size bone china mugs with pictures of dogs on them. A box full of china mugs from different countries all over the world. A dozen Halloween costumes, including three pirates of different sizes. A hand-knit blanket with six holes in it and an enormous patchwork quilt that looked big enough to cover three beds. An old Minolta SLR camera, three boxes full of dusty negatives, and seventeen photo albums filled with pictures.

That was not, in fact, everything; that's just what I managed to get through in three or four days. Every morning I got up, made myself a cup of coffee and some ramen noodles, watched ten or fifteen minutes of the morning news, then got my flashlight and let myself back into that hidden room and looked around. There was no overhead light and only one dim window hidden by all the detritus in the far corner, so whenever I found a box that looked like it might have something interesting in it—which was, in fact, all of them—I would shove it across the floor to the laundry room, and there I would unload it, examining each separate piece before adding it to the pile on top of the dryer. On the second day of this, I rigged up an improvised light source by running a long orange extension cord back to the plug in the laundry room and firing up a couple of portable electric photographer's lamps from my new favorite hardware store. The lamps gave off a fierce and uncompromising light, which was finally too unnerving to be tolerated. So I went on dragging each box into the light of the laundry room and squeezing the lives that had been hidden away there back into the apartment they had once inhabited.

My timing for this new hobby was good, as Lucy had decided to

give me a little break from her clever maneuverings, because she did
know that she had completely pissed me off about that injunction thing.
Then, after several days of peace and quiet, she started to slowly reappear.
First Alison called my cell phone, leaving a tight little birdlike message
about wanting to see how I was and speculating that maybe she and
Daniel could drop by with some carry-out so I wouldn't be all alone
over here. I didn't call back, so she called again and left a message virtually identical to the first one, which I was a hundred percent sure she
left only because Lucy told her to. When I didn't return that call either,
Daniel phoned and said he was worried about me and that he and Alison were coming by later that day. I knew everyone was acting on
Lucy's orders. So I called Alison back and got her voice mail and left a
short cheerful message about how I was fine and everything was fine
and they shouldn't come over. So then Daniel left another message
about wanting to talk to me, which I didn't respond to, and then Lucy
left a message saying Daniel and Alison were coming over and she had
heard that I told them they couldn't, which was not okay because even
though I was staying there that didn't mean I could control access to
the apartment. The apartment belonged to all three of us, and I could
not say that they couldn't come over. So then I left a message on Lucy's
voice mail saying I didn't think I owned the apartment, and my understanding was that nobody knew who really owned the apartment until
the courts made a ruling, but that this was not a good time for me and
I didn't want anyone to come over right now because I had some things
I was doing. At which point Lucy called back and left a message saying
that she and Daniel and Alison would come over that evening at six.

Which would have been fine—I was planning on letting them in,
for Chrissake—but Lucy got herself so worked up over my arrogance
that she decided she'd better come over early and yell at me some more.
So she showed up in the middle of the day, well before I was expecting
to have to let anybody in. And she couldn't get in, because I had locked
it from the inside with my slide bolt and the two chain guards.

Honestly, I had not predicted that Lucy would get so offended by
my defiance that she would just arrive, which was why I was all the way

in the back of the apartment, crawling around in the secret room, looking through boxes with a flashlight and trying to determine which one
to go through next. I had already gone through six boxes that day, and I
had not yet thought about packing it all up and hiding it away again, so
flatware and shoes and fifty-year-old Halloween costumes were strewn
all over the laundry room. I had just found the first box of photo albums
when my cell phone, which I kept clipped to my belt loop, started to
buzz. I looked down, saw that it was Lucy, and decided not to answer.
After about three minutes it buzzed again, and I ignored it again, figuring I had already gotten one shitty message from her and that was plenty.
I mean, why listen to her snipe at me on the phone when I could just
wait and get it in person? So I was truly immersed in my studies when
the phone buzzed a third time. I decided to finally answer it.

"Yes, *what,* Lucy?" I said, annoyed as hell.

"I am out in the hall, let me in," she demanded.

"Wait, you're what?"

"I'm in the hall at the front door and I can't get in. I told you to
take those extra locks off the door, we don't need them. I'm not going
to talk to you about this while I'm standing out in the hallway. Just let
me in. Right now." She was calm but furious.

"You said you were coming at six," I said.

"I don't have to get your permission to come over, Tina!" she said.
"And I am not kidding around! You have to come and let me in immediately!"

Lucy is so good at bossing people around that sometimes I actually
do whatever she's told me to do before I've even decided to do it. So I
had squeezed through the doorway of the secret room and out into the
laundry area before I paused to consider what would happen if I let her
in. I kicked aside a pile of sweaters I had unearthed, which were now
strewn all over the floor. One of them, a rather small olive green pull-
over, had a lot of charming cables all over it, and one of the rows of
cable was all screwed up—it went one way and then the other, and then
it twisted around and kind of collapsed into a knot, and then it came out
the other side and held steady for the rest of its journey up the sleeve.

Right then I realized that the sweater was handmade and that the mother of those two boys had knitted it, that she was a knitter.

"Tina, where are you?" Lucy snapped, because I hadn't said anything while I considered the hapless cable on the sleeve of the little sweater on the floor.

"You have to come back," I said.

"Open the door, Tina," Lucy said, surprised.

"Come back at six, I'll let you in then," I said. And then I hung up.

Lucy is nothing if not persistent, and she did not go away. She called me back three more times, and then she stood out there and pounded on the door for ten minutes, trying the locks in between calls, pulling furiously at the doorknob and yelling, "Tina! TINA. TINA." I cautiously made my way to the front of the apartment so I could listen to the commotion for a little while, and it really did continue for longer than you would have thought possible, even given the fact that it was Lucy. Then I heard Mrs. Westmoreland come out and say something curt to her. Lucy said something sharp back. A door slammed, and I heard more pounding, and a little while later I heard the elevator ding and heard a soft rumbly voice that sounded somewhat confused and vaguely like Frank. And then Mrs. Westmoreland, who had apparently called Frank and told him to get up there, said something that sounded wounded and angry and filled with righteous indignation, and she and Lucy started to argue. Then there was more patient rumbling from Frank, and the next thing I heard was the ding of the elevator and then the slamming of the door across the hall, and then silence.

So I went back and picked up the sweaters, which I had strewn about with a ridiculous degree of disregard, and I folded them up, making two piles. I kept the little green sweater out, because it seemed kind of friendly and real to me now. When I held it up to my nose and sniffed it, I thought it smelled a little bit like fall air, but that may have been because there was no heat in that storage area, so everything was imbued with a sort of timeless chill. I looked around at all the sweaters and shoes and Halloween costumes, and I thought about all the other things stored in that room. And then I spent the rest of the day picking up everything I had excavated and putting it back into the room behind the laundry. I shoved the broom closet back in front of the door, and for good measure I pushed one of those half-empty boxes full of expensive wine in front of it and tried to make it look exactly as it had before my discovery.

When Lucy arrived for the second time that afternoon, she was predictably in a state. "This is completely unacceptable," she snarled, pushing right by me as soon as I opened the door. "You are *forbidden* to deny us entrance, Tina!"

"I'm not denying you entrance, I'm letting you in," I pointed out calmly. "Hi, Alison. Hi, Daniel."

Alison smiled at me with a vague air of apologetic goodwill. I could tell she'd already gotten an earful from Lucy, who really was ridiculously worked up about how horrible I was being.

"This afternoon was humiliating. Do you know I was asked to leave the building?"

"Oh for crying out loud," I sighed. "Would you stop yelling at me? What is the big damn deal? I'm not your apartment *slave*. I was doing something and I didn't want to see you right then! I didn't say you couldn't come in *ever*."

"This is coming off. Now," Lucy asserted, ignoring me and turning her attention back to my private set of locks. "Daniel, can you take care of this?"

"Well . . . I *can*," said Daniel, with a tone of such rational reluctance that we all turned and stared at him. He shoved his hands into his pockets, looking thoughtful, and squeezed up his face into a sort of regret-filled grimace. He's actually a fairly nice-looking guy, even though his hair is thinning and prematurely gray, and he has a fondness for corduroy jackets. So he looked like an excessively reasonable father figure who was about to step in and make the girls behave.

"You *can*?" Lucy repeated. "Then I suggest you do so."

"You know, Lucy . . . I think Tina might be right," Daniel suggested. "She's a bit at risk here. I personally can see why she'd want to have some degree of control over people coming and going. Besides, she's entitled to a bit of privacy, isn't she?"

"This apartment belongs to all of us!"

"It doesn't belong to us quite yet, actually," he pointed out.

"That's what I said," I started. He held up his hand, endlessly patient.

"Maybe we should take this away from the door," he suggested, waving everyone farther into the apartment, where the patently nosy Mrs. Westmoreland couldn't overhear absolutely every evil thing we might dream up to say to each other. It was pretty slick; in one fell swoop he looked saner and Lucy looked more out of control and nuts. The implication was not lost on her. But rather than snapping back, as was her clear instinct, she did as she was told.

"Of course," she said, tersely diplomatic. "Thank you. You are absolutely right."

"I just think we do have to be careful," Daniel continued, walking calmly to the far end of the great room. "You were asked to leave the building? That's bad, that's the sort of thing people talk about."

"That's my point. She should never have put me in that position," Lucy asserted.

"I didn't, I told you I was busy," I volunteered.

"Doing *what*?" Lucy hissed.

"It's not relevant, what she was doing," Daniel told her. I was thrilled to be on the winning side of this, but I'm not so stupid that I didn't get what he was up to. The power plays were flying thick and fast. "It's clearly important that we maintain a presence here," he continued, sounding like the most sensible guy on earth. "So far I think Tina's doing a good job. You told me she's already made some friends in the building, she knows people on the co-op board, she's gotten some jobs babysitting?"

"For the Whites, yes. Mrs. White is on the board too," I said. Daniel's hand went up again, keeping me from drowning them all in helpful, sloppy details.

"So Tina is in fact doing what we need her to do," he noted methodically. "And you want to kick her out?"

"Kick me out?" I said, suddenly not feeling so cheerfully helpful. "Did she tell you that? She wants to kick me out?"

"No one's kicking you out, Tina, that's what Daniel is *saying*," Alison reassured me, a little too nicely.

"You guys talked about kicking me out because I wouldn't let Lucy just barge in on me in the middle of the day?" I said, getting all worked up as fast as I could. "That is *ridiculous*."

"It is ridiculous and it's not happening," Daniel repeated, but he wasn't talking to me, he was talking to Lucy. Lucy looked him square in the face, unflinching, even though she knew she had overreached and lost.

"Well, then, maybe I'll just move in," she said. And with that she headed down the hallway, pulling out her CrackBerry and moving her thumbs over it. I looked at Daniel, reeling from whiplash and worried that maybe I had won the battle and lost the war. He shook his head and raised his shoulders in a slightly edgy dismissive shrug.

"Let it go, she doesn't mean it," he said. He was right. By the time we caught up with her, she was phoning an order for sandwiches to some deli, without asking any of us what we wanted. I got stuck with salami on rye, which I have a feeling she did on purpose. But for the next two hours the conversation stayed on boring lawyer issues, and everyone behaved themselves and I was nearly rid of them by eight, when Alison started cheerfully clearing the paper plates off the coffee table. She took the trash into the kitchen while Lucy droned on about our court date and the deposition schedules and how Mr. Long was going to testify on Mom's behalf even though the opposition's attorney had tried to have him barred from the proceedings because of a conflict of interest, but our attorney had pulled some unbelievably clever move and successfully quashed their motions. Seriously, it was so devious and boring I thought my head was going to explode, when Alison breezed back into the room and held up the little green sweater.

"What's this?" she asked, cheerfully curious.

I froze. I don't know why, because usually I am a much more fluid liar. "Oh," I said, feeling my face turn red. Lucy looked at me, her antennae at full alert.

"What is it?" she asked.

"It's a sweater, a children's sweater," Alison told her. "I found it in the kitchen, on the counter."

Why I had left that thing on the counter is anybody's guess. It was the only thing I hadn't put away, but why on earth did I leave it out in plain sight? I wracked my brain trying to figure out what I had been thinking, while Alison was holding it up and admiring it, running her fingers down one of the cables and smiling. She wants to have kids so badly that even holding a piece of kids' clothing can make her shyly hopeful.

"It looks like it's handmade," she observed. "Isn't it sweet?"

"Adorable," said Lucy, taking the sweater from Alison and looking at it, then looking up at me. "Where did it come from, Tina?"

"I found it," I said. My brain was full of oatmeal and molasses. The secret I was keeping from them was so large it was making me catastrophically stupid.

"I've been over every inch of this apartment, and all the closets are empty," Lucy observed, not buying it. "Where was it?"

"Oh, not here, I didn't find it here," I said, recovering finally. "I took a walk over to Amsterdam and there was a stoop sale."

"You bought it at a stoop sale? Why?" asked Lucy.

"For the little girl upstairs." What a relief, my brain was starting to function again. The lies were coming thick and fast. "It was only a dollar and I thought it might be a nice way to just, you know, build on the relationship."

"Very smart," Daniel said, nodding to himself. Lucy handed it back to Alison, who folded it up and set it softly on the arm of the couch. And then, ten minutes later, she mentioned that she was tired, and she and Daniel headed for the door.

Lucy did not follow immediately. She wasn't going to punish me any more for locking her out, but she knew it would look weak to leave when Alison decided it was time to go, and she was tired of looking weak. So she lingered on the couch, checking her e-mails yet again. I, however, jumped up and said, "I'll walk you to the door!" Which had the advantage of looking proprietary and affording me a moment alone with Alison while Daniel went over to the elevator.

"Hey, Alison," I whispered, yanking her back into the apartment for a split second. "Can I ask you something?"

She looked at me, surprised and immediately worried by my conspiratorial tone. When we were teenagers, I had tried once or twice to get her to side with me against Lucy, and it never ended well. Her default position in times of family conflict was a sort of worried neutrality.

"It's really late, Tina," Alison said, edging toward the door. "I have to be at work early tomorrow."

"Do you know how Mom met Bill?" I asked.

She blinked, startled, then glanced at the floor. When she looked up, she made a little face, like she felt sorry for me.

"She was his housekeeper, is that what you mean?" Alison said.

"You knew that she was his cleaning lady?"

"For heaven's sake. You know they don't call it that anymore."

"What would you call it?"

"I don't know. What did you call it while you were out there at the Delaware Water Gap—you were a 'caretaker' or something. A lot of people do it, it's a good way to make money without paying taxes."

"She needed money?"

"She always needed money, you knew that."

"I just don't understand why nobody told me."

"Probably because nobody could find you half the time. Look, is there a problem?"

"Did she clean for other people?" I asked.

"What does it matter now?" said Alison.

"I just want to know."

"Yeah, Tina," said Alison. "She was a cleaning lady. That's what she was doing when she met Bill."

"Elevator's here," said Daniel from the hallway. "Are you coming?"

Alison looked at the door and then back at me, and I realized it wasn't that she felt sorry for me. It was more like she thought I was stupid. "Look," she said. "Be nice to Lucy, okay? It's okay what she's doing, it's what Mom wanted. She wanted us to have something."

"Did Mom tell you that, that she wanted us to have Bill's apartment?"

"Don't make life so hard, Tina, *please*. It's always so hard with you. Daniel says that if you don't screw this up we have a really good shot at winning. It doesn't matter how it happened, we could win. We could win, Tina! We could win."

"Alison, I cannot hold this elevator forever!"

"I have to go, Tina. It's going to be fine!" she said. She squeezed my hand. "Don't screw this up! We could *win*."

16

I DISCOVERED LOTS OF BOOKS ABOUT THE ARCHITECTURE OF OLD New York in the boxes in that lost room, all with little scraps of paper taped to the pages that told the story of the Livingston Mansion Apartment, which is an important apartment, as apartments go. I had never thought of apartments as being important, but now that I was staying in this one, I could see their point. The Livingston Mansion Apartment was the grandest of the grand apartments in the Edgewood, which was the grandest of New York apartment buildings when it was built in 1876. The Livingstons were an important New York family, one of the four hundred most important, or at least one of the four hundred families who considered themselves the most important, and Sophie Drinan was a Livingston, the last of the Livingstons, in fact. The story of her life, as told by her photographs, was elegant and thrilling. Pictures from all those books, plus the photos of her childhood, showed a home so lavish in its grandeur that it took me a while to figure out that it really was my deserted and decaying apartment.

Sophie was a good-looking kid, but her school pictures were horrible. As she grew up, her dark hair looked more starched and insane, developing into corny little bouffants that were clearly someone else's idea of pretty, because no seven-year-old thinks her hair should look like that. The crazy starched hair unfortunately followed her into high school. In a bunch of formal shots, each evening gown was more astonishing than the last, but she had truly bad hair. A tidy stack of yearbooks from the Brearley School had pictures of her in plaid uniforms but her hair looked more normal. They showed her acting up a storm in some school play and giving a thumbs-up to the camera after a field hockey game, for which she was wearing baggy shorts and a T-shirt, with her hair in a ponytail.

In the next stack were more photo albums, and Sophie's look shifted suddenly and radically into hippie chick/Janis Joplin chic. Cowboy boots and long skirts, tiny little tank tops, hair down her back and in her face, boyfriends in beards and blue jeans hanging all over her. At one point she seems to have had one of those crazy perms that no one would even consider anymore, and in another photo she had cut her hair down to nothing. Then came the wedding album. This was my first look at Bill, the man who had commandeered my mother and left nothing to show for it but old underwear and mystery novels and some pretty good red wine. In the wedding pictures he looked young and terrified. He squinted, he had a bad haircut, and his suit was starting to wrinkle. The groomsmen, of whom there were seven, seemed smoother but unremarkable, all stiff smiles and identical boutonnieres, and the bridesmaids were equally unremarkable, wearing narrow pink sheaths with empire waists and matching headbands. The maid of honor's dress flushed into a darker, mustier shade of rose, but her transparent complexion was too pale for it, so she looked like a person standing inside a dress instead of wearing it. Bill looked hot and nervous next to all of them.

In the middle of all this upscale insanity, Sophie truly looked spectacular. Her wedding dress was pristine white satin, with a low scalloped neckline and a tight bodice that came to a perfect point at her waist, like the dress Sleeping Beauty wore when she pricked her finger and fell asleep in the Disney movie. Her gown had miles of train and she wore a huge tulle veil held in place by a ridiculous little pillbox hat. Somehow, she pulled it off, but I hated her for it. Honestly, I hated them all.

I did. I hated these people. I couldn't believe the haircuts, the phony grins, the expensive dresses that no one ever wore more than once—all the smug details that money could buy, I hated all of it. The cover of the wedding album was draped in white stuffed satin with a big heart fixed right in the center that actually proclaimed, in gold stitching, *Forever.* The whole thing made you want to throw up and then just throw the book at the wall. Instead I dumped it back into its box and went back into the room to see what else I could find. I couldn't stand these people, and I couldn't get enough of them. Sophie seemed just perfect. I hated her.

My hunt through the boxes yielded more cowboy boots—which, after seeing pictures of Sophie wearing them, seemed almost eerie in their reality—and lots of thin tights, the kind you wear under skirts and with boots in the winter. I also found four full boxes of wool yarn in about sixteen colors, some of it still in skeins, some of it knitted onto needles and abandoned—half-finished pieces of half-imagined sweaters. There was a box with watercolor paper stuck together at the edges, some matte cutters, and dried-up tubes of time-frozen inks.

All of the leftovers from so many arts and crafts projects started to get to me—my mom did that with us when she wasn't loaded, projects with yarn and glitter glue and linoleum cutters—why the hell do you think I tried to be a pottery major?—so my opinion of Sophie was swinging back in her favor. And then the ghost reappeared.

I knew it wasn't a ghost; I really did. Somebody in the apartment next door or on another floor even was having a crying jag right next to an air duct or something. But seriously, it sounded so much like a person stuck in a different time that it made your skin crawl. I was sitting next to the doorway, looking through the boxes by the light of the laundry room, and I could hear the ghost deep in the wall all the way across the room, buried by boxes I hadn't gone through yet. Her unseen and unintelligible argument was so drenched in heartsick rage that I decided she wanted to kill me for going through her stuff. So I quit for the night and went back to my sorry little adopted bedroom, where I stared at the sunset painted on the wall and wondered what had happened to that woman and why my beautiful apartment was so barren and lost that there was no room for anyone but me in it now. I lay there for a long time, wondering if the ghost would follow me, but she didn't; she was definitely trapped in that secret room. She was trapped in the night too. I heard her only after dark; during the daytime all was quiet.

Meanwhile, the legal machinations of all the various lawyers were churning away in some other cosmos, and for the moment Alison and Lucy and Daniel had decided to leave me be. I was free to keep pawing through somebody elses's stuff. And after spending a couple more days going through boxes of dishware and towels and children's toys and old ski boots, I found more photographs.

There were about six hundred of them, tossed into a box with a bunch of old negatives and also pasted in three chaotic photo albums with no concern for chronology whatsoever. One album, covered with dark blue leather, held dozens of photographs of two laughing little boys, followed by pages and pages of one laughing little baby, and then pictures of Sophie pregnant and holding the hand of one little boy, and then Sophie, alone, laughing at the camera, pregnant. After the strict chronology of the yearbooks and the wedding album, the chaos of photos had a startling effect; I thought, oh I'm going back in time, and then forward in time, and then backward and forward at once. The other two albums were the same, just a mess of people's lives with no sense of order.

Sophie's boys seemed to be having a pretty good time of it. She took a lot of pictures of them running in the park, eating ice cream, blowing out candles, riding scooters. As their ages leapt back and forth, the brothers maintained a goodwill for each other and the camera that was startling in its consistency, particularly given the grim weariness of the men I now knew as Doug and Pete Drinan. Even well into adolescence, both were blessed with what looked like wealth and happiness, cute girlfriends, fun birthday parties, and an unbelievably cool apartment to grow up in. Some people who may have been grandparents showed up occasionally, and a couple of girlfriends, or cousins maybe, were here and there. Bill was there too, grumpy, a little sloppy, often holding a glass of wine. And Sophie would show up still looking like a hippie chick in long sweaters and Indian-print skirts and cowboy boots. At some point she must have thought she was getting fat, because she started wearing big loose shirts open at the neck over a tank top. Then, when she felt skinny again, she would wear just the tank top without the shirt. In some photos she was wearing wire-rimmed glasses, but she didn't seem to wear them all the time. Or maybe all the back-and-forth with her weight and the hair and the glasses was because the pictures were so jumbled up. Her mouth was wide, her nose a little too long, and her eyes were large and expressive. At a certain point, it started to seem like she couldn't look at a camera without mugging a bit. Her hair was dark brown, and it never got gray.

So that is what the Drinans' lives looked like. After the high school proms and cotillions and the one big wedding, there were no formal pictures of Sophie or Bill. Except for one. She and Bill are holding hands and smiling at the camera. They are standing in front of a white marble mantel that has three golden glass vases on it and an antique black clock with tiny gilt feet. The wall is painted a kind of pearly dove gray, and you can see from the elaborate carving on the mantelpiece that it's the one in the great room; they are having their picture taken in their home before going out for the evening. The camera flash has caught Sophie and Bill slightly by surprise, but even so, both of them look traditionally glamorous; he is in a blue suit, and she wears a tight little black dress with pearls and low heels. Her hair is up in a classic knot, which shows off her neck. They look happy and excited for a night out. Except for the fact that they are standing in the greatest apartment I've ever seen, they look just like my mom and dad. You can practically see the kids in pajamas watching in awe while the babysitter frames the picture.

It took me a couple days to hunt it down, but then I thought a bit and pulled out the garment bag that was way in back of everything. Sure enough, the dress was there, carefully folded inside one of the flashier evening gowns from her high school days. So well protected, it looked pristine, almost as if it came straight off the rack. It was a gorgeous dress—black silk taffeta with a fitted bodice and a plunging back neckline. The shoes I found by going back to the first boxes I had looked through; they were slightly scuffed around the back of the heels, and they were crushed a little by having had something heavy placed on them. They were also a little dusty.

The pearls I finally found in another box, tossed in as if nobody cared what happened to them, even though they were clearly the real thing, not fake like the jewelry my mom wore when she got dressed up. But there they were, curled at the bottom of the box, a double rope of perfectly matched champagne-colored pearls held together by a heavy gold clasp encrusted with real diamonds. That necklace should have been carefully laid in some dark blue velvet-lined case from Tiffany's or some store so exclusive that people like me have never even heard of it. Anyway, there it was, in a brown cardboard box, a perfect pearl necklace, lost in a disorderly clutter of shoes, plastic dishes, everyday spoons, and more shoes.

17

I CARRIED THE PEARLS OUT INTO THE GRIM LITTLE TV ROOM AND sat on that lousy couch and wondered what to do. I was afraid to tell anybody what I had found, because I knew Lucy would insist that the stuff was all part of the estate, which meant, according to her, that it was ours. And then she would have appraisers from Sotheby's show up and paw through everything to see if they could find all the really valuable bits, and then those Drinan brothers would again lose everything they had already lost, only this time they wouldn't even know it.

I didn't know what to do. I didn't know what had happened in that crazy apartment, to Bill, or my mom, or Sophie, or those boys. The only person who might be able to cough up a few answers, I realized, was Len.

And that was when I realized I had not seen Len for some time. I couldn't remember the last time he had stopped by, but a quick investigation of the mossery confirmed that his absence from the apartment had been long enough to have a devastating effect. A dying mossery doesn't look like what you would normally call a disaster, in that there isn't a lot of spectacle involved, but when I poked my head into the kitchen and turned on the lights, an unmistakable air of doom hovered over all the beds. It was as if the breath of the room had tiptoed away; it felt kind of cold and dry and was simply too silent for anything to be growing. If you had never been in there before you might not notice anything, but the air wasn't moist, and the gentle tune of the water being pumped through the teeny-tiny irrigation system had gone silent. The pumps were dead, and the moss was slowly dying.

It is amazing how panicked a person can get over some dying moss. My heart started to race, and I began pawing around the counter to find the controls to turn the pumps back on. I had watched Len refill them once, so I knew the switches ran along the wall to the right of some beds of a normally purple-tinged forest moss, which had now turned a disturbing shade of gray. But when I turned the switches on, they instantly switched off, with a decisiveness that was frankly startling in an inanimate object. Because I was so worried about the moss, the water pumps' aggressive refusal to return to life seemed upsetting and perverse until I realized that they were clicking off because there was no water. There was just no water in the trays, in the beds, in the irrigation tubes, anywhere. I hurried to the sink, picked up one of the plastic watering cans lined up there, filled it from the tap, and immediately started watering all the beds. Then I refilled the three reserve tanks, which were tucked in corners around the room, and I tried turning on the irrigation system again. It clunked a few times, but then it started whirring and humming, and the sound of water running around the edges of the trays reemerged from the silence.

Once I had the water going, I felt better, but every one of those moss beds was in serious trouble. Most of them had gone brown; the previously spongy soil was hard and even brittle in places, and water was now pooling in little brown puddles instead of soaking in gently the way it was supposed to. Len had all sorts of moss-sized gardening implements lined up on the open shelves above the sink, but I had no idea what to do with any of them; watering was pretty much the end of my restorative capabilities. Besides, I thought, where in the world is Len?

After I checked my phone again, I tried to call him, but he didn't pick up, and his machine was turned off. So I went up to his landing and knocked on the door. For a moment, I thought I heard a vague rustle of movement, like someone was in there, so I pounded harder and yelled that the moss was in real trouble and he needed to come down and take a look at it. There was no response. So then I went down to the lobby.

"Hey, Frank! How're you doing?" I asked.

"Yeah. Tina. Hi," Frank said, with less enthusiasm than I was exhibiting. He was sorting through the mail and doing a crossword puzzle at the same time. "Haven't seen you in a while."

"I've been kind of busy."

"Good for you."

It was a little troubling to have Frank bristle at me, but I was worried, so I got right to the point. "Hey, have you seen Len?"

"Not today," he said, still not looking at me.

"Did you see him yesterday?"

"No, Tina, I didn't."

"Well, when was the last time you saw him?"

This conversation was obviously annoying the new, mean Frank. "It's not my job to keep track of people, that is not my job description."

"No, I know, I just—"

"And you don't have any rights here."

"What?" I said, surprised at how direct and horrible that statement sounded, coming from Frank. I was truly hurt. I guess my face must have made that clear, because he flushed a little, like he was privately ashamed for half a second, before the mean version of himself could take over again. It took the sting out of what came next.

"I just mean you're staying here, okay, obviously no one can stop you from doing that, but it's unclear what's going to happen next. People want to make sure you are aware of that."

"Of course I'm aware of that."

"All right, then."

"So like . . . what? Has the building been talking about us?"

Frank glanced up, then took a small step back, like he wanted to make sure he wasn't too close to me. "Yeah, the building has been talking," he said.

More than anything else, that little step smacked me in the heart, but there was nothing I could do about it. Frank worked for the building. I tried to remember why I had come down to speak to him.

"What about Len?" I said finally. "I really need to get hold of him, there's something he needs to know, and I haven't seen him for at least two weeks and now I can't get him on the phone."

Frank looked up at the ceiling as if he had to find the nerve to keep up the nasty edge, and it was hiding somewhere up there, in the corner maybe. "Like I said, it's not my job—" he started, still bristling.

"Okay, I got it, Frank! If you see him, tell him I need to talk to him, and it's *important*," I hissed. Frank turned all red, like I had really hurt his feelings. Like most nice people, he was terrible at being mean; he didn't know how to pull it off and he also didn't know how not to be hurt when someone was mean back. So of course I felt ashamed of myself immediately. It is no fun picking on nice people; I don't know why anyone ever does it, honestly.

Back up in my apartment, with no idea what I was doing, I did my best to fertilize and feed the dying moss. In the corner of the kitchen, Len had stashed dozens of plant nutrients—potassium, nitrogen, magnesium, something with an oxidized-silicate formula, arsenic, and bromides—all of which had different functions. His main supply of plant foods came in little glass bottles with droppers, and you had to mix them up into various solutions before you poured them into a thing that looked like an IV lead, which fed into the water supply. It took me three hours of following the pictures on the backs of the boxes and putting that information together with what I had seen Len do the few times I had watched him work in there before I felt like I might be making progress. I couldn't tell if I was giving any of the plants the right amount of these different versions of fertilizer, but since I still couldn't find Len—his phone just rang and rang whenever I tried him—I was left with my own haphazard guesswork.

After two days of working on the moss with mixed results, I decided I'd better get help.

I took the express train from Seventy-second Street to Park Slope, where the Eastern Parkway stop lets you off right at the front gate of the Brooklyn Botanic Garden. When I told the man in the ticket booth that I was looking for Charlotte Colbert, he didn't even make me buy a ticket, he just directed me to the conservatory, where another cheerfully helpful employee pointed me toward a side room that held a subdivision of bonsai trees.

The bonsai room was bright and hot and full of light. Long wooden tables along the walls held a series of bonsai trees, each more surreal than the last. There was a tiny maple with a whorled trunk and perfect five-point leaves, a miniature stand of beech trees with whittled bark, a tiny juniper with elegantly twirling branches. An impossibly miniature dogwood gracefully presented fresh miniature pink blossoms. An ancient bald cypress, I learned from the metal plaque on its base, was over three hundred years old. Even though there were no other visitors, it took me a moment to locate Len's daughter, Charlie; she had drifted into a tiny alcove just off the main display area, her entire attention focused on a miniature pine tree, which she was pruning with extraordinary care. As Charlie looked up, in the same plant-induced daze I had seen on Len's face, I realized that all of the trees in the room were growing in trays covered in moss.

"Can I help you?" she said, not recognizing me.

"Hi, I'm Tina, Tina Finn? I met you at your dad's apartment."

"My father?" She didn't actually perk up at this; what she did was more the opposite. She set her pruning shears on the table and looked down as if trying to decide whether or not to say something she might regret. "What about him?"

"Have you talked to him?"

"Who are you again?" Charlie folded her arms over her chest. When I first met her in the foyer of Len's apartment, she had struck me as a sort of friendly soldier. The friendly part of the equation had, unfortunately, evaporated.

"I live in his building, and he keeps his moss in my apartment, and I haven't been able to get hold of him for, well, a while. Have you heard from him?"

Charlie continued to consider me like a piece of stinkgrass. "No," she finally said, turning back to her miniature pine tree, as if that was all I could possibly expect out of her.

"Well, if you do hear from him, could you ask him to call me? Here, I can write my number down for you," I offered, trying not to sound too desperate.

"Look, I don't know what you think you're doing with my father," Charlie said, cutting me off. "But you've made a colossal mistake if you think I'm going to help you."

"I'm not doing anything with your father. I'm just helping him with his moss."

"That's the first time I've heard it called that," she said with a sneer.

"Look," I retorted. "There are plenty of people who have good reason to be mad at me, but trust me, you are not one of them. I'm telling you the truth. Why would I make something like this up? The kitchen of my apartment is just covered with moss beds, and the moss is dying because he hasn't shown up to take care of it for ages. I didn't even notice at first, because I was not paying attention, but now, I'm telling you, the moss is *dying*. It's dying and I don't know how to take care of it and I can't find Len. Did he go somewhere? Did he take a trip? Do you know where he is? And if you don't know where he is, can you at least tell me what to *do*? There's moss around all these little bonsai trees, and you clearly know what you're doing. I don't know *what* I am doing and the moss is going to *die*. My mother helped Len take care of the moss before she died. She was . . . she was a good person." This statement came out of my mouth so unexpectedly that I suddenly felt overwhelmed. "She took care of his moss. I don't want it to die."

While Charlie did not seem impressed, she was at least listening. "So you're not some sort of hooker?" she asked.

"Why does everyone think that?" I asked, pinching my eyes quickly so she couldn't see that I was crying.

"I don't know why other people think that, but the last time I saw you, you were hanging around my dad's apartment and he handed you hundreds of dollars and then told you to get lost. That would be why *I* think that."

"That was for the *moss*," I said, trying not to get too defensive. "Are you going to help me save the stupid moss, or are we just going to let it die?"

Unlike Len, Charlie was not much of a talker. She didn't say anything on the subway ride back to my apartment, and she didn't say anything in the elevator, and she didn't say anything even when I took her into the kitchen, flipped on the lights, and showed her the catastrophic mess that had once been a mossery. She took in the situation from the doorway for a moment, then took a step forward to consider each bed separately. She looked up and over, immediately spotting the open shelf with the itty-bitty gardening implements, as if she knew they would be there because that was the only logical place for them. She picked up a miniature trowel and turned back to the moss, gently press-

ing it and her fingers into the edges of the soil, searching for some mysterious force under the surface that I would never understand. She did that
for a full minute before I finally asked, "So can you fix this, or are they all
going to die?"

"You fed them," she observed, without answering the question.

"I tried."

"Do you remember what you did?"

"I did whatever the plant food told me to do," I said. I started pulling out all the different kinds of plant food and fertilizer from under the
table and handing them to her. "He's got the directions written on the
top of the containers, so I tried to do what they said, but who knows? I
didn't know if I should be mixing everything up or putting it on top of
the moss or underneath it, and he has these little spiky things, so I thought
maybe I should dig holes in the beds and then put the food in the hole or
something. I was kind of making it up as I went along."

"Yes, I see," Charlie said, opening one of the little plastic containers
and rubbing the black stuff between her fingers. She held her finger up
to her nose, breathing it in quietly, and then she tasted it with the tip of
her tongue. She looked at another container in her hand, then glanced
back at the moss. "Okay," she said. "Can you get me a ham sandwich?"

"A ham sandwich?"

"Yeah, I'm kind of hungry. There's got to be some sort of deli
around here. I'd like a ham sandwich."

"Oh. Sure. I'm just, I guess I assumed that people like you were
vegetarians."

"No," she said, and went back to work.

Three hours later, I was lying on the little bed in my bedroom, reading a passably interesting mystery novel about some detective who was as
screwed-up as the killers he was chasing. He drank too much and had
trouble opening up to people, and he had a cynical weariness that came
from seeing too much suffering, and he distrusted women, who all found
him irresistibly sexy. In short, he was such a dead ringer for Pete Drinan
that I could not help but wonder if they taught those specific qualities in
detective school. I picked up one of the photo albums from the lost room
and looked at the pictures of the young Pete and Doug when they were in

high school and grinning at the camera with all the money and good looks that New York privilege could buy. How could someone who grew up in the swankest apartment in New York and whose brother was some sort of big-deal egghead at the Dalton School end up in the NYPD?

"You're all right for now," Charlie announced, standing in the doorway.

I shoved the photo album back into its hiding place between the bed and the wall. Her eyes flickered as she watched me, but she didn't comment. Like Len, she apparently was not interested in anything in that apartment except the moss. She took a half step into the room and held out a sheet of lined notebook paper with tidy rows of information neatly inscribed in tight handwriting. "You need to make sure there's enough water in the pumps every morning and then add the minerals and fertilizers according to this schedule. You did a pretty good job faking your way through this."

"Then you think we can save most of it?"

She shrugged; it was a stupid question, but she seemed used to dealing with people who didn't understand plants. "Moss is pretty sturdy," she explained. "It goes dormant when humidity or ground conditions become hostile to growth. How long was it, that the water was turned off?"

"I don't know exactly. Maybe two weeks? Len always just came down and worked there every few days and then he . . . stopped."

That was the information she was after. She folded her arms and leaned against the doorjamb, acting like she didn't give a shit, but her crazy eyes were thinking.

"And you tried to get hold of him."

"I called him and I went up there and knocked on the door a bunch of times. I think he's in there, but he didn't answer. And he's not answering the phone, obviously. I mean, I wouldn't have come looking for you if he had. Is something going on with him?"

Charlie lifted her arms into the air, clasped them backward over her head, then let them float to her sides. It made her look really tall, like a tree spirit, standing in the doorway of my strange little room with the sunset on the wall and the stars and planets glued to the ceiling. Then she twisted swiftly back and forth at the waist and bent forward until her hands touched the ground in front of her, doing a few yoga stretches while she considered how much to tell me.

"Look," I said, trying to prompt her. "Do you think something's happened to him? I mean, do you think he's hurt or—"

"He's up there. I came by a couple of nights ago and watched from the park with a pair of binoculars. The lights were on and he's in there."

This was a pretty interesting piece of information. "You came by and spied on him?"

"Yes," she responded, completely without apology. "He stole something from me and I need to get it back."

"That plant you brought him? That little boy's plant?"

"Do you actually not know?"

"Of *course* I don't know," I said, trying not to sound too annoyed. "I mean, I think it's obvious I'm not a plant person, and since no one has told me anything, I don't know anything."

"It's possibly what's on the wall in your kitchen," she told me. I just stared at her. "The plate. From the *Sarum Horae. Madrigaris antiaris toxi-caria.*"

"The picture of the tree?"

"Yes. We're not precisely sure—no one knows what that plant really looks like. No one's seen it for a millennium."

"And you think that's what those seeds were—seeds to some medieval tree?"

"It's older than that," she corrected me, ignoring my incredulous tone. "There are records of it being cultivated on the island of Malta as early as the fourth century. Some people think it was one of the psycho-tropic plants used in the Greek rituals at Elysium, which, if that is true, would make it quite a bit older."

"Psychotropic," I said. "So it's like a drug plant?"

"It is historically understood to have promoted altered states, yes," she replied.

"So what do you do, you smoke it?"

"My impulse would be to study it. No one knows if the rumors about its ritualistic uses are accurate. No one has seen that plant in any shape or form for a long, long time. If it is what we think, it's worth a lot of money, which Benny could use. That's why I brought him over here. I thought he would be able to help us. And protect it. It's so improbable, but if it's true, we needed protection. So I took that boy, who trusted me, and I told him my father would help us. And now he, apparently, he has decided . . . I don't know what he's decided," she admitted, looking off. "I would like to kill him."

I didn't know what to say. I thought she was kidding, you know, but she was so tall and fierce and had those strange blue eyes, it certainly sounded like she meant it. In the few times I had been around Len and Charlie and that little boy Benny, they had all struck me as special. But now they were sounding and acting like everyone else, just people who had a hole in their hearts and only one thing could fill it.

Charlie smiled at me, one of those old smiles that admit things to people you barely know. "It's my fault. I should never have trusted him," she said.

"He's your father," I said.

"Yeah." She turned around and looked at the stars on the ceiling of the little bedroom. "This is a nice room. How come you don't have any furniture in this place?"

"It's kind of a long story," I said. "If I hear from Len, do you want me to have him call you?"

"I think it might be better if you just called me. My phone number is there." She tipped her chin toward the sheet of watering and feeding instructions in my hand. "Thanks for the ham sandwich." And with that she left.

18

Ira Grossman and his offices were the last word in swank. His waiting room was paneled in actual wood and had several low black leather couches and chairs with stylishly sloped backs, plus sleek glass coffee tables with international newspapers fanned out neatly across the glittering surfaces. You expected to see a murderous widow draped in front of the narrow, knifelike windows, which overlooked a particularly dense canyon of skyscrapers in Midtown. Unfortunately, it was just us, although each and every one of us was dressed better than we had been on the day we buried Mom and ended up in Stuart Long's crummy offices farther downtown.

Grossman turned out to be just as slick as his waiting room. He wore a flawlessly fitted double-breasted suit with the thinnest of pinstripes. His shoes were fiercely and evenly polished to a rich meaty brown. As he crossed the room with capable purpose, honestly, you couldn't help but notice the perfection of those shoes. So while everyone in my family was standing and greeting this killer, my eyes kept slipping back to the floor. Those dazzling shoes smiled up at me like crocodiles.

"You must be Tina," Grossman said, reaching out to shake. I looked up just in time to catch him giving me the once-over; Lucy had clearly filled him in on my questionable past, only the facts had, as usual, backfired on her. He held my hand about two and a half seconds longer than strictly necessary, and there was the slightest suggestion in his smile that he was thinking about licking his chops. No question, like many clever and successful men, Ira Grossman liked bad girls.

"Let's get to it, shall we?" he asked me.

"That would be wonderful!" Alison trilled, annoyed. It was always hard on her, the way guys flirted with me. She was the oldest, but from high school on, it was clear that Lucy was destined to be the smartest and that I was the one boys liked. Alison ended up with the cute, stable husband while Lucy lived alone and I careened from one loser to the next, but it didn't seem to make a difference, finally. Whenever creepy guys in suits started sniffing around me, Alison took it as a personal offense.

"Yeah, let's get to this, Mr. Grossman." I smiled, turning up the wattage. I even reached over and touched him lightly on the sleeve of that astonishing suit. "I looked through all those papers Lucy gave me, and I couldn't make head or tail out of them. I hope you can explain to me what really is going on here, because I *suck* at math."

"It is a bit complicated," Grossman told me, infinitely touched and turned on by my putative stupidity and maybe my emphasis on *suck*. "Let's go to the conference room. Would anyone like some coffee?"

"I'll take a Coke," I said, trying to make it sound like I wanted to have sex. I thought Lucy was going to gag and Alison would throttle me, or at least ask Daniel to do it. I didn't care. Both my sisters were really getting on my nerves. They didn't have a clue what was going on. I was the one who was living in the apartment, and I was the one who had found the lost room, and I was the one who knew everyone in the building, and they just didn't have a clue. This was my oh-so-enlightened position at the time. It gave me permission to be snarky and superior to them while they were being snarky and superior to me.

The meeting started simply enough, with piles of papers that we were told to sign for no apparent reason, in triplicate.

"Since Lucille has been acting as administratrix for the past two months, we do need to formalize that situation immediately," Grossman announced as we took our seats around the solid black conference table. "There's no need to backdate the documents since we don't even have a court date yet in the matter of the execution of your mother's estate, but in the negotiations with Mr. Drinan's estate it will occasionally be necessary for a representative of your mother's estate to make a physical appearance. She will need to be authorized to negotiate on your behalf legally as in fact."

"What?" I said.

"Just sign it, Tina," Daniel advised me, helpfully turning my copies of the docs to the signature pages. Alison had already bent her head over her set and was writing her name with a schoolgirl's determination, like she was trying to teach me a lesson by following the rules to a T.

Lucy was a little more subtle, but she was also doing what she was told as quickly and efficiently as possible, leaving me quite openly in the position of Problem Child as I sat there, pen in hand, not signing a thing.

"This makes Lucy *what*? 'Adminis*tra*trix?'" I asked. "How come she gets to do that?"

"It's just a legal designation; she doesn't actually 'do' anything," Grossman assured me, with just enough of a conspiratorial gleam in his eye to register what an administratrix might actually "do" in private. "The courts require that the estate designate a petitioner to represent all interested parties as a matter of expediency, but if there is a discrepancy in the wishes of the interested parties, you and your sister will have the opportunity to appear and object in court." Both Alison and Lucy pretended that they understood this nonsense and shoved their carefully signed documents across the table to him. He took them with one hand while passing different documents back to Lucy with the other. They all ignored the fact that not only had I not finished signing my documents, I had not even started. I had not even picked up one of the plain little ballpoint pens Grossman had so helpfully pushed in front of everyone.

"This authorizes me to act as your legal representative in this matter and to schedule payments of monies from the estate," he explained, quickly moving through the docs. "This authorizes the previous attorney for the estate to forward to me all files pertaining to the estate."

"What monies, there are no monies," I said.

"There will be," Lucy replied, signing away.

"Yeah, but when? How can we hire this guy—excuse me, Mr. Grossman—"

"Ira, please."

"Ira, I'm having a little trouble catching up with this."

"Which would be why Lucy is the administratrix," Alison muttered.

"Sure, okay, sure, Alison, fine," I started, getting testy. "I'm still allowed to ask a few questions."

"Absolutely, that's why we're here," Grossman reassured the room. "These situations are always complicated. The fact is, however, that the Drinans are moving ahead with the challenge to their father's will, and you and your sisters have already been designated as interested parties in that action. They've scheduled a deposition of your mother's attorney, and the likelihood is that they will attempt to depose all three of you. We're hoping to avoid that, which is why the documents need to be signed so that Lucille can be the point person, otherwise all three of you will have to give depositions. Of course, we don't think anything unsavory or contradictory would come out of a situation like that, but it's an issue of controlling the odds."

"Odds of what?"

"The odds of something coming out," Daniel inserted bluntly.

"What could come out?" I asked.

"The Drinans are claiming that your mother kept their father in a state of constant inebriation, during which she coerced him into changing his will, which disinherited them and left the entirety of the estate to her," Grossman stated bluntly.

"That's ridiculous," I said, out of loyalty. "Mom *coerced* him? He wouldn't let Mom out of his sight, she was his prisoner, and if he had a drinking problem that wasn't her fault."

"What makes you think he had a drinking problem?" Grossman asked me, suddenly serious.

"The first day we got there, alcohol was everywhere," I said.

"This was the day of your mother's funeral?"

"Yes. No furniture, just vodka and red wine."

"That was a full three weeks after her husband's death," Grossman said pointedly.

"Well, I didn't know exactly when Bill died," I started.

"She didn't tell you?" Grossman asked.

"Not right when it happened."

"When did she tell you?"

Lucy, Daniel, and Alison were all staring at me, silent, as if I were about to betray them. "She . . ." I started, and then I turned all red as the truth occurred to me. "She never told me that he died. I didn't know."

"What did you think when you heard that he had died? Didn't it strike you as odd that she never informed you of it?"

"I didn't actually think about it. I was upset about Mom. I thought Bill had died a long time ago." Lucy, Daniel, and Alison kept staring at me like a jury. It was really creepy. "What is the big deal? They didn't know either," I commented, defensive.

"I knew," said Lucy.

"How could you know?"

"I knew because she told me. She was very sad, and she called and told me that Bill had died, but she didn't want us to come to the funeral." Lucy stared at me coolly, like this was common knowledge. Next to her, Alison stiffened her spine fiercely.

"Did you know too, Alison?"

"Yes," Alison whispered. "I did."

"So that would be another thing you didn't tell me."

"Mom told her not to," Lucy inserted.

"Mom *told* you not to tell me her *husband* died? The way she *told* you both not to tell me that she was cleaning houses. She told you not to tell me any of that." I looked at both of them. Lucy looked back, unapologetic; Alison looked at the floor.

"Yes, she did," Lucy stated.

"Why?"

"I don't know," said Lucy, very plain. Alison's lips were pursed. Daniel just kept staring at me.

"This is good, this is good," Grossman explained smoothly. "It's wonderful to see you all work out the complications of this situation in terms of communication and confusion. Death is often like this. Certain people know things, others don't know those things. My understanding, Tina, is that you were out of touch with the family for a while. But your personal circumstances—where you were, what you

were doing—are completely irrelevant to the court case and have no
bearing on the details of the settlement. So you see why it would be
important to keep these personal discussions out of the court record."
Grossman continued smiling at me, like he and I shared a secret, even
though it was clear that we did not. "And the amount of alcohol that
your mother was keeping in the apartment, even though she was the
only person living there, is not something that the court is going to be
able to ignore, since it is at the heart of the Drinans' case."

"Bill was a big drinker," I said.

"By your own admission you never met Bill," Grossman reminded
me. "And your mother did not share information with you about her
marriage. Your testimony is not going to be helpful in this matter. But
please don't worry about this," Grossman hastened to reassure me, taking the opportunity to reach over and press my hand. "They don't have
much of an argument, given their own family history. The burden of
proof is on them. I'm just saying we don't want to help them out if we
can easily avoid it. The first step is making it difficult for them to depose all three of you. We need to name an administrator. Both Alison
and Lucy feel that Lucy is the right person for that job. And since you've
taken on so much responsibility for the daily upkeep of the apartment,
no one wants to burden you further."

This guy was a really smooth customer. It occurred to me that he
had been flirting with me because he thought it would get him what he
wanted, which was my signature and nothing else. It also occurred to me
that Alison and Lucy were lying—that Mom hadn't called anybody when
Bill died, because she just hadn't—and they had secretly consulted with
this new smooth lawyer, who told them they didn't need to put any of
this out there. So they had agreed among themselves to lie about it. It
occurred to me that maybe she didn't call me because I was out at the
Delaware Water Gap living in a trailer with another loser and I didn't
return phone calls. It occurred to me that maybe Mom didn't call any of
us because we weren't ever much comfort to her.

I picked up my sorry little ballpoint pen. Lucy let out her breath
with a sound that meant *finally!*, but I wasn't actually planning to go
along with this just yet. "What is . . . what . . ." I started to ask. "Just

do it, Tina!" Lucy snarled. "Alison and I have the majority vote, and we can do this with or without you! Just do it!"

"Now now, no one is being forced into anything. We absolutely want to present a united front here," Grossman announced soothingly. "Tina, do you have more questions?"

I did have a lot of questions, so many that I didn't even know where to start. Most of them were about me and my sisters and why we ended up abandoning each other and Mom, why none of us meant more to the others. But I didn't think that was what he was suggesting. I thought I'd better stick to someone else's facts for now. "When you said 'given their own family history'? The Drinans don't have much of an argument given their own family history, what does that mean?" I asked.

"Because of what happened with the first Mrs. Drinan," Grossman said, nodding like that was a very good question and he was glad I had asked it. "They may try to make that inadmissible, but it clearly relates to why and how the sons were disinherited."

"Didn't she die a long time ago?" Alison asked. "Do we have to deal with her relatives too?"

"Not at all. The apartment did, however, originally belong to her. Mr. Drinan came into possession at the time of her death. There was no question that he was the sole beneficiary. I think there were cousins or nieces, but they had no claim, then or now."

"Yeah, but if it was her apartment in the first place, doesn't that make it more of a stretch that we should get the place instead of her own sons?" I pointed out.

"You might argue that, but you could also argue that they were heavily implicated in her death," Grossman announced, like he was reporting the weather. "There were apparently a lot of recriminations between them and their father about it, but they both supported him when he made the decision to have her institutionalized."

"*What?*" I asked. "What did you just say?"

"I don't have the hospital records yet, and it's not clear that I'll be able to get them released, but according to Stuart Long they all were in agreement at first that she needed to be hospitalized. I'm told that all three of them signed the admission papers. It apparently wasn't until later that a lot of hard feelings emerged."

"Okay, wait, wait," I said, trying to catch up. It seemed an inconceivable end to the story that was lying around in scraps in my apartment. "She was *institutionalized*? And all three of them—okay—"

"The facts indicate that both his sons agreed that she should be admitted to a psychiatric facility, and then, after some period of time there—I don't know how long—she died. Obviously the hospital bears responsibility for the lack of oversight, but no legal action was ever taken. Anyway, upon her death the apartment, which was in her name, became her husband's property. That coincided with his rift with the sons, so there may have been some overlap there in terms of what they were all upset about. Our argument would be that Mr. Drinan disinherited his sons because of that situation, long before he met your mother. It's not even an argument; it's the simple truth. Your mother did nothing worse than fall in love with the man and take care of him in the last years of his life, long after his sons had abandoned him. There's no coercion involved, none that can be proven in any case."

"What was wrong with her? The first Mrs. Drinan?" Alison asked, touched and curious about Sophie's troubles.

Grossman shrugged; this part of the story wasn't relevant to the cash, so it wasn't relevant to him. "Long maintains that it was some form of depression, but there's no way to tell unless we get a look at the records, which they most certainly will not permit," he noted, looking through his papers. "And 'depression' covers a lot of ground. She could have been terribly sick or she could have just been angry."

"You can lock up people for just being angry?" Lucy asked. Like Grossman, she was not even vaguely interested; she was working her CrackBerry again. It was more of a rhetorical question.

"Well, that's a good question, but one that I have no jurisdiction to answer." Grossman smiled pleasantly. Having finished his gruesome history, he turned his full attention back to me. "Tina, do you have any more questions about the process? We do have a lot to cover today."

I stared at my ballpoint and the pile of documents in front of me.

There were three more stacks of documents at Grossman's elbow. I felt like Alice going down the rabbit hole. Nothing got simpler, it all just got weirder, meaner, richer. We were all getting richer, inch by inch, billable hour by billable hour.

"No, I'm fine," I said. "So where do I sign?"

19

The press conference at Sotheby's was dazzling. There were a lot of minions—men in suits, women in expensive, tightly fitted dresses, all of them completely confident that they belonged at Sotheby's and that you did too. Lucy was wrong when she told me I'd better buy myself some ugly clothes, because there was nothing ugly about any of these people. Maybe they were just a lot of normal people who worked for a lot of rich people, but we were the people they were working for now, so we sure as hell needed to look as rich as possible. I wore the black taffeta dress and the pearls and the low pumps that went with them. The Sotheby's minions were impressed.

Lucy managed to pull off an acceptable presence; she wore her best silk suit, gray as usual. Her hair was down, and she had had the foresight to put on a little blush and mascara, so she looked businesslike and thin but in a pretty way. Alison, unfortunately, didn't quite come up to the mark. She wore a nice red wool dress, which I know she likes, but it doesn't really suit her; it bunches around the waist and clings to her stomach in a tragic way that makes her look like a dumpy middle-aged housewife, which sadly had never occurred to her until possibly this moment. She kept looking around the room and smiling at everyone with such panicked eyes that I finally snuck around behind her and gave her a fast hug.

"You look beautiful, Alison," I said, holding her close.

"Really?" she said, hungry to believe me. She ran her fingers through her hair, which was losing its bounce because she had been fooling with it incessantly for the past twenty minutes.

"Absolutely," I told her. "That color is phenomenal on you. I wish I could wear red." She smiled at me with sad hope, which had become her habitual expression of late. Daniel came up behind us, looking around as if he didn't know her.

"I think they're about to start," he informed the air next to Alison. He was wearing a new suit, and he had gotten a haircut, short on the sides but sort of sexy and floppy over his eyes. His eyes raked back toward me and paused, impressed. "You look good, Tina," he said.

"Oh, thanks," I said, not appreciating the glint in his eye. "Look, you're right, they're starting."

The crowd seemed to be gently drifting toward the other end of the room, where a small podium awaited. We wafted along with the others, catching up with Lucy in front of the podium. "Where'd you get that?" Lucy asked, barely glancing at my dress but noting it with some approval nonetheless. As long as I showed up looking like someone who should inherit fifteen million dollars, she didn't care if I looked better than she did.

"Used-clothing place in my neighborhood," I said. "It didn't cost a thing."

"You look good, you look rich."

"That was the plan," I said. She actually smiled at this, and for a moment there was sincere relief between us that we were on the same page. I wasn't sure why we needed a big press conference before we'd even made it into court on one of these depositions or hearings or pleadings, but she and our snaky lawyer and our fancy new partner, Sotheby's, seemed to think it was a good idea. If that meant putting on a nice dress and drinking the Kool-Aid, I was happy to oblige.

Our host, someone big in Sotheby's real estate division, approached and took my hand, helping me take the last few steps up to the small staging area they had assembled for our inaugural conversation with the public. His name was Leonard, and he looked like a Leonard, all arching nose under a big head of fabulous white hair. I decided it was true that men age better than women. This guy was a skinny rich old hunk. "That piece is stunning," Leonard informed me, kissing me on the cheek. "Where did you get it?"

He was of course talking about the pearls, which were draped around my neck and held there with a fourteen-carat gold-and-diamond clasp.

"A tag sale," I said, smiling.

"The clasp is extraordinary."

"Thank you," I said, demurely.

"If you ever want to sell it, I hope you'll bring it here. We'll take very good care of you," he advised me intimately. I was about to say something sweet in response, when Alison turned and stared at me, and then the lights went haywire. The room began to pulse with a million flashes and the press conference was on its merry way.

"Thank you all for coming on this lovely day," Leonard announced into the microphone. "I feel very sure that we can make it worth your while." The small but attentive audience of reporters and real estate agents settled into an expectant hush laced with something that was either awe or greed as Leonard laid it all out for them.

"It is a rare occasion when a truly historic New York property comes on the market, one that reminds us of the very great privilege we here at Sotheby's enjoy as stewards of history. The great families of this country—the Morgans, the Rockefellers, the Clays, the Fricks—made their mark in finance, transportation, industry, the art world. They also left their mark in the bricks and stones and mortar that are the heart and soul of New York. Ladies and gentlemen, today it is my great privilege to introduce to you one of the finest historic properties in New York. The Livingston Mansion Apartment occupies seven thousand square feet of the eighth floor of the Edgewood Building at a prime location on Central Park West. Could we dim the lights, please?" The flashes stopped, and a large white projection screen came to life as the lights went down, revealing a stunning black-and-white photograph of the outside of my building. A horse and carriage stood in front, and women in long, sweeping gowns paraded sedately up the street. The Edge in all its glory stood alone—severe, gorgeous, Victorian.

"The Edgewood was built in 1879," Leonard informed us, "two years before they broke ground for the Dakota, nearby." A series of beautiful photographs of old New York wafted across the screen as he continued with his history, which was definitely educational but also a little boring. It got slightly more interesting when he started working in the specifics of the Livingston family, but as it turned out, Sophie's forebears were just a couple of brothers who made a ton of money by cornering the market on cotton fabric around the time when store-bought dresses became all the rage. The most noteworthy thing about the Livingstons, I discovered, was their continued inability to propagate. The slide show had several historic pictures of my endlessly sprawling seven-thousand-square-foot apartment with no people in them, and no matter how many stories Leonard told about the historically important Livingston family, they never seemed to have more than one or two kids, many of whom died childless. Which is how, apparently, the property finally came into the possession of the lone Livingston heir, our own Sophie, whose dress and pearls and shoes I was wearing while the head of historic properties at Sotheby's blipped over her quiet and terrible end.

"Eventually the family's prominence would fade," Leonard announced happily. "And the apartment would move into other hands. Today Sotheby's is proud to present this jewel of New York, an apartment almost unparalleled in architectural detail and beauty, to the real estate community."

The lights were gently coming up, and hands were being raised. Leonard tipped his head slightly toward a youngish guy with messy hair wearing a corduroy jacket, who was sitting in the front row. "Who are the sellers?" he asked, getting straight to the point.

"The sellers are the daughters of Olivia Drinan, the second wife of the Livingston heir, William Patrick Drinan," Leonard replied with simple confidence.

"Can we get the names?"

"The names of the heirs to Mrs. Drinan's estate are Alison Finn Lindemann, Lucille Finn, and Christina Finn, all of whom are with me today," Leonard replied. He turned and gestured toward us with an open palm. We smiled at the small crowd, as we had been instructed to do, and Lucy stepped forward. Leonard made an elegant little gesture in our direction and relinquished the microphone to her.

"On behalf of myself and my sisters, I would like to thank Mr. Rubenstein and Sotheby's for hosting us today," Lucy announced with clear and gracious confidence. Although she's relentlessly mean in private, there's a reason that public relations is her field. "It is a tremendous honor to be a part of this presentation," she proclaimed. "We are well aware that the Edgewood is one of the most prestigious addresses in Manhattan, and the Livingston Mansion Apartment has long been considered the centerpiece of the property. We very much feel the responsibility and privilege of our stewardship in helping it move into the hands of someone who will value it as much as our mother did." What utter horseshit, I thought, but the crowd did not seem to notice that so much as the one big detail that no one had yet mentioned.

"Our understanding is that there is a competing claim on the apartment from the Livingston heirs," someone called from the back of the room. I couldn't see who it was because the lights were in my eyes, but it was a woman and she wasn't kidding around. No one else was either; in the front you could see everyone stop scribbling and look up at us expectantly. This was the real show as far as they were concerned. Lucy looked over her shoulder, supremely confident, and Ira Grossman stepped forward, joining her and Leonard. Lucy, in her little gray outfit, was framed by two handsome men in pinstripe suits. It made an extremely reassuring picture.

"The apartment was legally bequeathed to Mrs. Drinan, who bequeathed it to her daughters," Grossman said simply. "The sons of the first Mrs. Drinan are investigating the terms of their father's will, as is their right. But as of now there is no reason to believe that there are any legal grounds upon which the will might be set aside. Our expectation is that everyone's concerns will be addressed expeditiously and that the sale of the apartment will not be affected."

"Is there a cloud on the title?" the invisible woman in the back continued.

"As of this moment there is no cloud on the title."

I had no idea what that meant, but they all bent their heads and dutifully scribbled it down. It all sounded so reassuring. I found myself feeling effortlessly confident, standing there in a pretty dress and listening to it all. My peculiar and precarious life seemed a million miles away.

"Is it true that one of the heirs is being harassed by the NYPD at the request of one of the counterclaimants?" asked the persistent guy in the first row. Grossman nodded, all disappointed and concerned now, not wanting to spread the bad news in the middle of this elegant party but only too willing to do it. "One of the heirs, Christina Finn, is currently living in the apartment, and she has experienced several harassing incidents," he admitted. "One specific incident is of particular concern, as it seems that one of the counterclaimants, who is associated with the police department, used illegal influence to have Ms. Finn arrested and held unlawfully in an attempt to intimidate and humiliate her." All of this was so bizarrely phrased that at first I didn't even know they were talking about me.

"Would you care to comment, Miss Finn?" the man in the corduroy jacket pursued. Everybody turned to look at me. This is when I got a clue. Daniel, who was standing next to me, gave me a look that said, *Tina, pay attention and don't fuck this up, please.*

"Oh," I said, stepping up quickly and unfortunately, tripping slightly because I forgot for a moment that I was wearing heels. "I'm sorry, what's the question? What do I think of getting arrested? I think it sucks." Out of the corner of my eye I could see Lucy's smile stiffen slightly in annoyance, but I was pretty sure that was because I got the only laugh of the afternoon, and it was my first line.

"Can you describe what happened?" Corduroy Jacket asked.

"Well," I started. Grossman had actually drilled a little speech into my head in case this did come up, so I was not completely unprepared. The guy waited, expectant, his crummy ballpoint in his left hand hovering over the narrow reporter's notebook in his right. The spill light from the stage hit him at a harsh angle, illuminating the lines of the wale in the dark brown corduroy and the furry edges of the suede patch on the elbow of his sleeve, and for a moment he almost looked like a statue hovering in front of me, the light glistening off the wide place on his forehead where his hairline was receding. He wasn't even looking at me. That's what tipped me off—the way he was waiting without look-ing, like he wasn't all that curious because he already knew the answer.

"I'm sorry," I said. "Who do you write for?"

Lucy turned her head at this.

"Who do I write for?" he asked, surprised.

"No, no, don't tell me, let me guess," I said. "You write for the city page of the *New York Times,* right?"

We were under the lights, so Lucy couldn't snap, "What does it matter, Tina," even under her breath. She just stood next to me and smiled, with a little perplexed look on her face, which said to both the audience and Grossman, isn't my sister silly and adorable. This guy was Lucy's friend. She'd told me about him. He was a plant. If I gave good answers, they'd all get into the *New York Times.*

"Yes, I write for the city page of the *New York Times,* is that all right?" he asked smugly.

"Oh, that's sensational," I told him. "As far as being arrested, let me tell you, that was my fourth time, and honestly the other ones were a lot more spectacular. The one in Hoboken, in 2003, I actually slugged a cop! Although that was a complete misunderstanding. Anyway, I'd give this one two stars, it was a little boring by comparison."

The reporter nodded and wrote this down, smiling to himself. I got another laugh, but it was a tad uncomfortable as laughs go. Several flashes went off at once. Leonard leaned forward and spoke into the microphone, fluidly edging me the slightest bit out of the way with his shoulder.

"Are there more questions about the property itself?" he asked. Someone in another unlit corner raised her hand.

"What is it listing for?" she asked. And with that, my part of the song and dance was over.

20

"Nice dress," said the note. That was all, just the two words, "nice dress."

"Where did this come from?" I asked Frank.

He glanced up from his copy of Spanish *People*, but just barely. "Vince Masterson, he came by for his mail and then he left that, said for me to give it to you. He said you were on television." He went back to his magazine, but you could tell he wasn't really reading it. He had dark rings under his eyes, and his uniform didn't quite fit him anymore. The corny epaulets hung way too far over his shoulders, as if he had started to shrink inside it. There was no question that Frank was deteriorating.

"Are you okay?" I asked.

"Sure, I'm fine," he said, not much interested in the question. "I didn't get any sleep last night because my stupid brother was up watching wrestling on the television and drinking beer until three in the morning. Other than that, no problem." It sounded to me like there was a problem.

"You look thin," I told him. "Your uniform's falling off you, Frank."

"My uniform?" He looked down at his clothes, completely annoyed now. "It's not mine. Mine's at the dry cleaners. This is the extra one they keep in the storage closet."

"Well, that's a relief, but I'm not kidding, you look like you're not eating."

"Tina, you maybe should worry about yourself, huh?" Frank said, going back to his magazine but again not reading it. "Vince said to remind you he's in 5B."

I could have ignored this summons from the problematic Vince Masterson, but I was pretty curious about Vince having seen me on television. I knew there were news cameras, but the possibility that we would get on the evening news had seemed pretty far-fetched. I mean, I know that New Yorkers are a little nutty about real estate, but is the sale of an apartment something you would put on the evening news? I decided to go see Vince, partly because I wanted to find out about that, and partly because I was relieved that someone in the building would actually invite me over.

Apparently a press conference about real estate is actually big enough news to put on television in New York City. New York One, the local public-access news station, broadcasts things like city council meetings and roundtables about real estate developments in Brooklyn. They also have strange overwrought talk shows with slightly crazy-looking people screaming at each other about off-Broadway theater. That was the program Vince and his friends were looking for when my turn in front of the cameras popped up.

"Well, we cheered, as you can imagine," Vince told me, pouring an icy and perfect vodka gimlet from a silver bar shaker and expertly twisting a lime wedge over it. "I said wait wait wait that's the *girl*! The one who's squatting in the fifteen-million-dollar apartment! No one believed me. And then you started talking about how many times you'd been arrested, and you were wearing that incredible dress, and I thought, what have you been up to, Tina, and why haven't you come by to visit me?"

"I've been busy," I said, taking my gimlet from him with both hands so I wouldn't spill it.

"So I gather, darling," he said, smiling. "Come and meet my friends!"

He took me by the hand and led me like a prize from the perfectly appointed black marble kitchen and into the equally well-appointed living room of his father's apartment. The walls of this room—what you could see of them behind the floor-to-ceiling bookcases—were painted a deep maroon. There was an enormous blue-and-gold Turkish rug on the floor, plus a leather couch, a coffee table, coffee-table books, two dark brown leather chairs, and eleven gay men. Which would have been intimidating in any room, but it was particularly daunting in this one because in contrast to my apartment, which was cavernous and fascinating and incoherent, Vince's father's apartment was gorgeous, coherent, and quite small.

"We're so excited to meet you, Vince has told us all about you," one of the men announced, standing and reaching to shake my hand.

"Not *everything*, I hope," I said, trying to laugh and feeling completely out of my element. I took a sip of my gimlet. It was, no surprise, perfect.

"That dress is amazing, is it a Chanel? It looks antique," said a second man.

"It's pretty old," I said. "But not Chanel. The tag says Ballen-something."

"Oh my god it's Balenciaga," someone sighed. "Of course it is."

"Where did you find it?" asked a fourth.

"In a closet," I said, wondering how long I might be able to just tell the truth to these guys and get away with it.

"And the alligator clutch was just tucked away in there as well? Look at this, Lyle, how much is this worth?" A fifth guy took it from my hand and held it up, waving it to someone across the room.

"Stop it!" said Lyle, making his way over to eye the clutch.

"You were hilarious at that press conference," said a sixth. "Have you really been arrested?"

"Yes," I said.

"Could someone show some manners here?" said a seventh, walking over to me. "Hi, my name's Jonathan." He stopped, shook my hand, put his arm around me, and steered me toward one of the chairs. "Could one of you ladies be a gentleman and offer her a seat?" Two men leapt up and offered me one of the leather chairs. I sat down, and they took my shoes off, handed me another gimlet when I finished the first, and we watched the recording of the Sotheby's press conference six times. Every time I announced, on television, "The one in Hoboken, in 2003? I actually slugged a cop!" everybody cheered, and then, when I said, "Anyway, I'd give this one two stars, it was a little boring by comparison," they cheered again. I do think most of them were drunk—I certainly was, after my second gimlet—but they were fun and excitable and happy to have me at their party.

"Vincent says your place is completely gorgeous, twelve-foot ceilings and marble arches and mirrors everywhere and square footage galore," said one of them.

"That's actually pretty accurate. Except the arches aren't marble, they're more that kind of dark red wood."

"Cherry?" asked another.

"Walnut," Vince observed, and three of these guys moaned, like walnut door frames were some especially appealing kind of pornography.

"Yeah, they're pretty nice," I admitted. "Can I have one of those?" There was a bag of fancy potato chips behind Jonathan's arm, on the floor.

"Absolutely, have you not eaten?" he said, handing the bag over.

"Sotheby's didn't feed you?" Vince tossed over his shoulder. "Shame on them." He went off to the kitchen with the authority of someone who knew there was really good food in there, but all he came back with was a cell phone. "How about sushi?" he asked, dialing. The men murmured some kind of assent, but he wasn't really paying attention; he was already talking to some underling. "Hi, I'm over at the Edgewood and we're going to need a couple platters," he announced. "Just some of those big ones that you do, tell the chef omakase is fine. Oh, and some of those little fried chicken appetizers. Do people want Japanese fried chicken?" he asked the room. Then he went right back to the phone, without waiting for an answer. "Just bring some of the fried chicken," he ordered.

"Christ, he is such a young god," Jonathan said under his breath. I watched him watch Vince with a kind of deeply amused wonder. Vince was leaning in the doorway with his head down, listening to the guy at the sushi joint repeat back his chaotic order, and then he turned, untucking his pale blue oxford shirt from his dark blue wool trousers, like it was suddenly too hot or something. Oblivious to the fact that every guy in the room was staring at him—or maybe not so oblivious—Vince tapped the phone off and went back into the kitchen. "Twenty minutes," he called back to us.

"Ooh la la," someone sighed. "I need a cigarette. I'm going out on the balcony. Tina, do you want to come?"

"Vince has a balcony?"

"It isn't a balcony; it's a fire escape, darling," my new friend informed me. "Although I like the competitive nature of the question. Come on, let me show you Vincent's apartment. His *father's* apartment, that is," he said casually but loud, so that Vince, returning from the kitchen, could hear him all the way across the room. Vince wagged a finger in our direction, which made everyone laugh, although it was a pretty edgy joke. I didn't have time to register whether Vince really was annoyed, because my guide was already narrating in my ear.

"I know he hates that, but please, how many people get to live in the Edge for *free*. He should just count his blessings, of which he has *quite a few*. Check out the closet, he has a walk-in *closet* that is bigger than my entire apartment, and look at this. Somebody painted the woodwork sage, it's genius, don't you think?"

"I do," I said. It was relaxing listening to this stranger blather on. He had the same attitude all these gay guys seemed to have: even though we had never before met, he assumed a level of complete understanding between us, which was surprisingly accurate considering that I was having trouble remembering his name.

The apartments on the fifth floor had been subdivided three times since the building was built, which meant that Vince's dad's apartment was only four rooms—a bedroom, a living room, a den, and a kitchen— and they were all rather small, even though the walk-in closet was, as my new friend Andrew noted, quite large. The bedroom had a sleekly square king-size bed that took up virtually the entire space, except for the three feet in front of an enormous flat-screen television, which was screwed into the wall like a giant piece of pop art. But the bathroom was enormous and a thing of beauty. Pink Italian tile rose up the walls and framed an actual Jacuzzi, which was tucked neatly into a corner so that unlike the bed in the next room it didn't take over the entire space.

"A Jacuzzi," I breathed. I suddenly felt completely exhausted. "A Jacuzzi."

"And he's mad because his father hasn't put the lease in his name. I'm going, *taxes*? It's not in your name, so who pays the property taxes, you could also look at it that way . . . oh, look what I've found!" Andrew plucked something off the bottom shelf of the tiniest teak cabinet I'd ever seen, which stood next to the pedestal sink. "This looks like a bottle of bubble bath with your name on it. Look, it says 'Tina Finn,' right here," he announced, waving it madly in the air and leaning over to turn on the faucets.

I admit that it's a little crazy that I took off my dress and got into that hot tub, but I was so tired and drunk on vodka gimlets that it seemed like a good idea. The bubbles smelled like lavender, and the Jacuzzi jets were whipping them into a complete state of frenzy, and those guys were being so nice to me. At first it was just Andrew, who, as I said, simply started filling the tub as if this were a done deal, and then Scott with the silver hair came in to use the bathroom, but he immediately got into the spirit of the thing and started running around looking for towels. Then Lyle (short) and Roger (buzz-cut) showed up, reporting that Dave and Edward *and* Christopher were *all* in love with Vince, and he was driving everyone crazy and he just didn't want to watch it anymore. So they were just coming back to say good-bye before taking off, but then they thought that having a Jacuzzi with Tina sounded like fun, so they decided to stick around, but we all needed another round of drinks. While they were getting the drinks, the sushi arrived, which they brought back along with the drinks, and then everyone took turns getting in and out of the Jacuzzi, but I didn't have to get out because they all thought of me as somebody truly special who deserved for one night to be treated like a queen.

And they wanted to know everything. All of it. Every time I tried to streamline the story, they would say I wasn't telling near enough.

"Okay," said Andrew. "Let's start at the beginning. Your mother died—"

"Yes, they said that on television, you know that."

"No, back up beyond that," said Scott, sounding slightly abrupt, but that was just his manner. "Where were you when she died?"

"I was out at the Delaware Water Gap—"

"The Delaware *Water* Gap? Why?" Scott demanded.

"I had this boyfriend, he had this idea that we would clean houses—"

"He had you cleaning houses? Back up," said Lyle.

"Well, we were supposed to be caretakers for the homes of rich people who had places out there. But Darren didn't have it worked out."

"Back *up*. What do you mean it wasn't worked out?" Lyle held his hand out to silence the other three, so he could get the information he wanted.

"Well, you know, he didn't really know anybody there, so we went out and there was no place to live, not even an apartment to rent because there just wasn't, so we ended up living in this trailer—"

"You went from living in a trailer to living in the Edge?" said Roger, clearly entranced by the magic of this.

"Don't rush her, we're not there yet!" Scott interrupted. "So then your mother died."

"Yes. My mother died."

"And when was this?" he continued.

"About two months ago."

"Two months?" someone murmured.

"It was just two months ago? Oh, sweetie. Oh, Tina. That's such a loss." All of them were silent for a moment, thinking about what a terrible thing it is to lose a mother. And it did feel like that suddenly. For the first time since she died, I knew I was talking to people who wanted to hear about my mom.

"It was," I said. "It really was. But the fact is, I had already lost her! I hadn't seen her in so long. Years. I hadn't seen her in years."

"So you lost her twice," said Andrew, mourning that double loss quietly with the question.

"I lost her even before that," I admitted. "She started drinking when I was in high school. And it wasn't her fault."

"Spoken like the true daughter of an alcoholic. I see some Al-Anon meetings in your future, darling," Scott observed.

"I don't mind that she drank," I said. "It didn't make her mean or anything, it just made her kind of dopey. Honestly, I thought it made her feel better. Nobody was really very nice to her. My father was a nightmare."

"Did he hit her? Did he hit you?"

"He hit everybody." Soaking in a tubful of bubbles, surrounded by nice gay men, somehow made it not so hard to admit that.

"Did he drink too?"

"Well, sure, he always drank. He drank beer. Her drink was vodka."

"God, I love vodka," Roger said with a sort of spiritual sigh.

"Okay, so he was always a drinker, and she started when you were in high school," Lyle narrated, making sure we were all on the same page.

"Yes," I said.

"It happens like that sometimes," said Andrew, the compassionate realist. "People don't know they have options and so they get dragged into it."

"Is anyone worried that we're all sitting here getting smashed while we talk about Tina's tragic and clearly alcoholic parents who both died terribly young? They died terribly young, right?" said Scott, the less compassionate realist.

"My father died in a car crash when I was twenty," I said. "He was forty-seven or something."

"Did you cheer?"

"No, everyone just pretended it was all so sad," I remembered. "It was weird. Lucy and Alison and I were all out of the house by then—"

"You were in college," Scott supplied.

"No, I dropped out of college."

"You *dropped* out of *college*?" Roger exclaimed, as if this were really astonishing.

"Let her *finish*," said Lyle.

"Yeah, so I was living with this guy," I fumbled.

"Darren?" suggested Roger.

"No, a different guy, there were—several—different guys," I admitted.

"I'm sure," Scott said, nodding.

"Anyway, Lucy and Alison and I went back to my parents' house after the funeral—there was like a little thing after the funeral." I had a terrible moment as I realized that we had had a little party for my oh-so-shitty father, and we didn't have one for mom. But I didn't want to stop and fill in all the ironic extra details anymore; as nice as these guys were, I was afraid that I might suddenly drown. "Anyway, there were neighbors and some friends of his from work, and people brought food and stood around. We lived in a little duplex, one of those places that has aluminum siding on it, it was pretty nice, Mom always kept it clean. And so people were there after the funeral, talking about how it was such a shame and what a relief that he didn't suffer, and then they all left. Mom was drinking by then, it was like one in the afternoon, and she was totally just—but she didn't really show it. She would go into the kitchen when no one was paying attention and come out with a glass of grape juice or orange juice, pretending like that's all it was. I mean, she never said, 'oh, I need another drink,' she would just disappear and come back and then eventually she would fall asleep. She would put her head down on the table and mutter something like 'whatever you do, it's not enough.' That was like her mantra, I used to hate her for it. She was such a quitter."

"Tina, shush, she's dead, sweetheart," Scott reminded me.

"So Alison and Lucy and I," I said, pushing on with the story, "we knew she was about to pass out, she kept disappearing into the kitchen, so we all assumed, and we were getting ready to take off. Alison had put all the dishes in the dishwasher and it was running, and we were leaving. And then Mom was, she just showed up in the doorway and said, 'Can you take that out of here?'" I couldn't believe I was remembering all this. Sitting there in all those bubbles, it all seemed so clear, like a movie playing in my head. "And she sort of lifted her hand just a little, because she was really drunk, she was, she was just smashed—" Okay, and then I did start crying, because that seemed like the worst detail of the whole story, that she was so drunk. "And she was pointing at his chair. He had this chair, it was so ugly, this brown plaid Barcalounger that he would just, he sat there all the time and got drunk and watched stupid sports on television, and it was like *him*. It was just *him*. And she said it, she didn't have to ask twice, we knew what she was asking. Just, get that *thing* out of here. Which we did, the three of us, we went over and picked up that horrible chair and took it to the front door, and I don't know how we got it out but we did, we took it out to the curb and left it there. And it sat out there for like a week and a half, and then the garbagemen got tired of ignoring it, I guess, because it was finally gone. Like him. No one could explain how it happened that we were all just—free."

Andrew poured another vodka gimlet into my glass. He had a little shaker tucked by the side of the Jacuzzi, on the floor. "Thank you," I said, clutching the slippery glass. I had to concentrate to do that, and then I was able to stop sobbing, which was a relief.

"Why didn't she leave him?" Roger asked. "That's what I don't understand. Honestly, what is the point of sticking *around*?"

"She had three kids," I offered, as if that answered the question. I was aware as soon as I said it that it answered nothing at all, but I was too exhausted and embarrassed and drunk to offer more.

"Did you inherit those pearls?" asked Scott.

"The pearls?" I felt my hand creep up to my neck, to make sure they were still there, although I could feel them heavy against my neck. Scott raised an eyebrow at me. He was sitting on the floor now, draped in a towel, and he looked a little like Zeus or Apollo or some severe god who was not going to be easily fooled by mere mortals.

"Yes, the pearls, Tina, don't look so guilty," he commented. "Did you steal them?"

"Did I *steal* them?"

"Goodness, you sound so paranoid! I was joking, I just wanted to know where you got them, you know they have to be worth a fortune. Is that a melo pearl in the clasp? How much are those worth?" Scott turned to Lyle, who was apparently an expert on all things women wore.

"If you have to ask, you can't afford it," Lyle said, without seeming to notice the questions inside the question. "Although I will note that the clutch you were carrying is a Rue Jacob and probably worth at least fifteen thousand. Does anyone want this last piece of sushi?"

"Fifteen—come on, for just the purse?" I asked.

"Well, that's probably what you'd pay for it in a vintage couture shop. You wouldn't get that if you sold it. You'd get maybe five."

"And the pearls?"

"You really want to know?" Lyle asked. You could tell he was wondering what on earth I was doing wearing them if I didn't even know what they were worth.

"I just borrowed them," I said, sliding down a little farther in the bubbles. The steam in the room was making everyone a little pink, so no one could see me blush. I am an accomplished liar, but I didn't feel like lying to these guys. They cared enough about me to respect the truth, which made it hard.

"Isn't that funny," I murmured.

"What's funny, Tina?" asked Andrew gently. I looked at him, surprised that I had spoken the words aloud, like in one of those dreams where you can't tell the difference between what you are thinking and what you are saying.

"It's funny that Lucy and Alison are so easy to lie to, but you're not," I said. "I don't even know you. Shouldn't it be the other way around?"

Before this could lead to any more truth-telling, however, our steam-filled reverie was interrupted.

"Tina Finn, in a hot tub wearing pearls, surrounded by men," said a sardonic voice. "Be still, my heart." Everyone looked up, and there was Vince, his shirt hanging open, lounging in the doorway. While it was true that I had been sitting in that hot tub surrounded by men and bubbles for a good forty minutes, no one had glanced at me that entire time with anything more intrusive than good-natured kindness or drunken bonhomie. Vince's lust curled and snapped through the room like a whip. I knew he couldn't see a thing below my breastbone, because the bubbles, frothed up by the water jets, were insanely thick by this point. But for the first time all night I felt naked.

"Go away, Vince," I said. "We're having a good time."

"I can see that. I can't believe I've missed all the fun."

But it wasn't fun anymore. I looked up at him slouching in that doorway, thinking about having sex with me, and he looked like half a dozen other guys I let myself get swallowed up by. I looked over at Roger and Lyle, who were rolling their eyes at each other; there's no mistaking a guy in heat, and if you're not the one he's gunning for, you may as well not be in the room. Our little cabal had turned into some sort of hot fantasy for Vince. As far as the rest of us were concerned, the fun was over.

"Well, we were just taking off," Lyle announced. "It's great to meet you, Tina. Take care of those pearls, those are a treasure. And so are you." He leaned over and kissed me on the cheek, dropping his towel carelessly as he did. He truly did spend a lot of time at the gym, so there was no reason not to be bold at a moment like that. Scott and Andrew cheered. "Have a good look, girls," Lyle said, raising his arms with a little flourish as he squeezed by Vince. Roger, who was a little shorter and stouter, held on to his towel, but he kissed me too.

"Bye, Tina, be a good girl," he said. And he gave me a little look, like there was no need to say anything about my past just now but also no need to pretend I didn't have one. Scott and Andrew were collecting their clothes as well. I reached out and kind of grabbed Andrew's wet fingers, and he lifted my hand to his mouth, kissing it sweetly while he raised an eyebrow at me. Vince watched the mass exodus of gay men with a smirk; there was no question in his mind that he was going to get a turn with me in the hot tub. And then the retreating Roger threw me a lifeline. "Are Dave and Edward still here?" he called from the next room.

This clipped Vince right across the back of the neck. He turned, caught out somehow, and his face got all thoughtful, like he really cared whether or not Dave and Edward were still there. "Yeah, they're in the kitchen, cleaning up, with Jonathan," he called back. Loose towels were lying around everywhere by this point, and I had one in my hand before he had time to turn back.

"You're not getting out?" he asked, petulant, as he slid into the bathroom and closed the door. "Come on, I just got here." There was a spoiled and wicked glint in his eye, and his bare chest seemed to immediately glisten as it came in contact with the humidity. This was a dangerous, soggy moment at the very least, a moment when one's weakness for hot, problematic men might be tested. The one thought that kept me from doing something stupid was the question that good-hearted Roger had flung over his shoulder just before Vince shut the bathroom door.

"What's the story with Dave and Edward?" I asked. "I hear they're both in love with you." Vince cocked his head at this, somewhat amused, and gave me enough time to wrap myself in that towel and step out onto the tiles. I wobbled a little, as the floor was slippery and I was drunk—a little less drunk, fortunately, since Vince had arrived and put a straight male damper on things—but class triumphed. Vince reached out, a perfect gentleman, and steadied me.

"Who told you that?" he asked.

"Roger and Lyle, they said that half the gathering is in love with you. Is it possible that you have not told those nice boys which side of the fence you fall on?" I asked.

"Not that it's any of your business, Tina, but Dave and Edward and some of the other men here have a fair amount of disposable income that they are considering investing with me. It doesn't have anything to do with fences. Or falling. You look very fetching, wearing nothing but pearls." He was hovering over me, and that thing had happened where I just fit so neatly into the curve of his shoulder it seemed inevitable that we were going to end up having sex on the floor. His arm was curling down my naked back, and his mouth was closing in on mine. Honestly, it was not the kind of situation I would have resisted under normal circumstances, but my loyalties were not to my past at this moment.

"Vince—I'm not going to have sex with you in your bathroom while you have guests in the next room who are in love with you, because you're letting them think you might be gay so you can get them to give you money," I informed him. His face was right up against mine, so I literally had to whisper it into his ear. "It's not going to happen, Vince. I like those guys. You shouldn't fuck around with them." I wobbled again and wheeled myself around on my toes, grabbing on to the front of his shirt as I did. For a second he thought he was going to get lucky even though I was telling him he wasn't, but then he realized I had just repositioned myself so I could grab my dress and scoot out the door.

Which is what I did. Lyle and Roger and Scott had moved back to the living room and the kitchen, to rejoin the party, which was still in progress. But Andrew was still there in the bedroom, pulling his ash-colored cashmere crewneck over his head carefully, to keep it from stretching. He looked up and smiled and reached out for my dress, which I handed to him. I finished drying myself off while he went back into the bathroom to find my underwear and stockings and heels, which I had dropped carelessly in corners when I took them off. Andrew helped me slip them on, and then my dress, and neither of us said a thing about Vince watching the whole operation from the door of the bathroom. You can watch all you want, I thought; this is as close as you're going to get to me or Sophie's dress or Sophie's pearls.

21

AFTER I KISSED ALL THOSE NICE BOYS GOOD-BYE, I WENT BACK TO my beautiful empty apartment and pulled on a T-shirt and crawled into my little bed on the floor and had a dream. It was not a very subtle dream. I was out at the Delaware Water Gap, standing in front of my trailer, alone. The wind was blowing the few trees around so violently that they looked like they might come down. I knew a terrible storm was coming, so I looked around for Alison and Lucy and Mom, but I couldn't see them anywhere. So I ran into the middle of the trailer park to see if I could find them. I could see people in the other trailers, but they were just moving around inside, I didn't know who they were, and every now and then one of them would come to the door to look at me and wave me away. Everyone wanted me to go back to my trailer. One lady started to yell at me and point, and when I looked where she was pointing, I could see a tornado coming, a real tornado with a funnel cloud that seemed to reach all the way to the ground. It was maybe half a mile away and coming right at us. She kept waving her arms, like you have to go home, you have to get to safety, so I ran back to the trailer, even though I knew no one was there, and I knew that a trailer is the last place you want to be during a tornado. I kept thinking, you should just get down on the ground, Tina, get down, that's your only chance. But when I looked at the door of the trailer, I thought someone was in there, maybe Alison or Lucy or Mom had come back and I needed to rescue them. So I went into that terrible old plywood and aluminum trailer, which was empty and dark, but no one was in there, and then the tornado hit and I knew it was too late for me and everybody.

Which of course woke me up. I sat upright, my heart pounding, and for a terrible second I didn't know where I was. That room was usually so dark, but for some reason light was spilling all down the wall.

Then I heard someone crying, like a child, long miserable sobs, and I didn't know if it was me or the dream or the ghost or someone breaking into my apartment; honestly, it was disorienting as hell. So I held my hand over my heart, trying to force it to slow the fuck down, and then I turned to see where the light was coming from, thinking I had just forgotten to turn off the hall light, and I saw someone standing in the doorway. A child, in a nightgown, holding a club. And she was real.

"Oh my *god*," I said. "Holy *shit*. Jesus God above, what do you want? Oh my god." I don't think I'd ever been so scared in my life. Truly. Over the past two months my mother had died, I'd been invaded, I'd been arrested, I'd met a ghost—and nothing tossed me into complete unblinking terror the way that kid standing there with a club did. I crept up the wall, hoping it would swallow me up and protect me from this unholy vision. It didn't. But rather than enter the room swinging, the kid just stood there and sobbed.

"What do you want?" I said. "Seriously. Seriously. What do you want?"

"You didn't come back!" the kid wailed. "Why didn't you come back?" And then she just stood there and sobbed even harder.

"Katherine?" I said. She stood there and cried, and then she dropped the club on the floor. It was in fact a flashlight, not a club, and another crazy beam of light careened through the room and caught the wall with the sunset painting, then me in the face. But by this time I was out of the bed and across the floor. I scooped Katherine up and held her against my chest.

"It's okay, it's okay," I said, while my heart tried to find something approximating a normal rhythm. "How did you get here?"

"Everybody's mad all the time," she told me. "And Jennifer won't get out of bed."

Working as best I could on the shreds of information the unhappy girl choked out between sobs, I picked up the flashlight and walked out toward the front of the apartment. "You said you would come get us," Katherine accused me. "You said we could see your apartment."

"So now, because you are so brave and impatient, you get to see it," I said cheerfully, flicking on the lights as I passed through rooms and hallways. "You are right. I was just too busy and I didn't come back and I promised I would, so now I will show you *everything*. Did you tell your mom where you were going?" I assumed the answer would be no, and I was already trying to figure out what on earth I was going to tell Mrs. White when I presented her errant daughter to her in the middle of the night.

"How come there's no furniture?" asked Katherine, looking around. "How come the secret room has all the furniture but there's none out here?" I stopped and looked at her.

"How do you know about the secret room, Katherine?" She looked back at me while I figured it out. "Is that how you got in?" I was standing in the great room now, and I could see, in the moonlight, that all my locks were securely fastened. "You came in through the secret room, through the trapdoor!" I exclaimed, like this was the smartest thing I had ever heard, giving her a little poke. She giggled, finally relaxing. "How did you get the trapdoor open?" I asked.

"We carved a hole in it," she said. "Do you want to see?"

"I do. I think I would like to see that, a lot."

So I turned around and carried Katherine back to the far end of the apartment, where the door to the lost room stood ajar, which was not how I had left it.

"Did you open the door?" I asked her.

"I had a flashlight," she said, as if this explained everything.

"Didn't the ghost scare you? Sometimes she's really loud."

"That's not a ghost, that's a person," Katherine told me. "She lives in Mrs. Westmoreland's apartment."

"How do you know?" I asked.

"Jennifer figured it out when she was trying to make the hole."

The kid was a font of information. She led me into the secret room, past the plundered cardboard boxes, and over to the far wall, where a cupboard had been jammed open, barely. With so many boxes stacked in front of it, I hadn't noticed that cupboard.

"Look," said Katherine. It's just steps." And sure enough, it was exactly as Louise had suspected that night not so long ago. The narrowest of stairways rose and turned within the wall itself.

"Wow," I said. "That is amazing. So you guys worked the plug out?"

"Jennifer did it."

"And how did you get this one open?"

"I just pushed it."

"Did Jennifer help you?"

"Jennifer's in bed. Can you come talk to her?"

"Well, it's kind of late," I reminded her.

"She's really sad," Katherine said again, her eyes wide. "She keeps getting yelled at."

"Why?" I asked. This was not sounding so good.

"Because she won't get out of bed. *Never.* You have to come *now.*"

"All right, all right," I agreed. "You have to go back to bed anyway."

Now that I realized how the kid had gotten there, the need to get her back without anyone realizing she'd been gone seemed pretty paramount. I most certainly did not want her mother, or her notoriously reactive father, to stick her or his head into Katherine's room and find her gone into a hole in the wall that led directly to my apartment. Obviously I was not the one who had cracked open the crawl space, but to someone who was inclined to look at it that way, this whole situation might look like I was the one doing the breaking and entering into the Whites' apartment. I looked up the stairwell and then back at Katherine, formulating the shred of a plan.

"Listen," I said. "Don't tell anybody about this, okay? For right now this has to be a secret, and if your mommy finds out about it we're both going to be in big trouble."

"Why?" said Katherine.

"I don't know, kid, that's just the way it is sometimes. We've got to get you back up there and plug the hole up and then think about this."

The ancient red brick stairs built into the wall were curled, claustrophobic, and vertical; I had to grab on to each step above with my hands, and I could hear and feel small living things moving around. Some of them, frankly, were not so small. I remembered from some grade-school history class that people in New York in the nineteenth century didn't have enough milk, so many of them died young, and those who survived were really short, which is doubtless how those Victorian workmen managed to fit into this horrifying space. They also lived in tiny, dark tenements, so climbing up terrifyingly claustrophobic hidden staircases must have seemed normal to them. Or maybe it's just that being poor in any century sucks, and if you have no money you have to do impossible things to survive. Anyway, climbing up that walled-in crawl space certainly seemed impossible, and by the time I tumbled through the hole in the wall onto the floor of Katherine's closet I was having trouble breathing.

"That's kind of scary," I admitted. When I glanced back at the thin snap of the stairwell as it wound its narrow way up the inside of the building, I saw the shape of an enormous rat slowly disappearing above us. "WHOA," I said, then tried too late to lower my voice. "Wow. Whoa, there's, that's scary."

"You said that twice," Katherine noted.

"That's because it's really actually pretty fucking scary," I said. "How does this work?" I looked at the wooden slab that Jennifer had somehow crowbarred out of the wall.

Before I could stop her, Katherine pushed it back in to show me. "It just sticks in the wall," she said. "See?"

"And how did you get it out?"

"Well. You put your fingers here," she explained, demonstrating with seven-year-old confidence. "And then you just pull it." She pulled. Nothing happened.

"That's how you do it?" I asked.

"It's stuck," she said.

"It can't be stuck, Katherine. You just did it ten minutes ago. How can it be stuck?" I gave it a try myself, and of course the plug was stuck. On one side, several gouge marks revealed where Jennifer had located its weak spot and managed to pry it out, but because Katherine had pushed it back at an angle, the handhold was now apparently useless. "Oh, boy," I said, trying not to panic.

"You just pull it," Katherine said, yawning. Which I did, about twenty times, twenty different ways. Nothing happened.

"Come on, Katherine, you have to show me how," I repeated hopelessly.

"You push it," she said this time, lying on the floor.

"Don't go to sleep—I'm not kidding, I have to go home, you have to show me how to open it. Katherine, open it. Open it." If she didn't get the thing open, I realized, I was stuck there for good. I could sneak out the front door and take the elevator down to my own apartment, but it was locked from the inside, as I well knew. I needed to get back down the way I had come up.

"Come on, Katherine, you've got to open it for me. Katherine," I hissed, shaking her shoulder. She looked at me, dopey with sleep. "Jennifer knows how to do it." She yawned. "She's the one who figured it out."

I had known where Jennifer's bedroom was when I babysat for the Whites, but in the middle of the night and with only the occasional night-light at floor level as my guide, getting back there wasn't the simplest trick to navigate. I took two wrong turns, one of which landed me in the psychotically pink bedroom of the middle-school monsters, who were sacked out and snoring. The other wrong turn brought me perilously close to barging in on Mr. and Mrs. White themselves, but as I was about to carefully turn the knob on their bedroom door, I heard someone moving around, and then Mrs. White asked some sort of question and Mr. White answered. A light went on, and I nearly cursed aloud, but instead I just took a quick step backward and gave thanks to the crazy genius who invented wall-to-wall carpet. The Whites continued to mumble back and forth as I looked around, got my bearings, and turned back one more time, finally locating Jennifer's bedroom at the far end of the next hallway.

Her room was both adorable and disturbing. Like Katherine's, it was painted a glowing yellow and there were stuffed animals everywhere, but in the middle of the room was an enormous bed with a white canopy, and the carpet was a dark and terrifying red.

I crept silently across the blood red sea and knelt down next to the bed. Jennifer, quite frankly, looked like a sleeping princess. "Hey, Jennifer," I whispered. "Wake up. Wake up." She didn't move, so I reached over and touched her shoulder. "Jennifer."

"I'm *awake,*" she announced, completely annoyed. I was so startled that I jumped a little and almost tipped over.

"Well, why didn't you say something?" I asked.

"What are you *doing* here?" she replied, with the authority of somebody who knows she has the better question. "It's the middle of the *night.*"

"Katherine opened the door to the crawl space and came down into my apartment," I told her. Jennifer turned her head and smiled but still didn't move. "When did you figure out how to open it?"

"A while ago," she said, seemingly losing interest all of a sudden. "I was going to tell you about it. But then you never came back."

"Well, I'm here now, and I closed it, but I can't get it open again, you have to show me how to do it."

"Why?"

"So I can get home!" I whispered. "Why do I have to explain this? What's going to happen if your parents find me hanging out in your apartment in the middle of the night?"

"They'll be pissed off," she mused, barely interested in the question.

"Well, that's not so good for me," I said. "Come on, help me get home, please."

She looked at me, and a little spark came into her eyes. "You were on television—everybody's mad at you," she informed me. "You're in trouble."

"What else is new." I sighed. "I'm not kidding, Jennifer, you have to help me. Now, right now."

"We're all in trouble," she observed, and looked up at the ceiling.

That's when this improbable situation started to make some sense. She was just so nonreactive, as if neighbors routinely showed up at her bedside in the middle of the night. There was definitely a disconnect between event and reaction. And she had the peculiar nocturnal coherence of the chronic nonsleeper. "Katherine says you won't get out of bed," I noted. She continued to stare at the ceiling.

"I get out of bed. I go to school. I come home, and I get back in bed."

"Your mom lets you do that?"

"My mom," she stated, with an evil, sardonic edge. "My *mom*?"

I wanted to pick her up and carry her home with me, but I knew that would not be an effective choice of action. "Jennifer," I said. I let my hand creep up onto the covers and find her fingertips. "Sweetheart, you're depressed. You need help."

"What do you know," she said.

A door opened and closed somewhere in the apartment. I looked over my shoulder just in time to see the hall light flip on, then shadows rippled across the floor where the light spilled in under the door. The doorknob started to turn. "Shit," I whispered, and rolled under the bed just as the door swung open.

"Hey, are you awake?" the hideous Louise asked. When Jennifer didn't answer, she asked again. "Jennifer," she insisted. "Are you awake?"

"If I don't answer, why would you ask again?" Jennifer said, reasonably. "Are you *trying* to wake me up?"

"I asked again because I knew you were awake," Louise observed, unimpressed by Jennifer's logic.

"Then why did you ask?"

"I heard voices. Who are you talking to?" Louise's question was fluted with suspicion. All I could see from my hiding place was the tail end of a frilly pink-and-white-striped nightgown and her bare feet, which made their way into the room and stopped, then turned and moved out of my field of vision again. I heard a door swing open.

"What are you doing; are you looking in my *closet*?" Jennifer asked. I was pretty nervous down there under the bed, but honestly it felt better to hear her yell at her sister than to watch her lie there like she couldn't bear to sit up and breathe.

"I heard *voices*, Jennifer; I know what I heard. There's someone in here with you." The feet were back in sight and the hem of the nightgown started to lower, as good old Louise, who was starting to seem like the teenage-girl version of the Stasi, was in fact bending over to look under the bed.

"Get *out* of here, you freak!" Jennifer snarled suddenly. Her feet appeared by the side of the bed as she inserted herself between me and certain discovery, actually shoving her older sister aside.

"Hey!" Louise snapped. "You are, you're hiding something!"

"You are not the boss of me, Louise!" Jennifer informed her. "MOM!" Okay, this was a little further than I wanted Jennifer to go to protect me, but I was hardly calling the shots at this point. Besides, Mrs. White appeared in the room so quickly that it seemed likely she had heard the argument and was already on her way to check it out, so I don't know that Jennifer put anything in motion that would not have happened anyway.

"What is going on in here! It's the middle of the night!" Mrs. White announced.

"I heard her talking to someone," Louise started.

"She is crazy! I was just in here sleeping!" Jennifer snapped.

"I heard someone, there's someone in here with her," the persistent Louise repeated, but the illogical nature of her statement undid her.

"That is ridiculous," Mrs. White hissed. "Go back to your room, Louise! And both of you go back to sleep this minute! Honestly. Your father is going to be really angry if he has to come in here, and then we'll all have to deal with it. Go to bed." Her feet stayed in the doorway while she waited for Louise to sullenly drag herself back to her room, and then the door swung shut behind them both. After an excruciatingly long moment of silence, Jennifer's blond hair swung down over the edge of the bed, and I saw her forehead and then her eyes and then the rest of her face make an appearance. She held her finger to her upside-down mouth.

Why is it that taking care of someone else makes you feel better? The listless despair had evaporated, and she was a different person; her eyes were alert with the delight of keeping my presence a secret, and then the prospect of getting me home without being discovered by the wearisome Louise was suddenly a fantastic adventure to be had. We waited in alert silence for a full fifteen minutes before she crept out into the hallway, passed by Louise's closed door, passed back again, waited to see if she was awake and reactive, and, when she proved not to be, waved to me in the half light of the hallway to follow her. She led me with assurance through the maze of hallways to the back room of the sleeping apartment, where Katherine lay asleep on the floor, just as I had left her. While Jennifer closed the door, I picked Katherine up and put her back in her bed.

"So how do you get this thing open?" I whispered, tipping my head at that blasted piece of wood stuck in the wall.

"It's really not very hard," she said with a trace of her former arrogance. And sure enough, she squeezed her fingers into the side of it and yanked. It popped out as if she had ordered it to. The entire operation took maybe six seconds.

"Wow, that is pretty easy," I exclaimed.

We both looked at the hidden staircase. I could hear the rats scrambling to stay out of the light.

"She wasn't supposed to try it without me," Jennifer noted, glancing back at the sleeping Katherine. "The little louse. So it does open into your place?" She leaned forward and tried to see into the darkness. The barest flicker of light seemed to touch the edge of that terrifying staircase from somewhere deep in my apartment, but that was all.

"There's a storage room down there," I explained. "Bill and my mom had shoved stuff in front of the door to the room."

"So they like hid things in the room?"

"There's a bunch of stuff in it," I admitted, "stuff from a while ago, like they needed to put it someplace, so they piled it all back there, and pulled a big cupboard in front of the door and then forgot about it."

"Like treasure?"

"Well, most of it's junk."

"But not all of it?"

I wish I could say that I was honest with this helpful and lovely young girl. I was not. "It's just a bunch of boxes, Jennifer, just a lot of, you know, stuff people don't want anymore."

"Why didn't you tell me? I was the one who found the door—you wouldn't even know it was there if it wasn't for me. Why didn't you just—call me or something?" She looked at me with such a simple sense of disappointment and betrayal that it took a moment to catch up.

"I couldn't just phone you," I explained. "Your mom would think it was weird."

"So? You don't mind people thinking you're weird. Everyone think's you're weird. So what?"

"Come on, I have to go home, it's the middle of the night, and I can't get caught here! It's like I'm breaking and entering. I could get arrested for this."

"You get arrested all the time, you don't care about being arrested," she observed. "You said it on television."

"I said that on like local-access television!" I noted with some exasperation. "Who watches that stuff?"

"Everyone in the building watched it tonight. Everybody knows about it. My mom was on the phone with the whole co-op board."

This was not good news. "What did she say?" I asked, worried.

"People think your mom was a con lady, she made Mr. Drinan give her the apartment—the same stuff. Not that they cared about him, they didn't like him to begin with, you know."

"They didn't like the Drinans?" This had never occurred to me.

"They were *Irish*," Jennifer explained, as if this made everything clear. "I mean, they liked it that he could get things done because he was hooked up with lots of people around the city, but they didn't want him to *live* here."

"Why not? What sorts of things did he do?"

"Look, I don't know, I just heard some stuff while she was on the phone." Jennifer sighed. The spark was going out of her, you could see it happen even before I was halfway through the wall. She was sitting on the edge of Katherine's bed, her shoulders hunched over like an old bag lady who didn't remember how to hold herself up straight anymore.

"Listen," I said. "You have to come to me. You have to sneak out and come down. To the apartment."

"You mean like . . ."

"Katherine did it. You can do it. You just have to be careful. And while you're at it, you have to find out if the co-op board is going to do anything like testify for the Drinans or against my mom or something."

"You mean like *spy* on my *mother*?" Jennifer asked.

"No, no, it's more like—yeah, actually, it's like spying on your mother," I agreed. Her eyes lit up, and she sat up for a moment, the wheels turning, as she considered how she was going to pull this off.

"Yeah," she finally said, with a sort of internal calculating confidence. She was already working it out. "Yeah, I can do it."

She needed a purpose; I gave her one. Her sly grin bounced back and released me into the darkness. I slipped my legs over the edge and scrambled onto that dark rat-infested staircase, feeling my way back down one foot at a time until I reached my own unknowable home.

22

THE MORNING FOLLOWING MY NOCTURNAL ADVENTURES I FOUND myself completely entangled in about eight conflicting concerns. The biggest problem, as I saw it, was what to do with all the stuff stashed in the forgotten room. It seemed unlikely that the room would continue to be overlooked. When Lucy had invited those real estate agents over, they had just breezed through and offered general ideas about how much the place was worth. But now I felt pretty sure that the subsequent walk-throughs would be more thorough, and the original floor plan surely would alert people to the existence of that back room. And once they found it, all of Sophie's stuff would be up for grabs. Including, perhaps, the pearls.

I called Lucy; it seemed the necessary first step.

"Hey," I said, trying hard not to sound too phony in my friendliness. "It's me! I just wanted to call and find out how you thought it went yesterday with the press conference. I thought it was pretty good."

"Yes, people seemed to feel it was a success. You made quite a splash, as usual," she said drily. "You probably didn't need to share quite so much information about your colorful past, but I guess I'm not surprised that you did."

"Oh, yeah, I'm sorry, Lucy, it just kind of popped out," I apologized, trying to keep the conversation on an even keel as long as I could. "Listen, I need to talk to you about when those Sotheby's people are going to start showing the apartment. Is that going to happen right away? Because I'm a little worried about the moss."

"I told you to get rid of that weeks ago, Tina, what is the problem?" she asked, exasperated.

"I know I know, but it's really important to Len, and he's on the co-op board, and I don't want to piss him off. You and Daniel and Alison wanted me to make friends in the building and that's what I'm doing, and I can't just throw it out, I think that would really be counter-productive."

"And he won't move it himself?"

"He's been hard to get hold of lately," I said, dropping a little truth in the middle of all the lies. "I'll keep trying, but it would really help if you could keep Sotheby's from showing the place for a little while."

"I don't know how much flexibility I have on that. The market being what it is, which is obviously not what it should be, we can't afford to set a lot of rules. The kind of buyer a place like ours might attract doesn't come along every day. You don't keep those people waiting."

"Yeah, but the market sucks. You've said so many times. Maybe it makes sense to wait."

"I hardly think you're the expert."

"I didn't *say* I was the expert," I said, trying not to get edgy. "I just mean maybe we should wait until I can get rid of the moss and then have a little time to clean the whole place properly."

"Sotheby's will take care of the cleaning."

"I need some time to get rid of the moss, Lucy!" I finally snapped. "Honestly, I get so tired of the endless go-round that the simplest conversation always turns into with you! Why do they have to come this week? You keep telling me the market sucks—"

"I also keep telling you to get rid of the moss."

"Oh, for crying out loud! Forget it. Send them over here today. Let's show the apartment with a ton of moss growing out of the kitchen, that'll really sell the place. In this shitty market that'll be a big plus."

There was a tense silence. Finally she sighed, but not a defeated sigh, more a "Tina's such a pain in the ass" sigh, which she long ago perfected and always has at the ready. "So were you going to tell me about the pearls?" she asked.

This I did not expect. I had to stop myself from blurting out something that would sound utterly defensive and guilty. I rallied my best tone of aggressive innocence. "What about them?" I asked.

"Where did you get them?"

"Where did I get them? Who remembers? Some thrift shop in Delaware."

"You said you left all your things out there with Darren."

"Well, you know what? That idiot Darren actually got it together to send me a box of my stuff finally. You kept telling me I couldn't have any money for new clothes, so I got Darren to send me my stuff."

"This is the first I've heard of a *package* from *Darren*," she observed, making it sound like the most improbable event of a lifetime, which it would have been, were it true.

"Well, I don't tell you *everything*, Lucy," I said snidely.

"I know that, Tina, and let me just say, it's a lot of work, trying to figure out what you do tell me and what you don't and what's true and what isn't."

"Lucy," I started. "I show up for these dumb meetings. I get dressed up and show up at the press conference. I'm nice to the people in the building. Whatever you ask me to do, I do it! Why am I still the enemy?"

"I didn't say you were the enemy," she responded, with so much undisguised bile it was impossible to mistake her conviction that I was in fact the enemy. "I'm just a little curious about those pearls. Alison said the Sotheby's curator was very interested in them. He seemed to think they were valuable."

"He was a *real* estate guy!" I said, inwardly cursing my insanely cocky decision to wear them to that stupid press conference. "What does he know about pearls?"

"I'm just telling you what Alison told me. She said—"

"I don't care what Alison said. I got those pearls out in Delaware at a thrift shop last summer, which is, by the way, the same place I got the dress I was wearing and the cute shoes. You told me to get dressed up, so that's what I did. And, by the way, it's a good thing Darren finally sent me that stuff, otherwise I would have nothing to wear, because as you have mentioned oh so many times, I don't have *any money*, and since you don't seem to think it's a good idea to give me money, and you also don't want me to get a job, I'm having a little bit of a problem figuring out how to *eat*, much less get dressed up."

"You seem to be doing just fine, Tina," she responded, completely without sympathy. "I thought you had found some jobs around the building."

"Oh, come on, I babysat for the Whites once, and the guy upstairs pays me to let the moss stay here. But you want me to get rid of the moss, so there goes that cash!"

"That's right," Lucy agreed. "The moss is going. You take care of it or I will, because they're coming over to clean the place on Friday."

"*Friday?*" I said, trying not to panic. "That's in three days."

"Wednesday, Thursday, Friday," she said. "Two and a half."

I had to make some more phone calls. Len was still not picking up, and neither was Charlie, although at least she had voice mail and I could leave her a message about the complications surrounding this moss situation. I also called the Brooklyn Botanic Garden and left a message for her. Then I spent an hour or so rearranging the storage space and going through the boxes to see if there was anything else I wanted to keep. The thought that I was stealing from a dead woman had evaporated; now I just wanted to save some of her stuff, and since I had just concocted the pretty good story about Darren sending a box of old clothes, I thought I might be able to legitimately pull out some of that stuff without having anyone ask too many questions about where they came from. There was no reason I shouldn't keep some of Sophie's things. Otherwise they'd just be thrown out.

I started with the clothes. Sophie's hippie phase especially had some great moments, and as I had discovered, her clothes actually fit me. So I picked out the best of the Indian-print and tie-dyed tops and skirts, and even a dress with little mirrors all over it. I chose a couple of pairs of cowboy boots and four or five pairs of shoes. I took out two boxes of yarn and knitting needles with the thought that I had always wanted to learn how to knit. And then I grabbed her old Canon, even though it was a film SLR and totally useless anymore.

So I spent the morning and early afternoon picking out stuff to use or save and hanging it up or hiding it in my little room. The way Lucy was talking, I thought, there's no telling how much longer I'll be here, and just going through Sophie's things made me want to turn that sorry old place into a home again. I found a table and a lamp that were old and beat-up enough to look like I might have bought them at a stoop sale. I even found a small Turkish area rug with funny little animals all over it; next to my equally small bed, it made the room quite cozy. I had already lifted a dozen or so mystery novels from the boxes underneath Mom's bed and lined them against the wall where I slept, so the room was beginning to look as if an actual person lived there.

I picked up Sophie's alligator clutch from the floor where I had dropped it, wondering where I could hide something that valuable. And then I thought, oh it doesn't look valuable, it looks like an old purse, nobody's going to steal it.

So it wasn't a big leap, frankly, to the next step. I was on the verge of money problems. I had come to that apartment with nothing, really nothing, and then I was lucky enough to find seven hundred dollars, and then I squeezed two hundred out of Len and eighty out of the Whites. I had been living on that for a little over two months! I was pretty much broke now, and that purse was worth at least five thousand dollars. And the dress, I suspected, was worth quite a bit as well. I found a shopping bag and put the clutch in the bottom and the Balenciaga on top of it. And then I dropped the pearls in there too.

In the elevator I took a couple of breaths and turned my brain over to reptile mode, which is what I do when I know I'm doing something wrong—like stealing—but I also know that I'm going to do it anyway. Not that I make a habit of stealing; if I did, I might not be so broke all the time. Or I might be spending more time in jail than the occasional overnight visit. In any case, I don't steal except in the direst circumstances. And in this case, I wasn't all that bothered about it. What good would it do Sophie or my mother or me if I just left the stuff back there and let it be tossed or grabbed up by lawyers or Sotheby's or Mrs. Westmoreland or someone else from the building? Why leave it for any of them? That is what my determined reptile brain was telling me when I stepped off the elevator: I needed the money, no one else needed the money. No one else was going to help me out; only Sophie would.

I didn't even make it through the lobby.

The response to our cocky little performance at Sotheby's had apparently been swift and decisive. Right there in the Edgewood lobby I found myself in the middle of another press conference, this one decidedly less civil, particularly with regard to me and my family and

what we thought we were doing there. The place was packed; there
were at least twice as many reporters and photographers as we had seen
the day before, shoved together in every available square inch from the
elevator bank past Frank's podium all the way to the front door. Everybody's backs were to me as they tried to take photographs and shoot
questions at the small but definite cadre of speakers gathered in front of
the giant fireplace and trying to answer the questions being thrown at
them. There were no microphones at this press conference, so people
were shouting.

"Mr. Drinan—Mr. Drinan—Mr. Drinan!" somebody yelled. "Has
any court issued a ruling on the status of the will?"

"The Surrogate's Court has not issued a ruling, but as of this afternoon a cloud has been placed on the title. The Livingston Mansion
Apartment, my mother's family apartment, is not being represented for
sale at this time. The announcement that Sotheby's will be representing
the Livingston Mansion Apartment is a complete fabrication," Doug
shouted. "The so-called heirs of Olivia Finn have no claim on it. The
will that purports to bequeath the apartment to Olivia Finn has been
determined to be fraudulent."

The alarming and decisive confidence of this assertion pretty much
scared the shit out of me for a second, but when I stood on my toes and
caught a glimpse of old Doug over the heads of the two gigantic camera
guys who were blocking my view, I could see that Doug wasn't so sure
of himself. His air of frustrated defeat had turned into something like a
permanent expression of deep unhappiness. His lips had almost disappeared, his hair was disappearing, and his skin was gray, which may
just have been the ugly fluorescent lighting in the lobby, but I had seen
Frank under those lights a thousand times by now, and he always looked
fine. Doug looked paunchy and angry, and while he made it sound like
he was winning, he looked like he was losing. But as Doug kept talking,
I remembered that someone who is losing has nothing more to lose and
is usually the worst enemy you can have.

From where I was standing I couldn't see anything but backs. There
were more camera flashes. Someone else asked a question I couldn't hear,
and somebody else, with a big voice, answered. "It's possible that the se-

nior Mr. Drinan was never intended to be the heir in the first place. We have not been able to ascertain that the will of the first Mrs. Drinan was ever probated, in which case the document being considered by the Surrogate's Court at the present time will carry no authority whatsoever. If that is the case, the sons of Sophia Livingston, who grew up in the apartment, are clearly the rightful heirs."

There were more mumbled questions, and the guy with the big voice made another announcement. "Why don't we let the board answer that question."

He and some of the others up there conversed among themselves, and then a third voice started to speak, but there was so much overlap he couldn't really be heard. The room was getting hot from all the camera lights, and people were starting to shove a bit, because it was so crowded and no one could see what was happening.

"We can't hear!" someone in the back yelled. After some more frustrated mumbling, the loud voice in the front spoke up again.

"Yes, sorry, sorry, here this seems to help," it announced. There was some shuffling, and then Len stepped up onto one of the lobby's wing-back chairs.

I just stared. It really was Len, and his hair was combed and he was wearing a lovely dark green suit and tie, but his eyes were crazier than ever.

"The Edgewood in no way supports the supposed heirs of Olivia Finn. Our understanding is that, contrary to the assertions made by Sotheby's, there is in fact a cloud on the title, but that doesn't matter because the co-op board will not endorse any sale at this time. These women are no better than thieves as far as we are concerned. It is disgraceful that they have succeeded in this dreadful misappropriation of property to any degree *whatsoever*," he hissed. "And it will not be allowed."

Some more mumbling at Len's feet apparently struck a nerve, because he became completely incensed. "Yes there is, there is someone living there who has no rights at all, and the building has very much taken note of it, and she is going to be evicted immediately!" he declared hotly. "This is a landmark building, and the indignity—the indignity of this *pretender* and *interloper*—will no longer be tolerated.

Unless these people vacate the premises within the week, the building will bring its own action against them!" There was some more mumbling, which made Len even madder. "Legality—there has been too much talk about legality! What about what is historic! What about what is right! What about that!"

In spite of the tidy suit, Len was starting to look and sound completely psychotic. I couldn't believe it; he was like a different person. I wanted to shout at him, I'm taking care of your moss, you asshole! But that would not have helped my situation. His angry exhortations were having their effect on the mood of the room. Some of the photographers in the back were shoving each other to get a decent shot; many were just holding their cameras above their heads and firing off their motor drives, hoping they'd end up with something worth printing. But some of the reporters at the back were feeling left out, so they started shouting questions really loudly, partly out of frustration and partly so they could be heard. "Has the building started eviction proceedings?" a skinny girl in a red jacket shouted. I wanted to hit her, but I was beginning to worry that someone would notice that the evil pretender and interloper was standing right there spying on the proceedings, and they'd mob me.

Which actually is what happened next, just not to me. Someone up front tried to answer the skinny reporter's question with what may have been the last shred of reason in the room. "No one is being evicted!" he shouted, but then there was a kind of swelling up and movement near the front door; one of the tenants was coming home, and those of us back by the elevators were getting shoved. Seriously, it's not like there were a hundred people there—I don't know how many were there, maybe thirty—but the foyer of the Edge is not a limitless space. That one extra person seems to have been the tipping point. Or maybe it was *who* she was, because suddenly all the reporters started to shout and turn their attention toward the doorway, where the beautiful Julianna Gideon was trying to make her way in.

I had seen her only a couple times, but this crowd was made up of the kind of society writers who know where you live and how much money you have and how old your family is and what parties you go to and what charity events you attend. In any event, they all knew who she was, and, more important, they cared. "Miss Gideon! Miss Gideon!" they shouted, which in the moment honestly sounded sort of obscenely polite, given that they were shoving around her like a crazed soccer mob and sticking their cameras in her face ruthlessly. "Can we get a comment about the controversy? Have you met any of the women who now claim part ownership of the building? Will you support the co-op board if they attempt eviction proceedings?"

I couldn't even see Julianna at first, but then I spotted that beautiful head of hair, her face tucked down against her shoulder, as she gently tried to make her way through the swarm. She wore a soft rose-colored coat, which had been pulled open by her struggle with the crowd, and she carried a couple of expensive shopping bags that kept getting caught behind her, so she kept turning back to murmur, "Excuse me, so sorry, excuse me." She would try to move forward, then get dragged back, people were shouting, and then she threw back her head, releasing her face from all those dark curls with an almost angelic despair. Her face went all white and her knees buckled and she started to go down.

Who knows what might have happened—she had fainted, no question, and people were being careless indeed. But Frank appeared out of the crowd and caught her. She fell into his arms, and he picked her up and shouldered his way through the mob, carrying her the last few steps to where I was standing in front of the elevators. Her head was tipped back, and her curls fell gracefully around the epaulets on his doorman's uniform. I had enough presence of mind to swing the elevator door open for them and swing myself in behind. The reporters were closing in, and Julianna wasn't the only one who needed to make an escape. "What floor is she on, Frank?" I said fast, reaching for the buttons.

"Eleven," he told me.

Just then a hand reached in and stopped the elevator door from closing. "No no no no," I begged, half under my breath. I actually smacked the hand, hard, and then tried to pry the fingers off the sliding panel as I shoved my body in front of Julianna and Frank so that no one could push their way in.

"Would you relax! Tina, *Jesus,* owww." I looked up from the fingers still clinging to the edge of the panel to see who was blocking the crowd of reporters, which looked small and insignificant now, a bunch of society scribblers trying to make something out of nothing. "You gonna bite me?" Pete asked.

"I was thinking about it."

"I'm sure. She dropped these." He shoved in the two elegant shopping bags—pristine, with corded handles, one from Barney's, the other from Bergdorf Goodman—which had slipped from Julianna's grasp.

"Thanks," I said.

"Wait wait, is this yours?" he asked. And he pushed in the bag I had been carrying—the brown paper shopping bag containing his mother's Balenciaga dress and alligator clutch and her pearls. I felt myself turning red, but he didn't know; how could he know.

"Go on, get out of here," he said, tipping his head toward the call buttons. He turned his back to me and held up his hands, blocking access to the shouting reporters. "Back up, *back up,* you fucking piranhas," he ordered.

"Is that one of the other heirs?" somebody asked, putting two and two together.

"I don't know, is it?" he wondered. I didn't hear anything further. The door closed, the elevator lifted, and we left him and the ensuing chaos behind.

23

High above the city, with sweeping views of the park similar to my own, the Gideon apartment was a haven of peace and light. Every one of the rooms had been "done," apparently by some famous designer, in a palette of gold and white. You walked into the living room and felt like you were floating.

Frank was still carrying Julianna in his arms. She had revived to the point that she could insist he put her down, but not with any real force. "I'm fine, really, Frank, I promise, this is so silly," she protested, as she leaned her cheek against his chest. I had opened the door with Frank's master keys, which he tossed to me in the elevator with almost alarming speed and accuracy, as if he had been preparing for this moment his entire life. In any case, he tossed me the keys and I knew what to do with them. I grabbed her bags and he held on to Julianna and we brought her safely home, where he laid her on a milk white sofa in front of a bank of windows overlooking the world.

"I was so frightened," she said, smiling up at him. Frank knelt beside her and pushed a strand of curling hair off her cheek.

"You're all right now," he said.

"I'm perfect now," she said. "Thank you."

She reached over and held his hand. Frank just stared at her, his face so full of wonder you truly thought the universe might stop. They had completely forgotten that I was back in the corner by the door; both of them were clearly so content just looking at each other. I almost shouted, "Kiss her! Kiss her!" but there was no time.

"What is going on here?" someone announced, behind us. Before I could even turn to say hello, Mrs. Gideon with the steely gray hair swept by me to join her daughter on that pristine couch. When Julianna lay on it, it looked like a bed, but as soon as her ferocious mother sat next to her it looked like a throne. It had strange paw-like feet that you noticed only when Mom was sitting there.

"Oh, mother, I'm fine," Julianna began. Mother cut her off.

"You're clearly *not* fine, someone just carried you into your own apartment. What happened?" Mrs. Gideon turned on Frank and me as if we were the problem here and not the solution. She was a fairly frightening person, truth be told. She kept asking questions, but they didn't sound a bit like questions; every word out of her mouth sounded like a complete accusation. She was honestly no fun at all.

"There was a crowd down in the lobby, things were a little upsetting," Frank explained.

"Yes, things are upsetting, people in the building are upset, my understanding is that it's being handled, Frank, I don't know what it has to do with you," Mrs. Gideon snapped, standing. "And I don't appreciate your bringing *her* into my home." She barely flicked her eyes in my direction; I was beneath her, and besides, she was having too much fun giving Frank a hard time. "Surely you know that I would consider that inappropriate."

Frank was completely mortified. "I . . . I . . . I . . . ," he began, but she was having none of it.

"You've done enough, *now go*," she ordered.

"Mother. Please." Julianna sat up, her cheeks turning the palest rose. I'm telling you, that girl knew how to blush. Her pink cheeks were just the slightest shade lighter than her rose-colored wrap. Sitting up on that white couch, she looked like a flower. "Frank took care of me, I don't know why you would speak so harshly to him," she said, laughing a little in a way that took all the sting out of her mother's accusations. "I don't know what I would have done if you hadn't been there, Frank. I was really frightened and it was so silly to faint."

"You *fainted*? I'm calling the doctor."

"I'm fine now, thanks to Frank. I am very grateful, Frank, really I am." She stood up and held her hand out to him with a simple elegance. He took it in both of his own, too overwhelmed to speak. Honestly, if her hideous mother had not been there, I think he would have fallen to his knees in a worshipful daze. But Hideous Mother *was* there. And she was done with us.

"Well, I don't know what happened," she said. "But if you say Frank was helpful, I'm sure he was. Here, Frank, wait there for a minute so I can get you something."

"Oh—no, please," said Frank. But Hideous Mother had already stalked to the entryway, where I was standing and watching, and picked up her purse from a useless-looking sticklike table perched just inside the door. She smiled at me tightly as she turned, making sure I knew that even if I had fooled her pretty daughter, I sure wasn't going to fool *her*. But she really didn't have anything to say anymore; she was just ready to get rid of both of us.

"Here," she said, holding out a five-dollar bill in Frank's direction.

Frank's face went white, then a deep, truly indescribable color seemed to pass over it like a wave. To give him his due, his expression did not change. But for a moment he seemed unable to speak or move.

"Mother," whispered Julianna, completely mortified.

"What?" said Hideous Mother. "He's the doorman and he was very helpful to you." She twitched the five between her fingers in an insanely insulting breath of a gesture. "You just said so yourself, sweetheart. I think it's completely appropriate to offer him a tip." She took another step toward Frank and gave the bill yet another little flick. The whole performance was so shocking I couldn't look away.

"You dropped your bags," I said, holding up the Bergdorf's and Barney's bags with a sudden humble but loud goodwill. "I'm going to leave them here by the door, okay?"

"Oh—" Julianna started.

"Frank, you were going to let me into my apartment, remember? I am so sorry, I locked myself out. So stupid. What a great apartment you have, it's so pretty, I didn't at all mean to barge in, I just, Frank was going to help me with my keys and then your daughter fainted." I reached out and grabbed Frank's arm, to get him to move. With a quick, sharp shrug he pushed me aside, but at least it got him going. He strode past Hideous

Mother, and me, with every shred of Latin American pride that was left in him and his uniform. As he clearly wasn't going to pause, I scurried along. He did not give himself permission to look back even when Julianna called after him.

"Thank you, Frank, thank you!"

"If you want to thank him so much, I don't know why you wouldn't let me tip him," Mrs. Gideon admonished her, behind our exit. "Honestly, Julianna, your affectations have gotten completely—" The door slammed her voice shut. Frank was at the elevator now, pressing the button with a fierce and uncompromising rage. Blessedly, it was right there, and we didn't have to wait. We both stepped into the elevator, and I hit 8. Frank hit L. We traveled in silence for a moment.

"Boy," I finally said. "What a witch."

"Hopeless," he whispered. "Hopeless." He sagged then, leaning against the paneled wall as if it were the only way he could continue to stand. When the elevator dinged for my floor, I reached over and pulled him up, put his arm over my shoulder, and half carried, half walked him out at my landing. Then I let us into my apartment, using his keys.

He was mumbling to himself, some sort of protest, I think, but my Spanish is not all that good when someone talks fast. It sounded sort of like, you have to let me go I have to get downstairs and do my job, but it could just as easily have been a grocery list. In any case he was in no condition to face anyone down in the lobby, much less that crowd of howling society reporters who were most certainly still on the premises. So I shut the door behind us and pushed him into my sweet empty enormous front room, propping him up against one of the windows that have the really good view of the park.

"Here, wait here, Frank, I'm going to get you something to drink, okay?" I said. He just kept talking to himself. I headed for the kitchen, where I knew there was a nearly full bottle of vodka stashed in the freezer.

As I raced through the little TV room, a head popped up off the couch. "Hey, you're home," said Jennifer as she cheerfully set down a mystery novel. I had forgotten that she was planning to show up, so her sudden appearance sent my heart rate through the roof.

"Oh, Jennifer," I said, holding my hand to my chest in an attempt not to die from the scare she gave me. "Oh."

"You told me to come," she reminded me, a little worried now.

"No, I'm really glad you're here," I said. "Oh. Really glad." And I was. Even though my heart was still racing, it was not lost on me that finally, maybe, I had an ally. At the very least, for the first time ever in the Edgewood, I had someone to come home to. "Come on," I said, heading for the refrigerator. "Frank's in the front room. He's a complete mess."

"The *door*man?" she said, following me obediently.

We took the vodka to the great room, and I poured Frank a stiff drink. He knocked it back without protest, and I poured him another.

"What's wrong with him?" Jennifer asked.

"It's complicated," I started, but the vodka had brought vitality back to his spirit, and he started rambling again, in Spanish. "Frank," I said, taking his hand. "Frank. Speak English, Frank."

"No, it's okay," said Jennifer calmly. "He's upset. He loves her, but it's hopeless, she is a goddess and he is nothing. And his father, there's some—*que quieres compartir con nosotros tu familia,* Frank?"

So it turns out that a private-school education in New York City is pretty thorough. Also, Jennifer was in the Spanish Club, so her comprehension didn't fall completely apart when someone started talking fast.

"He lives with his father and his two brothers in a one-bedroom apartment in Queens," Jennifer translated. "He came from the Dominican Republic six years ago and sent money to them faithfully, but they were never grateful, never—they became jealous. No matter what he sent, it made them unhappy and greedy for more and so they came here. He is here legally but they are not. He can't, they use up all the money—they—" He interrupted her with a long explanation, and she asked him some questions before continuing. "He doesn't blame them because the life they had in the Dominican Republic was nothing, there are no jobs there and they want to be men, but they cannot find work, and if the INS finds out that they're staying with him he's afraid he'll be deported too. He told one of his brothers—*como se llama tu hermano* horrible—"

"Manuel," Frank answered, trying to continue and contradict her about the "horrible" part, but she cut him off.

"He has a horrible brother who threatens him. He is supporting all of them, and this brother, Manuel, *threatens* Frank that if he doesn't bring home more and more money he'll have to turn himself in to the INS and they will all have to go back, even though Frank totally has his green card, I know he does because the building would never hire him if he didn't, and my mom was on the committee that interviewed him. They love him here, they'd never let that happen. Frank," she continued, turning her attention back to him. *"Es impossible, lo que se dice su hermano. El es un mentiroso. Un mentiroso,"* she insisted. He protested firmly, but I could tell he knew that whatever she was telling him was right. *"Porque no ayudan?"* she continued. *"Porque no trabajan, todo su familia viven aqui en Nueva York, aqui nadie le importa si usted tiene una tarjeta verde! Aqui a la Edgewood, si, es importante, but muchas otras lugares no no no. Todos los restaurantes en la cuidad, nadie le importa!"*

He disagreed with her. They argued back and forth. He finally started to cry. She put her arms around him and he wept about his hopeless situation, the trap of his family, his love for a woman who was so far above him that the only word he could use to describe her was *diosa*. Now Frank was drinking straight out of the bottle, and by the time we had the whole story out of him, he was stupefied with grief and completely smashed, so there was really no way he could go back to work. I got him a pillow and a blanket from my bedroom, and he fell asleep on the floor, with the light fading from gold to blue all around him.

Jennifer looked up at the changing light and checked her watch. "I've got to go," she said, nervous. "I left Katherine playing in her room and we locked the door and she knows not to open it? But she's seven, she could just forget and open the door and then anyone could come in and then what would happen."

I was following her back, through the kitchenette and the laundry room. As we moved, she quickly filled me in on what she had found out by just hanging around, hiding behind doors, and listening in on the flurry of phone calls that had come in and out of the Whites' apartment over the past two days.

"People are really mad," she said. "Mom told them she knows you and you're okay. I told her she had to tell them that, because you are such a good babysitter and a godsend, but you know there're a lot of rich assholes in this building, and they kept talking about you and your sisters and how this is such a famous apartment, that, um, you know— they can't just let it go down the toilet, shit like that."

"Oh that's lovely," I said. "Such swell manners they have here on the Upper West Side."

"Oh, you know people say things like that, and you know." She shrugged, not knowing how to say what came next. She decided to just say it. "You know, Tina, they didn't like your mom."

"Some of them did. Len did."

"I don't think you should trust Len, Tina," Jennifer suggested cautiously. "Mom said, she was talking to him in the elevator? And he said he knew your mom, they had a deal where he kept some plants here, so he came by all the time, and he saw her and Bill together, and she kept Bill drunk so she could get him to sign things."

"He didn't say that."

"That's what my mom said he said. He claims to be a real witness, like he *saw* all this and he's ready to testify. And he had some idea about having a big press conference? To get you out of here?"

"Yeah, I was down there earlier. It was a total scene down in the lobby."

"Well, Mom said that was his idea."

"It was his idea? Len's?" The sheer betrayal of it hit me like a fist to the stomach. I felt sick.

"That's what she said."

"It's lies. My mom wouldn't, she wasn't like that. She . . ." I stopped myself, completely caught by how much I didn't know about my own mother and what she might or might not have been doing for the last three years of her life. "I don't know why he would do something like this."

Jennifer looked kind of sad, like she was sorry that I wasn't savvier about people like Len. "They're all like that here, Tina. They're all, well, you know. They live in the Edge," she concluded lamely.

I gave her a quick hug good-bye as she glanced around the lost room at all the junk and the thrown-away details of the lives of the people who had lived there. Katherine was apparently still content; we could hear her up above, chattering to herself in some near corner of her room.

"Frank's right, you know," Jennifer suddenly announced, turning back for a second. "Julianna Gideon *is* a goddess. And I mean, in my social studies class they all talk about democracy and America and immigrants and New York being this big melting pot, but he's a *doorman* from the Dominican Republic and he's got a horrible family, and she's like, a *goddess*. And the Gideons just have pots of money, they are truly stinking rich, just like everyone else who lives here. You don't think about things like that. But, you know, it really is hopeless." And with that hopeless remark, she ascended to her sister's room.

24

In my enormous front room under a moonless sky, on a bed of horrible mustard-colored shag carpet, Frank slept the sleep of the hopelessly drunk while I considered the master keys he had handed me earlier. It was a relatively innocuous-looking set, five in all, two of them larger than the others. Those two clearly had some outdoor use; I was less interested in them. But I was quite interested in the three smaller keys, which presumably would let you into any apartment in the building.

Those keys were mine for as long as it might take Frank to sleep it off. Unfortunately, all three were stamped with the words DO NOT DUPLICATE, so I was relatively quick to conclude that any hardware store that didn't take bribes would refuse to duplicate them. So all I had was three or four hours before Frank woke up and wanted his keys back. I didn't waste a lot of time thinking about my options. Abducting that ancient plant might give me some leverage with Len, which I definitely needed. Jennifer's account of his lies, along with my own glimpse of his snarling rage, was unnerving, and while I didn't know what he was up to, I did know I had to get him to back down. I pulled out my throwaway cell and dialed.

"I have a way to get us into Len's apartment," I told her. "How fast can you get over here?"

There was a pause. "Twenty minutes," she said.

"Okay, do you know where the service entrance is?"

"I lived in the Edge for seven years," she said. "Of course I know where the service entrance is."

"Well, then can you tell me?" I asked. "I think it would be better if I met you there and we snuck up the back."

Twenty-five minutes later we were on the landing in front of Len's door. Charlie didn't ask a lot of questions about how I had gotten my hands on the master keys; she was blessedly uncurious about anything other than getting through the door of her father's apartment and making off with her plant. She stood silently behind me as I lay down on the floor of the landing and peeked through the crack at the bottom of the door to see if any lights were on inside. I hoped that Len was still downstairs with the rest of that hysterical co-op board, but I needed to be sure. After five minutes of utter silence it seemed safe to assume we were alone.

So within half an hour, I found myself standing in Len's silent greenhouse next to his tall, elflike daughter, wondering what we were looking for. The last time I had seen the plant, it was small, and in a little white plastic cup.

"Do you know what it looks like?" I whispered. A quiet breeze blew through the lush foliage of the deciduous room, but that was the only answer I got. Charlie glided ahead into the night, and before I could find my bearings and follow her, she was gone.

"Shit," I said, to myself mostly. "Charlie?" There was no answer, and the place was pitch black. I felt a wave of panic; this wasn't the plan, that she would just go off and leave me standing like a dope by the front door. Or maybe that was the plan. I realized that we hadn't actually made a plan, and Charlie did know the layout of the greenhouse since she had lived there for seven years. So I waited by the door for an exceptionally long time, and then I started to wonder if I shouldn't just leave.

That is doubtless what I should have done, but it didn't feel right. For a sick moment I realized that once again I had put all my trust in a person I barely knew, and maybe since Len had surprised me with his many unexplained betrayals, I shouldn't expect his only daughter to behave all that much better. What was she doing back there? Why was this taking so long? "Hey, Charlie," I whispered, taking a step forward into the darkness. "Come on. Charlie?" I waited for another moment, listening for any signs of non-plant-based life. I heard nothing but water and the strange omnipresent sense of things growing. Charlie had completely disappeared. I took another step forward.

Len had rigged up a series of night-lights, which cast spooky little glows in obscure corners of the greenhouse, but they were next to useless under the weight of that moonless sky. The foliage was dense, and lights from the street below were too far away to do any good; the few leaves I could make out were black against black, and only my fingers could really discern the subtle differences as I moved deeper into their jungle pathways. My eyes couldn't seem to get used to the darkness, so I finally closed them to keep from straining for sense, and slowly the logic of the conservatory, room after room, bloomed in my head. The kid had said the seeds were from Africa, and the Latin notes on the woodcut print mentioned Malaysia, so there were only a few places in the greenhouse it might be.

And then, past the orchid room, right on the edge of the poisonous plants room, on a small platform lit with a bank of dull purple neon lights, was a small shrub with thick, short stems and fierce shiny dark green leaves. The tiniest of bulbs was forming on one branch.

"Holy shit," I said.

It wasn't very big—nowhere near as big as the picture in the mossery indicated it might be. But even though it hadn't flowered yet, it was clearly the plant in the medieval print on my wall. There was something peculiar about how specifically it matched, almost as if it were a carefully manufactured bonsai version of something much larger but equally specific that had appeared on the earth two thousand years ago. It was the perfect example of the botanist's art; every scrap of knowledge that humanity had attained over centuries of cultivation had been showered on this strange growing thing, and it virtually quivered with its own perfection. That may have been the effect of the three separate humidifiers that surrounded its perch under the neon lights and breathed a hissing steam upon the leaves and branches; in any event, there was no question that this was the piece of greenery I was looking for. I reached out to touch it.

"How many times do I have to remind you, Tina," Len whispered, right in my ear. "It's called a poisonous plant for a reason."

I just about jumped out of my skin. "Man, Len, what the fuck!" I threw the words at him fast, assuming friendly aggression was the only path available in these dicey circumstances. "You're like a fucking snake hiding in the grass. How long have you been here?"

"Since I'm not the one who's been caught breaking and entering, I don't actually have to answer that," he said, unseen. "And as I recall, the snake encouraged Eve to pick the apple, even though it went against her best interests. I'm suggesting quite the opposite."

"I came up to talk to you," I said, tap-dancing wildly. "I've been calling about the moss, and you don't even pick up the phone."

"You broke into my apartment in the middle of the night so that you could talk about moss? I don't know that I'd take that approach with the police, Tina, it does not sound very likely. Especially since I can honestly testify that I found you sneaking around my apartment, looking to steal a rare plant that is very valuable to me."

"You know, Len, it's not right that you took that kid's plant. Charlie told me you just took it and now you're hiding up here, and you won't call her back. She's the one who should be calling the police." I looked around, hoping that Charlie would take this cue to reveal herself. She did not.

"She's deluded," the voice in the darkness observed.

"You stole it, Len," I said. He hadn't called the cops yet, and I was starting to hope that maybe he wouldn't. "Charlie said the kid needs the money. You just said yourself it's valuable, and you took it from him."

"Spare me the moral outrage, Tina; you've been doing nothing but taking things that don't belong to you for months, and there's always a good reason, isn't there," he noted, an amused sneer curling around the edge of his words. "You've got a criminal heart vastly more experienced than my own."

"There's nothing illegal about it. My mom—"

"You might also spare me the drivel about your mother, who by all accounts, including your own, you completely abandoned when she needed you most. Oh, by the way. I thought you looked terrific at that press conference over at Sotheby's. Wasn't that Sophie's dress you were wearing? And her pearls, another lovely touch. Does it make you feel more at home, since you've already stolen her apartment and her history, to be wearing her things as well?"

"They threw them away," I said, trying to sound cocky, but my criminal heart was abruptly less sure of its footing. "They threw her away too."

"And what do you think you know about that?" he asked, his voice hardening.

"What I don't know, I'm learning fast," I tossed back, hoping I sounded more secure than I felt. "Charlie brought that plant to you because she trusted you. She's your own kid. You stole from your own kid."

Len sighed in the dark. "Of course families betray each other, what would be the fun otherwise? Betraying someone you hardly know, it's not even worth it really."

"Was it fun betraying me?"

There was a kind of gleeful silence at this. "You are fun, actually," he told me. "You're so completely unmoored in the universe. And now you think you've found a home, only it's someone else's home, someone else's apartment, someone else's clothes, someone else's life. You could just as easily try to understand your own lost mother or even your lost sisters, but that doesn't attract you. You're too busy coveting . . . us."

"Is that why you're trying to get rid of me now? Because I don't belong? Because a place like this only belongs to the people who had it in the past? You're as bad as everybody else in this stupid building, they just want things to stay the same because they own everything and they think that sharing is for losers. Well, you know what? You *don't* own the Edgewood. Alison and Lucy and I are here fair and square."

"Well, you're not *here* fair and square, Tina, I caught you breaking and entering and trying to rob me. And while I find your philosophical musings about property and identity amusing, I suspect the authorities will not be in the least interested."

"They'll be interested in hearing what I have to say about that plant."

"That *will* be interesting. How many times have you been arrested? I couldn't really tell from what you said at that press conference. Does your record endear you to the police, make them trust you more? When you explain things to them, do they actually take your word for it?"

I didn't even bother to answer that one. By this point my heart wasn't pounding as hard; it wasn't pounding at all, in fact. Len *was* having fun; there was no sense of urgency to any of this at all.

"What do you want, Len?" I asked him. "What's the deal going to be?" For a moment one of the shadows shifted, and the barest reflection of the clustered purple lights picked up a hollow glint in his eyes, then slid back into the dark. His hand reached out and hovered over the *Madrigalis* like he was blessing it.

"If she could have made those seeds grow, don't you think she would have?" he asked, musing. "She didn't have the skill. That's what she's angry about. She brought me a boy, she brought me a seed, that's all she brought. A seed is nothing but potential. The rest is mine."

"She's your daughter."

"Don't come back here, Tina," he said simply. "That goes for Charlie too. My world is off-limits. You make her understand that. And maybe you'll be allowed to stay."

"Tell her yourself," I said. "She's right behind you."

The purple glint, which was all I could see of him, shifted to one side, startled, and none too soon, as something long and sharp sliced through the space where Len had stood a fraction of a second before.

"Holy shit," I said. "What the fuck!"

"Hi, Dad," said Charlie, raising her weapon again. "Nice to see you."

"Put that thing down. Jesus!" I said, really scared that she was going to give it another go. "What the fuck is that thing?"

"It's a pruning saw," Charlie informed me. "I'm going to murder my father with it." And then she brought it down again, barely missing him a second time. Len leapt back, falling into a black mass of something fernlike and dense but not completely losing his balance. From what little I could see in the shadows of the obscured foliage, he stumbled to one side, caught himself, and moved down one of the black paths that converged on this corner of the greenhouse.

"Your aim is not what it might be, dear," Len called back to her. "There aren't many who would have missed that chance."

"Maybe I'm hoping to drag this out," she countered. "It might be worth it to me to scare you a few times before I finish you off, you motherfucker." I couldn't see much of anything, but she was moving after him fast down that pathway, holding the pruning saw over her head as she aimed for her third try.

"Stop it, Charlie—man, come on, I'm a witness here!" I yelled.

"Don't kid yourself, Tina, you're an accessory!" she yelled back. I heard the blade swish through the night air again and make contact with something plantlike.

"Not even close," Len hissed, and now he sounded as if he were on another path in a different direction. "Your mother will be so disappointed in you," he observed with real pleasure. Charlie reappeared at my side, still swinging. I had to duck to stay clear of her.

"Mother will delight in every detail of this story," Charlie reported back. She swung the pruning saw blindly now, cutting another swath through the unseen foliage in front of her. "Oh, sorry, Dad, I think I just took out your *Heliotropus syncathia*. How long did it take you to root that? Oh well, you can spend another three years nurturing that one instead of me. Ooops. You don't have another three years, do you?" She swung the blade again, and I realized she wasn't blindly slashing at all; she knew where every single plant was in that place, and she was aiming. "Oh dear. There go the Asiatic lilies. Too bad, they are so *pretty.*"

"Stop. *Stop.*" This time Len's voice came from directly behind me. I didn't know where either of them was, but they did.

"I'm not going to stop, you fuckface!" she yelled, lunging yet again. And then, under her breath, to me, "Take it. Take it now. Get it out of here."

I didn't need to be told twice. While Charlie continued to destroy her father's greenhouse, I grabbed the *Madrigalis* and stumbled back

the way I had come. Behind me, the sound of the falling blade continued, cutting down the forest with glee.

Twenty minutes later, Frank was still passed out on the floor when
Charlie showed up at my door. "Thanks," she said abruptly. She had a
cut on her forehead, her hands were covered in dirt, and those spooky
blue eyes were unreadable. She slipped by me and Frank and headed for
the kitchen, knowing that was where I had stashed it.

"Look," I said, pissed, following her. "I said I'd help you get your
plant back. I didn't say you should *kill* him."

"Trust me, if I'd wanted to kill him, I wouldn't have missed," she
informed me. She flipped on the lights and looked at the *Madrigalis,*
which I had placed directly underneath its picture. "My god," she
sighed, "it really is beautiful." She put her arms around the plain terra-
cotta pot and lifted it carefully over to the sink. Then she took one of
the leaves between her fingers and held it delicately toward the light, so
she could get a better view of the one tiny bud hidden there.

"He got it to bud," she said. "He really is . . . amazing."

"You have to get that thing out of here right now," I told her. "I'm
serious. I can't be seen as an accomplice to this."

"Well, but you are very much an accomplice," she noted, barely
glancing my way. "I mean, *I* didn't call *you* and say let's go break into
my dad's greenhouse."

"Did you tell him that? Did you tell him that I called you?"

"He doesn't care. All he knows is that you crossed him."

"He crossed me first," I said, sounding like an eight-year-old. "Seriously, he was out there trying to get me kicked out of the building
before I did anything. All I ever did was help him and he—he—"

"Don't tell me about my own father," Charlie said as she examined
the leaves and stalks with care. "He probably wanted something out of
you, and he got it, and then he wanted something else. He wanted the
Madrigalis. And you saw me bring it to him. So he had to get rid of you,
because you knew he had it, and he saw that as threatening somehow.
And he was right," she said, finally smiling at me. "You were a threat.
You knew what he had, and you knew me, and you helped me take it

back. He was right to want to get rid of you." She turned back to the
sink and grabbed a small cup, filling it with water.

"So what's he going to do now?" I asked.

"Nothing right away," she said. She took Len's gardening gloves
that he had left there and slipped them on deliberately. "Tomorrow or
the next day, I don't know."

"What did you do to him?" I asked, a little worried.

"It's not what I did to *him*," she responded. "It's what I did to his
plants. You can do a lot of damage with a pruning saw if you're not
careful. And I wasn't." She pulled the leaves off one of the tiny branches
carefully, and then squeezed the stalk between her fingers. A sticky
white sap appeared. She studied it for a moment, then dipped the stalk
into the water and let it soak.

"Oh, you know, that's not—you know, I was trying to *help you*," I
said.

"Well, you did," said Charlie. "You helped me a lot." She rum-
maged around in the stack of miniature gardening implements on
the shelf above the sink and carefully selected one of the fertilizing
needles.

"Look," I said, finally sick of her and her cool disinterest in the
mess she had made for me. "I did this thing, for you and that kid. I was
trying to be nice, and you just, you—you're as bad as he is."

"You have no idea how bad he is," she stated. "I do." She placed the
fertilizing needle in the water.

"Then why did you even bring him that plant?" I said. "Why did
you ask him for help in the first place? Why did you trust him?"

She looked over at me, unimpressed. "I know a lot of talented
botanists, but he is the only one who could have gotten those seeds
to grow," she said, finishing her task with the needle. She touched
the slender, glistening leaves of the *Madrigalis* and smiled with a
cloudless and perverse delight. "He's right, I never could have done
it." She picked up the plant and headed out the door. "Don't touch
those things without gloves on," she called back to me. "That sap is
really quite toxic."

I didn't know what she was talking about until the next morning, when I glanced into the kitchen and understood what she had been doing while we talked. She had fed her quickly improvised solution from the sap of the *Madrigalis* into the irrigation system. Every tray of moss was dead.

25

It was kind of nice to see old Stuart Long. I hadn't laid eyes on the guy since the day we buried Mom, and there he was, sitting patiently in Ira Grossman's glamorous waiting room, looking like a friendly egg. He was reading a magazine, something financial and boring.

"Hey, Mr. Long," I said.

"Hello, Tina," he said, smiling with real pleasure. "It's been a while."

"Yes, a lot has happened," I agreed, sitting next to him. "What are you doing here, do you have business with Ira?"

"I'm giving a deposition," he informed me.

"Oh, so am I."

"Yes, I presumed so."

"Lucy and Alison are doing theirs tomorrow. They kind of didn't want me anywhere near the whole deposition thing in general? So we had to sign all these docs saying Lucy was the administratrix. That's the word, right?"

"I think it's a fine word."

"Anyway, they all decided that she should be in charge because I'm kind of a loose cannon, but now I have to give a deposition anyway."

"Sometimes it happens that way."

"I can't really follow it all that well. I pretty much just show up whenever they tell me to and do what I'm told."

"Very wise."

"It might be if I really pulled it off. Frankly, I understand why they'd rather keep me under wraps. I keep trying, over at the Edge, to be, you know, a good representative of the family, but it's not going as well as it might."

"Really?"

"Is that a surprise?" I asked.

"No," he said, closing his magazine carefully and setting it back on the table. This is the thing I find curious about lawyers. Even when they want to talk to you, they don't say very much. Mr. Long was clearly happy to see me and more than willing to talk to me while we waited to be called into our respective depositions; it's not like he was trying to ignore me so he could read his magazine. But he really wasn't going to say anything extra. After a moment I got embarrassed and decided to keep this going.

"Are you here for our case?" I asked. "I mean, I assumed you were, but maybe you're here on somebody else's case."

"I'm here on your case."

"Did I hear that the Drinans were suing you? I think Lucy told me that."

"Their lawyers have suggested it, certainly. It would be part of the case they need to build around the earlier wills."

"What kind of a case?"

"It's just one among several arguments they might make. That perhaps I was lax in probating Mrs. Drinan's will. The *first* Mrs. Drinan."

"I'm sorry about that, Mr. Long. I feel bad that you're being dragged into this on our account," I told him.

"Not on your account, no. Bill's wishes were very clear; he meant to leave the apartment and all his worldly goods to your mother, Tina. I am here because legally, as executor of his estate, I am required to enact his wishes."

"Yeah, but he didn't mean to leave the apartment to *us*," I said. Mr. Long tilted his head, like he had to sort of dramatically think about that, even though it seemed to me that all the legal shenanigans we were about to embark on were premised on that fact.

"Have you spoken to your lawyer about that thought?" he asked me.

"Not precisely," I admitted.

"Perhaps you should, in private," he advised. "Before you give your deposition. Opposing counsel will be present, and the deposition itself will be recorded as a legal document. So the question of Bill's intent, as you were aware of it, will surely be raised. Haven't you been prepped on this?"

"They're going to prep me just before I go in, some underling is going to run through it with me," I explained. But I was kind of touched that he felt like taking care of me. "What kind of things do they ask you in a deposition?" I asked.

"Well, they'll probably ask you about your mother, the last time you saw her, what she told you about Bill, things like that."

"Oh, no," I said. "I meant you. What kinds of questions will they ask *you*?"

"Oh." He nodded, as if that were a really intelligent thing for me to be curious about. "Yes, I will be deposed on completely different matters. Although there will be some overlap. I'm probably the only person who really spent time with Bill and Olivia together, and they'll want to know about that."

"You did?" I asked. I don't know why this hadn't occurred to me. From the start everybody had said he represented Bill and his estate. And I remembered Lucy saying he was Mom's lawyer, the day we found out about the apartment. "Of course you saw them together; they had to come into your office and sign things."

"No, no, they never came into the office," he corrected me. "Bill wouldn't leave the apartment. I went to them."

"You went to them? You went to the apartment?"

"Of course. I had dinner with them many times."

"You had *dinner* with them?"

"Yes, your mother was a lovely cook."

"My mother was not a lovely cook, Mr. Long," I said, almost laughing out loud. "My mother never cooked."

"Oh. Well. She cooked for Bill. And for me, when I would come by with a legal matter."

This was so far out of the realm of possibility I didn't know what to say. "Well, what did she cook?" I finally asked, trying not to sound utterly incredulous.

"She would roast a tenderloin or a chicken," he replied. "Once we had salmon fillets with some kind of sauce. I think it was an anchovy sauce, it was delicious. And Brussels sprouts in a Dijon mustard dressing, she made that once. There were concerns about Bill's diet, which she was quite alert to. No potatoes, whole-grain rice occasionally. Dessert was usually fresh fruit. Pineapple. Strawberries when they were in season. Or mango! With a little yogurt, we had that several times."

"Were there napkins? Napkin rings? Was there a *tablecloth*?" My incredulity had tipped over into a completely childish sarcasm and contempt. Mr. Long the Egg Man tilted his head thoughtfully for a moment and answered the question.

"We used paper napkins. There was no tablecloth because all they really had was that little coffee table next to the television set. I presume you've seen it?"

"Of course I've seen it."

"Yes. That's where we would eat, so mostly we held our plates on our laps. It was quite pleasant, really, sort of like a little picnic, except with lovely food."

"Made by my mother."

"Once Bill made the salad."

"You know what she used to cook for us? Fish sticks. Spaghetti with Ragú sauce from the jar. Hamburgers, the kind that came in those little flat frozen circles. When she really felt like doing something special for us, you know what we'd get? Frozen *waffles*."

"Really?" said Mr. Long.

"Yeah, really," I said. I felt like I was trapped in a cocktail shaker and someone was giving it a go; the inside of my head had become completely dislodged. "She was still drinking, right? I mean, *please* don't tell me, I don't care how shitty it sounds, but I really don't want to find out that once she was finished with the three of us my mother actually fixed her life. There was vodka all over the apartment when I got there, just vodka and red wine and and and nothing—like nothing else was there when I got there. She was still just a big drunk."

"They both drank." Mr. Long nodded, and like everything else it sounded like a fact coming from him. "But I would never have called either of them 'a big drunk.' Neither one of them, to my knowledge, drank before six." He stopped talking, like that was enough facts for now.

"What do you mean, they didn't drink before six?"

"I don't know if it was true when I was not present. But whenever I was present they did not drink before six. They had a certain reverence for the phrase 'cocktail hour.'"

"But then they kept drinking."

"We would enjoy wine with dinner and then I would leave. I don't know if they continued to drink after I left."

"Cocktail hour. When I was a kid, cocktail hour started at noon," I said. I sounded like a big whiner, and in fact my voice actually cracked in the most horrifying way, as if I were about to start crying. Mr. Long just stared at the floor with a sort of deliberate and embarrassed disinclination to continue the conversation. "I'm happy, no, I mean I'm really happy for them," I added. "You too. I'm happy you got to have these lovely dinners with Bill and my mom, that sounds terrific."

"It was, actually. She was a very good cook. Now that you tell me she didn't cook often before she met Bill, I understand the pleasure she took in it. There was always a real sense of surprise that she was good at it. And now I know why."

"Yeah, all those lovely dinners sound terrific." I picked up one of the magazines on the table so I could act like I didn't care. Like all the rest of the magazines in that swank office, it looked boring as hell; besides which, I knew I was behaving horribly, so I immediately put it back down.

"She was his cleaning lady. So you knew that, right, before he married her? She was just, like, his cleaning lady?"

"Yes, of course I did. I was the one who introduced them."

"You *introduced* them?"

"Oh. Yes. It hadn't occurred to me that you didn't know. Your mother was doing some cleaning for me, and I knew Bill was looking for someone as well, so I introduced them."

"Well, how did you know her?" I asked, feeling, inexplicably, more and more outraged by all this.

"She lived a few blocks from me in Jersey City. She advertised her cleaning services in one of the smaller local papers, and I responded to her ad."

"That's, this is all just—crazy," I said.

"Why is it crazy?"

"So you *knew* her? You *really* knew her?"

"I knew her in several different contexts and through several rather significant changes in her circumstances. So I know about those events, and her experience of those events. Is that what you mean?"

"I—don't think—I knew her," I said a bit lamely.

There was silence at this. I'm sure I was just embarrassing the hell out of old Stuart Long.

"Perhaps you should discuss the gaps in your information with your sisters," he finally suggested. "They seem to have had more consistent contact with her in the past few years."

"Yes, that's a good idea," I murmured, embarrassed for us both now. "Of course, that's obviously what I should do. I apologize, Mr. Long, really. Please excuse me. I think maybe I need to use the restroom. I don't, actually, need to use the restroom. I'm not kidding, you have to tell me. This is not, no. All you can say, go talk to Alison and Lucy because they were *around* more? I would but I sincerely doubt that they were paying attention. Nobody was paying attention, nobody was *talking* to her. You should hear the shit I hear from the people who live in that building— they can't get over the fact that she was a *cleaning lady* from *New Jersey,* and that meant something—that she was a thief and a liar and cheating Bill and keeping him drunk. Because there's no way it was about anything except the apartment, but that's not her either, it's not—it's not . . . None of it sounds like anything I remember. None of it." I stopped finally. "Sorry. Sorry. I don't know why I'm ranting, I really do sound like an idiot."

Mr. Long waited, probably to see if there would be any further useless outbursts. When there weren't, he folded his fingers together and considered his response. And then he considered some more. It seemed to take him forever to decide what to tell me that might rise to the level of some truth about my mother's life.

"She took very good care of him," he finally said. "His health was quite poor those last few years; that was why he never went out. He was afraid to be left alone, but she didn't seem to mind how much he needed her. And he appreciated everything she did for him, very much. He wanted her to have a home after he was gone. There was nothing dishonest or dishonorable in their relationship. They took great pleasure in each other. It was my impression that they loved each other very much. That at least is what I will report in my deposition."

"What was Sophie like?" I asked.

Mr. Long looked at me sharply—at least as sharply as a guy who looks like an egg can look. He didn't have a chance to tell me to mind my own business, though. One of Ira's legal underlings suddenly appeared and smiled at me from inside his suit. "Tina? Hi, I'm Jackson, I'm going to be prepping your deposition today. I'm so glad I poked my head out, no one knew if you were here or not!"

"Yeah, I kind of slithered in, forgot to tell the girl at the desk," I said.

"Not a problem, not a problem," he reassured me. He held out his hand like he was guiding me to my execution. "Right in here, please, we'll just get started."

26

JENNIFER WAS NOT ENTIRELY SYMPATHETIC TO MY POSITION ABOUT my mother, but that may have been because she didn't understand it. "Okay, so you were mad at her for being a drunk, but now you're mad because she *wasn't* a drunk?" she asked.

"I don't know that she wasn't a drunk," I said. "All he said was she stopped drinking. Which she didn't even, stop drinking."

"But she didn't drink as much."

"That's what he said. When I was a teenager, she like drank all the time and then passed out in the middle of the day. Then we grow up and she suddenly gets it together to fall in love with a total stranger and *not* drink except at like six o'clock, when everybody drinks?" I said, pouring a huge shot of vodka over a couple of ice cubes.

"My parents drink wine," Jennifer informed me. She was delicately perched on the minuscule counter in my little kitchen, her plaid skirt falling perfectly over her skinny knees, while she watched me make myself a cocktail. Her geometry book was lying open on the floor, where she had left it when I returned from my torturous afternoon. She had paid Katherine off with a series of minor bribes all week—a Tootsie Roll, a Blow Pop, a two-pack of Mint Milano cookies—so she could visit me for an hour each day while Katherine played in her room with the door locked. I thought it was a pretty clever bit of plotting, and I had come to find it unimaginably delightful to have her there. Lucy and Daniel and Alison were off giving depositions and living their lives, that cloud on the title had scared off the real estate agent for the time being, and Len was probably plotting revenge on me, so it felt pretty lonely in that big apartment. Jennifer was good company in a kind of sardonic teenage way.

"So what was this thing you had to do?" she asked. "You were being decomposed?"

"Yes, that's exactly what it was, I was being *decomposed* by a bunch of bloodless vampires also known as *lawyers*," I said. "It was *endless*. This total moron, *Jack*son, that was his first *name*, I hate it when people have first names that are last names. That became cool, *why*? You have to ask yourself. I'm not kidding. This guy, he's got like the most astonishing suit you've ever seen, and even though it's *my* deposition, *I'm* the one who's supposed to be answering questions, even so he manages to squeeze into the conversation his weekend in the Hamptons and where he gets his suit made. I mean, who cares? It's *my* deposition."

"He sounds like, you know, half of Manhattan," Jennifer noted.

"Right? Plus then the whole thing is about him telling me what not to say. They're going to ask you questions about your mother, and these are the things *not* to tell them. You know what I wasn't allowed to tell them? Everything. Seriously. Everything. Every question, he would say, 'what's your favorite memory of your mother,' and I would say, 'her perfume,' and he would say, 'no no, you can't say that,' and I would say, but that is my favorite memory of my mother."

"She had nice perfume?"

"She had the most expensive perfume in the world."

"Wow," said Jennifer.

"Yes," I agreed. "But she never wore it, because it was really expensive, so she couldn't afford to wear it, and besides my dad never took her anywhere to wear it."

"Well, that's a drag."

"Seriously," I said. "So I tried to explain that to this—asshole, *Jack*son—because he's all 'you have to be more specific.' And then when I tell him that, what I just said, which *is* specific, he's all, 'no no, you can't say that.' And I'm like, well what do you want me to say? And he's like, 'tell the truth, be specific, but don't give them any rope they can hang you with.' And I'm like, what do you mean, rope? And he's like— 'they are trying to prove that your mother had a questionable character. You cannot let them prove that.'"

"A 'questionable character'?" said Jennifer. "What does that mean?"

"It means, I don't know, it means—I don't know what it means," I said. "But I've, honestly, I'm really thinking that I just want to do this right, I don't want to screw things up again. My mom—this is my mom we're talking about, and my sisters—and *I*—I love this place! I love it! I don't want to screw this up. I don't want to give them *rope*. There's already been too much—and then of *course* the other lawyer—"

"There's another lawyer?"

"Yes. From the other side, representing the Drinans, who truth be told, I'm sorry, but what they did is also not so great."

"What did they do?"

"It doesn't matter. But this other lawyer—the questions—it's all so—the things they said. And tried to get me to say."

"Like what?"

"Nothing. Forget it."

"You're in a bad mood," Jennifer observed. She hopped off the counter and started to look through the cabinets. "How come you never have anything to eat around here?"

"I have things to eat," I said. "There's half a sandwich in the refrigerator."

"That thing is really old, Tina. I looked at it before you got back, and it is like truly disgusting. I'm not saying you're anorexic or anything, but seriously. If I were you I wouldn't wait until I was sixty to figure out how to eat."

I looked at the bottle of orange juice in my hand and actually considered throwing it at her. I'm not kidding, a wave of something truly evil came over me, I even raised the bottle for a moment and looked up at her with the thought in my heart, *just throw it at her*. I could feel the rage physically rise up the back of my neck; it was the way I felt the last time I did something truly worth getting arrested for. Jennifer just took a startled little step back and held up her hands, confused but sensible.

"Whoa, Tina, what's up, are you okay? I didn't mean anything. I just meant, you should go to the grocery store and get some eggs or something, crackers, carrot sticks, you know, stuff to eat when you get hungry. Or a chicken. Even if you don't like to cook, the grocery stores sell these roasted chickens; they're pretty good."

Honestly, what she was saying was so simple, but my head seriously wasn't processing. I set down the orange juice and looked around the counter. "You know what, though, is why, why isn't there a cookbook, then?" I asked her. I opened my arms and included the entire kitchen in my conversation, as if it, or Jennifer, or anyone, really, might know the answer to this question. "It's not like I haven't looked! Where are the recipes? How would you know what to do? If you never did it? How would you know?"

"You can buy cookbooks pretty much anywhere," Jennifer told me, strangely and wonderfully knowing what I was asking.

"Then why isn't there one here?" I asked. "Where did she learn how to do it?"

"I don't know," said Jennifer. "Don't people just know how to cook?"

"No," I told her. "They *don't*."

We looked. For forty minutes. We went through all the cabinets and in all the boxes under the bed in Bill and Olivia's bedroom. We looked under the couch. We looked in closets that had nothing in them; we checked the shelves over the washer and the dryer; we looked under the sinks in the bathrooms, and then we went through the boxes of books one more time. There were no cookbooks; Olivia seemingly never bought one.

"Or she threw it away after he died," Jennifer speculated.

Which is finally what made me cry. It wasn't like I was bawling or anything, but tears just started running down my face and I couldn't seem to stop them.

"Oh," Jennifer said, sort of embarrassed and surprised in a sad, sardonic way. "I don't know. I mean, what do I know?"

"I'm sorry," I said. "I don't know what's the matter with me."

"No, it's okay, you had a long day."

"You have homework," I observed.

"Yeah," she said. "Okay, I'll see you tomorrow." And with that she turned, grabbed her geometry book off the floor, and fled.

After an hour of sitting in my mother's little living room in front of the blank television screen, alongside her empty kitchen, I went out and bought myself a roast chicken. I couldn't eat it, unfortunately; once it was on the kitchen counter it just looked stupid to me. So I put it in the refrigerator and channel-flipped for half the night.

No matter what you do, it's never enough, I thought. *No matter what you do, it's never enough.* Mom said that all the time, that was one of my big memories, along with the perfume she never wore, *no matter what you do it's never enough.* And that's what I did with the entire next day. I sat around in my empty apartment, counting and recounting the last of my money, trying to think what I could to make more, having a cocktail, looking through someone else's photographs, channel-flipping, counting my money again, thinking, *no matter what you do it's never enough.* This went on for an entire day before I changed the mantra to *to hell with it,* got myself up off the couch, and walked to the store.

They have a grocery store on the Upper West Side called Fairway, of all things, and it's famous as grocery stores go, so that is where I went. I fought my way through enormous crowds of shoppers while trying to figure out what ingredients to buy to make a real meal for myself. As it turned out, they had little recipe cards perched everywhere, and they were free. It was like a service that the store offered for people like me who didn't have a clue: you take one of these cards, buy all the ingredients on the card, take it all home and follow the recipe, and then, presto, you've cooked a meal. Buying all the ingredients totally cleaned me out cashwise, but I managed to get everything I needed for pasta with scallops and pears in a lemon cream sauce. It sounds fancy, but the instructions made it seem not so hard to cook. I thought of inviting Jennifer to stay for dinner.

Frank was the first to warn me that the evening might not go as planned. "Your sisters are here," he said as he reached out to help me carry my groceries to the elevator. Not only was he back to being nice Frank, he was particularly nice to me. We had never spoken about what happened the day he confessed his love for Julianna Gideon, but it was there between us. I think just that much is sometimes enough to give people hope.

"Thanks for the warning," I said, holding the elevator door open so he could put my bags on the floor for me. "Did they say anything?"

"You know what, they did," said Frank. "They wanted to know what apartment Vince lived in."

"*Vince?* What did they want with Vince?"

Frank gave me a friendly little "who knows" gesture. "I told them I couldn't give out that information, but the pushy one didn't believe me."

"She never takes no for an answer," I said.

"No, she don't. Anyway she just went through the junk mail I leave by the radiator until she found it."

"Yes, she's clever too."

"Boy, she is," he said, tapping the elevator button and sending me off.

As I opened the door to the apartment, I actually felt my heart thump a little in anticipation. I hadn't seen much of Alison or Lucy lately, and I was getting lonely. It was hard to sit in that apartment night after night and wonder who I was. Plus things had gotten so complicated, with press conferences and clouds and screaming co-op boards, I was frankly hoping that Lucy might explain to me what was going on.

There was Alison, as soon as I stepped in, in the front of the apartment, scrubbing down the kitchen.

"I see you got rid of the moss!" she exclaimed, really happy and excited. She had never let go of her first impression, that the stuff was dangerous and would cost millions to get removed, and we might be on the hook for it even if we didn't win this case. And now the stuff was miraculously gone. After Charlie had poisoned it beyond repair, I had tossed all the trays into garbage bags and taken them straight out to the Dumpster so the stuff that had killed the moss wouldn't get everyone else in the building. Alison didn't know that, of course; all she knew was that the scary green stuff was gone. It made her cheerful.

"How'd your deposition go?" I asked.

"Terrific," she said. "Just great. I like that Jackson, don't you? He really thinks we're going to win this. He was very reassuring."

"Was he?"

"And so cute! I mean, not my type, I'm happily married! But that doesn't mean I can't look!"

"What can I do for you today, Alison?"

"Oh, Lucy and I just thought maybe we should come over and help you keep this place clean," she explained with that cheerful smile. "It just didn't seem fair that you should have to do all the work of keeping this big place presentable while the lawyers and the real estate people and the people who run the building try and work out their problems. I mean, who knows how long that is going to take! And you're not a slave!"

"There's not that much to do, actually," I told her, trying to figure this out. "Most of the rooms don't get used. The moss thing, as you've noticed, has been taken care of."

"So that man who owned it—Len, is that his name?"

"Yes?" I said, wondering where this was going.

"Len Colbert?"

"Did I mention his name to you?"

"I just, I saw a Len on the names for the co-op board, and I wondered if that was him."

"Yes, that is him. He was the one ranting at that press conference they threw in the lobby, where they told the entire city of New York that we're white-trash interlopers. That was his phrase, I think. He got mentioned in all the articles. Lucy's friend over at the *Times* especially gave him a lot of ink."

"Well, I didn't read any of it, because I knew it would upset me, but Daniel did, and he did mention that this Len person seemed particularly upset. And if he's angry already, we don't want to make him any angrier. I was going to suggest we should leave the moss where it is."

"No, it's gone."

"Well, maybe you should let him know that if he wants to keep it here, he is welcome," she said, smiling at me brightly, like a Girl Scout leader.

"Listen, Alison, is something going on?" I asked. She was being so cheerfully weird I had to comment on it.

"What makes you ask?"

"Oh—nothing." I could tell that she didn't want to be the one to deliver whatever bizarre news she and Lucy had come to unload on me, so I decided to spare her for now. "Is Lucy in the back?"

"No, she had to run out for a moment," Alison reported, nervous.

"Really? Frank said she was up here."

"She was. She'll be right back. Would you like some tea? I think I saw some in the closet in the back kitchen. I would love a cup of tea," she enthused, clearly working to get her act back on the rails.

"Terrific," I said. "Let's go do that, then."

We hiked through the great room and down the endless hallway to the other kitchen. "Hey, Alison, do you remember if Mom ever cooked?" I asked.

"Mom? Cook?" Alison said, startled. The idea seemed as nonsensical to her as it had to me. "Well, she boiled water for spaghetti, I remember her doing that. But that was pretty much the extent of the cooking."

"Do you cook?" I asked.

"Daniel and I both work, you know that."

"Lucy doesn't cook," I observed.

"When you live in Manhattan, you don't have to cook. Manhattan is thirty-five square miles of room service!"

"Well, I think I'm going to cook tonight," I said. "I bought a bunch of groceries because I thought I'd like to try it. You want to stay for dinner?"

"Oh," she said, like this was a really bad idea.

"You don't have to stay. I mean, you can stay if you want. It's probably going to be a disaster. But you never know. I'm making scallops and pears in a lemon cream sauce. I read the recipe, and it doesn't look as hard as it sounds. You just boil some pasta and sear the scallops and the pears—do you know how to sear?"

"No, I don't, I really don't," she said, inexplicably getting all upset again.

"It's not that big a deal, I can figure it out."

"I think that's Lucy," she said, picking up the tiny change in the atmosphere that occurs when someone opens the front door of the apartment. "LUCY! IS THAT YOU?" she asked, and then she scurried away.

Even after Frank's forewarning, I couldn't put together what their plan was. Lucy had to just come out and announce it to me. She breezed into the kitchen with Alison hovering behind her and tossed it off like a fancy new pair of leather gloves.

"I was just down on the fifth floor talking to your friend Vince," she told me, as if this were the most natural thing in the world.

"You were what?" I said.

"He really likes you, Tina. Well, we knew that."

"Okay, can we back up for a second? You went down to see Vince Masterson?"

"His father is the president of the co-op board."

"So?"

"So we—Daniel and Ira and I, and Alison—think that's a good relationship to build. Obviously, no one is happy about the co-op's response to this situation. That press conference they held made a big impression on the media, and Sotheby's has, well, I think it's obvious that their interest has cooled. We were all set to move ahead with the renovation, and that, all of it, has been put on hold."

"What renovation? You want to renovate this place? With what?"

"There are investors willing to come on board with us. We told you this."

"You did not tell me this."

"If I didn't tell you all the details, it's because you can barely hold on to the three or four in front of you at any given time."

"Stop talking to me like I'm an idiot, Lucy—"

"I'm not talking to you like you're an idiot. I'm telling you the facts. You're angry because we don't always give them to you; well, I'll give them to you now if you'll stop whining long enough to listen."

"That's charming."

"Please, please don't fight," Alison interrupted, suddenly near tears. "It's terrible, Tina. You don't know how bad things are. We're going to lose everything. We're going to *lose*."

"Relax, Alison," Lucy warned her. "We're not losing anything. It's just going to take a bit longer to win. We have to be both wily and tenacious, and as you and I both know, Tina is completely capable of that."

"Oh great. I can't wait to hear what I'm capable of," I said. "Keep going, Lucy."

"Vince would really like to have dinner with you."

"So you arranged for that. For me to have dinner with him."

"You have a reservation at Neal's, for seven-thirty. He'll meet you there."

"And then we can cab back home together," I observed, picking up on the genius of the plan fast enough.

"Well, that would be up to you, but since you live in the same building I don't know why not."

"Perfect," I said. "I'm really looking forward to sharing a cab with that octopus."

"He's quite attractive," Lucy told Alison, ignoring my tone. "He looks like a supermodel. I can't believe he looks like that *and* he has money! Oh, you put water on for tea! Is there enough for me?" She sailed back into the kitchen and started looking around for the tea bags.

"Yes, there's water. I don't think it's ready yet, but maybe it is," Alison twittered. "I don't know how long you keep it on."

"You keep it on until it *boils*," I said. "Are you kidding me? You really don't even know how to boil *water*?"

"We don't have tea very often, Tina," she replied, with an air of offended dignity. "I just heat up the water in the microwave."

"Well, let me clue you in to something. The microwave uses up sixty zillion times as much energy as you need, and it *doesn't get the water hot enough.*"

"Don't yell at her," Lucy warned me.

"How about if I yell at you?" I said, furious.

"What, what?" said Alison. "What's wrong?"

"Oh, stop acting like an idiot, Alison," I sneered. "I'm being pimped out by my own sisters, and you want me to act like there's nothing *wrong*?"

"Inflammatory language is not going to be helpful here," Lucy announced.

"Inflammatory language is *never* helpful, that's not why I use it!" I hissed. "You want me to fuck that guy. I'm supposed to fuck Vince Masterson because his father is on the fucking co-op board."

"He is the *president* of the co-op board."

"No one said you had to sleep with him," Alison protested. "We just thought that since he liked you already, that you could ask for his help, Tina, that's all we were talking about."

"Alison, grow up and get a clue, would you, please? Vince Masterson does not want to have *dinner* with me."

"A couple of months ago, I almost walked in on you and Vince doing the deed right out front on that hideous shag rug," Lucy pointed out, unimpressed with my moral outrage. "I don't think it's unreasonable to assume that if you decided to follow through on that impulse, it might put things on a friendlier footing. Between us and the co-op board."

"Why don't *you* have sex with him, you think it's such a great idea."

"Why would I when you and he have already established such a rapport."

"You don't have to have sex with him, Tina, come on," Alison interjected with a note of pleading. "Just have dinner with him, that's all, and remind him that we're really good people and we want to do what's best for the building and the apartment, we want it to be safe and have it go into the right hands. That's really what we want, and they don't have to worry about that."

"Great, that's great, I'm sure that will make a big impression on old Vince," I said, not really caring about any of this, I found the whole scenario so depressing. "My sisters are pimping me out," I muttered. "That's great. My sisters are pimping me out."

"Please stop saying that, it's just not true," said Alison.

"You know, Mom would not want this," I said. "You know that."

"She doesn't get a vote," Lucy said.

"What do you think?" I said to Alison. "You think Mom would want me to do this? Just go have sex with this guy because Lucy thinks maybe that'll help?"

"It's because of what *she* wanted. You don't know, Tina, Mom wanted—"

"Alison—" Lucy began.

"No, we have to tell her. If we don't tell her, how will she know?"

"Know what?" I asked.

They stared at each other. Lucy was clearly both furious and calculating, while Alison pleaded with her sad, puppylike eyes. Lucy looked up at the ceiling, like Pontius Pilate about to dip his bloody hands into a plate of water in the picture my mother had on the wall of the living room when we were kids.

"Well, now you have to tell me," I pointed out.

"Fine," said Lucy. "Alison, be my guest."

"Mom called me," Alison whispered. And then stopped.

"Mom *called* you? When, like last week? From the grave?" I knew it was mean, but I had had it with both of them by that point.

"Before. Before the grave. But just before."

"Alison, stop beating around the bush!"

"I'm not, I'm telling you! She called me. She was feeling sick. And she was worried. She felt like she couldn't stay here, that she was living in someone else's home. But Bill had left it to her, he wanted her to have it, and she wanted to stay here and be close to him, but she was worried that something might happen to her and she wanted to make a will. She wanted to make sure, make sure that his sons would get their home back."

This revelation landed with some authority.

"When was this?"

"It was just a few days. Before she died. Like three, even," Alison admitted.

"And—"

"Yes. She wanted to make a will, but she didn't make a will. We weren't sure, we thought maybe she called that lawyer—"

"Mr. Long?"

"Yes, him, we thought maybe she had called him and told him?"

"But we've seen his deposition, and it wasn't there," Lucy narrated. "They asked him specifically, did she ever make statements to the effect that she felt the property was deeded to her improperly. He said no."

"So we think she never said it to him. We think she only said it to me, then didn't do it."

"And you didn't tell anybody. You didn't tell the lawyers or the Drinans. Or me."

"No, she didn't," Lucy said. She went to the refrigerator and with one icy motion opened the freezer door and grabbed the vodka bottle, then pulled the cork out with her teeth. I felt like I was in Russia suddenly. "She didn't tell anybody at first because she didn't know what Mom meant," she continued. "And then when Mom died, we started getting these phone calls about a house—"

"They said 'apartment,'" Alison added. "But Mom had called it a house. That's why I was confused. She said it was a house."

"So you didn't tell anybody."

"I told Daniel and Lucy. But they, they said not to tell anybody else. Because if Mom really had wanted to leave it to someone else, she'd had plenty of time to do it. Or she could have called her lawyer. She could have done that anytime. So maybe she was drunk or something. When she called me. And if she was drunk, then she maybe didn't really mean what she said, and if I told people it would just confuse things."

"It doesn't sound too confusing to me," I said. "You tell somebody—like, Mr. Long, say—that she wanted the Drinans to have the apartment? That kind of statement would make things significantly *less* confusing. You tell them that and all the turmoil goes away, Alison."

"Yes, people suspected your unpredictable conscience might choose to see things that way," Lucy said, downing a straight shot of vodka from one of my few clean glasses. "Which is why people felt that the right thing to do, to protect you and your interests, was to keep it to ourselves."

"What's that supposed to mean?"

"It means sometimes you get on a high horse and sometimes you get on quite a different horse, and no one knows which you're going to choose on any given day."

"That's not what I do."

"Tina. Your immediate reaction to this story is to run off and tell the lawyers? This is what Mom wanted, so that's what we should do, 'it's not confusing,' 'it makes all the problems go away.' But it doesn't. It's hearsay. Alison can't remember exactly what Mom said. And you weren't on the phone call, you weren't even on the call list, so you don't know what Mom may or may not have wanted. So you can't testify to what Alison just told you anyway. But if Mom called anyone else?" She shrugged and poured herself another vodka.

"Can I have some of that?" I asked.

"Of course," she said, finding the second clean glass and pouring the shot, which I tossed back. It tasted good.

"You mean one of the Drinans," I said. "You think she called one of them and said that she wanted to do the right thing and leave them the apartment."

"Whether or not she did, that would be hearsay too. Unless somebody has it in writing, none of it is admissible."

"Which is why—what? Which is why the co-op board is the bigger problem today?"

"They're all problems," Lucy said. "But today the co-op board is the big one, yes." She poured me another vodka, rather more than I needed. I knew she was trying to get me drunk so I'd go along with her crazy plot, but I almost appreciated the gesture. "Listen, Tina," she said. "The Drinans are not going to win this. The one piece of evidence they need—that Mom intended to leave the apartment to them—doesn't exist! So if the co-op board takes some crazy position against us, it won't do anybody any good. It will just complicate things. You'll be doing everyone a favor if you can straighten this out."

"Lucy says Vince is really nice," Alison said sadly. "She thinks he wants to help us."

"Oh, for crying out loud," I said. "I was going to make a dinner."

"You can do it tomorrow," Lucy told me. "Maybe you could wear that black dress you wore to the press conference at Sotheby's. You really look terrific in that."

27

I WENT TO THAT RESTAURANT TO MEET VINCE. WHY NOT? I thought. The honest pleasure I had felt when I saw Alison poking around my mossless kitchen had completely evaporated; I didn't want to even try cooking now, I just wanted to get away from my sisters. Plus, even though I didn't know what the dead people who had put all this in motion had wanted, I knew that handing the apartment over to the building was what they *didn't* want. Plus the food would be good. Plus I was out of cash, and under the circumstances Vince would definitely have to pay for it.

"Tina, hi," he said, smiling, as I walked into the bar. He stood up from his stool and leaned over and kissed me on the mouth, quick but deliberate. There would be no mystery around the assumptions of the evening. "That dress really is stunning; I was hoping you'd wear it."

"My sister suggested you might feel that way," I replied. "We aim to please."

"And you do," he said, slightly gallant but also slightly creepy. Then he turned to the bartender, who of course was right there waiting for his next command. "A vodka gimlet for the lady," Vince told him. "And can we have some of those cheese things that keep wandering by? I'm *starving*."

Those "cheese things" turned out to be some sort of cheddar cream puff, which was all we ate while Vince poured vodka gimlets into me at the bar.

"Aren't we going to eat?" I asked, as the bartender delivered my third gimlet. "I'm getting drunk."

"But you're so charming when you're drunk," Vince reassured me. "I confess I was hoping to get you a little inebriated and then lure you back into that hot tub. I can still see you there, surrounded by naked men. I can't believe I missed that."

"A little louder, Vince, I don't think the entire restaurant heard you. And by the way, I do understand what the intentions of the evening are, but can't you at least pretend?" I leaned over the bar and spoke to the bartender. "We're going to be eating at the bar," I told him. "I'd like a big steak, the best one you've got, medium rare."

"Yes, ma'am," he replied discreetly. Vince raised his Scotch glass, which was empty for the third time.

"I'd slow down, Vince, you've got a long night ahead of you."

"I'm looking forward to it. You'll not escape me again, Tina Finn, and while we're on the subject, I have a bone to pick with you. Why are you playing so hard to get? I know you like me."

"Yeah, I love it when people try to extort me into having sex with them. That's my favorite, favorite thing."

"If your sister hadn't interrupted us, we'd have consummated our friendship the first day I met you. Nobody was extorting you then."

"What can I say, Vince? Somehow the mystery's lost," I said, but when I glanced over at him, honestly, I had to admit in my heart that maybe he had a point. His jacket hung beautifully across his back, and his blue eyes considered me with a kind of animal intelligence it was hard not to appreciate. The guy just radiated money and charisma. When he caught on to the fact that I was sizing him up, he grinned, which made him look both better and worse.

"Extortion, my ass," he said, leaning in and kissing me. This time there was nothing fast about it, and it involved a lot of tongue. On top of the three gimlets, it made me see stars, but I was not ready to hurl myself down the rabbit hole just yet. I pushed him back.

"Let's get out of here," he said.

"I have a steak coming," I reminded him.

"For crying out loud, I'm jumping out of my skin here," he informed me. "How long am I going to have to wait for this?"

"I don't know, Vince," I said, "but the whining is not doing it for me at the moment. I thought we were having dinner. You need to slow the train down."

This pissed him off. "You need to be nice," he said darkly.

"I *am* being nice," I retorted. "As nice as I get in situations like this. So what is going on with your stupid co-op board anyway? Lucy was acting like six years of legal hassle is nothing compared to what those jerks might be cooking up."

"Well, they're legally evicting you this week, so she might have a point," he informed me, continuing in the tone of careless nastiness we had both been taking. As soon as he said it, he half regretted it, I could tell, but only because it meant he wasn't going to get laid until he explained what that idle but utterly specific comment meant.

"What do you mean, they're evicting me?"

He looked away for a second, annoyed, but it was too late to take it back. "It's in the bylaws of the building," he said, reaching for his drink. He shrugged, like this was common knowledge.

"What's in the fucking bylaws?"

"What I just said! If you don't have any legal standing—and you don't, you have none until they settle all the confusion over the wills—"

"There isn't any confusion over the wills—"

"You have no legal standing, no right at all, Tina, to be in that apartment—"

"Pete Drinan said it was okay. They had an injunction, but it got removed—"

"They don't get to say! They have no legal standing either! The building gets to say! And the building wants you out."

"Why? Why?"

"Because you can't just waltz into one of the most exclusive addresses and take it over; it doesn't happen that way."

"I'm hardly taking it over."

"You're living in the Livingston Mansion Apartment. It will not be allowed."

"Tell that to the courts."

"You're gone, Tina. Get a clue."

"Unless what. I'm gone unless *what*?" I asked, feeling a little desperate at the sureness of his knowledge of how places like the Edge worked.

"Unless *nothing*," he said, laughing now. "It's a done deal."

"Then why am I supposed to sleep with you, asshole?" I said. "Why would I do that if they're kicking me out anyway?" Vince was suddenly caught in the mess of lies he had been telling my sisters and the truths he had been telling me, and his mouth dropped open. It was pathetic. "You can't do anything for any of us, can you? And you told my sister, you made my sister think that if I slept with you it would make a difference. You got her to sell me out for nothing."

"No," he started.

"You're a fucking piece of shit, Vince," I told him. And then, louder, as loud as I could, so the whole restaurant could hear me, "You're a fucking lying piece of *shit.*" And with that I left.

He caught up with me two blocks later, as I stalked up Broadway. I hate heels—they look great on the exit, but then you can never keep it up; boots are much better in a getaway. Unfortunately, though, I was wearing those stupid heels because I was supposed to look all beautiful and sexy for that lying shithead, which meant I could hardly walk, which meant that lying shithead didn't even have to break a sweat to catch up with me as I stumbled along the sidewalk.

"Tina, I'm sorry. Tina, stop, just stop and listen to me for a second."

"No."

"Yes, come on, I'm sorry. I exaggerated. It's not true what I told you."

"It sure sounded like the truth. At least, it sounded completely different from all the bullshit that comes out of your mouth otherwise."

"They *are* kicking you out. They had the vote scheduled for today. But my dad couldn't be there, so they had to reschedule."

"Liar."

"I'm not lying. They need a bunch of signatures to engage in legal action, and he's the board president so he had to be there. So I did tell your sister I'd put in a good word—"

"If I slept with you."

"Yes, I did tell her that," he said, having the grace, finally, to be the tiniest bit embarrassed. "But the fact is, even if he votes for you, it won't make a difference. They have eleven votes against you. Even if I could swing him your way, you're gone."

"Well, then who owns the apartment?" I asked.

"It will take them years to figure that out, and the longer it takes the better it is for the building. I mean, they never liked the Drinans either."

"It doesn't matter if they *liked* them or not, it was their apartment!"

"It was the *Livingston* apartment," Vince corrected me, quite serious for once. He looked startled; there was something about the import of this whole insane situation that I wasn't getting. "Those people, they came into the building, they weren't vetted, they just came in."

"I think they were born there, Vince."

"It's not like citizenship, Tina; it's not like if you're *born* in a building you have property rights. I didn't think I'd have to explain that to *you*. And if that first will wasn't probated? The building has more of a claim than anybody. And maybe they should—you know the story about what happened to the mother, they put her in some loony bin and threw away the key and then she *died* in there. It's totally Victorian."

"It's a Victorian building," I reminded him.

"Well said, but why should they get the apartment? It was her apartment."

"What's your point, Vince?" I asked.

"My point is, neither you or the Drinans is going to get that apartment, I don't care how hard you try," Vince said, all convivial now. "It's the *Livingston Mansion Apartment*, Tina! You might have had a chance with one of the minor apartments. But that one, no way."

"I see," I said, although I did not.

"Listen," he sighed, suddenly filled with pity and goodwill toward me, god knows why. "I'll see if I can buy you some time. I really can put in a good word, and it might keep dear old dad on the fence for a little while."

"How many times do I have to sleep with you for that whopping favor?"

"It's for free," he said, grinning at this. "Come on, Tina, let's grab a cab, you can't walk all the way home in those shoes. I won't bother you. I promise."

"Your promises," I sighed, indicating that I didn't think much of them. But I wasn't too mean about it.

28

"So how did it go?" Lucy cooed on the phone the next morning.

"Just great, Lucy," I said. "Vince is definitely on board."

"I knew you could do it," she replied smugly. "Thanks, Tina. I owe you one."

"Anything for the cause," I said. "You need anything else, just let me know."

I hung up and stared at the ceiling. I thought about calling her back and telling her everything Vince had said—that we would never win this, the building didn't want *any* of us, their goal was to boot both the Drinans and the Finns, the building was going to win, and we needed to come up with a better strategy than having Tina sleep with everybody on the board. But she never listened. Alison didn't listen much these days either; they both seemed like people I had known slightly a very long time ago. I wondered if that might have been why I had just disappeared finally: because nobody was listening anyway. And then I thought about Mom, and what she would say, and what she would want me to do, and I wished I had called her just once from out there at the Delaware Water Gap. Then maybe I would have been the one she called when she needed to talk to someone about doing the right thing, keeping that beautiful apartment for the people who had actually lived there. But I didn't call her; I just never did. I was too busy running away.

Finally there wasn't anything else for it. I went to the Ninety-first Precinct and marched up to the front desk. "I need to talk to Detective Drinan," I told the desk sergeant. He barely glanced up at me; he was busy opening mail with a plain silver letter opener that looked like a really boring dagger. He took his time, sliding the pointy end into the top of the envelope and moving it carefully all the way across. I don't know why people think mail is more important than people, but they certainly do. In any case, this desk sergeant finished opening his manila envelope, considered the first three pages of the contents, paper-clipped the docs to the outside of the envelope, and set the whole event down on the other side of his desk. Then he deigned to talk to me.

"He expecting you?" he asked, picking up a phone on his desk carelessly, like he might make a phone call in the middle of our conversation, that's how unimportant I was.

"I don't think he's expecting me," I said. "But you know, he might be. Actually, he actually might be." My fascinating conjectures held no interest for the desk sergeant, who just nodded and hit a few buttons as he shouldered the receiver.

"What's your name?" he asked.

"Tina Finn."

"Yeah," he suddenly said into the receiver, bored as hell, "somebody named Tina Finn is here for Pete." He paused. "Uh huh." Another pause. "Uh huh." Pause. "Yeah, okay." He hung up the phone and reached into the bag of chips that was sitting alongside the pile of mail. He put a potato chip in his mouth and crunched it a few times, then he picked up his letter opener and started slitting the end of another manila envelope.

"So, should I wait here for him?" I asked. The desk sergeant didn't even look up.

"He's not here," he said.

"He's not," I said.

"He have your number?"

"No, actually, he doesn't."

"You can leave it if you want," he said, pulling out some more docs and glancing through them.

"What kind of police station is this?" I said, a little loud. He looked up, raised his eyebrows at me. I swear, I never did know how to talk to the cops. "I could be a *witness* for a *murder* or something, and you can barely talk to me!"

"Are you?" he said.

"No. I am not." And then I held up the brown paper bag I had brought and dropped it into the middle of his mail call. "This is for Detective Drinan. This is important. It is important evidence for a case that he thinks is really important, and you need to give it to him as soon as he gets back."

"You can wait for him if you want," he said, completely unmoved by my theatrics.

"No," I said. "I'm not going to wait. He knows where to find me."

Which he most certainly did. Seven hours later he was at my front door. In his left hand he held a child's green hand-knit sweater with a broken cable on one arm, evidence from a previous life, which I had left in the brown paper bag at the front desk of his precinct. "So," he said, "you have my attention."

I already had that, I thought. What I said was, "Come on in."

I had spent the afternoon unloading what I could from that room and piling it all over the television area. There was stuff everywhere: clothes and shoes and dishes and books and photos and art projects and knitting.

"Holy shit," he said when I walked him back there.

"Yeah, it's a lot of stuff," I agreed.

"Where'd you find all this, that room in the back he used as a storage space?"

"I—"

"You took all this out of the boxes? Why'd you do that?"

"I thought you might want to see it," I said, feeling stupider and stupider. I looked over at him as he looked at all the stuff. There was a thin streak of color across the top of his cheeks, but otherwise nothing. He looked like he was viewing a corpse. "I really did, I thought, this is your stuff, this is your—here, I left a space for you on the couch. I thought maybe you'd want to look at the pictures. There are like four boxes of pictures." He stared at me, then walked over to the space on the couch I had cleared for him. I had stacked the albums neatly on the coffee table next to the boxes of loose photos and negatives. He stood there for a moment, considering the arrangement, then he reached down and flipped open the top album. Still without sitting, he turned the first page, and then the second, sort of casually, like he was only half interested. He looked up, and his eyes flicked over the room again, taking in the piles of stuff, the dusty collected bits and pieces of his childhood, and then he wavered on his feet for a minute, like he was going to fall over maybe.

"Are you okay?" I asked. "I'm sorry. I just thought you would want to see these things, I really, I . . ."

"Yeah," he said, holding up his hand to stop me from talking. "I know. I'm just going to need a minute." And then he turned and walked back down the hallway.

I felt like an idiot. I sat down in the middle of all the crap and wondered what to do. I wasn't even sure he was still in the apartment; that stupid place is so big you can't tell half the time if anyone is in there with you; it's like a mausoleum, just a big empty monument to people who came and went. When he didn't come back after ten minutes, I went looking for him. And there he was, in my room that used to be his room, sitting on the little bed on the floor and looking at the sunset painted on the wall.

"I used to dream about it," he said, not even acknowledging me, more like he was saying something out loud to himself just when I happened to show up. "In all those upside-down ways you dream about things. It would come to life sometimes and try to drown me. She thought it was so cool when she did it. Far as I was concerned, it was like a nightmare painted on the wall."

"Did you tell her?"

"Come on. She loved it," he said. "And it's really not very good, is it? I mean, really. It's just crap."

"I like it," I said, stepping inside the doorway and considering the sunset. He laughed a little, like he thought I was stupid but he appreciated my attempt to say something nice about his mother's dreadful painting. "I do," I insisted. "I'm not kidding, I really do."

"Well, you're wrong. Because it's shit."

"Are those real constellations?" I asked, pointing up at the star stickers on the ceiling.

"No," he said. "We tried. She was all, let's put up the ones no one knows, Taurus and Perseus and the Archer, only she was so bent on being original it ended up not looking like anything. It doesn't really mean anything."

"But her stuff. I thought you might want her stuff."

"All that shit in the other room?" he said. "Really. You think I might want that."

"Yeah, well, you know what? It's not all shit," I told him. I went to the closet, picked up that crumpled brown shopping bag, pulled out the pearls, and handed them to him. He turned them over in his hand, considered the clasp, and looked back up at me, raising an eyebrow like he was waiting for me to explain this again. "Those are real pearls, they're worth a fortune. I'm not kidding. There's a lot of stuff out there, who knows how much it's worth. There's an alligator purse, someone told me you could sell it for five thousand dollars. And some of her old dresses, they're probably worth . . . Sorry. I'm sorry."

"No, it's fine," he said. "People need money. I assumed you needed money." He continued watching me with those impartial eyes. I wished he would laugh again, but I figured that would be an uncommon event.

"Look," I said finally. "You should go look through that stuff. Even if you don't want it because of whatever your reasons are, even if it all seems like—nothing to you—you should go through it. It's yours."

"Our lawyers have been telling us for months that it's *not* ours. According to them, any way you look at it, it's all yours." He held up the pearls to hand them back to me; they hovered there between us for a moment. He wasn't kidding. I took the pearls, and then I took a breath.

"My mother. Called my sister," I told him. "Before she died."

"So?"

I sat down next to him on the bed. The pearls were lovely to hold, cool and round and heavy. They seemed somehow confident in my sweaty hands, like they knew I could get through this.

"She knew that she was, that maybe she was dying," I said. "Anyway, that's what I think. I don't know for sure, because I didn't talk to her. She didn't call me; I was out there in hell at the Delaware Water Gap, no one knew how to get hold of me."

"But she called your sister," he asked, like a detective reminding a witness to keep the story moving forward.

"She called Alison. She said something like the will wasn't right."

"No. It was right. He told us we weren't getting anything. The will was right."

"Yeah, but wait. Mom told Alison that she wanted to make a new will for herself, so that you and your brother would get it. If anything happened to her. She was going to make a will."

"Did she call a lawyer?"

"I don't know. I talked to that Mr. Long just last week. He didn't say anything."

"He didn't say anything in his deposition either. I saw it."

"Yeah, but she told Alison—"

"It's hearsay, Tina," he explained. "It won't hold up in court."

"You don't know that. You're not a lawyer."

"I'm a police detective; I think I know a few things about how the law works. Hearsay is inadmissible. Even if Alison would admit it."

"She admitted it to me."

"She won't admit it in court, and they wouldn't enter it as evidence even if she did. And then it would only complicate a legal situation that already has way too many complications. I wouldn't bring it up, if I were you. When did Alison tell you this?"

"Yesterday."

"So she knows how to keep a secret. Good for her. Tell her to keep her mouth shut in the future about your dying mother's phone call."

"Look," I said. "We have to start getting a clue. The co-op board wants both of our families out of here. They're trying to steal it out from under all of us. If we got together on this we could at least—"

"Keep it in the family?" he asked, with a sardonic roll of the eyes.

"I know you have every reason to be mad at me, but I'm honestly trying to do the right thing," I informed him. "Don't you want this? Don't you want the apartment?"

He looked over at the painting, and his eyes creased with the worry and sadness of the past. You could see that he didn't want to think about any of it, but that he wasn't a coward when called upon to do so.

"A lot of shit went down here," he said. "So no, I'm not sure that I do want it. And you know, I lived here for a long time, and then I didn't live here for a long time. So I'm not so sure I need it."

"Whether you need it or not, it's worth a lot of money!" I insisted. I was tired of his version of the facts. He kept skipping the one fact that had been twisting through everything that had happened since the day my mother died: the money. "Even if you don't want the stuff, this place is worth a total fortune. It's worth *millions*. You could sell it. If you didn't want it."

"Would you sell it?"

"Me?" I said. "It's not mine to sell."

"So, if you could, you'd just live here forever?"

I thought about this. I had never even let myself think it, because I knew from the start it couldn't happen. But if it could? "I like this place," I admitted. "It's beautiful. Things happen here. It's kind of weird, with all the hallways and rooms and hardly any furniture. I really like living here."

"People don't live here, they die here," he reminded me.

"People die everywhere. And this apartment is considerably better than the other places I've found."

"Yeah, I've seen your record," he said. "It's pretty interesting."

"I like living here," I said again, looking around the room, which was quite cozy now with the collection of little pieces I had pulled together to make a home for myself. "I'll be sorry to go."

"You don't need to be in such a hurry," he said. "It's going to take years to get this through the legal system."

"No, I'm being kicked out. The co-op board is kicking me out. It's part of their big plan to get the apartment."

"How is kicking you out going to accomplish that?"

"I don't know, I'm getting all my information thirdhand. Presumably they have more shenanigans up their sleeves."

"Who's behind this?"

"I don't know. They keep saying 'the building,' like it has a mind of its own."

"Yeah, they used to do that to us too," he remembered. "They'd get all bent out of shape about something or other, send notes to my dad signed 'The Building.' It really pissed him off. My mother screaming all the time, seriously bloodcurdling shit, horrible, and *loud,* and then we'd get these messages from The Building about appropriate noise levels. I think they threatened to kick *us* out a couple times—and her family built the place. Assholes. It was always presented in such a creepy way, too. Like, that woman who married beneath her is a little *loud* when she has her psychotic breaks, but the real problem is those Irish guys who are being rude. They're a bunch of 'feckin' bigots'—that was Dad's phrase."

"Wait a minute," I said. "You mean he was *really* Irish? Like, Irish Irish?"

"He grew up in Galway. But he was legal, at least after he married her. That was another one they kept tossing around: he married her for the green card. Somebody, or maybe it was 'The Building,' tried to argue that he wasn't allowed to inherit when she died. Our lawyers dug into it, because if he couldn't inherit it, then he couldn't leave it to your mother, and that meant it would come to us straight from her. But there's no legal standing for that one. They may go there anyway, who knows." He looked around the little room, thinking about all this, then he grinned as a thought occurred to him.

"That why you're trying to give it away?" he asked. "To stick it to all of them? If you can't have it, why not me?" This idea pleased him.

"I wasn't trying to stick it to anyone. I'm trying to do the right thing."

"The right thing." He laughed. "You're a criminal."

"Oh, please," I said. "I'm such a dumb criminal. I am the lamest of criminals."

"You have your points," he said. Then he leaned back, considered the stars above, and stretched his arms over his head, happy. He really was one of those guys, the truth made him happy. I had never seen him so relaxed. "I like criminals," he admitted. "I mean, some of them are jackasses, and some are truly bad people who should not be on the street. The rest of them—they're people who want things. I respect that. I mean, they go too far, they don't understand rules, but they want *life*. I get it."

There wasn't any point in waiting for more of an invitation. Sitting next to him on that little bed, I felt the same as I had the moment I first saw him, like I could just leap on that guy at any second. So that is what I did. Or at least, I reached over, took his face in my hands, and kissed him.

"Well, hello, Tina," he said when I let him come up for air.

"I was getting tired of waiting for you to kiss me," I said. And then I kissed him some more. For about fifteen minutes we made out like teenagers on his bed that was also my bed, which is when he stopped for a moment, pushed my hair out of my face, and considered me.

"I'm not sure I want to do this here," he said.

"Oh, yeah?" I said. "When will you know? Because like I said, they're kicking me out any minute now."

And because neither one of us was all that interested in living in the past, we went ahead and did it, and didn't let the death all around us take the day.

29

We spent the weekend in the apartment, going out only once to buy more scallops, which I cooked, and we got drunk on red wine and picked through Sophie's treasures. We lay together in the dark and told stories about our dead mothers, what we knew of them, what we didn't know, how they failed us, how we failed them.

Reality eventually reasserted itself; on Monday morning Pete took a shower in the bathroom with the good water pressure and then put his clothes back on so he could go off to his precinct. As he disentangled himself from me at the front door, he stuck his hand in his pocket, looking for his car keys, and his fingers curled around something he found there. "Oh, yeah, I thought you might want this," he said, and he handed me a little black perfume bottle.

"So," I said, "you knew all along that it was mine."

"I did know that," he admitted. "That's why I wanted it."

I looked at it. It was cool in my hand, like a big pebble, but black, unknowable. The word that had once scrolled across the opaque glass was long gone. I opened the bottle, smelled it for a moment, shook out a drop of the precious oil, and touched the back of his neck with it.

"Oh, great," he said. "Now I'll hear about that all day."

"I want you to," I told him.

After he was gone, I went back to bed. I woke up to the sound of that throwaway cell ringing away.

"It's been four days. Have you heard from Vince?" Lucy started.

"Not since we had dinner, no."

"Have you called him?"

"No"

"Tina, you have to follow up! And push a little! Have you met his father yet?"

"No," I said.

"Well, that needs to happen. You can make sure he understands our position and supports it, and then, if he does, maybe we can enlist him to speak to other board members on our behalf. Call Vince right now and let me know what he says." Then she hung up. Twenty minutes later Alison called.

"Hi, how are you!" she chirped.

"You know, I'm pretty good, Alison," I started. "I had a terrific weekend and I learned quite a bit about this place."

"About the co-op board?" she asked. "Lucy said you were calling Vince, have you talked to him?"

"No, I haven't really called him yet."

"Well, then, what good was it?" she started, almost crying with frustration. "It is so important to just work with the building! It's what Mom would have wanted, I know it."

"Mom told you specifically that it wasn't what she wanted," I reminded her.

"She wouldn't want them to have it!"

"No," I agreed. "That's not who she wanted to have it."

"So you're going to call him, right?"

"Who?" I asked, getting confused again.

"*Vince,*" she said, almost crying again. "For heaven's sake, Tina! This is no joke!"

They called four more times that day and then twice on Tuesday. I stopped answering the phone. I realized that any minute they would be coming over to harass me in person, so I needed to pack Sophie's stuff back into those boxes and haul it all back to the storage room. That took most of the day, and by the time I was finished, I was exhausted. I took a moment to sit in that lost room and think about what to do next. The boxes were in place. The light was evaporating. And then the ghost started up, mournful and frightened and inevitable. She murmured inside the wall, gently complaining about her traps and her losses and the impossibility of her life. She wept and worried in her unknown language, right there with me and unbearably far away. I let her go on, thinking that maybe she

would be able to explain something to me, even though I didn't understand a word she said. She couldn't explain anything at all.

"What are you doing in there?" I asked. "Why are you so stuck?"

"I'm not *stuck*," said a friendly voice. "It just takes a minute to get
out of here. It's pretty tight." And with that, the ghost voice disappeared
and Jennifer clambered into the room, dusting herself off with teenage
disgust. "Ugh, it's so gross in there. There are *live things* in there. We
have to figure out a better way to talk to each other."

"You could call me on the phone," I reminded her.

"It's too dangerous," she said, quite serious. "Someone might hear
me. There's no privacy in our apartment. You wouldn't believe the stuff
I heard *today*. They're going to try to kick you *out*."

"I know that part."

"You do? Because it's supposed to be top secret."

"Vince Masterson told me they were going to try it last week, but
his dad couldn't be at the meeting."

"Well, he's going to be there tonight," Jennifer informed me grimly.

"Tonight?" I said, startled. "It's *tonight*?"

"They're meeting at six. Oh. That's ten minutes ago."

"Thanks for the notice," I told her, not sounding particularly
grateful. "And thank you, Vince," I muttered to myself.

"So where are they meeting?" I asked her.

"The Gideons' apartment on eleven," she told me.

I looked up at that horrible bricked-up staircase, inhabited by rats
and spiders and god knows what else. My hands started to sweat.

"This thing goes all the way up through the building, right?" I asked.

"How am I supposed to know?"

"Look," I said, "if I don't come back in six hours, tell somebody
I might be stuck in the wall. Tell Frank."

"You're going *up* there?"

She sounded aghast. And why not? It was an idiotic idea. No one in
their right mind would even consider it.

"I think I am," I said. And with that I climbed up onto the edge of
the tiny doorway, put my fingers on one of the steps, crouched forward,

and started to climb. "You need a flashlight!" Jennifer called after me. "It's dark in there! What if the Gideons blocked off the entrance? What are you going to do when you get there? What if someone . . ." Her voice trailed off as it became obvious that I was going through with it.

There are advantages to being someone who thinks rules are made to be broken. Finding yourself stuck in an airless, dank, Victorian crawl space that might very well lead nowhere is not one of them. Even though Jennifer had opened the wall plug in Katherine's room, only a faint amount of light came in, and once I climbed beyond its friendly solace—the last moment that I might have bailed out of this insane endeavor—it was pitch black. I had to lead with my hands, which more than once landed on something crunchy and alive, and then my face went through some weblike, sticky stuff filled with little nublike things that were probably dead bugs. At some point I realized that I didn't know how far I'd have to climb to get to the Gideons' apartment and that I might have passed it already. I didn't know if I should go back down or continue up. Then, when I reached over to steady myself against the wall, I grabbed at something that moved and actually hissed; terrified, I jumped back and hit the wall, which had somehow transformed itself from brick to wood. It made a big thump.

"What was that?" someone asked. I froze.

"Did you hear something?" the voice asked again.

"Margarita thinks there are rats in that old crawl space," another voice announced. It was Mrs. Gideon, and you could tell even without seeing her that she thought Margarita was a moron. "I'll mention it to Frank."

"Frank's the doorman, Mother," the other voice, the beautiful Juli-anna, replied.

"You really are sentimental about him," her mother replied with a little sneer.

"I'm not *sentimental,* I'm *respectful.*"

"You encourage him, and it's ridiculous."

"We are not talking about Frank, Mother, please! I think I heard something, I know I did. It sounded like a rat or something in that crawl space. I think Margarita is right, there's something in there. You need to mention it to the super—or why don't you tell the board, since they're all here anyway."

"We are not gathered to talk about rats. Or perhaps we are," Mrs. Gideon observed. Then Julianna said something I couldn't quite pick up, as she clearly had moved away from the wall and the giant rats inside it. There was some further murmuring and then silence, as the two women apparently went into the next room or someplace beyond.

Here is where the true stupidity of my plan revealed itself. I had succeeded in landing right in the middle of the Gideons' apartment without anybody knowing I was there, but I had no way to get out of that wall. I hung in there, my heart pounding, my head leaning against some sort of old cabinet, and let my fingers probe the wood. I found a giant bolt, but there was no way to open it. My fingers continued to probe it, and I told myself that if I were anything like a functional thief I would have brought picks for the lock. But then I thought, it's a *deadbolt,* you can't open it from this side, you'd have to saw through the wall to get that thing off—or an axe, a short-handled *axe,* or a gun, maybe a gun would do it. I ran through all the possible solutions for opening a deadbolt, none of which were feasible in any kind of reality other than the movies. I was stuck in the wall; there was no way to get out.

Then a voice whispered, right next to my head, "Tina? Are you in there?"

It took me a second, honestly. I couldn't quite catch up.

"Tina. Tina. If you're in there, knock or something. I don't have a ton of time."

"Jennifer?" I said.

"Knock where you are, knock where you are, I can't tell, and we have to do this fast," she told me. I rapped gently on the wall several times.

"Okay, that's good, that's good," she said, rapping on the panel right in front of me. "Is this it? This is the doorway?"

"There's a bolt," I told her. "Right in front of you, they've got a deadbolt holding it shut."

"Yeah, I see," she said, working on it. "It's painted shut. Shoot. It's—oh. Hang on. I have to find something—oh wait. Not so bad, the paint's pretty old. Oh!" And with that, the door swung open three inches

and she smiled in at me. "Come on, come on," she said, excited, pulling
the door open against the resistance of the paint, which was half of what
was holding it in place. She reached in and grabbed me by the arm, forcing me to climb out. "It's a good thing you're little," she observed.

"What are you doing here?" I whispered. I was shaking, half with
relief and half with the sheer terror of what I had just been through.
"God, it's horrible in there. Don't go in there anymore."

"Yeah, it's not nice. I knew you weren't going to be able to get out of
there. You didn't think of that. Get down, you don't want them to see
you," she advised me. She shut the cabinet door carefully, holding it in
place with her shoulder while she flipped the ancient deadbolt back into
place. The kid was a marvel. She was grinning with delight at her own
cleverness. "Anyway," she said, dropping down to the floor so she could
talk to me, "as soon as you left, I knew you were going to need me, so I
took the elevator and interrupted the meeting and said I needed to talk
to my mom. So she came to the door, and I told her I had a fight with
Louise, and she told me they were busy and to go home, so then I told
her I needed to use the bathroom, which is supposedly what I'm doing
now. I've got to go. They're all in the living room, it's down that hallway,
you pass the dining room and some sort of den, and then it's right there.
There's a whole lot of them in there. The whole board, and then a couple
others, they look like lawyers. We'll make for the den, you can hide behind the door and hear everything, I checked it out on the way. Come
on, we have to go. I'll make a lot of noise when I go back out through the
meeting, so I can distract them while you're finding some place to listen.
Ready? Let's go."

I was still so freaked out from being stuck in the wall that my
brain was not functioning fully, so I was glad to have an excited teenager telling me what to do. She breezed ahead of me silently, glancing
back to make sure I stayed down and hidden by furniture in case anyone suddenly appeared looking for a glass of water or something; then
she took me into a dark room with plush couches and low lighting, all
done in red with the slightest touches of gold sprinkled through. I got
nothing more than a sense of its opulence as Jennifer quickly waved her
hand behind her, pointing to a corner behind the open door. She stood

in the doorway for a moment, waving her hand impatiently, and then she marched deliberately into the next room.

"Thanks for the use of your bathroom, Mrs. Gideon," she announced to the whole room. "Mom, can you at least *call* Louise and tell her that I don't *have* to put Gail and Mary Ellen to bed, they're big enough to get themselves to bed *anyway,* and it's not my job and plus I have a lot of homework."

"That's fine, Jennifer," Mrs. White noted tersely.

"Well, she's being horrible. Can you call her at least?"

"Jennifer, I said go home," Mrs. White told her with finality.

The door from the den to the living room was wide open, and a couch stood against the wall, just inside. Behind the door and beside the couch was a clever little area of carpet invisible to either room: that was my spot. Fully half of the room was out of my line of sight, but the other half was completely visible. I could see Jennifer scoot into the hallway by the front door, passing that ridiculous table with the spindly legs where Mrs. Gideon had given me the evil eye, then she quickly disappeared from view. The sound of the door opening and closing behind her was obscured by the rustle and settling of fifteen people in the room next to me.

"Thanks to everyone for making this a priority," announced a tall, absurdly handsome man who was standing to address the others, most of whom I couldn't see. He was clearly Vince's father; he looked just like him and he carried himself with even more self-involved confidence. Next to him, his son looked like a cheerful puppy. I immediately understood why Vince hated him so much.

"The petition to have the illegal tenant in apartment 8A removed is being passed among you for signatures," he explained. "We have asked everyone to sign, because if a lawsuit should result from this action, we want to make it clear that the entire board is in agreement and no one can be singled out for culpability."

"Can they sue?" asked someone unseen on the other side of the room.

"Why don't we let our lawyer answer that one, that's what he's here for," Vince's creepy dad responded. "Gary?"

Another good-looking guy in a suit stood up. I swear to god, he looked like every other lawyer I had met during this fiasco except Stuart Long, the Egg Man. These guys all looked like the suits they were wearing. "From what Roger has told me, and what I've gleaned from phone calls with many of you, these people are aggressive and determined," announced Gary the lawyer. "Under these circumstances, lawsuits are always a possibility. Lawsuits are, however, expensive. It is clear that they have few resources other than the speculative value of the Livingston Mansion Apartment. We've spoken to the legal department at Sotheby's, and they have reassured us that they will not support any action on behalf of the so-called heirs of Olivia Finn until the co-op has had the opportunity to state its legal position concerning the property."

"Do we have a position?" asked Mrs. Gideon, sounding like she was standing in front of the door right next to me. "Other than we wish they would go away?"

"That's what we're here to discuss," Vince's hyperconfident ice cube of a father asserted.

"My husband told me not to sign anything until we have our lawyer look at it," came another voice from beyond my sight line. But I recognized this one: it was Mrs. White, who sounded nervous and kind of unhappy.

"We can have copies sent to your lawyer, certainly, and wait a few days for your signature," said Mr. Ice Cube. "The reason we asked Gary to be here was to set your mind at ease about the legality of these documents."

"But he's not our personal lawyer. He doesn't represent me or my husband. And the interests of the co-op are not necessarily *our* interests, are they?" continued Mrs. White, insistent. She really sounded bothered, like she might secretly be on my side. That is what I told myself anyway. I wished I could see her face for a moment. I wondered what color suit she was wearing.

"No one should sign anything they're not comfortable signing," said the lawyer, trying to be soothing and looking more like a shark than ever. "I am happy to interface with anyone's attorney around all of this."

"He's already spoken to my guy," someone offered up.

"Mine as well," Mrs. Gideon purred. "I'm completely satisfied this is the appropriate move to make."

"Look, we can get her out of here with a simple majority of votes, and legally we don't *need* more than six signatures," Gary explained. "But if the co-op wants to send a message to these people and to the real estate community and to the city in general, my recommendation is that it be loud and unanimous. That's why I hope to have everyone's signature on the documents of removal."

"I want to support the building, I do," protested Mrs. White. "Maybe I could call my husband at the end of the meeting and just make sure it's okay."

"You do whatever you need to, Alice," said Ice Pop. "We all have a lot at stake here."

"Once they're gone, though, does it really change anything?" a woman asked. "I saw all the things on television and the papers, and it sounds like these two sets of heirs are going to fight it out whether we like it or not, and we're going to be dragged into the press for who knows how long. Is there anything we can do—beyond asserting our right to have the apartment remain empty?"

"That's an interesting question, Jenny," Ice Pop agreed. "And it's why I made sure that all of us could be here tonight. As it turns out, there is something we can do. Len, maybe you could explain the situation." He made one of those graceful little gestures that mean "the floor is yours," and Len stepped out of the invisible side of the room and into the front and center. He was wearing the dark green suit coat I'd seen him in at the press conference, and he carried a cream-colored folder with some papers in it. He had a big bandage on his left hand. Their nocturnal confrontation had taken place almost two weeks ago. For all her claims that she wasn't trying to hurt him, Charlie must have scored a real hit.

But Len wasn't acting wounded. With his calm, treelike posture and wry smile, he radiated strength and gentle wisdom to the entire gathering. "I do have some rather interesting—some exceptionally interesting— news about the legal status of the Livingston Mansion Apartment," he claimed. "As some of you know, I was quite friendly with Bill and his wife

Sophie for many years before her death. I was in fact a confidant of them and their sons."

"And the second wife, the one who made all the trouble?" someone called.

"I knew her, yes, and yes she was—problematic. Some of the things I saw her doing to her husband made me very unhappy, because of the degree to which she was maneuvering him around these questions of inheritance and the apartment."

"Could you be more specific? You actually saw—"

"I saw a lot, and I'm willing to testify to that," Len claimed, with seemingly sincere regret. I wanted to rip his face off or at least give Charlie another go. But before he could continue to tell spectacular stories about how evil my poor lost mother was, Vince's dad leaned forward and whispered something to him. Len tilted his head and listened, then nodded with bemused respect. "I quite agree. I quite agree," he murmured. Then he looked out at his audience and held up the little packet of papers.

"Our esteemed board president, Roger Masterson, has made the excellent point that a discussion centering on Bill's more recent wife, who actually never held any rights in regard to the Livingston apartment, is not the most useful way to spend our time together this evening. What's more important to all of us is the status of the apartment as designated by the last will and testament of the first Mrs. Drinan."

Something was up. Len was curling his sentences on top of each other so deliriously that the whole thing sounded fishy before he even started telling the story. But everyone in the room was eating it up. There was a pause and a hush. He sighed and looked down, sad. "Those of you who lived here then know that there was some difficulty surrounding Sophie Livingston. Those who knew her remember a woman filled with passion and delight. At times she was unhappy, and at times her spirit was greatly troubled. Today some might choose to label these fluctuations in temperament as mental illness. And indeed, her unhappiness led her family to make choices for her that were questionable, and they were questioned."

People shifted in their seats. He was taking too long. I could see old

Roger Masterson twitching, trying to figure out how to get Len to move the story along. But Len was enjoying his moment. "One evening Bill came to me, explaining his plan, which was to have his wife admitted to a psychiatric facility in the city. I was appalled. My experience with Sophie would never have led me to believe that such a drastic action, a *removal,* was called for. What I could see, from my vantage point, was that there were problems in the marriage, and the truly rational solution for everyone would be for them to divorce. But Bill was having none of it. What would happen to Sophie, he asked, if she were left alone in that glorious apartment? He was convinced she would do harm to herself. I thought this was nonsense. He didn't want to talk about it; his mind was made up. And he told me that his two grown sons supported his decision. The most I could do was insist that the facility to which Sophie was taken be the best possible home for her. I contacted a friend at the university where I was teaching, pulled some strings, and got her placed in a wonderful, wonderful treatment center."

He paused dramatically and considered the documents in his hand. The room was silent, expectant, waiting for the story to fulfill itself. "I visited her there often," he explained. "Bill, and Pete and Doug, her beloved sons, did not. They moved on with their lives. But I never thought she belonged there. We would have long talks about her life growing up in the Edgewood, the happiest times and memories for her centering on the building, which was so precious to her parents. And I said to her, Sophie, you belong in your home with us. She felt it was too late for that. And so she asked me to help her make a will."

He stopped and held up the little folder. "Which left the apartment to the building." No one said anything for a moment. Masterson and the lawyer glanced at each other, expressionless.

"Okay, wait a minute," someone finally said. I was really wishing I could see that half of the room, filled to the brim with people I knew and didn't know. *What a load of nonsense,* I thought, *I can't believe anybody is going to fall for this.* But there was money in the air now, and that crowd was particularly attuned to its potential. "You helped her make a will?" the questioner asked.

"No, no, I am not an attorney, I cannot legally 'help' anyone make a will. But I did alert a member of the staff, who wrote down her wishes. She was agitated but definitely in her right mind. So I agreed to serve as a witness, as did the nurse's aide who helped us. And I was given a copy of the document for safekeeping."

At this, Gary the lawyer stood up holding a stack of papers, which he proceeded to hand out to the group. "We have copies," he announced. There was a rustle of pages as each person obediently passed the copies on to the next, and the lawyer took over the narrative for a moment. "We have contacted the other witness on the will, who is willing to testify about the legitimacy of the document."

"This counts? It's more like a letter," someone behind the door said, worried.

"It states her wishes clearly. It counts," the lawyer asserted.

"Is this will later than the one that left the apartment to her husband?" someone else asked, also worried.

"It is the *only* will," the lawyer reassured the room. "When she passed six years ago, some questions were raised about when and why her will had not been probated properly. Because of the recent dissent between the two so-called sets of heirs, investigation was made into the failure to probate any will. Court documents indicate that there was no other will and that the apartment was improperly awarded to the husband as the next of kin."

"If all this happened six years ago, why are we only hearing about it now?" The unseen questioner was clearly not happy with this situation. He was getting pushy.

"That—was—my mistake," Len asserted with a regretful sigh. He was really a better actor than I'm making him sound. He was quite deft during this part of the performance. "Bill was truly bereft when she passed. There was bitterness and recriminations, so much sadness, and finally a real rupture between him and his sons. For years they didn't speak to each other! So I confess that my friendship with Bill overwhelmed my sense of loyalty to Sophie. I thought, what would be the harm in letting him spend his last years in the home he made with her in better times? He was so lonely. And so isolated there. I thought that when he died I could bring the will forward at that time."

"You were taking a lot on yourself," the angry guy noted with some asperity.

"Yes, I was, I most certainly was, and I regret it deeply," Len said. "I wasn't sure what to do. I consulted several people about the correct course. I spoke to Delia Westmoreland about it at the time; she was such friends with Sophie, and I knew she would understand the dilemma."

"Delia, is that true?" asked Mrs. White, as if this possibility might actually change her opinion about this improbable story.

"Yes, yes he did, he came to me, I can't remember when exactly—"

"It was six years ago, just after she died," Len provided.

"That's exactly right," Delia agreed. She was nervous, but almost everyone seemed to be going along—at least they were listening pretty intently—so she plowed ahead. "I wanted to tell people right away, though. I didn't like the idea of holding back information about Sophie's wishes. I never thought it was fair of them to put her away like that and then make a grab for the place, that seemed really bad to me."

"He was her husband," Mrs. White reminded her.

"He was *Irish*. He wasn't even American. And it wasn't what she would have wanted. Well, she wrote that down, I guess, that it wasn't what she wanted. And you know she was a feminist, Sophie would never have agreed that Bill could just *grab* her family's heritage, she wasn't into all that male power stuff, that's why it was so terrible, what he did to her. That he and those boys just sent her off to the asylum, I know that's not what they call it anymore, but let's face it, that's what they *did*. It's appalling really. And you know, her parents never liked him. So I wasn't surprised when Len told me about this. I thought, it serves them right, after the way they treated her, that she would not stand for them getting the apartment too. No, I was not surprised at all."

"Did you see the will, did Len show you this document at the time?" prompted Roger Masterson.

"Yes," said Mrs. Westmoreland. "He most certainly did." I was watching her through the door crack; she was right in my line of vision, and she had gotten the hang of it by then; she was confident and even defiant. "Len showed me the will, but also he told me his concerns, that Bill wasn't well and that he didn't have a lot of years left in him and that maybe it would be cruel to just kick him out. Even if it's what he deserved. Like I said, I thought we should bring it to the board right then. But then Len pointed out he would die soon enough. Certainly neither one of us thought some cleaning woman would show up and try to make off with all of it. That I *know* Sophie did not want."

"But no one else has a copy of this document?" asked the persistent questioner from the corner. "Was it registered anywhere? I just don't think it looks good that someone in the building had it all along and didn't bring it forward before now. That doesn't seem right." I wish I knew who that person was; he seemed to be the only one in the room with a shred of a clue.

"I think you need to leave that part to the lawyers," soothed Gary. "Stranger things have happened over the years with regard to wills and inheritances. And we have several witnesses. Len here, Delia, the aide from the nursing home. We can verify the history of the document. Our case is strong."

"Could you tell us what it even means?" Len asked, sweetly mystified. "I never really considered the question, even though I helped make it happen. How can a building own an apartment?"

"We hold it in trust and arrange for its sale. The proceeds go into a fund that we can use as an endowment of sorts to support the maintenance of the building," Roger Masterson explained. I thought he was going to start licking himself any second, he was enjoying this so much. "It's quite an exceptional situation. It gives us the opportunity to protect and restore a historic property and also support our own investment in the building as cooperative owners of the property. And you all should know that it's our importance as a historic property that is in play here. Sotheby's, Christie's, Corcoran—all the brokers of important properties—have agreed to wait and let our own interest play out here. No one is going to provide any real opposition to our position. It is not in their interest to do so."

"Isn't that like price fixing?" the malcontent in the corner called out.

"Not at all," Gary said with a cool, knowing smile. "Here, let me walk you through the legalities of a situation like this."

"You have to go," someone breathed into my ear. I almost fell over I was so startled, but she reached out and held my arm firmly to keep me steady and to keep me from giving myself away. I turned slowly. The most beautiful face I've ever seen was right next to my own. "Before they finish," Julianna whispered. "They can't find you here." And then she stood and silently reached her hand out to me. I took it and followed her into the kitchen, where she moved with graceful assurance to the cabinet door that opened onto that terrifying crawl space. I looked around, realizing that I would have to get back in there. But Julianna passed right by the cabinet as if it were invisible.

"I presume you came up the fire escape," she said, opening the kitchen window onto the night air. "Quickly, quickly!" she urged.

30

IT WAS SIGNIFICANTLY EASIER TO CLIMB DOWN THE RICKETY OLD fire escape than it had been to climb up the twisting staircase trapped inside the walls of the building. The skeletal ladders fit together like a perfect wrought-iron jigsaw puzzle, and within seconds, it seemed, I was on the landing outside the window of my own apartment. The euphoric sense of relief I had experienced as I clambered down the outside of the building waned slightly when I realized that I once again was unable to get into the apartment because, not surprisingly, the window was locked. I stood there and pondered this for a moment. And then I saw the ghost.

She was right there at the window, looking at me. At first I didn't know what I was seeing; I thought I was looking into a pair of disembodied eyes afloat in an undifferentiated and murky universe. They frightened me so completely that I pulled back and careened for a moment near the edge of the space that opened on the landing beneath me, at which point she held up a hand, instinctively, to warn me to be careful. Then she looked over her shoulder and back at me, and I thought, *the ghost, it's the ghost.* Her hair was pulled back under a kerchief, and her skin was as dark as the air around her. I took a step forward and reached my hand out to the window she stood at. There were bars across it. She looked like she was in a cage.

We considered each other for just a moment, and then I knew what to do. "Stay there," I said. And I took off my shirt, wrapped it around my fist, and stuck my hand through my own window, which was right next to hers. Then I reached in, turned the window latch, yanked the window up, climbed inside, and found my cell phone.

"You have to get over here now," I said to Pete when he picked up. "Now, right now, you have to come *right now.*" Then I ran through the apartment, undid all the locks, and headed down the stairs, because I didn't want to wait for the elevator.

"Frank," I said. He looked up from his little stand, where he was reading yet another magazine. "You have to come. You have to bring the master keys. There's a person trapped in Mrs. Westmoreland's apartment, she's locked in there, you have to help me get her out."

"Tina—look, I don't know," he began. "You know they're saying you're not supposed to be here. I'm not allowed to help you with anything. They told me I could get fired if I did."

"She's an *illegal,* Frank," I said. "Westmoreland's got an illegal up there, locked in a room. She's an *illegal.*"

That was all it took. Frank and his master keys got us into Delia Westmoreland's apartment, where we found the ghost hiding in a closet and praying to the gods of her homeland to come and save her. She was so lost in that other universe she didn't fully recognize the real thing when we showed up. She fought and cried and insisted in some strange tongue that we had to go, that they couldn't find us there. Then Mrs. Westmoreland showed up and insisted that she was calling the police to have me arrested. I told her there was no need, as they were already on their way, which she didn't take too well. Then when Pete arrived, Mrs. Westmoreland went into a rage and claimed to have sponsored the ghost—whose name was Gcina—for citizenship, out of the goodness of her heart.

In the middle of all the yelling, Pete took us all down to the local precinct, where I dragged him into a corner for a minute to tell him what I had heard at the board meeting. You could tell he didn't really believe me, but before I could explain, I was dragged into an interrogation room and asked about the ghost. I told them I had been hearing her in the wall for weeks and I knew she must be in some kind of trouble, but I didn't put it all together until I saw her. Meanwhile Gcina was giving up her story in an interrogation room down the hall. And then some cop asked me what I was doing out on the fire escape, and Pete said go ahead, tell them about the other stuff, so I told them about the co-op board meeting, and rather than laughing me out of the room, the cops went back to the building and asked Julianna Gideon to come

to the precinct and verify my story. Her mother, predictably, threw a fit
and insisted on coming with her and calling a lawyer and generally
screaming at everyone in the most horrible way possible. She especially
reamed out Frank, who was just sitting in a corner quietly waiting to
be told he could go home. Then when the lawyer arrived, the cops
wouldn't let Mrs. Gideon go with Julianna into the interrogation room,
where she apparently validated every detail of my story about what was
said at the board meeting. They took all of that back to Mrs. Westmoreland and told her she was going to be on the hook for abduction
and harboring an illegal alien, but that conspiracy to defraud the courts
was even more serious, and if she would flip on the whole cabal of board
members at the Edge they'd take that into consideration.

So she gave up everything and got a walk on the other charges,
because Gcina was from Somalia and no one knew who she was or
where her family was, and in the end she didn't matter as much as the
Livingston Mansion Apartment did. The police issued warrants for the
arrest of every member of the board, including Roger Masterson and
Len, who was in especially hot water because Westmoreland had admitted that the whole will scenario was a fake, and she claimed it was his
idea. Then Gary the lawyer showed up and explained that Roger Masterson did not have to come down to a police precinct in the middle of
the night and they could speak to him in his office the next day. Then
some uniformed officers brought Len in and walked him right past me,
as I sat in the waiting room with Pete. Then some lady from INS arrived and took Gcina off, and when I asked Pete where they were taking
her, he admitted that she would be put in jail, and they would hold her
probably for months and then send her back to Somalia unless she
could prove that she needed asylum.

"They can't," I said. "Come on. You can't put her in jail. She's been
in jail for months. We don't even know how long. But at least months."

"I still can't see how you put that together," Pete said, checking his
nails. "You really didn't have any evidence, just somebody crying in the
next room. You know, if you had brought that to me, I couldn't even
have gotten a warrant on it. It's a good thing you got Frank to open the
door for you. No cop in the city would have done it."

"Because she's nobody?"

"Because you didn't have any evidence."

"I'm on the same landing with them. I could see, when Westmoreland opened the door going out or coming in, that the place was getting cleaned every day. And no one ever came. I never saw anybody."

"Still not enough."

"I cleaned houses myself," I said. "I know what it's like to be locked in a trailer out at the Delaware Water Gap." And then I went on a crying jag, and Pete said he'd take me home.

Which is where we were the following morning when Doug showed up. Unfortunately I had not, for once, locked the door from the inside, both because I was so tired and because I had my own cop, and I wasn't worried about someone bursting into my world. I had not counted on Doug Drinan getting a tip-off from Len Colbert, who had used his one phone call to tell Doug that his brother might be here, fraternizing with the enemy, and he might want to come see for himself.

"I don't believe it," he said. He was standing in the doorway of the bedroom, watching us wake up. At least we weren't having sex, I thought, but Doug didn't see the upside of that. He was already in a state. "What the fuck," he seethed. "What the *fuck* are you doing with *her*?"

"Oh, shit," Pete muttered, groggy.

"Get up," Doug hissed. "Get up so I can hit you."

"Dial it down, Doug. I'm still waking up," Pete said.

"In our apartment," Doug exploded. "In our *room*! With her! You know what she is! You know what her mother did to our family!"

"My mom didn't do anything, she was a really nice person and she took really good care of your father," I started.

"Tina, stay out of this," Pete warned me.

"We know what she did. She stole our home," Doug informed me. "We have evidence—what she was doing, we know what she did, and we know what you're doing, at least those of us who aren't thinking with our dicks have something of a clue—"

"Hey hey hey, I said dial it back," Pete repeated. I opened my mouth to say something that would not have been helpful, but Pete put his hand up in a fast silencing gesture as he stood.

"We're not going to talk about it this way, Doug," he stated. "I want you to step out into the hallway."

"Don't you fucking 'cop' me," Doug sneered. "I'm not the crook in this fiasco. I can't believe you're this stupid. Or yes I can, actually, I can believe it. After what you did—what you did, to Mom—"

"Come on, don't start this again."

"It was your idea! What happened? You were the one who, you and Dad, she didn't want to go, I told you don't do it—"

"That's not the way it went down and you know it—"

"And then she died in there alone. She was *alone*—"

"She was there because she needed help! She couldn't stay here! Christ, she tried to kill him, more than once, Doug—"

"So he said—"

"I saw it! You saw what she would do, you saw the bruises, come on, man, let's not relive this."

"He made that happen. She was defending herself. He would get drunk and start those fights—"

"I'm serious, Doug, don't do this."

"*You're doing it! You did it!* You're just like him. She used to say, your brother is just like your father, a a a lowlife and a drunk—she would tell me—"

"I know what she said, come on, Doug, let's just take this down the hall—"

"No! She needs to hear this! She needs to know what you are, what you did, what you—she—" His rage took over as he glanced at me, utter madness in his face. I crept back against the wall a little. This was not a good situation. And it just goes to show, I thought: pictures don't tell the whole story. I thought of all those photos of the happy boys and their cool, interesting, rich, hippie mother. They didn't tell this story at all.

"I could kill you for this," Doug continued, pacing in a tight circle in that tiny room. "This was Mom's, everything. This place. And you're just throwing it away! On those—that *woman,* who Dad let come in here, like it wasn't Mom's. When it was *only* hers. This place is *hers.* It was the only thing she really loved." The words hung out there like a curse as soon as he said it. I was embarrassed to have heard it.

Pete shook his head. "You know that's not true. She loved us. I remember how much she loved us. That's what I choose to remember. I make that choice every day."

"That's convenient. Considering what you did to her, what you and Dad—what you *did*."

Pete didn't answer at first. The whisper of loss was rising around them. Doug looked completely spent. He glanced up at the ceiling for a moment, that old trick of raking your eyes frantically to keep them from betraying you. He looked at that awful painted sunset on the wall and started to shake with a terrible and relentless grief. Pete waited, still, while his brother wept openly for what seemed a long time before he shook himself back into some semblance of control.

"Sorry," Doug finally said, abrupt and ungracious.

Pete nodded, pretending the apology was better than it was. "There was something wrong with her brain," he continued quietly. Doug accepted the facts as Pete recounted them. "We talked to a lot of people. You remember that. The chemicals went bad. It wasn't her fault, but it wasn't his fault either."

"She wasn't well."

"No, she wasn't. We got a lot of opinions, Doug, you know we did what we had to do." The two of them stood there looking at each other, mournfully resting in the end of an argument they had had far too many times. For a long moment they just looked at each other. Pete reached up to touch his brother's shoulder. And Doug slugged him, hard, right across the face.

31

"THEY'RE KICKING YOU OUT, TINA," FRANK INFORMED ME UNDER his breath when I snuck out past the doorman's station several days later. "They're real mad at you."

I wasn't surprised to hear it.

The pearls I left at Sotheby's. Leonard Rubenstein, the man who looked like a lion, gave me an official estimate of their worth, somewhere in the range of $350,000. The clasp, apparently, was much more valuable than the pearls themselves. He knew of a jeweler who would take the necklace quickly and essentially break it up for parts. He promised to call me by the end of the day with an offer. Then I called one of my friends from the hot tub, Lyle, who had had the foresight to slip his phone number into that little alligator handbag. He suggested he could come by the apartment and price out the rest of the stuff, so I said sure.

"Really?" he said, almost cooing on the other end of the line. "Can I bring Roger? Or Andrew? Or Steve? They'll kill me, they really will, if they find out that I got to see the apartment and they didn't."

"Whoever wants to come see the apartment," I said, "is welcome."

It was a good little party. Andrew brought champagne and foie gras, and Roger and Steve and Edward and Dave came too, and they loved every square inch of the place; they appreciated every strange corner and disastrous choice. They even loved the mustard-colored shag rug.

"It's so hideous," Andrew said in an admiring tone. "And who would have thought to use so much? It's a sea of mustard. I think it works, I really do."

"You're insane," said Edward, but he kissed him, so I knew he wasn't in love with Vince anymore, which I thought was definitely a good thing.

"Tina, can I talk to you for a second?" Lyle called from the hallway.

He took me back to the storage room so we could talk business. "All right. A lot of this—everything over here—it's sentimental value, I'm sure, but that's how you need to see it," he explained, waving at a pile of boxes full of old shoes and knitting paraphernalia and wrinkled cotton skirts. "The Salvation Army maybe would take it off your hands if they didn't have to come pick it up. It's not worth anything. Over here, on the other hand, we have some things that probably are worth quite a bit." He stepped back out into the laundry area and led me around the corner toward the TV room. There he pointed toward the doorway of Bill and Mom's bedroom, where he had used the arched pocket doors as a frame for a little fashion show.

"What a lovely presentation," I told him.

"Thank you," he said, smiling. "I think it's important, with beautiful things, to display them properly, so we can decide in an aesthetic way what is the best course of action."

"The only course of action I'm really interested in is money," I said.

"Yes, sweetheart, I'm well aware." He nodded. "You can be a philistine all you want. The rest is for me. Okay. The Balenciaga cocktail dress will bring in, conservatively, two thousand dollars."

"Two *thousand*?" I said, hoping I was hearing this right.

"The alligator bag, I already know who I can take that to, and there's no question he'll pay four. The evening gowns are a little more specific and not quite as classic or timeless as the gowns that bring in the big bucks, but they're in good shape, the sea green one is really a beautiful color, we'll stay conservative and estimate another two for both of them."

"So what is that, eight? That's pretty good. How long will it take to sell them?"

"Wait wait wait. First, my darling, first we have to talk about this." He walked over to the display area, reached up against the wall, and presented me with a piece of the ugliest luggage I had ever seen.

"What about it?" I said.

"Do you know what this is?" he asked.

"You can have it, nobody wants this stuff," I assured him.

"You know nothing! Nothing!" he said, incensed with delight at how much I didn't know. "Six pieces—a matched set of Hermès airline luggage from the sixties. I've never seen even one piece before today— you have a whole set! And it's pristine! It's in perfect condition! I don't know what you might get for it. I just don't even know." He was dialing away on his cell phone, he was so excited.

"But do you know anybody who would buy it?" I asked him. "I need the money fast. They're going to kick me out any second. I have to get this stuff out of here."

"We'll buy it, Tina, don't worry," said Andrew, handing me a glass of champagne.

"*You'll* buy it," I said. "No no, come on you don't have to, to to—"

"To take care of you?" he asked. "But we want to take care of you. And if Lyle says it's worth something, trust me, it is. I'm sure it's a terrific investment."

"Do not take less than twenty-five, Tina," Lyle warned me while he consulted with someone on the phone.

"Twenty-five," I said. *"Thousand?"*

Andrew gave me a check right then and there, then went with me to cash it. On the sidewalk outside the bank I called Jennifer on her cell; she was just getting out of school and walking home. "You have to sneak out tonight. Tonight's the night," I told her. "Be at my place at eleven."

"Eleven, like eleven *P.M.*?" she said, stunned.

"Actually, make it half past ten," I said. "We have a lot to do."

Six hours later there were five gay men waiting for her in the lost room. They helped her climb out of the crawl space and slip through the darkness into one of the many empty bedrooms, where there was a makeup station, a hair station, party dresses in three different sizes, four evening jackets, and eight pairs of shoes for her to choose from.

"What is this?" she said, laughing.

"It's party time," I told her. "We're going to a club."

She protested, but not too hard. "It's a school night."

"Yeah, you're going to have problems staying awake in history tomorrow," I admitted, picking up a pair of strappy heels, hoping we got the right size.

"What is this you're wearing?" Andrew asked her, a little worried about that plaid skirt.

"It's a uniform, I go to a Catholic school up on Ninety-eighth," she explained, eyeing the party dresses with undisguised hunger.

"Come on," Roger said, his voice drenched in disbelief. "They have Catholic schools in Manhattan?"

We dressed her up and took her out. Edward rented a limo, and we went to three separate clubs. Jennifer danced with everyone in our entourage, and then she danced with a bunch of more appropriate college guys, whom we met up with later at an all-night diner in the Meatpacking District. She flirted outrageously with one of them, and they ended up making out on a street corner until five A.M., at which point I thought I'd better get her home so we could perhaps end the evening without parental discovery and Catholic recriminations and have it just be a wonderful night for her to remember forever.

In the car she threw her arms around me and hugged me with happiness. "Thank you thank you thank you," she said.

"Thank you, Jennifer," I said. "You did as much for me as anyone I've ever known in my whole life."

"I have to tell you something," she whispered, and her hand slipped into mine as she put her head on my shoulder. "My mom voted for you."

"What?" I said, trying to remember what that meant.

"She voted for you. She didn't want them to kick you out. She said you did a good thing, telling the cops about the phony will, that was the right thing to do. And she also said you were really nice and a good babysitter. And she voted for you."

The next day Frank was fired when he told a representative from the co-op board that he would not hire a security firm to help remove me from the building. It didn't matter. I was already out of there, and I had a lot of money in my pocket, which was about to come in very handy.

A month later Julianna Gideon bumped into Frank at a restaurant where she was having lunch with her roommate from Princeton. Frank looked especially handsome; he was wearing an extremely well-cut Armani suit that cost three thousand easily. He explained that he had a new job with a small but well-regarded investment firm that was looking to expand their business in several South American capitals. Julianna's roommate had done her sophomore year in Spain, so she and Frank carried on a quick and intelligent conversation in that most romantic of languages. Julianna was even more charmed than before, and without notifying her mother, she agreed to have dinner with Frank the following week. By their third date, Frank felt comfortable enough to invite her back to his apartment, which was small but beautifully furnished. He lived alone, he explained, because his father and brothers had recently come into money and returned to their family home in the Dominican Republic. She spent the night.

Gcina Motufe, an illegal immigrant from Somalia, presented her petition for amnesty to the INS later that week. Her extremely clever lawyer convinced the INS that because Gcina was underage, she should be in foster care until her case comes before the courts. She's currently living with a nice, wealthy family out at the Delaware Water Gap.

Vince Masterson was angry that once again his father had dismissed his considered opinion and had voted with the board to have the Finns removed from the Livingston Mansion Apartment. He told his father so, rather more forcefully than usual, which his father took poorly, observing that if Vince didn't like living rent-free in one of the most exclusive buildings in Manhattan, he was welcome to leave. A few months later, Vince did. He moved to Moscow, invested every penny of his trust fund in the Russian banking system, and managed to triple his fortune within four years. Every spring he goes golfing in Dubai.

Five months after I left the Edge, I showed up at the Surrogate's Court in lower Manhattan. After a series of postponements, our probate, or at least the first of a series of hearings on our probate, was finally on the docket. It was a nice morning in mid-April; the warmth of the air seemed mysterious and lively, like something was truly about to be born if we just had the patience to wait for it. Who would go inside on a morning like that?

"Well, look who it is," Lucy said, clipping up the courthouse steps like a warrior, her hair pulled back, severe and businesslike as usual in her gray suit. "I guess I'm not surprised."

"Hi, Lucy," I said. "I'm glad to see you."

"You know, Alison's been worried sick," she informed me crisply. "You could have called. We had no idea whatsoever where you were."

"Neither of you guys really have room for me," I told her. "I needed to take care of myself for a while."

"And you couldn't be *bothered* to make a *phone call*?"

"I had a lot of things to take care of, and I needed to think," I told her. "And you know, could you tone this down? I came here to talk, and I don't need you going at me before anybody's even said anything, okay?"

"By all means, Tina, tell me how to behave, since you are such an ideal role model for us all."

"Okay, fine, if that's the way you want it, I guess that's the way things are always going to be," I said. "I'm sorry. I'm sorry we don't understand each other."

"And whose fault is that?" she said in a nasty tone. She didn't even look at me; she was too busy checking her BlackBerry.

"Yours," I said. "I think it's yours."

"Of course you do." She nodded.

"Where's Alison?" I asked, looking around.

"She's not coming, she's too upset. She and Daniel are probably splitting up. And since they were married for ten years, he still expects his share of the apartment, and he thinks Grossman is completely incompetent, so we have a whole extra set of lawyers to deal with now, which is an utter delight."

"Alison and Daniel are splitting up?" I said.

"Yes, Tina, you might have known that if you had been anywhere reachable, which of course as usual you weren't."

"Well," I said. "I'm sorry to hear it."

"You never liked Daniel," Lucy said, dismissing my regret like yesterday's news.

"No, I didn't like Daniel, but I do like Alison," I told her. "So she's not coming today?"

"No," said Lucy. "There's no need. I'm the administratrix. Neither of you needs to be here. As usual, I will do the work." She turned, dismissing me, and headed inside.

"Hey, Lucy," I said. "Count me out. I'm going to walk away from this. Okay? I want nothing to do with it. And you know, honestly—honestly, I think you should do that too."

"What?" she said, like this was the most insane thing she had ever heard.

"There's something wrong with that apartment," I said. "It's like, enchanted. Everything is so beautiful but you know, there's poison in the walls. You should just walk away."

"Well gee, Tina, thanks for the advice. As usual, you're so sensible."

"I'm not kidding, Lucy."

"Good-bye, Tina."

"I'm going to call Alison, okay?" I yelled after her. "Tell her I'm going to call." She disappeared into the courthouse entryway and didn't look back.

Pete didn't have any luck with Doug either. Doug and Lucy, neither of them was built to walk away from a fight, or the past. As it turned out, however, Pete and I were. After six months of wrangling with co-op boards and landlords and mortgage brokers and buildings all over the Upper West Side, we got a place of our own, farther uptown. It's a two-bedroom, with a tiny dining room, tiny living room, tiny kitchen, and a sliver of a view of the river, if you stand against one of the windows and lean over exactly right.

Jennifer White comes over to babysit for us now. And once in a while, Alison comes for dinner. She plays with the baby and then puts her to bed while I try to finish my homework so I can finally get through college. After we're done sharing our lives, she fills us in on all the legal wranglings and what Doug is up to and what Lucy is doing and what clever trick Ira Grossman introduced last week and what new witnesses Doug found who are willing to state definitively that Mom and Bill were unhappy and crazy and why the one will is meaningless and why the other wills—the crazy fake one as well as the ones that never got written—are not. And then we laugh and kiss each other good night.

A year after I moved in and out of the Edgewood, the anthropo-logical botanist Leonard Colbert was found dead in his penthouse. Appar-ently he had been regularly ingesting rare hallucinogens, which police suspected he was cultivating in his extensive greenhouse. Since it was clear that he had died by his own hand, a full investigation was never conducted. The penthouse apartment of the Edgewood was known to be worth fourteen million dollars easily. He did not leave a will.

Acknowledgments

My very good agent, Loretta Barrett, informed me two years ago that writing a second novel would most likely be the most difficult challenge of my writing life. She was right. Since then I have had myriad discussions with dozens of writers about this specific nightmare, and while I despaired when Loretta and my excellent editor, Shaye Areheart, urged me to just get on with it, I now know that I could not have done so without their pushy support. I thank them for that, and for their mysterious confidence in me. Thanks also to Georgina Chapel, Abi Fellows, Amy Brownstein, Kate Snodgrass, Laura Heberton, Misha Angrist, Bill Rebeck, Susanna Sonnenberg, and Scott Burkhardt for providing essential pieces to the ongoing puzzle of my life as a novelist. Ira Pearlskin explained the practices of New York inheritance laws over and over, until I barely understood them. David Colman explained the ins and outs of Melo clasps and Balenciaga dresses. Tamara Tunie and Gregory Generet also opened their lives and their home to me in this enterprise in so many sturdy and tangible ways it would take its own book to describe them.

Marisa Smith is my second reader, and Jess Lynn, my husband, is my first. Their unwavering assurance was bracing and cheering and ultimately the thing that kept me on my path.

Ten years ago, my dear friend Susan David Bernstein invited me to visit her at her aunt Sherry's ten-room apartment overlooking Central Park West. I never forgot it. To Susan and Aunt Sherry, I say thank you for opening the door to the beginning of this book.

About the Author

THERESA REBECK is the author of the novel *Three Girls and Their Brother,* and her plays include *Our House, Bad Dates, Omnium Gatherum* (a Pulitzer finalist), *The Scene,* and *Mauritius,* which won Boston's prestigious IRNE and Elliot Norton Awards and premiered on Broadway in 2007. Rebeck lives with her husband and two children in Brooklyn, New York.

About the Type

This book was set in Adobe Garamond, a typeface designed by Robert Slimbach in 1989. It is based on Claude Garamond's sixteenth-century type samples found at the Plantin-Moretus Museum in Antwerp, Belgium.